✝

AMBER KNIGHT

KATHERINE JOHN

Á

Áccent Press Ltd

For Phil Trenfield

Writer, events manager and very special and wonderful friend
who resurrected Katherine John by introducing her to Accent Press.

Thank you

ACKNOWLEDGEMENTS

I wish to thank the curators and staff of the Wolfschanze, the curators and staff of the Historical and Archaeological Museums in Gdansk and the managers and staff of the Grand Hotel and Casino in Sopot.

Also, I would like to thank all the amber and silversmiths who shared their knowledge and expertise with me when I was researching this book. But while acknowledging their assistance I would like to state that any errors are entirely mine.

Katherine John
September 2006

PROLOGUE

Hitler's Wolfschanze
Rastenburg, East Prussia
the dark hours before dawn
January 24th, 1945

HE STANDARTENFÜHRER HAD never experienced a winter like it. An intense bitterness was carried on winds that bleached and shriveled flesh and permeated bones and, as if the cold wasn't enough, despair had set in. He detected it in every communication from Berlin; recognized it in the faces of his fellow officers and unkempt uniforms of his command; saw it in the sluggish steps of the men hauling crates out of the bunker into the waiting line of trucks. Wrapping his fur-lined greatcoat closer to his numbed body, he waved his arms and stamped his feet to circulate blood to his insensate and frozen extremities.

"Can't they move any faster, Hauptsturmführer?" he barked.

His aide clicked his heels, cracking the frosting of ice on his boots. "Are you soldiers or snails? Move it! On the double."

"The boxes are breeding in there," a private muttered loud enough for a sergeant to hear. The Unterscharführer snapped a reprimand, which was drowned out by a boom from a Russian gun. Night hadn't slowed the Soviet advance. Even the birds were fleeing westwards. Possessing neither the men nor heart to fight, all the Standartenführer hoped for was survival and an uneventful retreat to the Western front where he could surrender his command to the British or Americans. After a few years in a POW camp, he and his men could go home—if they still had homes to go to.

A private stumbled, dropping a long, narrow box. The wooden casing shattered on a concrete step revealing a panel that glowed gold against the silver snow.

"You stupid oaf, Schutze! Do you know what that is? How valuable..."

The private snapped to attention, shivering as the Unterscharführer gave vent to his anger.

"That was a piece of the amber room Tsar Peter stole from Frederick the Great." The Standartenführer picked up the panel emblazoned with a darker inlay depicting an eagle which Third Reich historians had unanimously pronounced Prussian.

"You're not fit to wipe a pig's ass, Schutze! Retrieve the pieces."

As the private scrambled for the broken corner pieces an officer stumbled through the darkness towards them, sliding up the icy path that led from the SS barracks.

"The mines are in place, Obersturmführer?" the Standartenführer asked, irritated by the breakage that was going to take some explaining if they ever reached Berlin.

"The Sturmbannführer respectfully requests another two hours, sir. The cold..."

"The cold is freezing all our balls, Obersturmführer." The Standartenführer's eyes narrowed. "Tell the Sturmbannführer he has half an hour, after that he'll be on his own."

The Obersturmführer snapped to attention before back-tracking down the path.

"The snow chains..."

"Have been put on the wheels of all the trucks, Standartenführer," his aide reassured him.

The Standartenführer lost sight of the lieutenant in the darkness that shrouded the trees, but he could still hear his boots crunching over the drifts. The man was passing the ruin of the conference room where von Stauffenberg had planted the bomb he'd hoped would put an end to Hitler and the war. The colonel shuddered from more than cold. How many people, civilian as well as military, would have lived if von Stauffenberg had succeeded? He was grateful Hitler's scientists hadn't perfected a machine that could read men's thoughts otherwise he and most of the surviving officers on the Eastern Front would find themselves facing piano wire nooses suspended from meat hooks.

"Twenty-five trucks packed, Standartenführer."

"I'll inspect the bunker." Pushing past the line of bur-dened privates negotiating the narrow staircase that led into the bunker, he strode inside and stood on the threshold of what had been Hitler's living room. Blinking against the blaze of artificial light, he saw a clerk hovering, clipboard in hand over piles of packing cases. "What's left?"

"Only the modern furniture, Persian rugs and what you see, Standartenführer."

The Standartenführer scrutinized the chalk inscriptions on the chests. "Take the van Goghs and Rembrandts next and—" he looked at the largest case. Over two meters long and one and a half wide, it could have coffined a giant. "Helmut von Mau?"

"I left it until last, sir, because of the weight. The stone sarcophagus alone is enough to test the strength of any axle and there's the amber..."

The colonel reverently touched the box. As a twelve-year-old schoolboy, he and his classmates had been taken on a pilgrimage to Konigsberg castle to pay homage to the amber-encased body of the knight who had crossed the Vistula in the Teutonic crusade of 1231. They had sat around the glass case that held the coffin, listening as their teacher related stories they knew by heart. Helmut von Mau, the lieutenant of Hermann von Balk, conqueror, founder and savior of Prussia. Helmut, the heroic and fearless soldier who helped free Prussia from the barbarians before making the ultimate sacrifice; a man so handsome that the beautiful pagan princess, Woberg, only had to look upon his face once to change her name to Maria, her religion to Christianity and forsake her people to become his camp follower. A man who wrought vengeance against the pagans even in death, when desperate in defeat, his men had strapped his body to his horse and sent his corpse galloping into the enemy camp. Legend had it that every heathen warrior who had looked upon him had been struck dead. Pity he didn't have one or two von Mau's in his command now.

"This goes next, pack the paintings around it. Don't leave any case graded A. High Command would be displeased if any of them were lost."

"Jawohl, Standartenführer."

The colonel damned the transport department. If he'd been given a train and half a dozen wagons he could have delivered the more valuable contents of the Wolfschanze to

Berlin a week ago. What could possibly be taking precedence over the Reich's art and history?

It had taken him days to assemble the decrepit convoy that lined the narrow road outside the Führer bunker, thirty vehicles and none of them sound. One ambush by partisans and the entire consignment would be lost. If it happened it would be the fault of Hitler and the sycophants he surrounded himself with, but he and his men would pay the price. When he'd taken a commission in the SS, he hadn't envisaged Command assigning crack troops and a platoon of hand-picked engineers to nurse-maid treasure while allied bombs fell on Berlin, killing civil-ians—perhaps even his beloved wife Hilde and little Wilhelm...

"It's not going to be easy to make progress through the forest in this snow, sir," his aide ventured as he stepped out-side the bunker.

"No, Hauptsturmführer." His voice rasped; he hoped the captain would put it down to the cold. "Alert the escort, we'll move out in thirty minutes."

"Before the last trucks are loaded, sir?"

"Delay and we risk losing the lot." The booming of large-bore guns tore through the air, adding emphasis to his order.

The partisan leader known only as "Jan" even to his closest confederates, for fear of reprisals against his family and village, crouched behind a tree. He hadn't moved a muscle in four hours and was beginning to doubt he'd be able to do so again. The cold had seeped through his rags, freezing his blood; and still the road stretched white, naked and empty like a scar hacked between the trees. Was there another route out of the Wolfschanze he knew nothing of? A road that led directly from the western perimeter?

When he heard the rumble of engines coughing reluctantly to life, he dismissed it as a product of his exhausted mind, then the click of a rifle reverberated behind him and he realized it was real. Tension filled the air; the same nauseating mixture of fear and fragile bravado that marked the prelude to every skirmish he had fought. Willing his frozen limbs to move, he jerked his gun arm forward.

The trucks lumbered slowly out of the chalky mist towards the inner ring of security gates like gray, mechanical elephants. He raised his hand. It didn't feel as though it was connected to his body. Guns blazed. Shadows dived out from behind the trees alongside him. The largest force he had been able to muster in five and a half years of bloody guerrilla warfare, but a turning tide carries a lot of flotsam on its crest. Men who'd kept a low profile were now anxious to strike a blow before victory bells sounded and their apathy—or collaboration—was noticed.

"Hold your fire!" A tall, fair-haired German colonel brandishing a white rag stepped in front of the leading truck, his hat tipped back on his head, his greatcoat open to show he carried no weapons.

"What now, Jan?" His second-in-command's question echoed above the engines.

"We talk to the bastard before we shoot him, and his men, like dogs."

The silhouettes in the forest reminded the colonel of wolves—gaunt, ravenous wolves with rapacious eyes. Without turning his head he shouted to his aide,

"Stand by."

Mesmerized by the sight of the approaching partisans, the captain remained silent.

"They're at our gates because the Russians aren't far behind. As we're set to lose our cargo, I'll try to use it as barter for our lives. If they kill me, retreat to the Führer bunker, order the Sturmbannführer to activate the explosives in the outer ring and contact Berlin." Both he and his aide knew there would be no reinforcements from Berlin or anywhere else, but he kept up the pretence for the men's benefit. "Alert the Sturmbannführer."

The leading partisan raised his rifle and took aim at the captain as he ran back through the gates.

"If he doesn't deliver the order I've just given him, we'll all be blown to kingdom come in five minutes." The colonel stepped forward.

"Hitler would never destroy his Headquarters."

"Annihilation is preferable to surrender in the Führer's eyes."

"Then why didn't he blow this place when he left in November?"

"Because he and High Command refused to recognize the end and that the Russians were near." The colonel lowered his voice, "and because they needed a secure place to store the Reich's treasure." He offered a pack of cigarettes to the partisan leader; when the man refused he pushed one into his own mouth. The paper stuck to his frozen lips. He waved at the trucks. "They're packed with gold, silver, amber, paintings—the riches of every building worth looting in every German-occupied Russian and Polish town. Yours, commander—and mine, if we can stop fighting long enough to divide it." He surveyed the ragged horde ranged behind the leader and saw that at least a third were women and children. "The war will soon be over. We all have lives to pick up, homes to build. The contents of those trucks could go a long way to easing the problems of peace."

A shot rang out. The colonel dove beneath the nearest truck. When he opened his eyes the partisan leader was lying alongside him.

"Your men don't respect a white flag when their commander is beneath it?" The colonel spat out the remains of his cigarette.

Jan slithered over the snow and peered out between the wheels. He frowned, creasing a scar that ran from his temple to the corner of his mouth. "My men don't have American lease-lend boots, Standartenführer. The Russians have arrived."

"I have enough treasure to satisfy three armies. Shall we call an officers' conference?"

"You expect Russians and Poles to sit at the same table as Germans!"

"We talk, or I blow everything and everyone within a five mile radius of this place sky high."

"I could kill you."

"And then you'd be responsible for the blast. My men are watching. They know the signal," he lied. "Kill me and they won't even need the signal. They'll fire the explosives anyway."

"My men aren't used to standing idly by while officers talk."

"A couple of hundred meters beyond the perimeter of that fence is Hitler's personal quarters stashed with wine and packing cases. There are enough bottles and loot to keep your men happy while we discuss the future of my cargo. Will you invite the Russians? I don't speak the language."

* * *

"I warned them not to stray from the path." The captain ran at the colonel's heels as they led the Russian and Polish commanders towards what had been the officers' casino.

"Good," the colonel commented absently.

"They laughed at me, Standartenführer. I told them the area's mined."

"And we'll be out of it in an hour." The colonel hoped there were enough trinkets and wine bottles left to occupy the Partisans and Russians until he could get his men into the forest and on to a westbound road. He'd passed down the order that the first German to take a drink would be the first man shot, but would his troops remain loyal when they saw the enemy looting a cargo they'd been ordered to guard by the Führer himself?

He was so tired he couldn't even recall the last time he had undressed to sleep in a bed. Was his house still standing in Berlin? He closed his eyes, visualizing the rosewood furniture, the crisp white sheets, his wife naked, her long fair hair tumbling down her back. Wilhelm curled pink and perfect in his crib...

"You have gold, Fritz?" the Russian major enquired in heavily accented German as they entered the casino.

"Gold, diamonds, silver, jewels, amber, paintings—more treasure than you can imagine, Ivan."

"I have a very good imagination, Fritz." The Russian slammed a bottle of vodka on a table and pulled a chair towards him. Turning it around, he sat leaning on its back.

"Hauptsturmführer, bring the clerk and his lists here, and," the colonel glanced at the vodka, "something to drink and a set of glasses."

"We don't need glasses." The Russian pulled the cork

from his bottle with his teeth, spat it out and drank deeply before passing it to Jan. He was enormous, his dark eyes shining from behind a fuzz of matted, black hair and beard, his massive bulk swathed in layers that bore no resemblance to any uniform.

Jan handed the colonel the vodka bottle. He put it to his mouth, pursing his lips as a stream of burning liquid flowed down his throat.

"Used to French brandy?" the Russian mocked. An explosion boomed through the open doorway, pounding the air and breath from their bodies. The bottle slipped through the colonel's fingers, its contents splashing over the carpeted floor onto the Russian's boots.

The captain materialized through the smoke, the clerk behind him. "I warned them about the mines but they..."

"Our men, Hauptsturmführer?"

"Russians, sir. They left the path."

Day had broken, the thin, watery light heightened by the lustrous sheen of snow blanketing the ground, frosting the trees, and roofing the bunkers, illuminating anarchy. Bottles were being upended into mouths and smashed against trees; crates wrenched apart and plundered. Straw packing littered the ground as gem-studded, gold and silver altar crosses were attacked with knives and bayonets. One man was dancing crazily, his arms and neck festooned with ropes of pearls and amber. Others lay in wait for the cases that were still being dragged from the bunker.

"Over there, sir."

All that was left of two Russians were shreds of flesh and bloodstained clothing that decorated the lower branches of a conifer and the ground beneath it with gobs of glistening gore. The legless body of a third still moved, his screams muffled by the rumpus around the bunker. The Russian commander pulled his gun from his holster, aimed and fired. The mutilated body jerked once before slumping motionless. The men didn't even glance up from the looting. To his dismay the colonel saw as many Germans as Russians and Partisans in the melee.

"I couldn't stop them, sir," his aide apologized. "Not after they saw the others."

"Looks like there's no one left to shoot them, Hauptsturmführer, except you and me."

"The Sturmbannführer managed to keep his men out of it, sir." The captain felt the major's success with the engineers who'd been ordered to destroy the bunker complex reflected badly on his ability to control his own men.

"How many engineers are there?"

"Two officers, including the Sturmbannführer, three non-commissioned officers, and twelve men, sir."

The colonel eyed the line of trucks that stretched between the Führer bunker and the gates. "Order them to drive the transport to the Naval High Command bunker."

"There's gold in the trucks?"

"Valuables," the colonel answered the Russian. "The men are looting what we would have abandoned."

"All the trucks are loaded?" A smile cracked the frozen dirt on the Russian's face.

"All," the colonel concurred.

"Then we divide..."

"Not here."

"I say we do it here and now." The Russian conjured another bottle of vodka from his shirt.

"How would you rate our chances of keeping what's in them from our men, or hanging on to it once we leave? The German army will make a last stand, if not in East Prussia, then Berlin. And his," he jerked his head towards Jan, "is not the only partisan unit in the forest."

"What are you proposing?" Jan asked.

"That we take only what we can carry in our packs. The larger more valuable items we hide here. At the end of the war we return, unearth them and sell to the highest bidder."

"What's to stop someone from coming in and taking them after we've gone?"

"They have to find them and there are cellars in this complex that could lie undiscovered until the sun turns to ice. If you won't take my word for it, see for yourselves."

"We will, Standartenführer." The Russian attacked the cork on the fresh bottle. "But first we drink to the philosophy of 'survivors take all'."

"Starting with—" the colonel pulled out his cigarettes and looked to the last truck in the line, "The Amber Knight and Frederick the Great's Amber Room."

"Peter the Great's Amber Room," the Russian commander corrected.

"You're both wrong," Jan smiled. "It's our Amber Room now."

Avoiding the drunken mob around the Führer bunker, the engineers drove the trucks past the Teleprinter exchange to the Naval High Command bunker. At the colonel's suggestion, three men from each group were entrusted with the location of the hideaway. The colonel chose his immediate ranking subordinates; the major in charge of the engineers and his aide. Jan picked his lieutenant and his mistress, the Russian his second-in-command and his brother.

Dismissing the drivers, the colonel led them into a bunker opposite the one occupied by the Naval High Command. In the three years he had been stationed in the Wolfschanze, his aide had never seen the building open or occupied. It housed a single large, empty room.

The colonel produced a set of keys, pried a concrete block from the inner wall at floor level and uncovered a lever. He heaved it downwards. The Russian leapt in the air as a stone trap door opened inches from where he was standing.

"That, gentlemen, leads to a passage buried three meters below the cemetery at the rear of the Naval Command bunker. At the end of the passage is a room, airtight and bomb proof, fifteen meters square and two meters high. Suitably commodious for our purpose, it has only one entrance."

"Air supply in the tunnel?" the Russian asked suspiciously.

"There are vents connected to the air supply that feeds the main bunkers. I suggest two men from each party transfer the artifacts."

"While the others remain on guard." The Russian primed his rifle and aimed it at the colonel's chest. "Shall we begin?"

It took eight hours to fill the chamber. The last chest to be carried in held the amber-encased corpse of Helmut von Mau. It required the combined efforts of all nine of them to slide it down the improvised wooden ramp the major had set up on the steps, through the passage and into the secret room.

"Forgive me, old fellow." The colonel stroked the box. "But someday there'll be a different world."

"It's here." He turned to see the Russian grinning in the

torchlight behind him. "The only question is, Standartenführer, whose world will it be?"

At nightfall the Russians and Partisans who were sober enough carried their comrades into the forest. The colonel mustered his men. Half the trucks were abandoned. Nursing hangovers and bruises, the Germans stowed their booty in their pockets and rucksacks, boarded the trucks and prepared themselves for a long, cold and uncomfortable journey west. An hour later, only the major and his band of engineers were left in Hitler's bunker city.

The outlines of the towering, concrete walls softened into ghost shadows as he and his men flitted from gray mass to gray mass, checking cables, priming fuses, laying caches of high explosives, ten tons to each bunker. An hour before midnight they retreated, crawling back over the paths Hitler had trodden with his beloved dog, Blondi.

The last building the major checked was the bunker opposite the Naval High Command. He'd been more careful with his calculations there than anywhere else in the complex, laying just enough explosive to blow out the windows and doors, and cover the floor with debris that would settle, attracting leaves and dirt, an ideal host for weeds, and even trees, given the ravages of time.

The colonel reached the town of Rastenburg as the Major depressed the plunger. It set off a chain reaction that sent everyone who hadn't already fled the Russian advance scurrying to the air-raid shelters. The peasants in the countryside fell to their knees and crossed themselves. Columns of smoke and fire erupted into the night sky, obliterating stars as explosion after explosion blasted trees and tossed great clumps of concrete askew. The Partisans and Russians who crept too close to watch had their eardrums shattered and their skin seared. Afterwards, they looked for, but failed to find, the German major. If he and his men had left the Wolfschanze it was not by the main gate.

A group of partisans found the colonel and his men waiting on the outskirts of Rastenburg for the major and his engineers. The colonel's wife never gave up hope. Men were still coming home from the Russian POW camps in the sixties. She never remarried.

Jan disappeared at the end of the war. The men who had been with him since the beginning wanted to believe that he'd returned to his village and his old life. But there were rumors; that he had been tried for collaboration by the Stalinists and sent to Siberia; that he had been caught by the retreating Germans and shot; and the unthinkable—that he was a Jew. If so, the end of the war brought no peace for him or his kind— some were meticulous in carrying on the persecution.

The Russians lingered in the forest until the fires in the Wolfschanze died down. They discovered the German engineers had done their job well. Twelve men were killed attempting to reach the bunker with the trap door in the floor. Eventually their commander abandoned the site to the army behind him, consoling himself with the thought that only nine people knew of the existence of the cellar. There would be time enough after the war. But then, he hadn't reckoned on the battle for Berlin.

* * *

Another Russian unit came to the Wolfschanze. Lured by tales of Hitler's gold, they walked through the outer fence and into the minefield. The last sight they saw was the eight-meter-thick, steel-reinforced roofs of the bunkers lying drunkenly on their sides. The invading army posted signs in Polish and Russian, warning people to stay away. There was no need to post signs in German. Those who hadn't fled west had been killed or transported to Siberia. East Prussia was no more, its lands swallowed by Communist Poland and the Soviet Union.

The Wolfschanze's fences were replaced and the skull and crossbones signs remained until seven years after the peace treaties had been signed. It took that long to defuse the 54,000 mines the German engineers had left in the complex. By then the birds had returned to the forest.

Tourists visited the bunker city constructed to protect one man's life and comfort, while the rest of Europe was being destroyed by a war he initiated. They walked over the airfield, the power station and the railway station; examined the air purification installations, the tanks that had ensured a plentiful supply of clean water, and the drainage systems. They imagined the scenes played out in Goering's, Jodl's, Keitel's, Speer's, Todt's, Von Ribbentrop's and the Führer's bunkers while Europe burned. Their footsteps echoed hollowly on the concrete floors of the casinos, the guest bunkers, the saunas, cinema, brothel, barber shops, doctor's and High Command offices. They stood on the uneven ground of the cemetery trying not to think of the bodies beneath them.

They posed for photographs, marveling at the scale of the

place. Some drew analogies between the demise of the empires of old and Hitler's Third Reich in the Wolfschanze's shattered ruins, but none imagined the riches that still lay buried beneath the forest floor.

CHAPTER ONE

ADAM SALEN FLICKED up the corners of the cards that lay face down on the blue baize in front of him. The nine of clubs and the seven of hearts—sixteen. He glanced at the dealer's nineteen before flashing an insincere smile at the German businessman whose rolls of fat spilled over the stool next to his. Perspiration oozed from every pore of his obese body, but the man was smirking like a chocoholic in a candy shop. On the table between them and the dealer was twice the gambling allowance Adam allowed himself, which amounted to more than two months wages for most Poles. Did the German have twenty or twenty-one?

"Card."

The dealer slid one out of the shoe and across the table. Adam flipped it over. The five of diamonds. He used it to turn the others.

Furious, the German pushed his cards aside with pudgy, ring-laden fingers.

"You know what they say about being lucky at cards?" Helga Leman shoveled a neat pile of chips towards Adam.

"I know what they say." He picked out three high value chips from the pile and returned them to her. "Is it true?"

"How would I know? Goodnight, Herr Dobrow, better luck tomorrow," Helga smiled at the German as he heaved his bulk off the stool and waddled in the direction of the Casino dining room.

"With half-price meals on offer to gamblers, the casino will still lose money on that one." Adam turned to the tuxedo-clad waiter behind him. "Mind if I borrow your tray?"

"Not at all, Mr. Salen. Lucky night?"

"Luckier than you, by the sound of it," Adam replied, as angry voices escalated around the roulette table.

The waiter flexed his muscles and sized up the situation. But there were more able-bodied staff than patrons in the casino. The men were uniformly massive, six feet or more, their brawny bodies shoehorned into ill-cut evening suits, their bull necks constrained by starched collars and black ties. In contrast the girls were all small-boned, fragile; their Hollywood make-up and Barbie doll hair at odds with the severe lines of their black mini-skirts, white and candy-striped shirts and bow ties.

"You're going to lose everything!" The protester was thin-faced, with the dark skin and eyes of a gypsy. He had embraced the worst American fashion had to offer. His baggy Bermuda shorts and short-sleeved Hawaiian silk shirt would have driven off a parakeet.

"It's mine to lose." His companion elbowed him aside and proceeded to blitz the squares on the roulette table with high value chips. Adam did a rough calculation. There had to be more than three thousand American dollars on the table.

Two more waiters discreetly abandoned their trays and stepped closer. The diminutive brunette behind the wheel moved her hand downwards to press the panic button, but both the manager and assistant manager were already making their way across the floor.

"The idiot's dropped forty-six thousand dollars in the last two hours." Helga scooped the used cards from the baize in front of Adam and posted them through the slot in the table.

Adam glanced at the gambler. "Isn't that Brunon Kaszuba?"

"You know him?"

"His wife works for the Salen Institute."

"I hope you pay her well. It costs a lot to keep a man with his habits."

The manager nodded to the girl running the roulette.

"Last bets," she called, before setting the wheel in motion. With every eye in the room concentrated on the ball, it was a good time for Adam to study Kaszuba.

He conceded that women might find him attractive: thick blond hair, blue eyes, stocky, muscular frame without an ounce of fat. But his speech was slurred, and there were red-threaded veins in the whites of his eyes. Like the gypsy, he had ignored the dress code of the casino. His purple track-suit could have been bought in an exorbitantly expensive designer shop, or a back-street market. To Adam's undiscerning eye, the outfit had the tacky air he associated with both outlets.

Adam had heard rumors about Brunon Kaszuba, none of them good. He was a drunk and a clean-up man for the Russian Mafia and wasn't too particular what he brushed under the carpet as long as he was paid. Looking at him in the flesh, he could believe every word.

He tried to imagine Kaszuba and his wife together, and failed. Magdalena was efficient and businesslike, her clothes severe, her demeanor cool to the point of frigidity but, if

Kaszuba had been her first indulgence, perhaps she'd decided she couldn't afford any more. He turned away and noticed a tall, slim dark man hovering on the fringe of the crowd. A man with Slavic eyes who was watching Kaszuba even more intently than he was. A man he'd seen somewhere before but couldn't recall exactly where.

The rattling slowed to a series of clicks as the ball bounced from cup to cup. The silence shattered in a collective short-lived sigh. The assistant croupiers moved in to scoop the losing chips into black plastic refuse sacks and Kaszuba went berserk. The spectators melted against the walls. Responding to the manager's signal, two of the largest "waiters" stepped forward and pinned Kaszuba's arms to his sides. His companion ran in their wake mewing, "I told you so," as Kaszuba was frog-marched, red-faced and protesting, to the door that led to the wide stone staircase outside the building.

The manager disappeared through the restaurant into his private office. Adam knew the casino paid the police a generous retainer. Kaszuba wouldn't be allowed to linger outside for long. The floor show over, more gamblers drifted towards the door than returned to the tables.

"Kaszuba's experience has made them cautious," Adam commented to Helga as she helped him pile his chips on to the tray.

"Fifty thousand American dollars is a lot to lose."

"That depends on how much effort went into making it." He turned towards the cashier's kiosk. "I'll be in the bar when you finish."

"You know I don't like being taken for granted."

"I thought you might be interested in helping me disprove the theory on luck in cards."

* * *

After he had cashed his chips, Adam took a double vodka onto the terrace that overlooked the bay. The sea glowed a deep, phosphorescent green. Lights glittered in a looped necklace of shimmering brilliants on the double-tiered pier to the right of the hotel and in a circle on the paved area beneath him. Lovers' shadows entwined on the sands. It was easy to imagine Sopot as it had been in its heyday, at the turn of the last century before two world wars had shattered Europe. Then, the aristocracy of northern Europe had flocked to the town and the heirs of Tsars had slept in the suites of the Grand Hotel.

"I thought that shift would never end." Helga stood beside him, her shoulders swathed in a mink jacket that was too warm for the spring night.

He finished his drink and abandoned his glass on the balustrade. "I'll find a taxi."

"I don't understand why you don't buy a car. You can easily afford one," she pouted.

"It's easier to travel by taxi. There are no worries about whether the car will still be there when you need it. Besides," he wrapped his arm around her furry shoulders, decided he disliked the sensation and felt for her hand, "a car's a liability in the old town of Gdansk."

"So you walk, like a peasant." She scrunched her pert nose disdainfully.

"If I didn't, I'd end up with a stomach like Herr Dobrow."

"Then I wouldn't like you anymore." She slipped her hand beneath his waistcoat. Wriggling her fingers she slid them below the waistband of his trousers into his boxer shorts.

Extricating her hand, he gripped it hard. "You'd like me well enough if I had Dobrow's money."

"Not if you were as mean with it as he is. He won five thousand dollars last night and only gave Jadwiga a five dollar tip."

"Sounds about the right percentage for Jadwiga."

"You don't think she's as pretty as me?" she demanded, fishing for compliments.

"If I did, she'd be here and you'd be looking for a lift home." He stared wistfully at the beach. Knowing Helga would balk at the suggestion of a walk, let alone in sand that would scratch her three-inch heels he descended the steps, stumbling as his foot connected with something soft and pulpy in the dark corner at garden level.

"Careful, I think a drunk's fallen asleep here." He kicked out gently. When the body failed to respond he crouched down.

"Who is it?"

"Get the manager."

"Who is it?" she repeated, hysteria mounting at the serious tone of his voice.

"No one who can hurt you. Now get the manager, please."

"Trust a fucking American," Josef Dalecka complained as he abandoned his police car on the pavement in front of the Grand Hotel and negotiated a path between the tables and upturned chairs of the outdoor cafe to the shuttered ice cream kiosk where Adam was talking to the hotel and casino managers. "If a Pole fell over a body at this time in the morning, he'd wipe the blood from his shoes and carry on minding his own business like a sensible fellow, but not you, Adam. Oh no, you have to disturb the hotel staff just as they're coming off duty, and roust police officers out of their beds."

"It's one of the Mafia boys, sir." Josef's long-suffering lieutenant, Jankiel Pajewski, who'd arrived earlier, left the police doctor who was hauling equipment out of his car and joined them.

"All the more reason to leave him where he is until morning. Do we have a name?" Josef demanded.

"Rat is all I've ever heard, sir."

"Gypsy, tall, thin, dark?"

"That's him."

"I've given the surgeon my shoes. I've hung about dutifully waiting for your arrival, and I've told security and Jankiel everything I know, which isn't much, so can I go home now, please?" Adam looked across to the wall where Helga was sitting sipping brandy and regaling her fellow croupiers with an embroidered account of their discovery of the body.

"No way, Adam. If I'm not allowed to sleep, neither are you. Where's the corpse?"

"At the foot of the steps that lead down from the bar terrace, sir." Jankiel led the way to the side of the building. Josef shook his head at both managers who tried to follow them.

Josef beckoned Adam forward as they drew close to the spot where the surgeon had rigged up portable spotlights behind an inadequate screen of black cloth stretched over a wire frame. The gypsy lay on his back in a puddle of congealed blood, arms and legs flung wide. An obscene slash in his neck had half severed his head from his body, exposing his spine.

"You seen him before?" Josef asked Adam.

"In the casino tonight. He was with Brunon Kaszuba." Adam patted his pockets in search of a cigar. He didn't smoke often, but he felt in need of something to disperse the metallic reek of blood that tainted the still night air.

"That's a name to conjure with. Were they playing the tables?"

"Kaszuba was playing roulette. I didn't see that poor bastard place any bets." Adam tapped a cigar from a pack and offered it to Josef.

"Did Kaszuba lose?"

"Fifty thousand dollars, according to Helga." Although only the doctor and Jankiel were within earshot Adam lowered his voice. Casinos were notoriously cagey about their clients' business.

"Damn, there goes the obvious motive." Josef couldn't keep the disappointment from his voice. "No self-respecting thug would knife a gambler with empty pockets outside a casino. Did this fellow seem upset at Kaszuba's losing streak?"

"He didn't look happy about it."

"Give me a rundown on how he died," Josef asked the surgeon.

"By the quantity of blood and angle of the wound I'd say he was killed on this spot. Tufts of hair have been pulled from the front of his head, which suggests he was grabbed from behind. The cut was made left to right, probably by a right-handed man. The edges on the throat and the wind-pipe are clean, so the blade was sharp, either new or well-honed. Death would have been instantaneous."

"All the hallmarks of the professional, sir," Jankiel observed.

"I noticed," Josef responded.

Used to Josef's vitriolic tongue and temper, Jankiel continued. "There's no sign of a weapon and only one bloody footprint. It matches Mr. Salen's shoe." He held up the swathe of plastic sheeting the doctor had wrapped around Adam's offending shoe. "That," he pointed to a bloody handprint on the wall behind the body, "also belongs to Mr. Salen."

"You could have been more careful," Josef scolded Adam.

"It's dark in this corner."

"It is." Josef glanced at the ring of lights set in the paved area in front of the hotel. "How did you know you'd stumbled into a body?"

"I kicked it and it didn't move."

"Could have been a drunk."

"Drunks don't leak blood. I laid a hand on him."

"Were you alone?"

"Helga was with me, we were on our way home. I've had a long day and she'd just finished a ten-hour shift," Adam said.

"The luscious Helga. I must have a word with her."

"She didn't see a thing. When I realized he was dead I sent her into the hotel to get the manager."

"Were you with Helga all night?" Josef motioned Adam to join him as he walked over the hotel gardens towards the sea.

"No, I left her in the casino after Kaszuba was thrown out, cashed my chips..."

"You won?"

"Not a lot."

"What were you playing?"

"Blackjack, not that it's any of your business."

"And after you cashed your chips?" Josef prompted.

"I took a vodka onto the terrace and waited for Helga."

"Did anyone see you?"

"Anyone who cared to look," Adam snapped, exhaustion making him irritable.

"How long were you out there?"

"I don't know—five—ten minutes perhaps."

"Did you hear or see anything?"

"The usual, lovers on the beach..."

"I didn't know you were a voyeur."

"Josef, I've been up since five," Adam reminded him irritably.

"Haven't we all?"

"Can't this wait until morning?" Adam pleaded.

"I suppose so, if you give me your passport."

"What?" Adam glared at him.

"Your passport, you must have it. You wouldn't have been allowed to play in the casino without it."

"You can't be serious? Come on, this is an open and shut case. It's Kaszuba you should be looking for."

"We don't need to look for Kaszuba. We've got him. Took him into custody five minutes after he was thrown out of the casino."

"You bastard! You've been wasting my time asking questions you already know the answers to."

"Not exactly. That corpse was alive when the locals picked up Kaszuba. If you left the casino shortly after Kaszuba, he must have been killed during the time you cashed in your chips and bought a drink. How long was that?"

"It was five to two when I left the casino."

"You're very sure of that, considering you couldn't remember how long you were out on the terrace."

"I looked at my watch. I remember thinking Helga only had five minutes of her shift to go."

"And we logged the call at half past two. So if you were out on the terrace for ten minutes—say quarter of an hour at the most, the murder must have taken place in the five to ten minutes that elapsed between us picking up Kaszuba and you walking outside, unless he was murdered while you were on the terrace." Josef looked back at the hotel. "You were on the terrace outside the bar?"

"I've already told you I was."

"You would have heard something if the murder had happened then, don't you think? A scuffle? A cry?"

"That depends on how much noise they made about it."

"I don't think Rat would have died easy if he saw his killer beforehand. Perhaps the murderer knew Rat was in the casino, lay in wait and took him by surprise."

"Unless he had an old score to settle and came across Rat by chance."

"That's the Mafia for you. Cross them, and they never forget it."

"If I were you, I'd ask Kaszuba how he acquired fifty thousand American dollars. If he and Rat stole it, it's my guess there's one pissed-off person around somewhere."

"Perhaps more pissed off than you know. Kaszuba insists the money belonged to Rat."

"Perhaps whoever Rat stole it from, got to him. As they couldn't collect their money, they collected his life. A warning to anyone else who has an eye on Mafia money." Adam thought for a moment. "Do you really believe Rat stole the money and gave it to Kaszuba to gamble away?"

"No, but I can hardly ask Rat where he got it."

"So you're harassing me."

"Harass is a strong word," Josef countered. "So far you're our only witness."

"I didn't see a thing."

"You found the body."

"And now I'd like to go to bed. Goodnight, doctor, Jankiel..."

"Papers?" Josef blocked his path. Adam crossed his arms and stared back belligerently. "I could find you and the lady cells in Piwna Street for the night."

Adam reluctantly put his hand in his inside pocket and pulled out his passport.

"Thank you." Josef's thin-lipped, chiseled features creased in a rare smile. "Just one more thing, Adam. Don't stray too far from Mariacka Street. I take it the lady's going home with you?"

Not trusting himself to answer, Adam turned on his heel.

"And do yourself a favor," Josef called after him. "Don't expend all your energy before morning. You may need it for official questioning."

CHAPTER TWO

DAM PULLED A fistful of notes from his pocket. Peering under the light of a street lamp that was more decorative than functional, he handed the taxi driver a wad of zlotys that looked a lot more than the twelve dollars it was, and added a tip.

"...If the killer saw us and it was a Mafia killing..." Helga speculated after the cab drove off.

"One more word about murder, killers, Mafia, blood or bodies and I'll abandon you right here." Pausing to remove his remaining shoe and socks, Adam walked barefoot down the Fishmarket towards the Long Riverside walk that bordered the Mottlau Canal.

Helga's stiletto heels clattered over the cobblestones behind him.

"I've had a terrible shock and you threaten to leave me here, when there could be dangerous..."

"I'll be dangerous if you don't close your mouth." Too weary to console her or offer soothing flattery, Adam closed his ears to Helga's mindless prattling and immersed himself in the sights and sounds of the medieval quarter of Gdansk. No matter how many times he walked alongside the canal past the buildings studded with ancient gates that opened into picturesque streets crammed with meticulously restored houses, he always found something new. A different angle on a familiar building; a baroque carving over a door or window he hadn't noticed before; a quirk of light that brought fresh perspective to the streets he had grown to love. Even the night was perfect. On their right the moon dappled the waters of the Mottlau canal with silver beams, the stars shone brighter than they ever had stateside; the outlines of church spires and secular tower cast inky silhouettes against the navy blue sky. Random lights sparkled like jewels through leaded- and stained-glass windows...

"How much did you win tonight?" Helga inquired shrilly, shattering the romantic world of cloak and doublet, velvet gowns and secret assignations in the narrow alleyways that he had been creating in his mind's eye.

"Not enough to cover last month's losses."

"You always say that." She squeezed his arm hard to let him know he wasn't forgiven.

"I am bone tired."

"Me too." She took his admission as an apology and broached a subject that had preoccupied her all evening. "I called in Feliks's workshop this afternoon. He's working on a stunning pair of gold and sapphire earrings."

"Probably a commission." Adam found Helga's flagrantly mercenary attitude refreshing after the devious, money-grub-bing tactics of his ex-wife.

"They were, but he said if he was paid upfront he could make another pair just like them. It's my birthday next month."

"And how old will you be this year?"

"Twenty-one, same as last."

"Did you ever see anything as lovely as that?" He halted before the low archway of the Mariacka Gate. Cut into the façade of a five-story tower it offered a picturesque glimpse of the narrow street beyond. Moonlight cast cold, gleaming spotlights across the cobblestones and gothic stonework. Dragons with gaping mouths jutted out above carved stone panels on which strange beasts and angels vied for supremacy. Above them towered the tall, narrow, casement-studded façades of the twin medieval terraces that led down to St Mary's church. A breeze stirred, sending the leaves of the few trees that grew on the terraces shivering and trembling. Before he could return to his dream world, Helga interrupted him again.

"When the light catches the sapphires they shine the exact same shade as your eyes. If you bought them for me, I'd think of you every time I wore them."

"Even when you've moved on to a fresh victim?" Adam teased.

"Victim! You..."

He silenced her by placing his mouth over hers. She bit down viciously on his lower lip.

He jumped back. "That hurt." He dabbed the blood from his lip.

"It was meant to. Do I get my earrings, or not?"

"I'll think about it."

"Not good enough."

"I'm too tired to argue."

"I can see Feliks if you're busy. He can send you the bill."

"Not before I know what it is." Conscious of his neighbors sleeping behind the walls, Adam crept down the street to the last house on the right. "We'll go in the back way. And no noise on the stairs, I don't want to wake Waleria."

Helga stamped all the louder up the short flight of stone steps that led to the back door.

Adam turned the key. Mixed odors of cinnamon, goulash, paint fixative, wax polish and washing soda wafted out to greet them. "Stop behaving like a spoiled child, Helga."

"I don't know how you put up with living in her house," Helga hissed as they passed Waleria's apartment door on the first floor. "Having to see her wrinkles every day."

"Youth isn't everything and Waleria's conversation extends to more than eulogies on sapphire earrings."

"Living on the fourth floor is bad enough. But with no elevator..."

"I like foreplay in the stairwell." He pinned her against the wall. "Saves time when we get inside."

"It'll be more than foreplay, if you don't get a move on," she gasped, worming out of his arms.

The lights clicked off on the time switch before they reached his apartment door. Floundering in the dark, Adam dragged Helga up the final flight of stairs and fumbled for his lock. Grabbing her by the waist he burst through the door.

Lights shone through the uncurtained windows from the top floor apartment across the street illuminating a surprisingly large room given the narrow confines of the house. Pushing Helga on to a huge, squashy, calico-upholstered sofa, Adam sank down beside her.

"The door," she mumbled, trying to avoid his kisses as his hand slid up her skirt.

"Burglars are too tired to climb up here."

"Waleria..."

"I pay my rent." He kicked out. Catching the edge of the door with his foot, he slammed it shut.

Adam woke to blinding light and air filled with birdsong. He hadn't needed an alarm since he had dispensed with curtains and there were other advantages; like not having to pull, open or wash them, or decide what color they should be. All he had to do, to ensure the neighbors couldn't see in, was keep the lights off when it was dark and all private activity below windowsill level in daylight.

He turned his head and gazed at Helga. Her looks had definitely been designed with artificial light and evening wear in mind. His bedding as well as her face was adorned with streaks of black mascara, passion-red lipstick and chalk-white foundation and, as he didn't have a maid, that meant changing the bedclothes himself. Still, he permitted himself a smug smile as he threw back the covers, last night had been worth a little inconvenience. Then he remembered the sapphire earrings and realized inconvenience wouldn't be the only price he'd have to pay for Helga's passion.

He stepped out of bed and padded over to the wardrobe. Sliding open the mirror doors that reflected the steep-sided gabled rooftops of the house opposite, he flicked through his clothes. He recalled yesterday's heat and selected a silk shirt, lightweight linen suit and clean shorts and socks before walking down the spiral staircase that led from the mezzanine sleeping area in the attic into the living room. The apartment was small, but it held everything he needed. An upper section to sleep in and house his wardrobe, desk and computer, a living area to get drunk in, preferably with friends, and a tiny bathroom and kitchen. The living room took up three-quarters of the floor space and anything out of place constituted a mess in his eyes.

He tossed the cushions he and Helga had dislodged back on to the sofa and went into the bathroom. Showered, shaved, and dressed, he left Helga to her dreams, and ran down the stairs to Waleria's gallery on the ground floor.

"Heard you and your lady friend banging about in the early hours." Waleria's well-preserved features tensed as she wrestled a large shapeless bronze from a plinth.

"I tried to keep the noise down."

"You didn't succeed."

"Sorry." He rescued the bronze from her wilting arms. "Where do you want this?"

"In the packing case. It's been sold."

"Glad to see you're still servicing the local art industry by fleecing the tourists." He heaved the sculpture into a wooden box.

"Thankfully some people have taste discerning enough to appreciate modern art," she countered.

"Who bought it?" He was unabashed by her gibe. "Nouveau riche Russian or pretentious German?"

"Swede, actually."

"It'll go with their furniture."

"If you're going to insult the exhibits, clear off."

"No offer of coffee?"

"She still here?" Waleria quizzed, filling a mug from the jug in the coffee maker.

"Is who where?"

"Don't play innocent with me. Lady croupier. She still upstairs?"

"Why do you want to know?"

"Because if she is, I need to lock the silver in my safe and it's inconvenient to lose the use of my teaspoons for a morning."

"It's my silver not yours she's after." Adam took the coffee she handed him.

"With all the girls in Gdansk on the lookout for Americans to buy them a ticket out of Poland, why did you have to pick her?"

Adam sipped the coffee. "Because Helga wears her price on her sleeve, and unlike every other woman I've met, I know that's all I'll have to pay."

"Ever thought there could be a hidden tax?" she called after him as walked out.

"If there is, it's got to be less than my ex-wife levied."

Even the thought of last night's murder and the occasional whiff of foul air from the sewers failed to dampen Adam's spirits as he strolled along the length of Mariacka Street in the bright spring sunshine. The last building on the right, adjoining the gate, had been commandeered by the town's Archaeological Museum, and the young curator, Edmund Dunst, had been delighted to lease the top floor to the Polish branch of the Salen Institute. Without Salen Institute rent, loans and project funding, there would have been fewer exhibits in both the town's Historical and Archaeological museums.

Unlocking the door, Adam raced up the three flights of stairs to his office. After opening the windows on the Mottlau Canal side, he ground coffee, filled the machine and switched it on. Only then did he sit behind his desk and gaze at the daunting mountain of mail.

"Regretting playing truant?" Edmund Dunst walked in and added more offerings to the pile.

"Truant! It was hard work."

"I heard there wasn't anything worth looking at. All fakes and forgeries."

"That was the problem." Adam slit open an envelope with a paper-knife fashioned into a miniature Roman sword. "In my opinion, that particular rural museum should have closed years ago."

"Well, it's closed now. Did you buy anything?"

"A couple of pieces of amber."

"Good ones I hope." Edmund sat in the visitor's chair.

"Who said you were going to get them?"

"How many times do I have to tell you? Keep faith in me and we'll build a Salen Institute display to rival the Swedish exhibition in Malbork Castle." Edmund was proud of the museum's amber collection that had blossomed under his guardianship from a few forlorn scraps into a four-hundred piece historical panorama detailing the history and working of the resin. "Come on, what did you get?"

"A ring made by Krefta the elder in 1936. Nice piece of workmanship."

"Authenticated?"

"What do you take me for? I found it in this." He tossed Dunst a catalogue emblazoned with a swastika.

"'1936 Konigsberg exhibition'," Dunst read. "Please, tell me it's this one?" He pointed to a colored sketch of an enormous ring set with a hunk of honey-colored, opaque amber carved into an eagle's head.

"It is."

"I take back every evil thought I've ever had about you. And the other piece?"

"A seventeenth-century powder horn, engraved with the von Bach Zalewski coat of arms."

"You fell for that?"

"It was pretty."

"It'll be a nineteenth-century forgery, the amber will be melted or pressed, not carved from a single piece, the workmanship shoddy and the silver mounting will turn out to be gilt, and bad gilt at that."

"Probably," Adam agreed, with irritating complacency.

"But you couldn't resist it because your great-great-grandfather changed his name from von Bach Zalewski to Salen when he reached America?"

"Please, we're the decayed branch. I'm proud of my peasant origins." Adam scanned a begging letter from a beleaguered museum that had lost its government funding. Tossing the envelope, he stuck the letter into an empty tray before picking up another.

"For Magdalena Janca?" Edmund picked up the letter and read it.

"Haven't you got any work to do?"

"I could rearrange the exhibits on the ground floor to make room for a ring and powder horn, but as I don't know if I'm going to get them..."

"Who else would I give them to? Don't forget to close the door on the way out."

After Edmund left, Adam sat staring out of the window at the canal and the weed-choked ruins of a bombed-out warehouse opposite. The saviors of Gdansk had completed a Herculean task when they'd rebuilt the city from the rubble and ashes of World War II, but odd corners of dereliction still needed attention.

Another perk of living in Europe, he decided. Time to sit and think. Folding his hands behind his head he contemplated the evening that lay ahead. The casino and Helga's company were beginning to pall. Perhaps he needed a change.

"Hard at it, I see?" Edmund returned with a large brown envelope.

"Nine-tenths of this job is planning."

"On whether to bed the luscious Helga, or ripe Elizbieta?"

"Elizbieta belongs to Feliks."

"That's not what I heard." Edmund dropped the envelope on the desk. "By the way, when can I expect the pieces?"

"End of the month when the museum closes."

"I suppose it will have to do."

Pouring himself a coffee, Adam propped his feet on the desk and set to work.

Half an hour later his wastepaper basket was overflowing and there were three neat piles of papers on his desk, all destined for Magdalena Janca. In the first he'd stacked appeals from museums and academic institutions; in the second, pleas for funding to save works of art and historical significance threatened with export and, in the third, scholarship applications from students who would otherwise have to abandon their studies.

A sucker for a sob story, Adam knew his limitations. Magdalena Janca was better equipped to deal with begging letters, particularly Polish ones. If she resented him dumping all the appeals that landed on his desk on her, she hadn't complained to him about it. Her job description was to oversee all the educational and archaeological projects funded by the Polish branch of the Salen Institute in return for a salary and package that had enabled her to continue working in the Historical Museum. He had offered Magdalena the job after Edmund had told him that the trustees of the museum had been forced to let her go. But that didn't stop him from suffering the odd pang of conscience or the feeling that he was using her. Jobs in the artistic and cultural fields were scarce in cash-strapped Poland and, for all Magdalena's undoubted talent, if it hadn't been for his offer, she would be unemployed—a fact they were both aware of. If Magdalena Janca had one fault, it was a tendency to work too hard. He would have been happier if she'd complained to him once in a while about the workload he sent her way.

Adam took his director's position at the Institute more seriously than anything he'd worked at before, but he sensed that Edmund, for all his friendliness, considered him an amateur and wouldn't have tolerated his presence in the building if he hadn't held the Institute checkbook. On the other hand, Magdalena Janca kept everyone at a distance. If she had personal feelings about anybody or anything, he had never seen evidence of them.

Occasionally, after a bad day when they'd failed to save a significant piece of Polish art from export, or discovered an entire collection of unique artifacts had been stolen and replaced by fakes during the Communist era, he wondered what he was doing in Poland. He had arrived in Gdansk a year ago after shamefully milking his family connections to get himself appointed head of a three-month fact-finding tour for the Salen Institute.

The facts he'd found hadn't been good. The staff of practically every Polish museum, gallery and institute he'd visited were well-trained and well-intentioned, but neither their training nor intentions could compensate for lack of funding; nor could they stem the tide of corruption that was sending works of art and historical treasures westwards at an alarming rate.

* * *

His three months had stretched to twelve and, as he'd become acclimatized to the slower, more civilized, cafe-orientated pace of life in Gdansk, he suddenly realized he was in no hurry to return to the States.

He stared down at his desk. There was only one envelope left, the special delivery Edmund had brought up. It was heavy and, when he slit it open, photographs tumbled out, along with two folded sheets of paper.

Adam picked up one of the prints. A dark background and slight blurring at the edges suggested it had been taken with a flash. An old man held a copy of Time magazine above what looked like a stone coffin filled with tarnished gold.

He reached for the papers. One was a testimonial, short and to the point.

        I LUDWIG KREFTA, AMBER AND SILVERSMITH,
    HEREBY AUTHENTICATE THE RELIC IN THESE
    PHOTOGRAPHS AS THE THIRTEENTH CENTURY
    AMBER ENCASED BODY OF HELMUT VON MAU, KNOWN
    AS THE AMBER KNIGHT.

There was an indecipherable signature scrawled beneath the text. The second paper was a letter.

        FOR THE ATTENTION OF THE SALEN INSTITUTE.
        THE AMBER KNIGHT IS IN OUR POSSESSION.
    WE ARE PREPARED TO ACCEPT BIDS FOR IT IN
    EXCESS OF FIFTY MILLION DOLLARS. ALL BIDS
    TO BE PLACED IN THE PERSONAL COLUMN OF THE
    NEW YORK TIMES ONE WEEK FROM TODAY.
        IF SUCCESSFUL YOU WILL BE NOTIFIED
    TOGETHER WITH INSTRUCTIONS FOR PAYMENT.

CHAPTER THREE

DAM BUZZED EDMUND as he laid the photographs out on his desk. There was a view of the side of the stone coffin, the head, the foot, the lid—cracked across the middle—and two close-ups taken with the lid off, one featuring the old man holding a copy of Time International. Picking up a magnifying glass he scrutinized the magazine's cover and date. Unless the photographs had been faked, the pictures had been taken last week. A corner of the magazine was curled against the surface of the amber, presumably a calculated touch to convince skeptical buyers the knight was genuine.

"I've found just the place for the pieces you've bought," Edmund flung back the door, crashing it against the wall. "We'll have to adjust the lighting over the powder horn so no one can examine it too closely..."

"Take a look at this," Adam interrupted, handing Edmund a close up of the coffin.

"Is it a quiz? It looks like lumps of sausage in yellow pea soup."

"There's a certificate signed by Ludwig Krefta authenticating it as Helmut von Mau's body."

"The Amber Knight! Holy Mother of God! I never thought he would surface again." Staring at the photograph Edmund fumbled blindly for the others.

"I'm surprised at the authentication. I assumed both Kreftas died years ago." Adam pushed the photographs into Edmund's hand.

"The elder did. As for the younger, an amber-smith doesn't always die when he stops exhibiting, and the curtailment of government grants after the fall of Communism hit some artists hard."

"And the bad ones who relied on the subsidies hardest of all," Adam observed cynically.

"Who's to say what's bad?"

Adam killed the argument before it began. "I admit I'm a philistine. Could these be for real?"

"It would be marvelous if they were. My old tutor always believed von Mau's body and the Amber Room ended up in the private collection of someone like your Howard Hughes; a recluse rich and mad enough to gloat over his ill-gotten gains in private."

"Let's hope they did. Some of your countrymen are crazy and avaricious enough to break up anything for a quick profit."

"Touché. Can the Institute afford fifty million dollars?"

"Only if I earmarked the whole of the European budget for the next fifty years including my own and Magdalena's salary."

"Can't you persuade the trustees to view this as a special case?" Edmund pleaded. "If this is authentic it would set the museum on the international tourist map. The legendary Amber Knight, here in Gdansk. They'd pour through the doors. We'd have to employ another dozen guides just to herd them around."

"You mean more people would want to see the Amber Knight than your collection of Sudanese mud huts?"

Edmund had the grace to remain silent. When Adam had arrived at the museum its exhibits had comprised a motley collection of Roman fragments, Bronze Age bones and African huts and spears, all the museum could afford, and most of which had absolutely no connection with Gdansk or Baltic culture.

"Just think what this means if it is the real thing?" Carried away by the prospect of recovering the knight, Edmund began mentally re-arranging the museum's layout. "If we emptied the long gallery on the second floor and refurbished it—dark blue would look good and complement the amber—put in subdued lighting and raised the coffin on a dais, people could walk around the amber-encased body of the man who founded Christian civilization on the Baltic. We wouldn't need another exhibit on the floor, and we could double, if not triple, our admission fees. I bet we'd even have to put in ropes to control the crowds."

"Wasn't von Mau a German?" Adam wondered which other institutions would be interested—and rich enough—to make a bid.

"He was born in Saxony, but that's like saying St. Patrick's Welsh, not Irish. After he and von Balk vanquished the barbarians..."

"The Prussians, you mean."

"What's in a name?" Edmund questioned impatiently. "Everyone knows the original Prussian tribes were savages, and Prussia as a state didn't exist until the Teutonic knights founded it. It's our history, the history of this region that goes back over seven hundred years."

"I hate to dampen your enthusiasm, but you're forgetting two small technicalities. One, even if this is the real McCoy we haven't got anything like fifty million dollars to spare. And two, it could be a forgery. Even I know that medieval stone coffins like this," Adam tapped the photograph Edmund was holding, "are ten a zloty around old monastery sites."

"Not with those markings." Edmund picked up a chair and pulled it close to the desk.

"There are any number of pre-war photographs and sketches of the Amber Knight that could provide a blueprint for a skilled forger," Adam argued. "Modern methods of distressing are very effective. You should see my sister's Roman swimming pool in LA."

"Look at the amber."

"You can tell whether it's genuine or not, from the amber?"

"Not exactly. But from the descriptions I've read, the color is right."

"You've never seen a color photograph of the Amber Knight?"

"Only paintings, I doubt a color print exists," Edmund admitted.

"But you've studied the story and the period?" Adam pressed.

"Every child in Poland has."

"Enlighten me."

"You don't know the legend of the Amber Knight?" Edmund wondered if Adam was joking.

"Only that he crossed the Vistula from what is now

modern Germany with Hermann von Balk in 1231 on a Teutonic Crusade. When he was killed in battle his troops immortalized him by casting his body in amber."

"Helmut was Lancelot to Hermann's Arthur."

"The Round Table in the East? Come on."

"Just as Arthur and his knights were the epitome of chivalry in western Europe, so Hermann and Helmut represented heroism and Christianity in the East. There's even a Guinevere. The pagan princess, Woberg, who changed her name to Maria after Helmut converted her to Christianity."

"I thought the Teutonic knights were monks?"

"The Teutonic order had three levels. The knights were the highest, but there were also chaplains and menial brothers. All took holy orders."

"But they weren't averse to a bit of hanky-panky on the side?"

"Helmut and Maria's love was platonic!" Edmund protested.

"You expect me to believe that?"

"Not everyone has your failings. Hermann and Helmut captured every pagan stronghold on the Vistula before reaching the last settlement on the Baltic shore which was close to the site of modern Elblag. The pagans had sent for reinforcements from the east and they outnumbered the Teutonic knights ten to one, but that didn't stop Helmut from attacking. The knights fought for twelve days and nights losing more and more men in every attack, until on the thirteenth day, Helmut himself was mortally wounded. With his dying breath he made his men promise to strap his body to his horse and send it into the pagan stronghold. When they did, every heretic who looked upon his face died. Struck down by God..."

"Or shock at seeing a maggoty corpse riding among them," Adam interposed irreverently.

"Those who didn't die surrendered." Carried away by the legend, Edmund ignored Adam's skepticism. "When Hermann took possession of the stronghold he ordered the town burned. The amber in the treasure house melted and ran down the street in a golden stream. He ordered his knights to gather it and pour it over Helmut's body, preserving it for posterity."

"Posterity, or as a warning to the next tribe who stepped out of line?"

"Whatever, it proved effective. That battle marked the end of hostilities on the western side of the Vistula."

"What did Hermann do to the tribes he conquered?"

"If they converted to Christianity and swore allegiance to the Teutonic knights, nothing."

"And if they didn't?"

"He burned them."

"Alive?" Adam asked.

"The medieval church believed that burning the corrupt body was the only way to purify a heathen soul," Edmund lectured. "Maria built a chapel and convent on the site of Helmut's last battle to house his coffin and commemorate the miracle that had delivered the knights from the barbarians. She devoted the rest of her life to God and guarding Helmut's relics. The chapel became a place of pilgrimage until the last Grand Master of the Teutonic Knights adopted the Protestant faith in 1525. He dissolved the order, pulled down the chapel and dispersed the nuns."

"And Helmut?"

"His coffin was moved to Konigsberg castle where it remained on display until 1944. The Nazis admired Helmut von Mau, and the chivalry and heroism he represented, which was why Hitler personally intervened to save his body from the advancing Russian army. The Amber Knight was packed along with the Amber Room and the other contents of the castle."

"And sent where?"

"Do you think I'd be sitting here if I knew the answer to that?" Edmund looked down at the photographs again. "Whoever made this demand knows the market. There are people who would gladly pay fifty million dollars for the knight, especially American museums, not to mention the Germans, who think von Mau belongs to them."

"And the Poles?"

"I shouldn't need to remind you how impoverished we are. But we've learned to be grateful, even for the gift of our own history. Poland's and the knight's, only hope is that some kind benefactor might consider buying it and donating it to us," he said artfully.

"All things in life have to be earned." Adam pushed an international directory of museums towards Edmund. "Telephone and e-mail every contact we've made in Europe and America to find out who else has been approached and, try to gauge if they're in a better position than us to make a bid for it."

Adam pulled a set of keys from his pocket and unlocked a wall cupboard. Behind it was a modern combination lock safe. Turning the dial he opened it and removed a small gadget that fitted easily in the palm of his hand. After locking his door he keyed the gadget into the telephone before dialing the international code for America. Five minutes later he was through to his grandfather's private number.

"Who are you calling?"

He recognized the voice of his grandfather's private secretary. "It's Adam, Peter. Can I speak to my grandfather, please?"

"Do you know what time it is here?"

"Yes, I also know my grandfather suffers from insomnia."

A familiar voice crackled down the line. "That you, Adam?"

"How are you?"

"You didn't call me to find out, so cut the crap. Hang up that extension, Peter. What's happened?"

"Can you talk?"

"Who the hell do you think I've got in my bedroom at my age?"

"Eighty's not so old."

"It is for what I'd like to do."

"You got the scrambler on?"

"It's permanently on this phone, boy."

"Someone may have tracked down the Amber Knight. They've sent photographs and a suggestion that if we want it, we put in a bid in excess of fifty million dollars."

"You sure it's the real thing?"

"Not yet. I've only just received the bid."

"If it checks out, bid what you have to. There's one hundred million in the special fund in Switzerland. It can be converted into cash at twenty four hours notice."

"Depending on who else has been approached, a successful bid could wipe out the special fund."

"Then I'll have to top it up. I saw the knight back in '38 when my father took me on a tour of Europe and the old country. It's an important national piece, like the British Crown Jewels or the original American Declaration of Independence. Old Helmut will rotate in that amber shroud if he's sent away from the patch of dirt he died conquering. Promise me you'll do all you can to secure him for a Polish Museum."

"If it's the real thing, I'll get it."

"Good boy."

The phone went dead. Adam knew his grandfather too well to expect any pleasantries, like "How are you?" or "Goodbye." Removing the gadget he slipped it into his pocket and dialed the local police station. He gave the operator the extension number he waited.

"Dalecka," snapped down the line, against a hubbub of voices and clacking of computer keys.

"How would you like a real crime to solve?"

"Like a murder outside a casino?" came the caustic reply.

"Meet you in the Cafe Milan in ten minutes."

Adam replaced the receiver and picked up his keys. Packing up the applications for funding, he pushed them into a file and carried them into Edmund's office. "Send these over to Magdalena and ask her to find out all she can about the last known movements of the Amber Knight. Tell her I'll call into the Historical Museum later to look at what she's got."

"Am I allowed to inquire what you intend to do while Magdalena and I slave away at the boring bits?"

Adam pushed the envelope with the demand and photographs into his inside pocket. "Talk to the police."

"You're not naive enough to think they'll instigate a search for the knight?"

"They might have some idea where it's been kept since the war. If we can locate it, we might be able to claim it for the museum without handing over a zloty."

"Try searching the cells," Edmund advised. "The police could be behind the demand. All I hear these days is how hard up they are."

One of the museum guides stopped Adam as he reached the door.

"Telephone, Mr. Salen. They said it was urgent."

He took the call in the ticket office. "Adam Salen."

"Adam..."

"I'm sorry he's unavailable at the moment."

"That's the worst Polish accent I've ever heard, dear brother."

"What do you want, Georgiana? I'm busy." Adam turned his face to the wall. No matter how hard he tried to ignore his sisters, they inevitably managed to corner him, and always at the most inconvenient times.

"Guess where I am?"

"I'm in no mood for games," Adam said sourly.

"Go on, guess," she pleaded, in a voice bubbling with suppressed excitement.

"In a wedding chapel in Las Vegas marrying number nine, or is it ten?"

"What would I do without a little brother to tease me?"

"Buy yourself a whipping boy?"

"I'm in Paris."

"Shopping?" he guessed.

"Scouting for the Texas gallery."

Adam suppressed a pang of jealousy. The Salen Institute's Texas gallery of modern art's budget was one he'd dearly love to dovetail into his Eastern European fund.

"... and tomorrow I'm going to visit you."

"I hope by 'you' you mean Poland in general, not me in particular."

"Of course I mean you in particular. I've seen the most darling paintings in the most seductive colors. All poached pastels, crushed magenta, mombie and mauve..."

"What the hell's mombie?"

"You never know anything. Anyway, the agent here tells me he picked them up in the most primitive little gallery in Gdansk which I simply have to see for myself. Isn't it the most amazing coincidence? Would you believe this gallery is in the very block you live in? You do live at 52 Mariacka Street?"

Adam was tempted to deny his address, but Georgiana didn't give him an opportunity to ease a word in.

"... and the artist's adorable. I've only seen his photograph, but he has mournful eyes and the most seductive telephone voice. It makes my toes curl. He's called Casimir... isn't that a gorgeous name? Casimir Zamosc. I don't suppose you know him?"

"No."

"I've arranged to meet him. A man with that accent could change my life."

"I've no doubt you'll change his," Adam broke in, still smarting at the thought of Georgiana touring Europe on the Texas gallery's budget.

"Stop behaving like a Victorian father. I'll be with you soon, there's no need to put yourself out..."

"I won't. I'll book rooms for you in the Grand Hotel in Sopot. You'll love it, all Art Nouveau, past splendors, atmos-pheric decadence, combined with modern room service and a casino. And, it's only a short taxi ride from Gdansk."

"In that case tell your staff we'll need three rooms. I have the children with me... and Nanny of course... and my maid..."

"Five rooms?"

"Better make it six. I have the teeniest little surprise up my sleeve."

"Don't forget to tell whoever drives you from the airport, the Grand Hotel, Sopot. Everyone knows where it is..." He was talking to a dial tone. She'd already hung up.

CHAPTER FOUR

THE CAFE MILAN was opposite the police station in Piwna Street. In the evenings it was a hive of social activity and dispenser of Italian cuisine, during the day a civilized spot for tourists to linger over leisurely lunches, and a haven for police officers who needed to escape from the pressure and clamor of the station.

Josef Dalecka was already seated at a table in the darkest, most inaccessible corner when Adam walked in. The gleaming mahogany furniture complemented by pink tablecloths and sparkling cut-glass candlesticks was seductive, offering a promise of the evening to come, even at ten in the morning.

"You had any more thoughts on last night?" Josef enquired as Adam approached.

"None."

"I knew it had to be something else!" he grumbled as Adam took the chair opposite his. "Just don't ask for any favors. I'm not in the mood for dishing out anything other than coffee."

"And vodka chasers?" Adam laid his hand over the glass in front of him. "Not for me, thanks, but don't let that stop you."

"It won't." Josef picked up the bottle and refilled his own glass.

"Last night still bothering you, or things not so good between you and Mariana again?"

"Worse than ever." Dalecka stared gloomily into his vodka. "We had a foul quarrel last night."

"It would be a newsworthy event if you hadn't." Adam leaned back so the waiter could set a coffee pot and cups on the table.

"This time we quarreled before she went to work."

"I take it she's on night shift?"

"Yes, and she wasn't home when I got in this morning. I stopped off at the hotel she works in on the way down from Sopot last night. They said she'd left an hour before. As she wasn't home, where was she?"

"Trying to avoid your foul temper," Adam suggested. He, and everyone else acquainted with the Daleckas in Gdansk knew that Mariana was having an affair. The affair was a constant, her choice of a man wasn't. They changed at frequent intervals.

"My marriage is falling apart and all you can do is make bad jokes."

"If you really want to save it, you can start by developing a pleasant personality. I'll allow you to practice your newfound politeness on me. You could also try throwing your mother-in-law out of your apartment. If she wasn't there to look after the kids, Mariana would have to come home. Whatever problems you two have, she'd never risk leaving the children on their own."

"I can't throw Marta out, not while Mariana and I work the shifts we do."

"If you've no intention of taking my advice, there's no point in discussing your domestic problems. Here's something that will help you forget them." Adam handed over the envelope. He sugared his coffee and looked out of the window into the street. "Now that's a sight to see, your chief sharing serious conversation with your cousin, Melerski."

"The way things are in Gdansk the police have good reason to be serious."

"Judging by the look on Melerski's face, so do the Mafia. He still is the Godfather of all crooked Poles?" Adam asked.

"You Americans, you get all your ideas from Hollywood," Josef said dismissively. "Melerski's a businessman."

"And I'm a green walnut."

"The Amber Knight!" Josef let out a long, low whistle. "Poland's legendary miracle worker. By God, we could do with him now to ride out among the foreign speculators intent on buying up the country. Quite a few I've come across would be improved by death."

"Don't tell me a hard-headed police officer like you believes in the legend?"

"Of course. I believe in everything Polish, even the sausages." Josef continued to scan the demand. "All the same, fifty million dollars is a lot to pay for a corpse, even Helmut von Mau's."

"It is set in amber," Adam pointed out.

"I could get you a ton of amber for a lot less, and a fresh corpse for nothing."

"That a proposition?"

"Make me an offer."

"I take it you have someone in mind to play the corpse?"

"The manager in the hotel Mariana works in," Josef said seriously.

Adam refused to bite at the bait of domestic intrigue. "People might notice the corpse wasn't medieval."

"Is there a way of finding out if this is the real thing?"

"I'm working on it. I also have Magdalena piecing together the last known movements of the Amber Knight."

"You want me to fingerprint the envelope and the photographs?"

"Bit late, after we've mauled them about."

Josef turned the envelope over. "Berlin postmark. Given the volume of east-west traffic that passes through that city, I can probably narrow it down to the odd million or so people. Is that Krefta holding the magazine over the coffin?"

"I have no idea, but I intend to find out."

"What about the magazine?"

"It's last week's Time. Available by international subscription, not to mention on every station bookstall between here and Paris."

"This letter suggests they're holding an auction. Have you contacted any other museums?"

"Edmund Dunst is approaching them, but I doubt many institutions will be keen on pooling information. Everyone will want the knight for themselves. On the other hand, they might be prepared to talk to the police."

"So that's where I come in. You want me to do your legwork. You've got a lot of nerve..."

"Come on, Josef, what museum is going to talk to a rival?"

"I don't even know why I'm talking to you."

"It is the duty of all government departments to cooperate with foreign institutions prepared to invest in Poland. Directive number..."

"Don't ever try to pull rank on me, it turns me vicious. Can I can keep this?" Josef held up the envelope.

"No, but you can make copies."

"I may as well get it dusted for prints at the same time." Josef picked up his glass and drained it.

"If I were you, I'd go for the coffee as well."

Josef sipped the coffee, made a face and pushed it aside.

"I take it I'm paying?" Adam signaled to the waiter as Josef rose from the table.

"Put it down on your tax return as a police bribe."

"You do realize that if we find the Amber Knight it will go on display here, in Gdansk," Adam opened his wallet. "An exhibit like that will bring the tourists rolling in."

"And what makes you think the Germans will allow us to keep a Teuton? They're very possessive about their people, even dead ones," Josef warned.

"They won't have much choice in the matter if I get my hands on von Mau before they do."

"If I were you, I'd phone the German museums first. Fifty million dollars is small change to them."

"Good idea. You'll talk to them first?" Adam checked the bill and paid the waiter.

"Save your time and energy. Forget about the knight." Josef avoided answering the question. "I know Germans. They have the taste and money for culture. If this knight is going anywhere, it's Berlin."

"How much do you want to bet on it?

"A million."

"Zlotys?"

"Dollars," Josef corrected. "You're the rich American."

"And if you lose?"

"Sue me. Everyone knows no Pole owns anything worth paying legal fees." Josef held up the envelope. "Want to see if the print boys come up with anything? If they do, dinner's on you."

"Isn't it always?" Adam followed Josef across the road into the station.

Adam took no pleasure in being proved right on the finger-prints. The technician discovered nine discernable sets plus a number of smudges on the envelope and three distinct prints on the papers and photographs. He didn't need a detective to work out that one set was his, another Edmund's and the third Josef's. After extracting a half-hearted promise from Josef to sound out Melerski along with his other Mafia con-tacts and approach Warsaw on the off chance that another museum had notified the authorities of the reappearance of the Amber Knight, he retrieved his passport from Josef and left.

Turning right out of Piwna Street he made his way through narrow lanes to the Royal Way. If Mariacka Street was the most beautiful in Gdansk, the Royal Way and the Long Market were the most imposing. He lingered in front of the Neptune Fountain watching tourists pose for photographs before the gothic facade of Artus Court and wondered if the wealthy brotherhood of merchants who had built it had also paid homage at the shrine of the Amber Knight. Mulling over the possibility while drinking a glass of cold beer in a pave-ment café seemed infinitely preferable to the prospect of climbing the stairs to the top floor of the Historical Museum to confront the frosty Magdalena.

Changing direction, he bumped into the back of Helena, Edmund Dunst's very new, and very pretty, blonde wife, who was trying to sell one of her still-life paintings to a chic, middle-aged French tourist.

"I thought you were going to keep all the landscapes and

still-lifes for the gallery," he hissed in strongly accented school French.

A born actress, Helena shrugged her shoulders. "I have to eat, sir, your gallery charges so much in commission it is not worth my while."

The tourist pricked up her ears. While Adam inspected the paintings Helena had racked out on frames, the deal was concluded.

"Five hundred euros." Helena tucked the money into the leather purse attached to her belt. "Thank you. That will put a smile on the face of our bank manager."

"Want a beer? We can sit on the step if you're afraid of missing customers."

"A beer would be good."

He caught the eye of a waiter, gave him an order and joined her. "Do you know anything about a painter called Casimir Zamosc?"

"Polish?"

"Presumably. All I know about him is that he exhibits with Waleria."

"Never heard of him."

"You sure?"

"He not a member of any of the guilds I've joined, so that rules out most of the artists in Gdansk. Must dash, here comes another one." Taking her beer from the waiter's tray she joined a German couple who had stopped to look at her landscapes.

Adam took his glass up on to the terrace and glanced at his watch. Nearly twelve—an ideal time for a combination breakfast and lunch. On impulse he finished his drink and crossed the street to the delicatessen. He picked up a basket and raided the shelves for the ingredients for a picnic lunch. No need for drink, there were a couple of bottles of good German wine cooling in his refrigerator. His purchases piled into a bag, he retraced his steps through the cool, dark alleyways to St Mary's church and Mariacka Street. An erotic vision of Manet's "dinner of herbs" came to mind. It would be fun to recreate the scene. Helga always looked better divested of the leather mini-skirt and cropped top she wore when out of her croupier's uniform.

"She's gone," Waleria announced as he stepped into the gallery. "Left about an hour ago." She eyed the carrier bag. "Replacing your silver?"

"Lunch." He dropped the bag to the floor.

"For us, how thoughtful!"

"Edmund Dunst and I have to work through in the museum. I only called in to pick up a bottle of wine from upstairs. By the way, you heard of a painter called..."

"Casimir Zamosc? Someone from the Salen Institute of Modern Art telephoned from Paris. I presumed you'd be connected."

"My sister. You should warn this Zamosc, she devours artists, body and soul. And the body part always comes first."

"Never seen him."

"You exhibit him?"

"Only since last week. Russian from Riga. He sent me an illustrated catalogue. I liked what I saw and took half a dozen on a sale or return basis."

"Georgiana's meeting him here tomorrow," Adam warned her.

"Then let's hope he arrives. Like his stuff?" She pointed him in the direction of a framed acrylic depicting a pile of pastel sticks heaped on a black background.

"Crayons in repose?"

"You really are a barbarian."

"Perhaps something in the composition escapes me. Must love you and leave you."

"You can't fool me," she shouted after him. "I know you only dropped in to count your ornaments."

He ran up the spiral staircase, an art deco version of the one in the Historical Museum, and out on to the back stairs. His apartment was empty, just as Waleria had told him it would be, but there were signs that Helga had made full use of everything the place had to offer. Wet towels slopped in pools of water on the bathroom floor; the shower door was open, the tops left off his shampoo and shower gel and a fine scattering of talcum powder overlaid the mess.

Damp footsteps led out of the bathroom across the deep pile of the living room carpet to the sofa where a soggy imprint of her body flattened the cushions. They'd even been conveniently arranged at a comfortable angle for the telephone.

Coffee grounds littered the worktop of the tiny triangular kitchen cut from a corner of the living room. A bottle of wine was missing from the fridge. On the mezzanine the make-up-smeared sheets lay tumbled on the bed. Her hairs were in his brush. There was no note.

It took him an hour to restore order. After pushing the sheets into the linen basket and straightening the newly jacketed duvet on the bed, he checked around one last time, even opening the drawer where he kept his cutlery. Waleria had made him paranoid. The odd bottle of wine, yes, but there was no way Helga would take any of the utilitarian pieces he had furnished the place with.

Suppressing the urge to phone Helga and tell her precisely

what he thought of her personal habits, he locked the door and returned downstairs.

"About time, I was just going to throw whatever's in this bag to the birds," Waleria nudged the bag with the toe of her shoe.

"Be my guest."

"You serious?" Waleria picked up the bag and examined the contents.

"I'm not hungry any more."

"And Edmund Dunst?"

"He can send out for a sandwich."

"Feed you dinner tonight in exchange?"

"Flaki?" Adam asked suspiciously.

"I was thinking of pork cutlets but if you'd prefer tripe I'll get some." She knew he hated the Polish national dish. "Eight o'clock?"

"I'll bring my appetite."

CHAPTER FIVE

TEPPING ON TO the small veranda that fronted the street, Adam noticed that the door to Feliks Malek's basement jewelry shop opposite was open, and the glass case he kept his most modestly priced tourist pieces in set out on the pavement.

"If you're looking for Feliks he isn't here." Elizbieta Hirsz, the pretty, eighteen-year-old redhead Feliks employed as an assistant informed him as he descended the steps.

"Is he likely to be long?"

"Who knows? A supply of amber is due in. He's gone to see what he can get."

"From Kaliningrad?"

"Where else? No one's prepared to pay Polish rates while the Russians can mine it for a third of the price." She bent her head over the earrings she was working on, laying hair-thin gold wires onto beaten silver leaves.

"What do you know about Ludwig Krefta?" Adam asked, aware that Elizbieta's family's pedigree as silver- and amber-smiths was even longer than Feliks's.

"The younger or the elder?"

"Is the elder dead?"

"Since 1951."

"Then it has to be the younger."

"It doesn't make much difference. The younger hasn't done anything worth shouting about since 1970. You been offered some of his pieces for the museum?"

"Would they be a good investment?"

"The best. They're not classed as antiques yet, but they will be, and Edmund will tell you good antique pieces are rarer than green storks these days."

"He has mentioned it."

"And while we're on the subject, some of the modern pieces he's bought for the museum are hideous—and worse than hideous, junk."

"I have a strong back, but I'd appreciate you not airing your opinions around Edmund. He's sensitive about his amber."

"I've noticed. But you won't go wrong with genuine Krefta, the elder or younger. Their early output equaled the best produced by George Schrieber and the seventeenth-century Konigsberg workshops. My father always used to say that one day Krefta the younger will be recognized as the finest amber-smith of the twentieth century."

"Coming from your father, that's quite a compliment."

"Not really, my father trained in Krefta's workshop. Of course that was before Krefta turned to drink. Surprising really," she bit her bottom lip as she concentrated on laying the final strands of wire in place, "just how many silver- and amber-smiths hit the bottle, but from what I've heard, Krefta had a better excuse than most. His wife died of cancer, and according to my father she took years to do it. All of them painful."

"But Krefta's still alive?"

"Physically maybe, but from an artistic point of view he's dead." She spoke as though the only life worth living was the artistic. "He hasn't exhibited since the late sixties. So what pieces are you after? If it's one of his chess sets..."

"It's nothing of his. I received a note from him this morning authenticating the body of Helmut von Mau."

"Blessed saints! You've tracked down the Amber Knight?" Feliks walked down the steps into the shop and parked his short, squat body on the edge of Elizbieta's workbench.

"I'm interested in its whereabouts."

"Does this interest extend to the Amber Room? They disappeared at the same time."

Adam handed the well-thumbed envelope to Feliks who promptly tipped it out on Elizbieta's work bench.

"Feliks!" Elizbieta remonstrated as he sent her carefully positioned strands of wire scattering.

"Sorry, my pet." His baggy clown's face sagged. Elizbieta was eighteen to his sixty-five, but he was as besotted as a lovesick boy.

"Sorry! Is that all you've got to say..."

"Could it be the Amber Knight?" Adam cut into Elizbieta's tirade.

Feliks studied the photographs for what seemed like an eternity. Pushing a couple across to Elizbieta he picked up a jewelers' glass from the desk.

"That's Krefta all right." Feliks pointed to the man holding the copy of Time. "Older, thinner and more lined than when I saw him in the Moscow exhibition in '68, but definitely him."

"He looks as though he's lost his teeth," Elizbieta commented, peering over Feliks's shoulder.

"And the knight?"

"That's more difficult. I don't know anything about stone coffins."

"But you do know amber," Adam pressed.

"I have been known to recognize it," Feliks conceded dryly, "but I couldn't say for certain what's in that coffin without doing a few tests."

"What kind of tests?"

"Let's start at the beginning," Feliks pontificated, with an old man's exasperatingly leisurely attitude. "There are records detailing how Helmut von Mau's corpse was set in amber."

Adam repeated what Edmund had told him. "The amber in the treasure house in Elblag melted when the town was burned by Hermann von Balk."

"Then poured around Helmut von Mau's body which had been placed in a coffin. Amber melts at 280 degrees centigrade which couldn't have done the corpse much good. Perhaps it's just as well that most amber clouds when it cools. I doubt the old boy's a pretty sight."

"He was old?"

"Thirty-three," Elizbieta supplied swiftly.

"Don't tell me you're hooked on the legend as well?"

Elizbieta looked Adam coolly in the eye. "Of course. Haven't you noticed heroes are an extinct breed? Every girl needs a man she can look up to, one who's handsome, brave, chivalrous..."

"And heading for eight hundred years old?" Adam interrupted dryly.

"If this is a copy, it could have been made with artificial amber." Feliks dropped one photograph in favor of another.

"I didn't know there was such a thing."

"Take a good look at the exhibits in some of the smaller museums next time you pass through them. It's been around for centuries. A mixture of copal, camphor and turpentine."

"Can you tell if that's artificial amber from the photographs?"

"There are only two certain methods of differentiating between real and artificial amber. One is by heating. Artificial amber has a lower melting point. It also softens in cold ether. I couldn't tell whether this is real or not without handling it."

"What he's trying to say," Elizbieta interrupted, "is that it's impossible to authenticate a piece from photographs."

"It has occurred to me that all you'd need to reproduce the knight is an outfit of medieval clothes and armor—not impossible given the number of museums in difficulties," Adam said, "and a stone coffin, a body and enough amber to cover it."

"Carbon dating the amber wouldn't be any help. Most of the amber in circulation is a few million years old," Feliks pronounced authoritatively. "And a stone coffin?" He opened his hands and turned down his mouth. "How do you go about authenticating one of those?"

"But there are ways of distinguishing between a modern corpse and one that's almost eight hundred years old." Adam thought about it and realized he wasn't sure.

"After it's been in amber? I wouldn't know, I've never seen a human corpse in amber." Feliks squinted at the photograph he was holding. "But I agree it could be difficult to spot a forgery. Unscrupulous amber-smiths have been putting insects into amber for centuries, so why not a body? Amber's the easiest thing in the world to mould. All you have to do is heat a pile of shavings and crumbs, melt them and pour them into a mould. You wouldn't believe what can be done these days with microwaves and dyes. Double or treble the size of a nugget at the push of a button. Name your color and you can have it in amber."

"And sell it off to unsuspecting tourists as a rare and perfect piece," Adam suggested mischievously.

"Tourists should research before they buy." Elizbieta opened a drawer. "Here." She handed Adam a bracelet set with a paperweight-sized polished nugget of amber. "Tell me what's wrong with that?"

"It's hallmarked silver."

"Any fool can imprint a hallmark. It's pewter, can't you tell by the sheen?"

"I'm no silversmith."

"And you're in charge of the Institute's budget?" She shook her head in dismay. "Now look at the amber."

"It's a large piece, which it makes it more valuable."

"It's made of three pieces which have been heated and welded together, can't you see the lines?"

"Can't those occur naturally?"

"In that irregular pattern? Now turn it over."

"There's indentations in the back."

"Caused by shrinkage after it was heated. There's also a rough join in the middle. The edges are splintering."

"You make this with anyone in mind?" Adam frowned.

"I keep it to show tourists what to avoid."

"You're all heart."

"We sell top quality goods at a fair price," Feliks declared. "I like people to go away happy. Give me the Amber Knight for a couple of days and I'll give you an opinion on whether it's genuine or not, but it will only be an opinion. Amber-smiths, like art experts, can be fooled."

"Then what chance do poor devils like me stand?"

Feliks handed Adam his glass. "Look at where the amber meets the sides of the coffin. It's splintering."

"Like the bracelet?"

"That's not surprising given that we know the amber was heated and melted in a fire," Elizbieta contributed. "And I doubt whoever covered him was that fussy about air getting between the layers of amber."

"The whole thing looks real enough." Feliks retrieved his glass and picked up another photograph. "It's also somewhat the worse for wear. As well as the splintering, there's evidence of deeper cracks. See the way the flash has broken up the light on these fissures in the surface. They could be the result of exposure to frost, or damage that occurred when it was moved out of Konigsberg Castle. If it was a fake I think they would have taken more care with its appearance."

"Or they could be cleverer than you think," Elizbieta suggested.

"Or it could be decay," Feliks said thoughtfully.

"I thought amber lasted forever." Adam's mind was racing to absorb the implications of what Felix and Elizbieta were saying.

"After it's been exposed to air it can deteriorate with age if it's not cared for properly."

"But we've got two thousand-year-old Roman beads made of the stuff in the museum," Adam protested.

"Which Edmund keeps in a glass case at a fixed temperature."

"So, after listening to you two for half an hour, all I know for certain is that this might, or might not be a forgery?"

"Does it matter?" Elizbieta retrieved her threads of gold wire and laid them on the workbench beside her. "Put it on display anyway. People love corpses. They'll flock to see one in amber."

"That's supposing I can track it down."

"You don't have it?"

"Whoever has it sent a demand along with the photographs. They want bids in excess of fifty million dollars."

"American?" Feliks asked.

"Oh, yes," Adam confirmed.

"Old zlotys and you might be talking." Feliks picked up a ruler from the desk, measured the magazine in the photograph, scribbled down the dimensions and began measuring the coffin. "Give me the magazine and I'll give you a rough estimate as to the quantity of amber you would need to fill that coffin."

"You don't know the size of the body."

"To get in there he has to be short."

"Or they chopped his legs off," Elizbieta said practically. "Father Ignatius told me that medieval monks often used to cut down bodies to fit the coffins they had in stock. It was easier to re-shape the body than carve out a larger coffin."

"If this is a fake made with real amber, they would have needed more than the supply used by an average workshop in a year. I could ask around for you. See if anyone's been buying in unusually large quantities lately, lucky sods."

Elizbieta looked up. "You didn't get any today?"

"The consignment was hijacked."

"Stolen!" Adam exclaimed.

"Too late to make this, if that's what you're thinking." Feliks returned the photographs to Adam. "It left

Kaliningrad last night, but failed to arrive in Gdansk this morning."

"How was it being brought in?" Adam stowed the photographs back in the envelope.

"I value my poor hide too much to tell someone outside the business that. You want to know, go ask the Mafia, or a certain high ranking official. He's paid enough to look the other way when it comes in."

"I don't suppose either of you has Krefta's address?" Adam asked hopefully.

"Last I heard he was in Konigsberg," Feliks answered.

"Kaliningrad, Feliks," Elizbieta corrected him.

"I can never remember new-fangled names."

"The Russians renamed it in 1945."

"Yesterday."

"Only to the senile." Elizbieta gave Adam the benefit of her most winsome smile. "Krefta moved to Kaliningrad after his wife died. I met him there a couple of times, but only at his workshop. I still have my father's old address book. Do you want me to look it up?"

"If it's not too much trouble."

She disappeared up the stairs.

"She likes you." Feliks opened a door set below a display cabinet and pulled out a bottle of vodka.

"And she's living with you."

"Only because she wants the trade secrets I keep up here." Feliks tapped his head. "I love her," he declared mournfully, "and I'd do anything to make her happy. Sleeping with you would make her happy."

"That's ridiculous."

"No, it isn't. She doesn't get enough sex from me."

"I don't sleep with my friends' women."

"Damned western morality."

"Here it is." Elizbieta, who had overheard the last part of their conversation, slid her forefinger along Adam's thumb as she handed him Krefta's address. "You going to write to him?"

"I thought I might look him up in the flesh."

"In Kaliningrad? You don't speak Russian," Feliks reminded him.

"He's probably moved on since Elizbieta last saw him," Adam replied.

"And even if he hasn't, you might have difficulty recognizing him from that photograph. You'll need an interpreter. If you like, I could go with you," Elizbieta offered archly.

"That could be helpful, seeing as how you've met him."

"Only a couple of times, a long time ago when my father worked for him. But Feliks is right—he might not still be at this address."

"It's somewhere to start."

"When are you thinking of going?"

"Tomorrow."

"Perfect, I could do with a day off. But Americans need a visa to cross the border."

"That's not a problem. I'll pick you up here. Be ready at six, we'll leave before the heat sets in."

Felix accompanied Adam up to street level. "Enjoy yourself with her."

"I'll have her back before nightfall and, just to ensure there'll be no hanky-panky, I'll take Magdalena along."

"You Americans never know when you're well off."

"We're worse off than most Poles think we are, which

reminds me. Helga said something about a pair of gold and sapphire earrings?"

"She was taken with them, but then she would be, a collector like her, and I don't mean jewelry. Why don't you find yourself a nice girl..."

"Like Elizbieta?"

"At least she doesn't charge for her favors."

"If there's one thing I've learned about women in the last twenty-eight years, it's that they always present a bill for their services. How much are the earrings?"

"The ones she saw were a special order for Radek. He's paying three thousand dollars."

"American?"

"No, Mickey Mouse money," Feliks mocked. "What do you think I am? A miracle worker? You want top quality goods; you have to pay the price."

"Not three thousand dollars, I don't. What can you do for three hundred?"

"You expect me to answer that?"

"Come on, there can't be that much gold in them."

"Now you're telling me my business."

"Haven't you anything you can substitute for sapphires?"

"Nothing that will fool Helga or the jeweler she'll sell them to."

"Three hundred's my limit."

"I could do crystal for that price."

"Only if it's blue."

"I'll see what I can find."

"Adam!" Waleria waved to him from across the street. "Josef Dalecka's looking for you."

"Probably to warn you against buying any hijacked

shipments of raw amber." Feliks was still smarting at the loss. Adam presumed because he'd have to buy in Polish amber at an inflated price in order to continue trading.

"Whoever has the knight has offered it to more than one museum. Do you think they could have stolen the shipment to make a copy?" Adam asked.

"Could probably make a few, certainly two, on what went missing."

"What price the knight when every major museum in western Europe has one?" Adam murmured.

"I'm in the wrong business. Amber-encased bodies at fifty million American dollars a time have to be a better investment of time and resources than three hundred dollar earrings."

"You'd need a body, Feliks," Adam reminded him.

"This is Poland. They're commoner than amber nuggets if you know where to look."

Adam started to protest, remembered Rat, and waved goodbye.

CHAPTER SIX

DAM FOUND JOSEF waiting for him in his office in the Historical Museum, coffee cup in hand, wearing an even gloomier expression than he had in the Milan.

"Feliks told me last night's amber shipment has gone missing." Adam shrugged off his jacket and hung it on the back of his chair.

"So much for trying to keep anything that happens in this town quiet." Josef reached for the coffee jug and poured Adam a cup. "Have you also heard that Brunon Kaszuba's skipped custody?"

"You let him go?"

"Not exactly, although we couldn't have held him much longer."

"After he dropped fifty thousand dollars in the casino?"

"Gambling is a stupidity, not a crime. He refused to shift from the story that Rat gave him the money, and as we had no evidence to the contrary, we had to take his word for it."

"But Rat was murdered."

"While Kaszuba was in custody, and you can't get a better alibi than that. All we had to hold him on was the fracas in the casino and you know how reluctant casino people are to prosecute. Kaszuba's a good customer."

"So he walked?"

"We were going to release him at midday, but he beat us to it. When the duty officer took down the morning coffee he found an empty cell."

Adam sat back in his chair and rested his chin on his fingertips. "Could Kaszuba's fifty thousand be connected to the missing amber shipment?"

"How?"

"You're the detective."

"If Kaszuba took the amber, which seems unlikely given that he was gambling in the casino before the loss was discovered, he would have had to move like lightning to negotiate and collect on the sale by two in the morning. Now if it had disappeared last week, I might have bought a link with the sudden reappearance of your knight."

"When did the amber go missing?"

"All we know from Melerski is that it was loaded on to a boat in Kaliningrad yesterday afternoon and it wasn't on board when the ship came into Gdansk this morning."

"It's shipped in?"

"You didn't think they brought it in overland?"

"I've never thought about it at all. Brunon and Rat could have stolen the amber to order."

"And got paid up front?" Josef questioned skeptically.

"What about the crew? Didn't they see or hear anything?"

"Probably."

"They're not talking?"

"When I said the boat came in, I should have mentioned that it was towed in by the coastguard. The crew and the deck had more holes in them than a hooker's panties, courtesy of a Heckler and Koch sub-machine gun, according to ballistics." Josef finished the coffee in his cup and poured himself another.

"Isn't that an army gun?" Adam asked.

"I doubt whoever fired it was wearing a uniform. There were three bodies on board, but as someone said in the station this morning, that's three less for us to worry about."

"Russian or Polish?"

"Who cares? I don't see a tie-in between Kaszuba's fifty grand and the hijacked amber shipment. Instinct tells me Kaszuba's money came from a killing. It wouldn't be the first time he and Rat had 'retired' someone for cash."

"I thought the going rate was a couple of hundred American." Adam held out a cup and Josef filled it for him.

"Depends on the subject."

"If the subject was important why entrust the job to third-rate hoodlums like Kaszuba and Rat?"

"I was sorting this nicely in my mind until you walked in."

"Then you're letting the vodka do your thinking for you."

"And I think I'm encouraging an amateur to get above himself."

"You're here for the coffee?" Adam switched the almost empty machine off.

Josef fell serious. "I came to tell you there's a price on Kaszuba's head. Ten thousand dollars dead, twenty alive, courtesy of the Russians, according to Melerski. The silly sod's really annoyed someone this time. Warn Magdalena, I'd hate to think of anyone taking it out on her."

"Warn her yourself."

"How can I, when we've had no notification through official channels?"

"I thought Mafia channels were the official ones these days."

"Very funny. I asked Melerski to pass on the message that Magdalena and Kaszuba lead separate lives and she knows nothing about him or what he does, but as I don't know who we're dealing with, it might not have any effect."

"But you get a clear conscience for playing the honorable police officer."

"I've done all I can, Adam," Josef asserted defensively rising from his chair.

"It has occurred to me that the amber might have been stolen to make a couple of fake knights."

"A couple?" Josef stopped in his tracks.

"Feliks reckons there'd be enough to make more than one."

"What about the coffin?"

"Not difficult to get hold of."

"Neither are corpses," Josef reflected. "After last night there's four lying unclaimed in the mortuary right now. Be interesting to see what happens if three knights turn up after the auction. A word of advice if you do fork out fifty million dollars—make sure you get the real thing."

"Tell me where to get hold of fifty million dollars and I might risk bidding."

"Don't forget to warn Magdalena about Kaszuba, and to let us know the minute she sees him." Josef opened the door.

"I'll talk to Magdalena, but I make no promises. You know what she's like."

"Impossible, like all damned women," Josef snarled.

Edmund entered Adam's office as soon as he heard Josef leave. "Berlin's had the same offer as us."

"They biting?" Adam asked.

"Wary, same as you. I spoke to the assistant curator. They're running around in circles trying to authenticate the photographs."

"They won't succeed. There's no way of doing it without access to the piece."

"You checked with Feliks?"

"He and Elizbieta identified Krefta. If you want coffee I'll make fresh," Adam offered.

Edmund shook his head. "What Feliks doesn't know about amber isn't worth knowing. So, are we going to make a bid or not?"

"Let you know nearer the date." Adam picked up his jacket. "If anyone wants me I'll be with Magdalena."

"You wouldn't give the knight to the Historical Museum?" Edmund was horrified at the thought of the archaeological museum losing out to its rival.

"Let's get the knight in Gdansk before we start arguing about where it's going to be exhibited, shall we?"

The Historical Museum was housed in the old town hall of Gdansk. Adam had never seen the facade for the simple reason that it had been swathed in scaffolding and plastic sheeting since his arrival, but he couldn't resist glancing up at the stone lions on the coat of arms above the door. Legend had it they turned their gaze in the direction of the rightful Polish king. Whatever the von Bach Zalewski's status before their arrival in the States, it clearly hadn't been royal, because their eyes had never swiveled in his direction.

Nodding to the burly ex-police officer who steered the tourists towards the ticket booth, he ran up the stairs to

Magdalena's office which was tucked away in a corner of the top floor. The rest of the floor housed a conference room and an apartment the Institute used to house visiting professors, historians, archaeologists and anyone who expressed the slightest interest in investing in a Salen Institute project.

Guilt at Magdalena's workload had led to the recent appointment of a new secretary. Magdalena had been all in favor until she had met Adam's choice, Wiklaria, the pretty, blonde niece of his landlady, Waleria. Wiklaria was orally proficient and literate in five languages, a whiz with computers and had impeccable references from the private commercial college her aunt had sent her to, but all Magdalena saw were a pair of long slim legs, blue eyes, and the mooning looks Wiklaria sent Adam's way on the rare occasions he ventured into the Historical Museum.

Adam smiled at Wiklaria as he entered the reception area. After asking how she was settling in, he sent her out to get coffee and sandwiches from the restaurant next door. Steeling himself for Magdalena's chilly reception, he tapped at the inner door. Her sharp, "Come," alerted him that she had overheard, and disapproved of, his conversation with her assistant.

Magdalena was sitting at her desk; wire-rimmed reading glasses perched on her nose, light brown hair scraped back into a net, the bare minimum of lipstick and mascara accentuating the stern expression in her steel-gray eyes.

"Edmund delivered the file and your instructions."

"It was a request for help, not an instruction. Any problems?" He was never as abrupt with the rest of the staff, but Magdalena had made it plain she disliked conversation that could be construed as personal, and that included comments on the weather or simple inquiries after her health.

"None, other than lack of time." She moved a pile of books uncovering a heap of newspaper cuttings that had turned brown and brittle with age.

"Edmund told you about the letter and authentication that arrived with the photographs?"

Adam folded his long frame onto the uncomfortable upright chair she kept in her office to discourage visitors. Before she had time to answer, Wiklaria knocked and carried in a tray loaded with coffee and rolls. "Thank you." Adam took it from her and deposited it on the window ledge, the only clear space in the room.

"I don't remember asking for coffee, Wiklaria," Magdalena snapped.

"You didn't, I did," Adam said. "Sorry, I should have checked with you, only I haven't had lunch and I assumed that you'd worked through too."

Wiklaria gave Magdalena an apologetic look before she closed the door. The staff liked Adam, but they were in no doubt as to who was in charge of the Salen Institute offices in the Historical Museum.

Adam poured out the coffee and laid two of the rolls on plates.

"Just coffee for me. I never eat lunch."

"You should."

"I prefer not to get butter smears on my papers, and in answer to your question, yes, Edmund told me about the photographs of the knight and the demand. After sixty years I really would urge caution…"

"Before we start on the Amber Knight, I have an unofficial warning from the police."

"Josef?"

He nodded, aware that the Daleckas lived in the same tower block as Magdalena and her younger brothers. "Your husband is in trouble."

"Brunon's always in trouble," she said dismissively.

"He was gambling in Sopot Casino last night with a man who was found murdered shortly after Brunon was escorted out of the place."

"Did Brunon kill him?" Her knuckles whitened as she locked her fingers together.

"No, he was in police custody when the man was killed."

"Then if he didn't kill this man..."

"Brunon dropped fifty thousand dollars on the roulette table in under an hour. Have you any idea where he got that kind of money?"

She continued to sit, pale-faced and tight-lipped. "None."

"The police don't think it was his money. It could also be the reason why his companion was killed. He might be in danger," he added, deliberately choosing not to mention the price on Brunon's head.

"Are the police still holding him?"

"He skipped out of a cell this morning."

"Skipped?" She stared at him blankly.

"Skipped—escaped," he explained. "It looks like he's annoyed some ruthless people. The police are afraid they might come after you and the boys."

"What for? Everyone knows Brunon doesn't live with us."

"When did you last see him?"

"Weeks ago."

"If he did steal that money..."

"What my husband does or doesn't do is no concern of yours. You're my employer, not my priest."

"No one is interfering in your private life. Josef and I are worried about you and the boys."

"We can look after ourselves. Now if we can discuss the information you asked for, I can get on with evaluating the appeals you sent me this morning."

Adam bit into his roll. He should have known what to expect. Experience had taught him that trying to get through to Magdalena on anything other than a work level was like trying to dig a clean-sided hole in fine sand.

"I asked the Berlin Document Center to fax us copies of the last orders issued by the Reich, relevant to the artifacts kept in Konigsberg castle. They were in the care of an SS brigadeFührer who according to this—" Magdalena produced a fax from the piles of paper on her desk and pushed it across to Adam, "oversaw the removal and packing of the castle contents. They were entrusted to a transport detail and taken out of Konigsberg in November 1944."

"Any documentation as to the destination?"

"None. But there are eyewitness reports that the only convoy that left the castle in November headed south."

Adam left his chair. Picking up another roll, he walked over to a large-scale map of modern Poland pinned to the wall opposite Magdalena's desk.

"South doesn't make sense. In November 1944 the Russians were massed on the borders of East Prussia. All logic dictates that High Command would have sent the convoy west on the Elbag road. It's the most direct route to Berlin."

"Direct by road," she interposed. "The brigadeFührer was captured and interrogated by the Russians in January 1945. He told them that the convoy was sent south to mislead any partisans and thieves who might be watching into thinking that it was a routine supply transport."

"This brigadeFührer didn't accompany the transport?"

"No, he stayed to defend the city against the onslaught of the Russians. And there are no documents to support his assertion that the castle contents were entrusted to the care of another officer, a Standartenführer. Either he didn't want to, or couldn't, identify the particular officer." She picked up a newspaper clipping. "There are no more official documents concerning the transport, only rumor and newspaper speculation."

"I bet there's plenty of that."

"The only hard evidence surfaced at the end of the war. A few minor pieces from the Konigsberg treasure, including a gold altar cross that had lost its rubies and sapphires, and a couple of gold rings purported to have once belonged to the Grand Masters of the Teutonic order, were discovered hidden under a pile of logs in the home of a Polish peasant."

"Discovered? Did the Russians search every farmhouse and cottage in the area in an effort to track down the treasure?"

"They were tipped off by a jealous neighbor. The farmer had been boasting about his find in the village, and the village—" she left her chair and stood next to him in front of the map "was here."

"Outside the town of Ostroda." He checked the scale of the map and made a swift calculation. "A hundred and twenty kilometers south of Konigsberg?"

"As the crow flies. Distances in wartime depended on the location of the front. The peasant was also interrogated by the Russians. He insisted he had discovered the pieces lying abandoned in the forest between Ostroda and Allenstein after the Russians had advanced and left the area."

"So the Russians attacked the baggage train and took everything?"

"If they had, they would have shipped it back to Moscow and exhibited it by now," Magdalena said authoritatively. "They've already held one exhibition of paintings lost since 1945, and their craftsmen have recreated the amber room in Tsarskoe Selo. Why would they have bothered if they had the original stashed away? If the Russians had the Amber Knight and Amber Room, they would have boasted about it to the world."

"So what happened to them?"

"The only document I've been able to unearth is a delivery note signed by a Standartenführer who received a consignment from a transport three days after the treasure transport left Konigsberg Castle. The note details the date and time of delivery. No mention of what the consignment consisted of, or place of handover."

"Was the colonel captured?"

"He and his men disappeared. It wasn't unusual, isolated units in the Prussian forests were frequently ambushed by Polish Partisans and Russian troops towards the end of the war. The forest is littered with mass graves."

"So, you've unearthed nothing new."

"You expect me to solve one of the great mysteries of World War II in a morning?" she taunted.

"It wasn't meant as a criticism," he said hastily.

"Edmund told me you received photographs along with the demand."

Adam handed her the envelope. She emptied it on to her desk. "So this is the Amber Knight."

"Or so they would have us believe."

"Edmund said you would have trouble raising the money?"

"There's no way the Institute can afford fifty million dollars for something that may not be authentic. And, before you ask, the man in the photograph is Krefta."

"It's not Krefta I'm looking at, but the background."

"It looks like gray concrete," Adam glanced at the photograph again.

"It's what's on the concrete that interests me. Have you noticed this?"

He looked over her shoulder. Scratched on the wall behind the coffin was a faint but unmistakable swastika.

"Just the sort of thing you'd expect to find in a war-time bunker," she mused.

"Or, given the rise of the neo-Nazis, a modern underground parking lot or cellar," he commented.

"I suppose so. It's just that," she picked up the photograph and went back to the map, "south from Konigsberg will take you to this area." She traced a line down the map.

"Olsztyn?"

"It was Allenstein in 1945, the second city of East Prussia and east of there..."

"East! Aren't you forgetting that in the winter of 1944/45 the Russians were advancing and the Polish Partisans were rising? Only a lunatic would consider carting valuables towards an advancing enemy army."

"A lunatic who built the largest bunker complex of World War II." She jabbed her finger on the map again.

"Ketrzyn."

"Formerly the East Prussian town of Rastenburg. Eight kilometers east of the town where Hitler built his Wolf's Lair."

"It's open to tourists. Every inch of the place has been fully explored and mapped."

"Perhaps," she said thoughtfully, "perhaps not, but in 1945 it was the obvious place to store valuables. The Wolfschanze had its own airport, railway station and garrison. Trains ran between Rastenburg and Berlin after the Russians had captured the roads. Planes flew in and out of Berlin when the city was surrounded. If you wanted to safeguard valuables would you risk sending them overland from Konigsberg via Elblag and Gdansk with the British bombing the ports and the Russian army advancing? Or would you secrete them in a secure bunker city with its own railway station and airport? A bunker city that could hold out for days, if not weeks."

"What happened to the Wolfschanze?"

"German engineers blew it up on the night of the 25th of January, 1945."

"Then, if the treasure was there, it must have been shipped out beforehand."

"If there was time. The Russians advanced quickly on that front. Prussians left their houses and ran for their lives leaving half-eaten meals on the tables. It's possible the troops in the Wolfschanze were caught out the same way."

"And the trains and planes?"

"Perhaps none came. Perhaps they were destroyed by bombing, in which case the treasure could well have been hidden in the bunker."

"For sixty years?"

"Hitler was a megalomaniac. God alone knows what he built in that place. I worked there for three summers when I was a student. I don't believe a quarter of it has been fully explored."

"If you're right, why would anyone who knew where the Amber Knight was wait sixty years to float it on the market?"

"Because whoever hid it couldn't get to it until now?" she suggested.

"Is this whoever, Polish, Russian or German?"

"Does it matter?"

"The location of the knight does. If it's still in Poland I might be able to make out a case for refusing an export license."

"You're going to look for it?"

"I'm going to make a start by visiting Krefta in Kaliningrad tomorrow."

"Do you expect him to be there, sitting, waiting for you, after having his photograph taken with the knight?"

"No, but I may meet someone who knows where he is. I'd appreciate your company," he hinted.

"I don't speak Russian and I know nothing about Kaliningrad or Krefta."

"Elizbieta Hirsz does. She's coming with me and I need a chaperone."

"Afraid of being propositioned, Adam?" For the first time he saw the shadow of a smile in the upturned corners of her mouth. So she did have a sense of humor after all.

CHAPTER SEVEN

AWN HADN'T BROKEN when the alarm Adam had borrowed from Waleria roused him. He surfaced still savoring the memory of the evening. Waleria had cooked a superb meal, the wine had been smooth, the sex gentle and sensuous after Helga's frantic grappling and it had the added advantage of taking place in Waleria's bed so he didn't have to change the sheets. He might have been tempted to risk his peace of mind in a long-term relationship, if Waleria had been willing to give up her independence.

The bell was ringing as he emerged from the shower. Wrapping a towel around his waist he pressed the buzzer that released the lock on the communal street door before climbing the stairs to dress. He barely had time to pull on his trousers and shirt before there was a knock on his apartment door. He opened it to find Elizbieta standing in the hallway.

"I told you I'd pick you up," he reprimanded her.

"Why are you always so nervous around me?" Slinging her bag over her shoulder she wandered past him into the living room and blocked his path.

"Because I'm wary of predatory females, especially ones who live with my friends."

"Feliks doesn't care who I sleep with."

"But I do." Disentangling her arms from around his neck, he retreated to the bathroom to finish dressing.

"Shall I make coffee?" She moved into the tiny kitchen.

"No time."

"I can't face the day without breakfast."

"We'll stop on the way."

"At a roadside van?" she made a face.

"I've ordered a picnic."

"Wonderful, we can watch the sun rise over the forest while we eat. I hope you remembered Buck's Fizz. There's nothing like champagne first thing in the morning to aid romance." She pursed her lips and eyed him seductively.

"If there is any Buck's Fizz it's all yours and Magdalena's. You know how strict the laws on drinking and driving are in this country." He grabbed his jacket, slipped on his shoes and checked his wallet, keys, passport and visa.

"Magdalena?" she enquired icily.

"Magdalena Janca, from the Salen Institute." He held the door open. "Didn't I tell you she was coming with us?"

Magdalena was waiting at the rental garage. As Elizbieta was the only one who spoke Russian, Adam insisted she sit in the back of the car to get as much rest as she could before they reached Kaliningrad. Brooking no argument, he opened the front passenger door for Magdalena, handed her the map and told her to navigate.

The road between Gdansk and Elbag was reasonably new and fast, so they made good, if strained and silent, time until they turned off on to the secondary road that meandered up to Braniewa and the border. Adam pulled up in a forest clearing outside Frombork soon after dawn broke. Heeding Josef's advice that the most public areas were the safest, he parked the car between a truck bearing the logo of a west German company and a battered kiosk that dispensed rolls and coffee. Opening the trunk he lifted out the picnic basket. Magdalena poured coffee from a flask into plastic cups and distributed salami rolls as the shadows between the trees lightened from dark to pale gray-green.

They crossed the border at Mamonowo. Joining the line for travelers with Western passports, Adam wondered why an hour spent at a border post crawled by at the same snail's pace as an hour under the dentist's drill. Magdalena buried her head in a book on the Deutsche Ostmesse, the huge trade fairs that were held in Konigsberg between the wars, and Elizbieta either slept, or pretended to. Being Polish they would have been waved through if Adam hadn't been with them and all three of them knew it.

As soon as Adam's passport was returned to him, they crossed into Byelorussia and Adam felt as though they had entered a colder, starker world. The buildings were utilitarian, the atmosphere sterile, even the forest seemed less green, as though spring had chosen to bypass the country.

"We're almost in Kaliningrad," Elizbieta muttered from the back seat after an hour of steady driving. "I can smell the river Pregolye."

"How do the locals stand it?" Adam fought to overcome his revulsion at the stench.

"Used to it, I suppose," she suggested.

"No one could get used to that." He pressed the button set in the door and closed all the car's windows.

"Is that the cathedral ahead?" Magdalena checked the map as Elizbieta finally opened her eyes.

"What's left of it."

"Wasn't there some talk of rebuilding it?" Adam asked.

"Talk has always been plentiful in Russia." Elizbieta produced a packet of cigarettes.

"No smoking in my car," Adam ordered.

"Would you prefer the smell of the river or tobacco?"

"The river." He joined the flow of traffic that twitched sluggishly over the bridge. Choking in a fog of exhaust fumes, they looked down on the river island and the skeletal ruins of the old cathedral, the only discernable structure in a desert of dereliction.

"Pity they didn't rebuild the old quarter after the war, like they did in Gdansk." Magdalena flicked through her book until she found a nineteenth-century etching of the cathedral tower rising out of an undulating plain of medieval rooftops.

"What the hell is that?" Adam stared at an enormous H-shaped building that dominated the skyline.

"That is what the Russians built on the site of Konigsberg Castle," Elizbieta informed him.

"The Russians blew up the Castle in 1964." Magdalena reverted to her book, preferring the etchings to reality. "It had stood on the site for over seven hundred years."

"There wasn't that much left to blow up," Elizbieta chipped in.

"There goes every idea I had of looking for clues as to the fate of the Amber Knight here, but you haven't said what that monstrosity's supposed to be."

"It was the House of the Soviets, there's talk of turning it into a business center."

"The guide book describes it as the ugliest creation in Soviet architecture." Magdalena snapped the book shut as if she. could no longer bear the comparison between old Konigsberg and modern Kaliningrad.

"I didn't think anything could be uglier than some of the monuments the Communists built in Poland, but I have to admit, it wins hands down."

"For God's sake don't stop here," Elizbieta begged when he slowed the car, "between the traffic fumes and the river I'll throw up."

"Which way do I go?"

"We want the other side of the city. Turn left at the next junction, then right."

Magdalena folded the map away as Elizbieta directed them through the traffic-clogged streets of the center into a wilderness of giant, high-rise apartment blocks. Adam's sense of direction failed completely as they traversed concrete roads flanked by towering walls of windows set neatly one upon the other. The only variation between one gargantuan edifice and the next was the degree of weathering and graffiti, and an occasional favored block that could boast the luxury of balconies.

"Turn right here." Elizbieta leaned over Adam's shoulder.

"Beats me how you can possibly know where we are when there are no landmarks." Adam turned a corner occupied by a gang of jeans-clad youths.

"This is the street. Look for number 193."

"This isn't that different from some of the estates around Gdynia and Gdansk." Magdalena craned her neck in an attempt to read a faded number painted on a wall.

"Yes, it is," Adam argued. "These people don't have the old quarter to visit."

"They're allowed to travel now, same as us." Elizbieta sat up and dabbed blusher on her cheeks and perfume on her neck.

"Krefta's an old man," Adam teased.

"You know me and old men." Elizbieta winked at him in the mirror as he reduced the car's speed to walking pace.

Even after they found the block it took twenty minutes to locate Krefta's apartment. Less than a quarter of the doors bore numbers and none had name plates, as though the occupants wanted to live as anonymously as possible. After Adam had wasted five minutes in fruitless knocking, Elizbieta tried the neighboring doors, eventually rousting out an old woman who purported not to know Krefta by name, but deigned to identify him from Adam's photograph. She insisted she hadn't seen him in weeks, had no idea where he was, or if he was coming back, and her parting shot, before slamming her door, was that Krefta could be dead for all she knew or cared.

"Nice neighbor." Adam returned to Krefta's door. It was at the end of a blind, windowless corridor. Four out of the five light bulbs designated to illuminate the area were missing, and, whether it was the gloom or the unnatural silence, he had the uneasy feeling that there were hostile, listening ears behind every door. After checking the ceiling for CCTV cameras, a ridiculous exercise given the age and state of the building, he slipped his hand into his pocket and pulled out a multi-bladed penknife.

"You're not thinking of breaking in?" Magdalena was horrified.

"I didn't drive all this way for nothing."

"This is Byelorussia."

"I'm carrying enough money to bribe the police."

"Sssh!" Elizbieta glanced around nervously, "it's not the police you have to worry about."

"You two can go back to the car," Adam attacked the door.

"If you're intent on behaving like an idiot, I'll keep a lookout," Elizbieta whispered conspiratorially.

"Thank you."

"I'll stay but only for the sake of the museum. Your successor might not be as amenable in funding projects," Magdalena declared practically.

Adam slid a long thin blade between the lock and the post. The door was so flimsy, one good kick would have finished it and, if it hadn't been for the noise and the mess he'd make of the door, he might have been tempted. As it was, it took him a few minutes to pry the lock from the frame.

"The river must flow under the building." Elizbieta reeled back as Adam entered the apartment.

"The poor little thing." Magdalena stooped down beside the corpse of a kitten. Skeletally thin, its fur writhed with spirals of maggots. "How could anyone have left it?"

"Perhaps Krefta didn't realize it was locked in." Adam looked around. The room was a reasonable size but it was crammed with rubbish and moldering furniture. A single, small window was set in the wall opposite the door. In front of it a table held piles of papers and the remains of a grayish, rock-hard slice of bread. A rickety, worm-eaten chair stood next to the table and another had been placed in front of a dust-coated work bench in the corner. A sagging sofa covered with blankets, so blackened with ingrained dirt it was difficult to see what color they had originally been, filled the space in between. The threadbare mats on the concrete floor felt spongy underfoot. Adam almost expected to hear a squelch as he tip-toed to the window. There were only two doors, the one they had entered by and another that opened into a cupboard-sized, filthy bathroom that contained a grimy toilet pan without a seat and a chipped and cracked sink. The smell was even more overpowering in there than the living room, which suggested its origins lay in more than the decomposing kitten. Adam turned to see Magdalena covering the tiny corpse with one of the blankets. Elizbieta was examining the work bench.

"If these are Krefta's tools it's no wonder he hasn't exhibited in years. No amber-smith worth his salt would attempt to work with this junk." Elizbieta held up a cutter blackened with neglect and eaten by rust. "There are some amber nuggets too."

"A lot?" Adam asked, thinking of the missing shipment.

"Not enough to keep the average workshop going for a day." She picked up one of the pieces. "The quality's appalling, the sort of thing beginners are given to practice on."

Adam kicked aside the debris of rags and trash that littered the floor, sifting through it patiently with his foot, too fastidious to touch it with his fingers.

"What are you looking for?" Magdalena asked.

"Something that might indicate where he's gone and when he left."

She rose to her feet and looked behind the door. "There's a small key hanging on a nail that might open his mail box."

"I'll go," Elizbieta took it from her. "If anyone stopped either of you, you wouldn't have a clue whether they were offering you a good time or asking the time of day."

Steeling himself against the smell, Adam returned to the bathroom. On a shelf behind the door he found a piece of cracked, dried, red soap, an old jam jar filled with water and a pair of hideous, grinning false teeth. "He left his teeth behind." He showed them to Magdalena.

"There's an old bus ticket here." Magdalena continued to sift through the papers piled on the table. "But there's no passport, no identity card..."

"And not even circulars in the mail box." Elizbieta closed the door behind her.

"Looks like your Mr. Krefta doesn't believe in the principles of basic hygiene." Adam flushed the toilet in an attempt to alleviate the smell.

"I think moving the cat out might do more than that," Elizbieta suggested.

"We should bury it."

"Under the garbage in here is as good a place as any."

"I meant outside," Magdalena broke in, unimpressed by Adam's attempt at humor.

"I'm not touching that cat," Elizbieta announced firmly.

"Adam." Magdalena looked expectantly at him.

"Be practical, there's nowhere to bury it in this concrete jungle."

"Then we'll take it to the forest."

"I'm not getting into the same car as a dead cat," Elizbieta snapped.

"We can't leave the poor thing lying here," Magdalena insisted.

"My mother says I'm too easy-going for my own good." Folding the blanket around the pathetic remains, Adam lifted it from the floor. "Open the door."

"I'll come with you," Magdalena offered.

"There are some things a man should do alone." Negotiating the maze of corridors to the outside he abandoned the blanket on top of a bank of trash bins.

"What did you do with it?" Magdalena demanded when he returned, hands outstretched and made a bee-line for the bathroom.

"What's the difference?" Adam had always thought of Magdalena as a hard-headed woman. Hardly the type to turn sentimental over a dead cat.

"I hate to think of a corpse, any corpse, left lying in the open to be kicked around."

"Do you realize you're talking about a cat?" Elizbieta was already at the door. "I've had enough of this place. You two coming?"

"As soon as I can raise lather on this damned soap," Adam answered.

"Break a piece off," Magdalena advised. "It will be softer inside."

"Westerners, they've never had to cope with poverty or shortages," Elizbieta sneered, giving Magdalena a conspiratorial glance.

"Oh shit!"

"Give up, Adam. I doubt even a dead cat carries enough germs to kill."

"This damned soap has just sliced my palm."

"Not even Russian soap can do that." Magdalena went to the bathroom door and saw blood seeping out of a cut in Adam's hand. "Let me look at it."

"It's nothing." Avoiding her eye, he wrapped his bloody hand, still clutching the soap in tissues before thrusting it into his trouser pocket. "There's a first-aid kit in the car. Let's go."

The return journey was swifter than the drive to Kaliningrad. Even the border crossing took only thirty minutes. While Elizbieta dozed fitfully in the back, Magdalena continued to immerse herself in her book and maps.

Adam broke the journey at the same clearing outside Frombork. Leaving Elizbieta and Magdalena the remains of the picnic, he walked into the forest in an effort to clear his lungs and head, of the stench of Kaliningrad. Crunching stale bread and warm salami, his thoughts turned to the hot savory soups, sauces and meats in the Milan. Overwhelmed by a sudden desire for the familiar streets of Gdansk he tossed aside the remains of his roll, picked up the basket, ordered the girls back into the car and climbed into the driver's seat.

As they moved out of the lay-by he caught sight of a large black car pulling out of a side road behind them. Wondering if it was plain clothes police, he remembered local traffic regulations regarding forest driving and switched on the headlamps before winding down the window.

The weather was glorious, the air sweet and untainted after the fetid stench of the city and the foul cloying smell of death in the apartment. He looked across at Magdalena. She was leaning against her door as though she couldn't get far enough away from him. Adjusting his rear-view mirror he caught a glimpse of Elizbieta sprawled inelegantly across the back seat. This time she really had to be asleep. Awake, she would never have lolled with her head thrown back and her mouth gaping wide. He pushed the mirror back into position and saw the black car again.

He slowed his speed to ten kilometers below the speed limit. He'd heard too many stories of foreigners being stopped and forced to pay on-the-spot fines that amounted to the contents of their wallet to want to tangle with officialdom.

The car continued to follow them. When Adam accelerated, the black car accelerated, when he slowed, it slowed, the distance between them as constant as if the vehicles had been linked by a steel tow-rope. When he dropped his speed to forty kilometers an hour the black car still refused to overtake. Adjusting the rear-view mirror he attempted, and failed, to read the Russian number plate while trying to recall all that Josef had told him about rental and Western cars being forced off the road, and the occupants robbed.

Finally deciding his best option was to put as much distance between the black car and his as possible, he pushed his foot down on the accelerator.

It happened when he was least expecting it. As he reduced his speed at a sign signaling crossroads ahead, the black car shot forward and swerved in front of him, forcing him to brake. The front passenger door flew opened and a man dressed in casual clothes emerged. A second man appeared from the back. Adam had time to register the tip of a gun barrel poking out from beneath his jacket before slamming down the central brake with his elbow and ramming the car into reverse. He did a handbrake turn and whirled around, speeding back along the road they had just traveled down.

"What the hell are you doing?" Elizbieta shouted angrily as she was thrust rudely out of sleep by the squeal of brakes and an impact that sent her reeling from one side of the car to the other. Adam was too busy trying to steer and check his mirror at the same time to answer. Magdalena, who had sized up the situation, pulled down her sun visor and peered into the cosmetic mirror.

"Check the map," Adam commanded. "There has to be a town or a village close by."

"Do you think people like that," Magdalena jerked her head to the back of the car, "would worry about the occupants of a small village?"

"They friends of your husband?" he enquired dryly.

"Take the next right."

"Back to the border?" he queried.

"There are police there," she pointed out.

"And whose side do you think they'll be on?" He checked the mirror. The car was gaining. It had a larger engine than the rental car. "Strap yourselves in and hold tight."

"Adam!" Elizbieta screeched as he plowed off the road onto the forest floor. "Now they have us cornered like eels in a trap."

"Not yet they don't." Pressing the accelerator to the floor, he charged between the trees at breakneck speed, scattering last year's leaves in his wake.

"And to think I won't even ski in the woods because the trees are in the way," Elizbieta wailed.

Adam didn't hear her. He was too busy watching the black car slowly but inexorably gain on them. Ahead was a steep-sided gully. Adam saw it, but didn't slow for an instant. Elizbieta and Magdalena wrapped their heads in their arms as he headed straight for it. There was a nerve-wracking moment when all four wheels left the ground, swiftly followed by a bump and the whirr of tires skidding over soft earth before they moved on.

"Just as I thought," Adam continued to charge recklessly ahead.

"Just as what?" Magdalena was white from shock.

"They haven't got four-wheel drive. That's the one thing I've learned about Polish roads. It's essential to rent a four-wheel drive vehicle."

"Watch out!"

Elizbieta's scream alerted Adam to a black transit van parked ahead. He spun the wheel frantically as the black-suited driver turned a rubber-masked face towards them. There was a sickening crunch of metal on metal as he lost control, followed by another scream, a long, loud piercing sound he thought would never end.

CHAPTER EIGHT

DAM OPENED HIS clenched eyelids to see a cloud of black smoke billowing from beneath the hood of the car. Relaxing his grip on the steering wheel, he flexed his muscles to confirm he was in one piece. "Everyone all right?" he shouted above Elizbieta's hysterical screaming.

"All right! Are you insane?" Elizbieta ceased screaming to turn on him. "You could have killed us!"

"Perhaps they'll finish what Adam started," Magdalena said as the door of the van they had crashed into slid back. Twin black-suited figures, their heads concealed by gas masks, lumbered towards them through the smoke.

"Ever feel as though you'd strayed onto the set of a science fiction movie?"

"How can you make jokes at a time like this?" Elizbieta wailed as one of the men attacked the handle on Adam's door only to be foiled by the central locking. Adam reached for the ignition key and a shadow moved across the windscreen. He glanced up to find himself looking down the barrel of a semi-automatic shotgun.

"You can't go out there." Elizbieta clutched his collar as he reached for the door button.

"You'd rather be shot in the car?"

"For God's sake, drive off."

"Even if this thing is capable of moving, I doubt the windshield is bullet proof." He opened the door and stepped out. To his amazement a white and trembling Magdalena followed suit on the other side. He barely had time to give her an encouraging wink before his face was slammed on to the roof of the car and his hands wrenched painfully behind his back.

"Identity card?"

The question, muted to a metallic whisper by the mask, was the last thing Adam had expected.

"In my jacket."

A gloved hand retrieved his passport from the inside pocket.

"Adam Salen? American? Director of the Salen Institute, a charitable institution?"

"Who's asking?"

"You are in a restricted area."

"I didn't see any signs."

"Barriers have been erected on all roads leading into this zone."

"A car forced us off the road. It's behind us—" Adam lifted his head to see the woods stretching around them, mockingly devoid of life. "It was a black Mercedes with Russian plates. The men in it were armed with sub-machine guns." He could feel the gun barrel digging into his neck, but it didn't prevent him from looking to Magdalena to check she was faring no worse than him. He knew that his story sounded pure Hollywood, and bad Hollywood at that. Handcuffs snapped over his wrists. "You're arresting us?" His question was drowned out by Elizbieta's shrieks as she was unceremoniously hauled from the back of their car. Minutes later Adam found himself sandwiched between Magdalena and Elizbieta in the sealed rear compartment of a second van that had pulled up alongside the first. With no windows to look out of, he had no way of knowing whether they were heading east or west, and he was left clinging to a dwindling hope that they were in the hands of the Polish authorities, not the Russian Mafia.

"I've never been so humiliated in my life. They stripped me, took away all my clothes, made me march naked into a shower, scrubbed me until my skin was raw, then a doctor, at least I hope it was a doctor—it was difficult to see under the mask—pushed me into a cubicle and stuck needles into my most tender parts before poking smear sticks over every inch of me—inside as well as out." Elizbieta glared at Adam who was wearing an identical white boiler suit to the ones she and Magdalena had been issued with.

"I suppose you were given the same treatment?" Magdalena asked Adam.

"Men weren't given any extra privileges, if that's what you're thinking," he replied.

"Did you ask what they were vaccinating you against?"

"Yes. They insisted we'd been exposed to a life-threatening disease but they wouldn't say what."

Elizbieta started screeching again. "They could have injected us with anything..."

Adam was tired of her complaining. "If they'd wanted to kill us, they could have done it with a lot less fuss in the forest."

He examined their surroundings. The best that could be

said was the hall they were in was clean and well-lit. Too well-lit for eye comfort. To their right an area had been divided into half a dozen open-fronted cubicles, walled on both sides by panels pushed tight to a glass wall threaded with steel mesh. As if the meshed glass wasn't enough, beyond it, floor to ceiling steel bars the thickness of his arm lent a zoo-like atmosphere. Behind the bars lay a corridor tiled with the same clinically white ceramic floor and wall tiles as the hall and cubicles.

Each cubicle housed a narrow steel bed, plastic chair and table. Nothing else. The end cell, which offered no more privacy from the corridor or the hall they were in than the others, was furnished as a bathroom with a shower head set on the wall above a drain, a stainless steel toilet, sink, liquid soap dispenser and paper towel holder. There were no windows, but Adam looked for, and found, the probing eyes of camera lenses set alongside the light bulbs recessed in the ceiling, and he had no doubt they carried microphones.

"Let's hope our keepers remember to feed us." He turned to the nearest cubicle and sat on the bed.

"We could have been exposed to radiation or AIDS..." Elizbieta's high-pitched voice reverberated hollowly around the hall.

"If we have, it's the first I've heard of a vaccine being developed against either condition." He pressed down on the bed with his fingertips.

"...they could be using us as guinea pigs. We could die here, no one would know, and it would be your fault. "Come to Kaliningrad," you said. "Nice little trip, visit Krefta," you said. And now look at us..."

"You ever heard of anything like this happening to anyone else?" Adam interrupted, looking to Magdalena.

"Not recently."

"Pity. I hoped it was some quaint Polish custom so you could tell me what to expect next."

"...they've taken everything." Elizbieta's ranting continued to intrude on Adam's attempts to make sense out of the events of the past few hours. "My one good suit, underclothes, money, cosmetics, perfume, papers—even my best tweezers..."

Adam pulled the pockets in his overalls inside-out to prove he had fared no better.

"Perhaps they're checking our ID," Magdalena suggested in an attempt to alleviate Elizbieta's panic.

"This bed is solid," Adam declared, lifting the single paper sheet that covered it. There was no mattress, blanket or pillow, but lying down proved less tiring than standing. A masked and suited figure appeared before the bars with a tray of coffee and sandwiches.

"You recognize the insignia on the shoulder?" Adam turned to Magdalena.

"Only from my nightmares."

After pulling his gun and training it on them, the guard unlocked a grill set in the bars and pushed the tray towards the glass wall.

"There's a glass door at the opposite end. I'll unlock it electronically after I leave."

"How long do you intend to keep us here?" Adam asked.

The guard re-locked the grill and holstered his gun.

"Why are you holding us?" Adam persevered. "I get claustrophobic in rooms without windows. If you leave me here for any length of time I'll turn into a gibbering idiot," he shouted after the retreating man.

They heard a click. By dint of pushing with her fingertips Magdalena found the door in the glass wall. She picked up the tray and carried it to the table in the cell Adam had commandeered.

"And I thought I'd mastered the Polish language," Adam complained.

"That depends on how you like your Polish." Drawn by the sandwiches, Elizbieta condescended to join them.

"When you can't influence the situation there's only one thing to do." Crossing his arms behind his head, Adam lay back.

"You're not going to sleep?" Elizbieta demanded.

"I intend to try."

"Want some coffee or a sandwich?" Magdalena held up two pieces of dark bread wrapped around a bright pink filling.

"Can you guarantee that serum we were given will protect me against the bacteria in that salami?"

"You want guarantees in this situation?"

"I'll pass. Wake me if something happens."

If Adam had been given access to a pencil and paper he might have been tempted to work out a new theory on the nature and substance of time. Existing in a world devoid of color and clocks under the glare of constantly burning lamps made the artificial divisions of hours and minutes irrelevant and, after listening to Elizbieta's tirades for what felt like eternity, he was prepared to discount the evidence of his beard and believe anyone who told him weeks had passed since they'd been picked up in the forest.

Pillows and blankets appeared alongside the third monot-onous meal of coffee and sandwiches. Magdalena and Elizbieta used the blankets to rig up a curtain around the shower, although he made a point of lying on his bed whenever either of them moved into the bathroom area.

Nothing intruded into their closed, sterile world except the masked guard who brought them food. Clean overalls appeared with the fourth tray. Even allowing for the amount of time he spent sleeping, or, more frequently, pretending to, Adam became closer acquainted with Elizbieta than he'd ever had the desire to, while Magdalena remained as enigmatic, cool and aloof as ever.

He never saw her with her hair or her guard down. Like him, she spent most of the time lying on her bed, apart from an hour between every meal during which she exercised as vigorously as the confines of space would allow. Just watching her go through a punishing routine of power walking and push-ups made him tired. By tacit agreement they limited their conversations to the absolute essential and, from the number of times Magdalena glanced up the ceiling, Adam assumed that she, too, had noticed the cameras.

In contrast to Magdalena, when awake, Elizbieta rarely remained still or quiet. Vitriolic ravings about his shortcomings and cowardice alternated with tearful outbursts for the men she had loved and believed she would never see again. She never mentioned Feliks. After their fifth meal of coffee and sandwiches she began entertaining him and Magdalena with doom-laden predictions of their imminent, extremely painful, slow and lingering deaths.

Just when Adam was beginning to wonder if he'd died and been consigned to a hell, custom-tailored by a vindictive deity as retribution for his particular sins, he was beckoned to the glass door at gunpoint by the guard, who'd abandoned his mask for the first time since they had been seized in the forest.

He opened the door in the glass wall and stepped tentatively towards the bars. As the guard unlocked the grid, he glanced back to see Magdalena standing next to her bed watching him, but it was left to Elizbieta to exploit the full drama of the moment.

"Adam, don't go! You can't leave us." She flung herself theatrically through the door, only to retreat when the guard waved his gun towards her.

"They probably want to give me a shave." He rubbed the stubble on his chin, debating whether it was two or three days' growth.

The guard motioned him to walk ahead. The corridor stretched, ominous and silent, before him. The guard's boots stamped behind him as he shuffled around corner after corner in his paper slippers and still the corridor yawned ahead of him. White, empty and threatening. All the stories he had heard about the Communist years came to mind, especially the ones about the final walks of hapless prisoners down corridors, walks that ended with a bullet in the back of the skull.

Then he heard a cacophony of voices, one loud, indignant and so blessedly familiar he almost whooped with joy. He ran down the tunnel the guard motioned him into. Through ragged joins in hooped, Perspex sheets he caught tantalizing glimpses of a garden—trees—leaves—grass—red and golden flowers—and finally, standing in a reception area at the end of the passage, the stocky figure of Josef Dalecka.

"You just can't stay out of trouble, can you, Adam?"

"I try to live a quiet life." Adam held out his hand. It seemed an odd gesture to make to a man he felt had just saved his life.

"Not hard enough. I've had it with nurse-maiding you. Next time get yourself out of your own scrapes."

"We're free?"

"It took a great deal of time and effort, my time and effort," Josef emphasized harshly, "but yes, they're going to let you go."

"That's generous of them considering we did absolutely nothing."

"I don't know about America, but in Poland we stick to the roads. It's an offense to drive across the forest. Apart from the inconvenience caused to walkers, deer and wild boars, think of the ecological damage."

"What about the damage done to us? They didn't decontaminate us to test their equipment. What exactly did we drive into?"

"Classified," Josef muttered, deferring to the uniformed figures ranged behind him.

"Did we stray into a biological warfare site?" Adam addressed the official sporting the most elaborate insignia.

"A virulent form of foot and mouth disease, sir," came the bland reply.

"I thought you needed cloven hooves to catch that."

"An anatomical advantage you Americans have over us Poles." Josef flashed Adam a warning look.

"You're free to go, Mr. Salen, just as soon as you sign this document."

Adam took the sheet of paper the man handed him and began to read it.

"It's the usual indemnity form used by the authorities, certifying that you suffered no injury while in our care."

"I'm not sure about the after-effects of those sandwiches..."

"Sign it," Josef barked.

Adam picked up a pen from the desk and scribbled his name at the foot of the page.

"Oh my God!" Elizbieta appeared at the head of the tunnel and stared aghast at a table behind Adam. On it stood three sorry piles of rags, but Elizbieta had recognized one as what was left of the clothes she had been wearing when they had been detained. The crimson designer suit she had been so proud of had been shrunk to child-size, its color bled to the palest pink. Beneath it, her white silk cami-knickers had been transformed to a hideous gray. "Those clothes cost me three month's wages, they were dry-clean only. What have you done to them? I'll sue you, you bastards..."

"Elizbieta," Josef broke in. "Sign the form, there's a good girl. I have a car waiting."

Adam and Magdalena's outfits had fared no better than Elizbieta's so they traveled back to Gdansk in boiler suits and paper slippers. Rather than fill Josef's car with the stench of disinfectant, they left their clothes behind, but it took the promise of a substantial check from Adam before Elizbieta could be persuaded to abandon her beloved suit. Even the girls' handbags, their shoes and Adam's leather wallet had been ruined. The only recognizable items in the neat piles that had been made of their possessions were their identity cards, passports, private papers, and a lump of dried soap that had been scraped away from a bullet, in Adam's pile.

"I'd be careful with that if I were you, Mr. Salen," one of the officers warned as he abandoned the soap and picked up the bullet. "The edges are sharp."

"It's a lucky charm." Adam pocketed it and followed Josef to his car.

When they reached the main road to Gdansk, much to Elizbieta's annoyance, Adam closed the glass partition that separated the front from the back of the police vehicle and looked at Josef, who was concentrating on driving.

"What's the real story?

"As far as I can make out you drove into an area contaminated with anthrax. They've found a couple of corpses."

"Animal?"

"Presumably deer or cattle. I couldn't get past the rumors. Not my department."

"You mean there isn't anyone in the know you can threaten into talking," Adam guessed.

"Special forces always have been a law unto themselves. You really are a bloody fool for tangling with them. I had a hell of time tracking you down. No one would admit to seeing you after you crossed the border back into Poland. Feliks, Magdalena's brothers and Edmund have haunted my office for three days…"

"We've been missing for three days?" Without access to clocks, watches or windows Adam couldn't have hazarded a guess as to how long they had been kept prisoner.

"They all know you're safe. As soon as I got word where you were being held last night, I sent messages."

"Last night! Why didn't you come for us then?"

"Because they wouldn't release you. I spoke to a doctor who insisted you had to remain in quarantine for a minimum of seventy-two hours."

"Lest we spread foot and mouth among the cloven-hoofed population of Gdansk?" Adam raised a skeptical eyebrow.

"What were you doing driving around the forest? They told me some cock and bull story about guns and a black car chasing yours. Couldn't you invent something better? A child of three would have a hard time believing that one."

"We went to Krefta's place in Kaliningrad, drew a blank and headed back. When we left a rest area outside Frombork a black Mercedes with Russian plates followed us. A couple of miles up the road it forced us to stop and two men got out. I took one look at the gun snout nosing from beneath one of their coats and headed into the forest. It seemed the safest place at the time." Adam turned his head. Magdalena and Elizbieta were curled up on opposite ends of the back seat, their eyes closed. "The plates were definitely Russian."

"You get a number?"

"I was too busy trying to avoid trees to make a note of it."

"Brunon Kaszuba still hasn't surfaced. It takes a special bastard to leave even an ex-wife to the mercies of the Russian Mafia."

"You think the Mafia could have been following us?"

"You saw them, I didn't."

"It wasn't a trade fair. They weren't wearing name badges." Adam glanced out of the window. The sun was still low in the sky. A family was breakfasting at a log table and bench at the side of the road. Mother, father and three beautiful blond children, the standard, nuclear family so beloved of advertising companies. Further along a group of teenagers were thumping a volleyball over a net in a school yard. He opened the window and breathed in the scents of morning and pine woods. The scenes and the day were peaceful and normal, but that didn't prevent him from checking the mirrors either side of the car. The road was empty behind them, but he didn't relax until they joined the two-lane highway out of Elbag.

"Another hour and we'll be in Gdansk." Josef adjusted his rearview mirror. "Elizbieta looks exhausted."

"With any luck she'll sleep until we return her to Feliks."

"Don't enjoy troilism?"

"I don't enjoy hysterical females."

"You can hardly blame them after what you've put them through."

"I don't blame them for anything, only Elizbieta. Magdalena's either a very brave, very cool cookie, or just plain stupid."

"I grew up with her. She's not stupid, which is why I'm putting a guard on her as soon as we reach Gdansk."

"You think she's at risk from the Mafia?"

"I'm not taking any chances."

"She's not going to like it."

"Then you'll just have to explain why a guard's necessary." Josef slammed his foot on the accelerator and overtook a car being driven by an elderly woman.

"Why me?" Adam demanded

"You pay her wages. People listen to their paymasters."

Adam turned his head again to see Magdalena sitting tense and awake behind him. He opened the glass panel.

"You think those men in the Mercedes had something to do with Brunon, don't you?" she asked.

"From what Adam's told me they could have been anyone, Magda," Josef prevaricated. "They were probably just thugs looking to mug a couple of tourists."

"But if they were after Brunon they could be at my apartment by now. My brothers..."

"Have police protection," Josef interrupted.

"To guard against kidnappers? Or in the hope they'll lead you to my husband?"

Josef maintained a tactical silence.

"Brunon's grandmother is frail. She won't be able to cope with this..."

"She left to visit her sister the morning you disappeared. We were hoping you could help us with an address."

"Oltzyn."

"Oltzyn?" Josef repeated, hoping for more.

"That's all I know. She goes there two or three times a year, usually after she's had a letter pleading for help. Her sister's an invalid."

"Those men in the Mercedes were heading for my side of the car, Magdalena," Adam reassured her. "I'd lay a zloty to a grosz they're holding the Amber Knight and they're pissed off with us for going to Krefta's apartment."

"I didn't see any sign of them on the way to Kaliningrad."

"We probably picked them up there. I should have realized they'd watch Krefta's place after putting out his photograph with the information on the knight."

"You don't expect me to believe those men want to protect that filthy apartment in Kaliningrad?"

Irritated at being excluded from the conversation, Elizbieta opened her eyes. "Something tells me you didn't tell me the whole story on this knight of yours."

"I told you all I know," Adam protested.

"You know how rental cars attract attention." Josef turned off onto the exit that led into Gdansk. "It's probably the old story, broke Polish peasant sees three well dressed people sitting in a car with a sticker advertising a rental company..."

"No broke Polish peasant I know drives a Mercedes with Russian plates," Magdalena interrupted.

"There's a bottle of brandy in the first aid kit under my seat. Why don't you open it?" Josef suggested, tired of speculation that wasn't taking them any closer to solutions.

"You're a policeman and you're driving," Adam reminded.

"You aren't, and Elizbieta looks as though she could do with a medicinal belt."

Adam turned around and touched Magdalena's arm as she reached for the brandy. "You all right?"

"Perfectly well," she replied in a strained voice.

He wished he could believe her.

CHAPTER NINE

ISREGARDING THE NO entry signs, Josef drove directly to Mariacka Street and dropped Elizbieta outside Feliks's shop, but not before she'd extracted a check from Adam's wrinkled checkbook.

"Conference in my office?" Josef suggested to Adam.

"I refuse to go anywhere in a white boiler suit."

"We should talk."

"Give us a couple of hours to eat and change."

"I have to see my brothers," Magdalena insisted.

"If it will make you any happier, I'll check with their guards now." Josef picked up the radio telephone and made contact with his control office. After a few minutes of static-filled conversation he was able to reassure her. "The boys are safely under escort at school, and you have my word they'll stay that way." He glanced at his watch. "If you won't come back to the station now, how about lunch in the Milan?"

"We'll be there." Adam opened the car door. "Know any good dress shops around here?" he asked as he helped Magdalena out of the back. "If you do, I'll get Waleria to buy you an outfit."

"I'd rather go home."

"Like that?"

"It's the utility look."

"Don't be ridiculous. You can't go anywhere, especially the Milan, dressed like a window cleaner."

"I'd rather not go to the Milan at all."

"You have to eat, woman. If you'd rather go somewhere else, say the word and I'll call Josef," he offered impatiently as he led the way to his back door.

"It's not the Milan that's the problem, it's you. I don't want you to buy me outfits, and I don't want to be seen with you, especially in a restaurant. You know how people talk. You run the Institute and I'm an employee, a married woman..."

"Which your husband seems to have conveniently forgotten."

"My private life—"

"Is private," he interrupted. "I got the message a long time ago. Let's get a couple of things straight. I'm not making a pass at you, only offering you a replacement outfit, which is no more than I've given Elizbieta. I got you into a mess, the least you can let me do is foot the bill. And both of us have to eat..."

"And wash. There's a bathroom in the apartment in the Historical Museum. You can send the clothes over there."

"I'm not leaving you on your own until Brunon's back in custody." Adam opened the back door to his building.

"You can't be with me every minute of every day."

"No," he agreed patiently, "but I can stay with you until Josef posts a round-the-clock guard to shadow you as he's done with your brothers."

"Adam..."

"For once you're going to do as you're told." He pulled her into the building after him.

"Despite what you said in the car, you think those men in the Mercedes were after me, don't you?" It was phrased as a question, but both of them knew it wasn't one.

"Whether they were or they weren't, neither Josef nor I will regard you as safe until Brunon's been found."

"And if they were after you?"

"You can protect me," he answered glibly.

She waited while he locked the door behind them. "Brunon never told me anything about his affairs even when we were living together."

"I believe you, but it looks like there are a few other people who need convincing."

"He's always been a thief. Ever since we were kids." She followed him up the stairs. "If he wanted something and didn't have the money to buy it, he took it. I thought things would change after the Revolution. They did, but for the worse. There were more things for Brunon to want, and less money than ever to buy them with."

"At least he seems to have stolen from his own kind this time."

"I suppose you're wondering why I married him."

"Is that an invitation to ask, so you can tell me to mind my own business again?"

"No," she answered seriously. "An attempt to tell you that I'm honest and I've brought my brothers up to be the same."

"You wouldn't be working for the Institute if I thought otherwise. It also might be a good idea for you and your family to move into the flat in the Historical Museum until this Brunon situation is resolved one way or another."

"Don't be ridiculous."

"The Mafia isn't going to stop looking for Brunon just

because Josef's put a guard on your family. If you won't consider yourself think of your brothers..." He froze in the stairwell as voices drifted down from the floor above.

"Are those coming from your apartment?"

"Run down to the gallery and ask Waleria to call the police."

"You can't go up there alone."

Waleria walked up from the gallery to meet them. "I thought I heard you coming in. Your sister's arrived."

"And you gave her the key?" Adam ran up the final flight of stairs. The door was ajar, his apartment in chaos. A tall, effeminate man, with shoulder length blond curls, dressed in a black leather biker suit, was hovering over Georgiana who was lying on the sofa. She had a glass of wine in one hand, a telephone in the other and was haranguing the international operator. As Adam picked up a bottle of duty-free bourbon that had scarred the surface of the limed oak table next to her, a crash resounded from the gallery. He looked up to see his nephew Niklas sitting at his desk banging away at his computer.

"If you've cracked my security code and messed up my records, I'll kill you." Ignoring Georgiana and momentarily forgetting Magdalena he pounded up the stairs.

"A bozo could have cracked your code," the thirteen-year-old goaded him. "No one uses 'Open Sesame' any more—it went out with steam driven computers."

"This shirt is tasty."

Adam whirled around to see his eleven-year-old niece wrapped in his most expensive silk shirt and very little else.

"Janine, get that off this minute!"

"Mom, Uncle Adam wants me to strip naked."

"Really, Adam, you're behaving like a bear," Georgiana drawled, not bothering to cover the mouthpiece of the telephone. "You haven't even allowed me to introduce Casimir, or told us the name of your friend."

He looked down to see Magdalena hovering in the doorway. "Come in, Magdalena, but don't shut the door. My sister and her entourage are leaving."

"Looks like we'll have to." Georgiana waved a manicured hand in Magdalena's direction. "I sent Nanny and the maid to investigate this Grand Hotel of yours. Why didn't you tell me that you live in one room? The woman downstairs said you don't even have a housekeeper. Really, Adam, what are you trying to prove? That you can slum it like the natives?"

"Magdalena happens to be a native."

"No insult intended. They're accustomed to a rudimentary lifestyle, we're not."

"I happen to like my lifestyle just the way it is." Pulling the plug on the computer, he yanked Janine's hand out of his wardrobe and slammed the door. "You two, down the stairs, stand by the door, and don't touch a thing until the taxi arrives."

"What taxi?" Georgiana asked.

"The one I'm going to call for you."

"I'm not leaving here until Nanny calls back with her judgment on the hotel." Giving up on the operator, Georgiana replaced the receiver, and buried her hand in Casimir's hair.

The bathroom door opened and a ravishingly beautiful woman, with flawless skin, a perfect figure and a shimmering halo of blonde hair stood in the doorway. She summed up the chaotic scene in a single smiling glance. "I'm Courtney von

Bielstein Salen, Adam's wife." She held out her hand to Magdalena, but her attention remained riveted on Adam.

"Magdalena Janca, I've been seconded to the Salen Institute from the Historical Museum."

"Then you work for Adam."

"We both work for the Institute." Adam didn't bother to conceal his irritation at Courtney's presence.

"You must show me around this museum of yours, Magdalena," Courtney continued smoothly. "We'll be here for a while, and I intend to take in all the sights."

"From the Grand Hotel," Adam said firmly.

"Your grandfather's been trying to get in touch with you for a few days, darling," Courtney purred, very much the caring wife. "He's been worried…"

"I'll call him." Adam cut her short and dialed the local taxi service. "As you won't all fit into one car, I'll order two. They'll be at the back door in twenty minutes. I suggest you wait for them in the gallery downstairs."

"Twenty minutes!" Georgiana rolled her eyes to the ceiling.

"In case you hadn't noticed, you're not in the States." He turned to Niklas who was creeping back up the mezzanine. "Touch that computer again and I'll get Granddad to suspend your pocket money for the next ten years."

"Mom gives me my pocket money," Niklas countered.

"Granddad gives her hers."

"Aren't you going tell us what you've been doing in this God-forsaken neck of the woods?" Georgiana complained as he pounded up the stairs.

"Magdalena and I have an important lunch date. Business," he elaborated, reading the expression in Courtney's eyes. "We only stopped here to freshen up."

"I take it white boiler suits are all the rage in Gdansk?" Courtney beamed at Magdalena.

"Ladies first." Adam threw a robe down the stairs. "I'll get Waleria to send out for some clothes."

"Jeans and a shirt, please. I could do with a new pair. And size 42 shoes." Magdalena caught the robe and disappeared into the bathroom, locking the door behind her.

"And before either of you say a word," Adam glared at his sister and Courtney, "we lost our clothes in an accident. The only thing between Magdalena and me is work."

"I didn't doubt it for a moment, darling." Courtney walked slowly up the stairs towards him. "No capitalist playboy could possibly be interested in a woman who wears boiler suits and scrapes her hair back in that unbecoming fashion. And she's so tall, practically the same height as you."

The phone rang. Before Adam was halfway down the stairs, Georgiana was cooing into the receiver, her hand still fondling Casimir's thick curls. Taking advantage of the distraction, the children ran back up on to the mezzanine. Adam shouted yet another dire threat to Niklas before retreating into the kitchen. Opening the refrigerator he pulled out a bottle of vodka and downed a stiff measure before remembering it was early morning, and he'd only eaten half a dozen salami sandwiches in the past three days.

"I didn't come all this way for you to ignore me." Courtney closed the door, effectively imprisoning him in the tiny triangular space.

"If you'd warned me you were coming I would have set aside some time. As it is, I'm up to my neck in business that won't wait."

"Aren't you always? I must have left hundreds of messages

on your office voicemail in the last year, not to mention all the e-mails. I would have phoned here, but no one had the number."

"I've only just had it installed," he lied.

"I hoped for something at Christmas. Just a card..."

"This isn't the time, Courtney."

"When is? We have to talk."

"I thought we had before I left America."

"That was then, this is now."

"I can give you five minutes," he snapped.

"I need longer."

"I'll call you."

"Tonight?"

"No chance."

"Adam." She stepped forward. He retreated, slamming his spine into the stove. Her hands went to his neck, smoothing the creases from the collar of the boiler suit. "I know I hurt you but..."

Taking her hands into his, he held her stiffly at arm's length. "I left you, remember. You agreed at the time that it was for the best."

"I was mixed up. You were hurt. I had behaved badly. But I realize now that our life together was too perfect. It made me uncomfortable with myself and our marriage. I was over-whelmed by a happiness I had done nothing to earn. I was carrying so much guilt I simply couldn't accept that I deserved our life together, so I took your love and put it to a test. But we've come out of it with flying colors, darling."

"We have?" he mocked.

"That little incident with Prince Vladimir taught me that sex without love is as meaningless as life without therapy. I appreciate that when you saw me with him, you were wounded and angry enough to run as far and as fast from me as you could, but there's no need to keep on running, darling. You love me, Adam. Imperfect as I am, you love me, and out of that love will come forgiveness. Not immediately, that would be too much to hope for, but in time. And, if you feel the need to continue punishing me, that's all right too, as long as you don't exclude me from your life. You're not alone any more. We can fight this thing together. And," she ran her fingers down the front panel of his suit, "as you see, I've used the time we've been apart to good effect. I've never been in better shape." She wiggled her hips and pushed out her breasts. "I've also been in therapy. I'm a more complete, whole and rounded person than the girl you married. I've arranged for Dr. Marsden to take you on as well, so we really will be able to work this thing out together. We have a wonderful future—darling—what are you doing?"

Adam pushed her as far away from him as the kitchen would allow. "You still don't get it, do you? I didn't leave because I was upset by the sight of you and that phony Russian having it off in the summerhouse..."

"Of course you did, darling, and it's all right to be angry. Dr. Marsden..."

"Listen, for once in your life, because I have no intention of repeating myself a third time. I left because I realized I couldn't give a damn who you fucked."

"You're only saying that because you're in pain."

"You can't be hurt by someone you don't give a shit about. And I don't give a shit about you, Courtney. Do us both a favor. Take the houses and the New York apartment and half of whatever you have left in my American bank account and get a divorce."

"I'll never divorce you."

"You'll lose it all if you try hanging on. I've told my father to suspend all payments from my trust fund. For the first time in my life I'm living on my salary, and there isn't a court in the world that will order me to make alimony payments out of what I earn. In fact they're more likely to direct you to support me."

Her face contorted, turning ugly. "Who is it, Adam? Some scrubby little Polish tart? I warn you, I'm not going to give you up without a fight, and looking the way I do, people will think you're crazy to throw me aside. Your grandfather..."

"Take the money, Courtney." He edged around her and opened the door.

"You'll come to the hotel?"

"There's no point." He picked up the shirt Janine had discarded from the sofa. "Both houses, half the bank account and the New York apartment. It's the best offer you'll get from me. Georgiana, Casimir, I need this space, go wait for the taxis downstairs."

"She's very beautiful," Magdalena said to Adam.

"My sister?" Adam looked up from the Milan's menu.

"Your wife."

Adam sat back in his chair and looked out of the window of the cafe. He was exhausted, as much from the belt of vodka as the trauma of the past few days. "She should be. That little work of art cost more in upkeep than the Sistine Chapel." Picking up the bottle of red wine he'd ordered he filled her glass.

"Why do you joke about everything that's important to you?"

"I'm not joking." Taking his spare wallet from the inside pocket of his jacket he removed two photographs that had been returned to him along with his papers. "Before and after. I carry them around to remind myself not to repeat my mistakes."

Magdalena eyed them curiously. The first picture was a head and shoulders, college-type snapshot of a skinny girl with buck teeth and ash-blonde hair. The second a glossy, Hollywood-style handout, of the Courtney von·Bielstein Salen she'd just met.

"That was Courtney before she embarked on her hobby of plastic surgery and had a nose job, lip implants, new breasts, rib removal to narrow her waist, buttock firming and hair extensions."

Magdalena continued to study the photograph while the waiter brought soup and salads. Too hungry to wait for Josef, Adam had ordered the day's special for both of them on the premise that it would require the least preparation time.

"I can't believe this earlier photograph is the woman I've just met."

"The one and only real her." He replaced the photographs in his wallet.

"Even knowing about the surgery, it must be hard to walk away from a woman who looks like she does now."

"Brunon's a good-looking guy and you walked away from him."

She took a deep breath and for a moment he thought he was about to receive another curt directive to refrain from commenting on her private life. "He left me. I believe in the sanctity of marriage vows, Brunon doesn't." She picked up her spoon and stirred her soup.

"How long have you lived apart?"

"You make it sound like it was planned." She crumbled her bread roll into tiny pieces. "Brunon stopped coming home six months after we were married. At first I wasn't even conscious that he'd left. I simply assumed he had to make more trips than usual. I knew what 'business' he was in even then. When I found myself celebrating our first anniversary alone, I realized we'd spent only one weekend together in six months."

"Do you miss him?"

"I have my job, my brothers and his grandmother."

"How old were you when you married?"

"Twenty-one. Old enough to know better."

"I was twenty-five and I went like a lamb to the slaughter."

"Unlike you with Courtney, I can't even accuse Brunon of changing. I've lived in the same apartment block as him all my life and he's always been the way he is now."

"Then why marry him?"

"Because he said he loved me, and I thought I needed someone to provide a home for myself and the boys. I didn't realize I'd be adding to my responsibilities by taking on Brunon's grandmother as well. She does what she can, but she's an old lady, and unfortunately her pension doesn't cover the cost of her food and medical bills."

"Brunon doesn't help?"

She leaned back so the waiter could remove her soup bowl. "Not with money, only useless gifts that we dare not sell because we're never sure where they've come from."

"What about your parents?"

"My father and Brunon's were idealists. They believed in

and worked for Solidarity. Both were involved with the protests at the shipyard and both were goaled. They died in prison along with scores of others."

"Murdered?" he asked.

"No one can prove anything. It was a bad time. Not only people but even tombstones disappeared in the 1980s. Brunon can remember his father. I have a mental picture of mine and that is all."

"Their names are on the memorial?"

"No, because they died in prison, although both were regarded as martyrs. Unfortunately their heroic status wasn't much comfort to Brunon's grandmother or my mother, but my mother managed to hang on to her job despite the politics. We survived well enough until she remarried. My stepfather and I didn't get along, so I spent as much time out of the apartment as I could. That's when I started going around with Brunon. In those days he was fun and always had a pocketful of money. I knew he was involved in shady dealing, but so were a lot of people. It was the only way to survive. I moved in with him and his grandmother when I was offered a place at university. Shortly after I received my degree, my mother died of cancer. My stepfather stopped paying rent on the apartment they'd shared and ran out on the boys, there wasn't anyone else to take them in." She poured dressing on her salad.

"You've had it rough," he sympathized.

"Better than some, no worse than most. Brunon's grandmother has been kind to me and the boys try hard."

"It couldn't have been easy for you and Brunon to start with a ready-made family."

"The worst thing was the lack of privacy. His grandmother's apartment only has two rooms. He and the boys slept in one, Maria and I in the other. The first thing I did after I began work at the Institute was save to have the balcony boarded in. It's pleasant in summer and freezing in winter, but I needn't have bothered. As I said, he rarely visits."

"I'm sorry."

"Why?" she looked across at him. "Your marriage is no better."

"When it works, marriage can be good."

"Name me one good marriage?" she challenged.

"Edmund Dunst is happy with Helena."

"Because they've been married three weeks. As soon as the honeymoon period is over, they'll move on in different directions."

"So young and so cynical, but when I think of my family I can't argue with you. You're shattering one of my last illusions. Ever since I was a child I've wanted to believe in 'happily ever after'. It probably stems from having five stepmothers, four stepfathers and six half-sisters who all seem set on repeating our respective parents' mistakes."

"You don't have any brothers?"

"One full brother, Peter. Now there's a case in point, he's happily married, or at least he was when I saw him a year ago."

"How long has he been married?"

"A year. I last saw him at his wedding. Careful," he warned.

"There's someone here?"

"No, you almost smiled," he joked.

"I don't often have something to smile about."

"Married to Brunon, I can see why."

"I'm resigned to Brunon, but I worry about my brothers."

"They're great kids."

"That's all you know after three chance meetings in the museum. It's not easy trying to bring up teenagers in Poland now."

"It's not easy anywhere."

"Some places are better than others. You live in the old town; you have no idea what it's like out in the suburbs. Practically everyone is unemployed, the only people with money are crime barons, the price of everything is rocketing. I have to pay school fees for the boys, and that's without the text books and examination costs. I want them to go to university but..." she suddenly realized she was telling Adam far more than she'd intended. "I'm sorry. I don't know what's got into me. I'm not complaining about my salary. I'm well-off compared to most people. The only excuse I can offer is that I'm tired."

"You'd be superhuman if you weren't."

"Mr. Salen?"

Adam looked up to see a policeman at their table. "Captain Josef sends his apologies. He would like you and the lady to join him in his office. He told me to tell you it's urgent."

CHAPTER TEN

"IT'S CUSTOMARY TO knock before barging into a room," Josef admonished, when Adam ushered Magdalena past a protesting clerk into the captain's office.

"You must make allowances for Americans. They have no manners." Stanislaw Melerski rose from his seat as Magdalena entered. He bowed over her hand, managing to kiss the tips of her fingers before she tugged them free. "Have you met Grigory Radek, the Russian art dealer?"

The square-built Russian creased his Mongolian features into a smile and offered Magdalena his hand. She shook it coolly. .

"We've done business. Radek." Adam nodded an acknowledgement and stepped between Magdalena and the two men. "This is Magdalena Janca, deputy director of the Polish Branch of the Salen Institute."

"And wife of Brunon Kaszuba or so Melerski tells me," Radek said in heavily accented Polish.

"Estranged wife." Adam answered for Magdalena. He took the seat Josef offered and looked around. "Isn't this cozy? I assume by the company you've switched sides, Josef?"

"One day your mouth will get you into serious trouble, Adam."

"I'm sorry, but no one told me the police had seconded the Mafia to the force."

"We're simply citizens doing our bit to maintain law and order," Melerski offered a pack of Cuban cigars around.

"And the priest in the confessional believes you?" Adam asked seriously.

"I was telling our friends about your encounter in the forest," Josef interrupted, steering the conversation on to what he hoped might prove a more useful track.

"Did you see what gun they were using?" Radek asked.

"Only the tip of the barrel. It had a short snout," Adam divulged

"Like a Heckler and Koch?" Josef suggested.

"Possibly, but I know nothing about guns," Adam lied.

"The man who was carrying it threatened you and Miss Janca?"

"We didn't wait around long enough to hear what he had to say. Josef told you they were in a black Mercedes with Russian plates?"

Radek pushed a cigarette between his slack lips. "I wouldn't draw too many conclusions from that, if I were you. If they had been Russian Mafia, you wouldn't be sitting here."

"And to think I gave myself credit for shaking them off," Adam said dryly.

Melerski produced a gold lighter and lit the cigars Josef and Radek had taken. "Exactly what have you been doing to annoy the Russians, Mr. Salen?"

"Absolutely nothing."

"So it was Miss Janca they were after?"

"I'm not too sure." Josef poured Magdalena a coffee and handed it to her. "As we all know, Mr. Salen has some very annoying habits."

"Mr. Radek, could you please pass on the message to whoever came after us that Brunon Kaszuba's wife has no idea where he is, or what he does with his time?" Adam asked.

"And what makes you think an honest art dealer would be acquainted with gun-toting men who drive black limousines, Mr. Salen?"

"There's something you don't know about Kaszuba," Josef broke in quickly before Adam could frame a retort to Radek's question.

"There are a number of things I don't know about Kaszuba and don't want to." Melerski flicked the ash from his cigar onto the floor.

"What I do know is that he rarely visits his grandmother or wife," Adam interrupted.

"Is that true, Mrs. Kaszuba?" Radek asked.

"The name is Janca, and I've only seen Brunon twice this year. Captain Dalecka lives in the same apartment block as me. He'll verify that Brunon doesn't live there."

"When did you last see him?"

"The twelfth of March. He paid his grandmother a birthday visit."

"Did he give her a present?"

"A silk scarf."

"Anything else?"

She shook her head.

"Think carefully," Josef urged. "Any money..."

"Brunon's never given me or his grandmother a grosz. All he ever does is borrow or steal from us."

"We think that fifty thousand dollars you saw him drop on the roulette table..." Josef looked to Radek who nodded,

"...was part of a consignment that came in with the amber shipment."

"To be laundered?" Adam asked.

"Invested," Radek contradicted.

"And your people tried to pick up Magdalena to put the screws on Brunon Kaszuba to hand back the amber and anything that's left of the consignment?"

"I know nothing about the people who came after you and the lady, Mr. Salen, that's if they even exist outside of your imagination," Radek retorted

"We didn't come here to argue," Melerski said smoothly. "Only to volunteer our services to the police."

"On a murder inquiry, missing amber shipment, or art fraud?" Adam asked.

Radek narrowed his eyes. "Are you inviting us to take our pick?"

"I want all the employees of the Salen Institute to be able to sleep at night."

"I've set a watch on Miss Janca's family and apartment." Josef punched the keyboard on his computer, "and I've stretched our resources to cover personal escorts for her and her two brothers."

"Against the kind of jokers who ran us off the road?" Adam demanded.

"Would you prefer it if I locked her in a cell?"

"The same one Kaszuba escaped from?" Adam opened the door and held out his hand to Magdalena. "Just remember, whoever comes after her will find themselves tangling with me."

"I'm sure they're quaking in their boots at the thought," Radek mocked.

"They should be," Adam called back, guiding Magdalena out through the door.

"You'll remain with her every minute?"

"It'll be more than my job's worth to leave her for a second, Mr. Salen," the burly policeman Josef had assigned to watch over Magdalena assured him, as they stood in her office at the Historical Museum.

"And you're going to stay here all afternoon?" Adam glanced out of the window at the stream of tourists pouring into the building. He realized that between the guard and the high profile police presence stationed in tourist areas to deter pickpockets, Magdalena would be safer here than anywhere else in Gdansk.

"Yes," Magdalena agreed irritably.

"I'll be back in an hour." Adam went to the door.

"There's no need..."

"One hour," he repeated.

Adam made his way down the alleyways to Mariacka Street, pausing to check every fifty yards or so that he wasn't being followed. He looked up at his window before walking up the half dozen steps that led to the gallery. The place was crammed with Americans flicking through cradles of scenic views of Gdansk painted by local artists.

"You wanted something, Mr. Salen?" Waleria always tried to get rid of Adam as soon as he appeared in the gallery lest he put off customers with his wisecracks.

"Has the American delegation returned?"

"No."

He tapped an oil painting one of the tourists was

admiring. "Helena's going to be enormous in a year or two. I buy all I can for my New York gallery. A superb artist..."

"But they could return at any time," Waleria interrupted when she realized what he was doing. Adam's attempts to boost her sales had a habit of backfiring, leaving her with full stock and an empty till.

"If you'll excuse me, ladies." He heard the tourists clamoring to see more of Helena's work before he reached the back staircase. He smiled; if Helena made a killing it might stop Edmund Dunst from pressing for a more generous stipend from the Institute.

Despite Waleria's assurance that his apartment was empty he heard the unmistakable sound of a voice. Standing behind his door he tensed his fists and his muscles, only to end up feeling foolish when the answering machine clicked off. He unlocked the door, walked in and inspected every corner before playing back his messages.

Courtney's voice, low and sexy, filled the room, inviting him to dine with her at the Grand Hotel. The initial message was followed by a second, warning him to be no later than eight, and finally a third informing him she'd thought better of the idea and would pick him up in a taxi at seven thirty so he could show her the old town at night.

He ran up the stairs to the mezzanine and filled a sports bag with sufficient clothes and toiletries to last him a week. Leaving the bag at the foot of the stairs he went into the kitchen. He pulled down the window blind and wheeled the dishwasher out of the short bank of units. Set in the floor beneath the space it had occupied was a safe. He turned the combination lock, opened it and lifted out several, neatly-tied bundles of papers, and two sizeable wads of twenty dollar bills.

Nestling in the bottom was a Glock pistol. Heeding warnings from experienced travelers in the Eastern Block, he had acquired it when he had first come to Poland, principally because it was a model that could be carried safely when loaded and had the added advantage of being made of a light polymer that didn't show up on metal detectors.

The military academy his father had parked him in had taught him about guns, but he'd never felt the need to carry one—until now. The shoulder holster felt uncomfortable and once he'd added the weight of the Glock, disconcertingly conspicuous, even after he slipped on his jacket. He pocketed two boxes of ammunition and one of the wads of cash, replaced the documents, re-locked the safe and returned the machine to its housing. Opening the fridge he emptied the contents into a cooler and carried it downstairs with the bag.

Waleria was counting the money in her till. "For once your ploy worked. I sold all the canvasses of Helena's I had in stock."

"Present for you." He dumped the box on to the counter beside her. She looked into it suspiciously.

"Do I look as though I need feeding up?"

"Just going away for a few days."

"Again?"

"The last trip was unexpected."

"Is this 'away' business, or a ploy to avoid your wife and sister?"

"Business. If there are any messages pass them on to Dunst at the museum, I'll be keeping in touch with him."

"What do you want me to tell your wife if she turns up?"

"That I've taken all the keys to my apartment, and you don't know where I am, or when I'm coming back."

"She's a very beautiful lady."

"So was Lucretia Borgia."

As soon as he reached his office he locked the door, opened the safe, removed the scrambler and attached it to the telephone.

"So, you finally remembered you have a grandfather." The old man's querulous voice was testier than usual.

"I was a bit tied up."

"Knowing you, in bed sheets. Why you have to chase skirts with a wife who looks the way yours does..."

"I was not in bed sheets. I just couldn't get to a phone."

"A likely story," his grandfather sneered.

"They're still scarce in country areas. I was trying to authenticate the photographs of the knight."

"Spit out whatever it is you have to say, boy."

"Everyone I've spoken to agrees that the photographs look genuine, but one of the most experienced amber-smiths I know insists it's impossible to be sure without actually handling the piece."

"Buy it, then he can handle it all he likes. The one thing I've learned about experts is they never agree when it comes to verifying a work of art. Bid now, today. The whole one-hundred million in the special fund, to be sure of getting it."

"That would be crazy."

"What's crazy about it? A piece like that..."

"I said it looks authentic. But just to disprove your theory about experts, everyone I've consulted agrees that given a stone coffin, enough amber and a body, it wouldn't take much to make a copy."

"That's a risk I'm prepared to run."

"It could cost you the whole of the emergency fund."

"So what? It's my decision."

"I'm aware of that, but we have three more days. Please, leave it with me for..."

"Damn it all, boy, I want that knight for Poland!"

Adam wasn't a Salen for nothing. Unlike his father and grandfather he'd learned to control his temper but he never kept it in check when it might turn the tide to his advantage. "And I want to make sure it's the real thing, so the Salen Institute doesn't become a byword for fakes and forgeries."

"Two days, and if you don't issue the code word tomorrow morning to release the money in Switzerland I'll put someone else on the job. That's not an idle threat. I have an expert standing by."

"I'll be in touch."

"If you want to hang on to the directorship of the Institute, you'd better be. I'll fly out to see the knight next week. I'll expect it to be there."

"I'll do my best."

"Make damned sure your best is good enough."

Adam pocketed the scrambler and replaced the receiver on the cradle just as Edmund knocked the door.

"Your wife's been in."

"Is she here now?" Adam was already reaching for his briefcase.

"No, but she said she'd be back."

"Send all my correspondence and messages over to the Historical Museum for a couple of days, and don't tell a soul— a single soul," he warned, "where I am."

"Wouldn't it be easier to talk to the woman, she's very..."

"Beautiful?" Adam finished for him. "If you think she's

that gorgeous, she's yours. I give her to you. As an added incentive I'll even throw in my house in New York on condition you live there and keep her away from me." He opened his case and emptied his in-tray into it.

"I thought this might come in useful." Edmund handed him a file. "Two dozen listings of all the Konigsberg treasures that disappeared along with the knight and the amber room. There's a separate appendix giving the history of the few pieces that have surfaced."

"Recently?"

"Nothing since '65."

"I should have thought of doing this earlier. It's probably worth passing it on to Josef so the police can check the antique shops for the smaller stuff."

"Already done. I made those for you to give Feliks and the other amber-smiths."

Adam sat on the edge of his desk and faced Edmund. "All I've done since we had the demand is run around in ever-decreasing circles. I'm glad one of us has taken the time to plan a strategy. I'm more grateful than you know for this."

"I could take the credit but it was Wiklaria's idea. She's a bright girl and she insisted she had nothing else to do as Magdalena was away with you."

Adam looked for and found no hint of sarcasm in Edmund's voice.

"Dare I ask if there have been any developments?" Edmund pressed.

"I haven't found the knight, if that's what you mean."

"Word has it Warsaw and the Smithsonian have been offered the same deal as us."

"Any ideas on bids?"

"If you were about to make a bid, would you be broadcasting the amount?"

"Sorry, I'm tired. Not thinking straight."

"You do realize there are only three days left to the deadline?"

"Yes."

"So are we going to make a bid, or not?" Edmund demanded, finally allowing his exasperation to show.

"Tell you when I know." Adam hesitated before leaving. "If there's any trouble over the next couple of days phone Josef right away. Whatever you do, don't try and handle it yourself."

"What kind of trouble are you expecting?"

"Nothing in particular, but if you see any unsavory people hanging around..."

"You seen any of the other kind in Gdansk lately?" Edmund interrupted.

"I'm serious."

"Trouble in Kaliningrad?"

"Not really."

"Then why did the trip take so long?"

"The car was wrecked in a contaminated area. We were quarantined."

"Josef couldn't track down any accident reports."

"That's the Polish police for you."

"You didn't see Krefta?"

"No."

Edmund frowned. "You would tell me if you were in trouble?"

"OK, it's not me. It's Magdalena. There's a possibility that Kaszuba's on this month's Mafia hit list."

"Kaszuba? I saw him at lunch time."

"Where?"

"In the main square."

"I don't believe it. Every police officer in Gdansk is looking for him and you see him in the main square. Did you talk to him?"

"Just waved. He was walking towards the torture house with another man. Looked like he was showing him the sights."

The phone rang and without thinking, Adam picked up the receiver.

"Adam this place is ghastly..."

"What place, Georgiana?" he asked impatiently.

"The whole country," she retorted. "The Hotel's fine, although the décor's not quite to my taste..."

"Too refined?" he interrupted caustically.

"—but at least they do room service. However there's a problem with the children's food. The burgers and fries don't look like the ones back home, and you know how fussy Niklas and Janine are."

"Try the brats on real food, Georgiana. You never know, you might improve their personalities."

"Niklas has this thing. He'll only eat chicken burgers. They were fine in Paris..."

"Call a taxi. There are McDonald's in Gdansk."

"Really? It's all right, Nanny, Adam says there are McDonald's here. But Adam, the children need more than just a place to eat. There's nowhere for Nanny to take them when I'm working. She's read all the brochures and there doesn't seem to be a Disney park between here and Paris..."

"Try the real thing."

"What real thing?"

"Sorry, Georgiana, must run, important meeting."

"We'll see you soon? Courtney is..."

He hung up to see Edmund grinning like a chimpanzee in a truckload of bananas. "You as much as drop a hint to my sister or wife where I am, or give them the telephone number of the Historical Museum, and you can kiss every exhibit on loan from the Institute goodbye. I am not joking." He picked up his bag and briefcase and walked out of the door.

CHAPTER ELEVEN

DAM HESITATED WHEN he reached the ground floor. He looked down the narrow street towards the impressive, red brick, Gothic bulk of St. Mary's church. Tucked away on the left just in front of the building were the display cases from Felix Malek's shop. The last person he wanted to see was Elizbieta but it certainly would be worth leaving a copy of the list Edmund Dunst had given him with Feliks. After glancing at his watch, he decided he could spare ten minutes. If whoever had the knight was employing help of Brunon Kaszuba's caliber, there was no telling what had been lifted from the hiding place and with luck, sold on, possibly leaving a trail for him or Josef to follow.

Going on the premise that the more public the place, the safer it was, he gripped his briefcase and stepped into the center of the narrow street, dogging the steps of a party of tourists who were stumbling over the cobblestones as they headed for the church.

To his relief there was no sign of Elizbieta in the jewelry store. Feliks was chatting to an elderly German couple over a counter filled with samples of his most elaborate and expensive work. Adam went to the back of the tiny shop and pretended to study an amber sculpture of a fully-rigged sailing ship while Feliks closed a large and lucrative sale.

"That will pay the rent for the next three months." Feliks grinned as he pocketed the bundle of euros the couple had given him.

"Where's Elizbieta?" Adam asked warily.

"Out shopping for clothes to replace the ones you ruined, and possibly cyanide to flavor the coffee the next time you visit. Where did you take her?"

"A country hotel that didn't live up to expectations."

"A likely story. One mention of your name was enough to send her into a frenzy, so I didn't push for an explanation, but Josef said something last night about you being quarantined because you'd strayed into an area contaminated with foot and mouth."

"Government accommodation is rather basic."

"Basic?" He laughed. "It must have been hell. Elizbieta actually hugged and kissed me when she came in. My heart's still throbbing along with a few other delicate parts that aren't used to so much excitement."

"I suggest you make the most of her enthusiasm."

"I always do but unfortunately kissing is about all I'm up for these days. From Elizbieta's reaction I take it she's over her crush on you."

"I have that impression, too." Adam opened his case and removed the file Edmund had given him. "Here are a couple of lists of the artifacts that disappeared from Konigsberg the same time as the knight. If they've been stored together for the last fifty years it's possible something else might reappear on the market. Could you distribute these among the dealers and wholesalers? I'd be grateful if they contact Edmund at the museum if they come across any of them."

"How grateful?"

"Full market value, plus twenty percent for their trouble."

"That's what I call grateful. You given the list to the police?"

"Edmund has."

"I take it you're thinking of the more unorthodox dealers?"

"I know your friends."

"I'll see what I can do." Feliks scanned the list. "Considerate of you to categorize them by gold, silver, amber, painting and sculpture, but did you have to put the Amber Room and Amber Knight on top? Anyone who gets offered either of those is likely to go to the police anyway. There's no way they could be shifted on the open market."

"Unless they're broken up."

"That would be sacrilege," Feliks asserted indignantly.

"Not every amber-smith has your integrity."

"I'll take that as a compliment, even if it wasn't intended as one." Feliks continued to read. "The missing thirteen beads from the necklace of Princess Dorothea manufactured in Gdansk 1610."

"The size of golf balls. Clear amber, crystal cut. I've seen the ten surviving ones in the Swedish exhibition in Malbork."

"So have I. Who do you think cleaned and prepared them for the exhibition?" Feliks ran his finger over the inventory. "Three rings, two bracelets, four sets of earrings and one head-dress, all amber and silver, and all made for Princess Dorothea. Lucky lady, she must have had a big jewelry box. Nine amber caskets, four from the seventeenth-century workshop of Michel Redlan, altar crosses, crucifixes—a dozen fif-teenth-century goblets, with bowls of amber and stems of gold, once the property of the last king of Poland—I like the sketches by the way. Frames, figurines, panels—cabinets—anyone who reads this will be wary of buying anything pre-war."

"Not once word of my offer gets around. Let's hope the present guardian of the knight is either broke or employs a few greedy helpers."

"Talking about greedy," Feliks opened a drawer and removed a small leather box. He opened it before handing it to Adam. "Blue stone earrings."

Adam lifted them out. Ornate, highly-wrought gold mounts snaked around stones the size and shape of quails' eggs. "Too large, too French Empire and too vulgar."

"Vulgarity is your Helga's middle name."

Adam held them up to the light. Even to his untrained eye they looked too pale to be sapphires. "The stones are the wrong color."

"Aquamarines," Feliks explained, "the best I could do for the price."

"Helga will know the difference."

"She would have found out when she'd sold them. Ladies like her never keep their jewelry long. Next year, if her looks last that long, she'll be wearing platinum and diamonds, not eight hundred dollar..."

"I gave you a ceiling of three."

"Seeing as how it's you, I'll forgo my profit. Five hundred."

"No way."

"A man has to eat. Besides, you deprived me of my assis-tant for three days. I deserve compensation."

Adam knew when he was beaten. He reached for his checkbook.

"I prefer cash."

"Cashier's check is the best I can do."

"Just this once I can make an exception."

Adam pulled out his pen and cleared a space on the counter. "Now these are much more elegant." He picked out another pair of earrings. Elongated, fluted raindrops of amber dangled from art deco silver cones.

"Crystal cut amber, an absolute swine to do. The technique hasn't changed since Princess Dorothea's day."

"How much are they?"

"Helga will never wear amber."

"I wasn't thinking of giving them to Helga."

Feliks grinned. "I heard your wife was in town."

"How much?"

"For you, two hundred dollars."

"A hundred."

"I'd be robbing myself. Do you have any idea how many hours of work went into those?"

"Knowing you, they weren't your hours, and I can guess what you pay Elizbieta. A hundred and fifty, that's my final offer. And, while I'm here, have you a couple of pieces of amber that I can borrow for a week or so?"

"My stocks are low. You want amber, you buy it."

Adam looked around the shelves. There was a large paperweight with a small panorama of insect life caught in its shimmering depths.

"That will do. With everything, shall we call it seven hundred dollars?"

"Eight-fifty."

"Seven-fifty."

"You drive a hard bargain. What do you want amber for, anyway?" Feliks rummaged in the depths of a cupboard for a case for the amber earrings.

"To get used to the feel of it. When I finally lay my hands on the knight, I want to make sure it's the real thing."

"I'm glad you're back." Magdalena looked up from her desk as he walked past the police officer into her office.

"That's a first."

"You remember I asked the Berlin Document Center to forward us all the documents relevant to the treasures in Konigsberg Castle? This was waiting on my desk."

Adam sat on the windowsill and read out the fax. "Standartenführer Dieter Meyer was in command of the Wolfschanze in January 1945." He looked across at her. "So?"

"Don't you remember the signature on the document I showed you? Dieter Meyer signed a receipt for an unspecified consignment of goods four days after the treasure was sent out of Konigsberg."

"But there's no proof that the consignment he signed for was the treasure?"

"No, but don't you think it's an incredible coincidence? What other transport could have warranted the personal attention of an SS Colonel?"

"Arms, ammunition—any one of a dozen things the Germans wanted to keep out of the hands of the Russians."

"They would have given priority to the treasure over a shipment of military hardware," she persisted.

"You can't fight an invading Russian army with amber rooms and knights."

"In my opinion Dieter Meyer signed for the Konigsberg treasure because it had been sent to the Wolfschanze for safe-keeping and, as there's no record of his orders being rescinded, Meyer and the treasure were probably there until the Russian invasion."

"You said he disappeared at the end of the war?"

"As did the treasure."

"He could have run off with it."

"All forty truckloads? More likely he hid it in the Wolfschanze before his command was wiped out by the Russian army."

"You won't let go of that idea, will you?" Adam pulled out his wallet and removed the bullet he had found in Krefta's apartment.

"What's that?"

"It was hidden in the soap in the Kaliningrad apartment. Careful," he warned as she took it from him. "It's sharp."

She turned it around slowly. "Russian markings, but nothing that shouldn't be there. The edges are sharp because the cap's been pried off at some time. Want me to open it?"

"You might damage the contents, or worse, they could be poisonous."

She had the cap off before he'd finished speaking. It took two taps against her desk to dislodge a small wedge of damp, swollen paper. "Someone soaked it in water."

"You were the one who made me carry out the dead cat. I had to wash my hands."

"And destroy the only potential clue we've found?" She produced a pair of paper tweezers.

"I didn't know it was in the soap at the time. Can you do anything with it?"

She cleared a space on her desk and attempted to unfold the bullet-shaped, compressed wedge. The paper disintegrated at the first touch of the tweezers. "Not here." She laid the torn fragment on to a tissue. "It's too fragile. But it would be a different story if we had our own fully equipped laboratory in the museum."

"Put forward a case for one and I'll try to persuade the board."

"In the meantime, this will have to be sent to Warsaw." She took a clean envelope from a tray and transferred the paper, the corner she'd torn off, and the bullet, into it.

Adam scrutinized the plan laid out on her desk. "Is that the Wolfschanze?"

"You've never been there?"

"I've seen photographs. The knight's no small trinket. You're looking at something twice the size of this desk. Do you really believe it could have lain undiscovered in a tourist attraction for fifty years?"

"Unlike you, I refuse to dismiss any possibility."

"OK, we'll go to the Wolfschanze tomorrow."

"Time's running out and it could turn out to be a wild goose chase," she warned.

"Now who's getting cold feet?"

"I hate 'I told you so's'."

"There won't be any. If I could think of a more constructive move, I'd make it," he said flatly.

"And if we're forced off the road into the forest again?"

"You're forgetting you have protection. I doubt even the Mafia will follow a police car."

"We'll hardly be inconspicuous."

"The more conspicuous the better. That way no one could possibly mistake me for Brunon."

"I shouldn't leave my brothers, not now. I've only just got back."

"Have you considered that your brothers might be safer without you around?"

Their eyes met. She looked away first. Sealing the envelope she left her desk. "I'll tell Wiklaria to send this to Warsaw."

"Express," he ordered.

"It could take days to process. The museums use the same forensic laboratories as the police, and police work has priority."

"I'll talk to Josef, see if he can pull strings. And afterwards we eat."

"Again?"

"We never saw the food we ordered at lunch time," he reminded her.

"No, we didn't," she recalled.

"And, after we've eaten, I'll take you home."

"I have a guard."

"I'm not leaving you."

"My apartment only has two rooms and there are three of us sleeping in them as it is. Four if Maria has returned from her sister's."

"Then I'll sleep in the hallway outside."

"You'd be a fire hazard. No one would be able to get in or out of their apartments."

"I'm not leaving you and that's the end of it. Pass me the telephone." He suddenly remembered Edmund's story that he'd seen Brunon in the city. "On second thoughts, I'll send Wiklaria out for coffee and use hers."

* * *

Adam and Magdalena ate with Josef, but not in the Milan. Adam insisted on driving out to the suburbs as far from the tourist path, and his wife's and sister's likely orbits, as he could get. As always, when he shared a meal with Josef he found himself stuck with the bill, and also that of the guards, who had eaten at a separate table.

"You'll send a car first thing in the morning?" Adam reminded Josef as the waiter poured out three complimentary coffees in appreciation of the tip he'd been given.

"Six early enough?"

"Make it half past."

"You'd better warn the driver to be prepared for an overnight stay," Magdalena cautioned. "Unless we're lucky it will take us two or three days to check out the Wolf's Lair; that's time you haven't got, Adam, if you're going to put in a bid for the knight."

"My grandfather threatened to bring in someone else to run the Institute if I don't secure the knight for Poland. Which reminds me, I'll be out on my ear if I don't make the call I promised him I would, right now." Adam checked his watch. He knew his grandfather had been serious about firing him if he didn't contact Switzerland. And, with everything else that had been going on, he had forgotten. Hoping that his grandfather had given him a couple of hours' grace, he went to a booth and dialed the bank.

Josef was peeling paper from sugar cubes and dropping them into his coffee when Adam returned to the table. "You have a hotel in mind for the overnight?"

"There are plenty of hotels around the Masurian lakes," Magdalena answered carelessly.

"German hotels?"

"Why are you asking?" Adam inquired suspiciously.

"I like German hotels. The beds are clean and comfortable, they're run like clockwork, and the food's always good."

"I take it that means you're thinking of coming with us?" Adam stirred his coffee.

"Mariana and I could do with a break."

"You two are talking?"

"Only just. The problem is we never see one another long enough to do otherwise. I hardly ever have any free time, and when I do the children and Marta are always around."

"You won't be able to guard Magdalena and romance Mariana at the same time."

"Magdalena has a guard, on a trip like this I'll double the detail, but they'll still need back-up." He glanced across at the officer who was sitting alert and poised next to the door. "He can drive you. I'll follow in a second car in case yours breaks down."

"Mariana won't be thrilled at the thought of an expedition to the Wolfschanze." Magdalena had been in school with Josef's wife. Shopping trips excepted, Mariana had never walked a willing step in her life.

"Oh, we won't be going to the Wolf's Lair with you. The guards will do that."

"While you..."

"Check out the security of the hotel," Josef interrupted Adam.

"Especially the bedrooms." Adam lifted his eyebrows.

"Trust me. I'll find us a good hotel. You know my car, Magda. I'll be outside our block at six thirty. We'll pick you up on the way, Adam."

"I'm staying with Magdalena."

"Really?" It was Josef's turn to raise his eyebrows.

"There's no 'really'," Magdalena snapped, irritated by the expression on Josef's face.

"I saw the men in the black Mercedes, you didn't," Adam reminded Josef, "and I'm not leaving Magdalena alone until you've resolved this case."

"Find me Brunon, and I'll soon settle the case, and in the meantime Magda has police protection."

"So did Brunon when you had him locked in the cells in Piwna Street."

"There's no room for either you or a guard in my apartment," Magdalena protested, angry at being discussed as though she wasn't in the same room, let alone at the same table as them.

"Don't worry about the guard, we'll give him a chair in the hallway," Josef asserted dismissively.

"All I'll need is a few inches of floor space in the boys' room," Adam countered.

"I have no bedding."

"We have some you can borrow." Josef earned himself a frown from Magdalena.

"I can take care of myself," she insisted.

"I've no doubt you can, but just this once, humor me." Adam left the table and Josef followed him into the men's room.

"That sighting of Edmund's didn't check out," Josef informed him.

"You got blind policemen on street duty?" Adam asked.

"You know how crowded the main town gets. Dunst could have seen someone who looks like Brunon."

"If this guy resembled Brunon enough to fool Edmund,

who knows him, why wasn't he picked up and questioned by your people?"

"Because it wasn't him," Josef suggested caustically.

"My money's on Edmund."

"I hate to agree with a woman," Josef retorted, smarting at Adam's criticism, "but what would you do if someone did break into Magdalena's apartment and tried to grab her?"

"You'd be amazed."

"I don't doubt it, but I'll double the night guard outside the block just in case."

CHAPTER TWELVE

WO ARMED POLICEMEN, one of them Josef's lieutenant, Pajewski, were sitting in the corridor outside Magdalena's apartment when Adam escorted her home. They assured Magdalena that her brothers were safe and confirmed that Josef had assigned a double guard to watch over them during the night. As Magdalena inserted her key into the door, Pajewski winked slyly at Adam, a gesture Adam only just managed to ignore.

Adam followed Magdalena into a room that served as both sitting room and kitchen. It was furnished in a style that hadn't been seen in the States since the middle of the last century. A shiny, teak-veneered Formica worktop stretched along one wall, topping two white painted cupboards and a refrigerator. A gray and white gas cooker stood next to a sink, a gas water heater screwed to the wall above it. Despite the open window there was a strong smell of tripe and onions.

An old woman was slumped on a bed, one of two ineffectively disguised as sofas. Wiktor and Jan, Magdalena's half-brothers, were sitting at a Formica table surrounded by piles of books.

"This is our neighbor, Mrs. Dynski, who looks after

Wiktor and Jan when Maria and I aren't here. Mrs. Dynski, this is Mr. Salen, the Director of the Salen Institute."

"Please, call me Adam." Adam shook the old woman's hand and smiled at the boys to let them know that applied to them as well.

"So you're the American who pays Magdalena her wages?" Mrs. Dynski's face had more cracks and crevasses than the Arizona desert, but her eyes sparkled like glass beads caught in candlelight.

"Guilty."

"I can't imagine what she does that's worth so much."

"You already know my brothers," Magdalena interrupted.

"Pleased to meet you again, sir." Both boys rose politely from their seats.

"I'm glad to see you doing your homework." Magdalena looked over Wiktor's shoulder at their books.

"What's Brunon done this time, Magda?" Jan demanded. "We've had police officers following us everywhere, and they won't tell us a thing."

"If they won't tell you, what makes you think they'll tell me?"

"You have police officers following you too, one of them told us that much."

"I also have Mr. Salen and that's even worse. Jan, your writing gets more like a spider's crawl every time I look at it. I can barely understand this essay."

"Most of the other boys print their work out on computers now," Wiktor said archly. "The school is selling off three of the old ones. Professor Jablonowski says they're going very cheap. Brunon promised to buy us one when they came up."

"We'll talk about it some other time," Magdalena said sternly.

"They'll be gone by the end of the week. Everyone is after them."

"I said some other time."

"When, Magda? You're never here..."

"I said some other time," she reiterated. "And it won't be tomorrow. I have to go away again on business."

"You don't want to go spending your money on a second-hand computer, especially if it's been used as heavily as school ones are," Adam warned.

"Jan and I have been saving for a new one, but at the rate we're going it'll take us twenty years, and by then they'll be twice the price they are now."

"If you're interested in computers, there's one in my office you can use," Adam said. "I'm never there after three in the afternoon. Why don't you call in after school, the Archaeological, not the Historical, Museum? The curator, Edmund Dunst, will show you where it is."

"You mean it?" Wiktor asked excitedly.

"I wouldn't have offered if I didn't."

"That would be great," Wiktor enthused.

"You have a printer as well?" Jan, the practical one, asked.

"A laser. In fact, come to think of it, there may be a computer coming up that you can have in a couple of weeks."

"If there is, it will be going for more than we can afford," Magdalena broke in sharply.

"Edmund is upgrading," Adam protested. "He was going to throw it out. I'll talk to him about it when we get back."

"We couldn't possibly accept it."

"Trash from a dumpster?" he questioned.

"Are all the computers in the museum connected to the Internet like Magda's?" Jan asked.

"Whether they are or not, is no concern of yours," Magdalena lectured. "The museum computers are not there for you to play with. Now take your homework into your bedroom and finish it there."

"But Adam's only just got here."

"It's Mr. Salen," she corrected, "and he's staying the night."

Wiktor opened the door that led into the second room. Three single beds, placed a foot apart were lined up in a row. Two wicker baskets at their feet left barely enough space to walk between them.

"Wiktor, take the mattress from Brunon's bed out on to the balcony. Jan, get the spare bedding..."

"You said you didn't have any spare bedding," Adam reminded her.

"I lied."

"Either way, I don't need anything, it's warm enough," Adam asserted, disliking the fuss his arrival had generated.

"Get the bedding," Magdalena repeated, disregarding Adam's protest.

"I'll get the dice out after we've finished our homework." Wiktor dragged a foam mattress across the living room floor. "Brunon taught us this terrific game. We'll show you how to play it, Magda."

"You have school tomorrow, Wiktor," Magdalena reminded him.

"Magda, we're out of toothpaste," Jan called from the bathroom.

"And soap," Wiktor chimed in.

"Here." Adam unzipped his case and threw his toilet bag at Jan. "There's soap and toothpaste in there."

"Maria's always complaining that you never remember to buy the essentials, Magda," Mrs. Dynski grumbled. "And you know soap and toothpaste are cheaper in the bigger stores in Gdansk."

"It's my fault she hasn't had a chance to do any shopping," Adam apologized. "I dragged her off to Kaliningrad."

"And had an accident, or so young Josef Dalecka said. The boys were worried out of their minds." Mrs. Dynski glowered at Magdalena as though she didn't believe a word of Josef's story.

"The car broke down," Magdalena said, not entirely untruthfully.

"I suppose you're hungry," Mrs. Dynski muttered.

"We've just come from a restaurant."

"Where you've eaten fancy food that has no nourishment at a price that would feed a family of four for a week. The sooner the Communists come back into power, the better. They'll put the rents down to what they should be, and get everyone back to work. Proper work, not this tourist rubbish where people are expected to work for tips, not wages. Then there'll be no more street gangs hanging around corners with nothing to do all day except plague old ladies, steal things that don't belong to them and make mischief." She wagged her finger at Adam. "You and your American ways! Lot of nonsense. Shops crammed to the ceiling with useless kitsch people can't afford and don't need, but are persuaded to buy by stupid advertisements on the television. And what happens when the penniless idiots see the goods in the shops? They become discontented with what they have. Democracy, bah!" She stared at him, daring him to contradict her.

"We're very tired, and we have to be up early tomorrow. I'm afraid I have to go away again for a couple of days, Mrs. Dynski," Magdalena apologized. "Will you and the boys be able to manage until Maria gets back?"

"And if we can't?" Mrs. Dynski challenged.

"I'll get someone in to help. Mrs. Milosz..."

"...is a lazy slut. I'm not in my coffin yet. You do what you have to, I'll see to everything here."

"We can look after ourselves tonight if you'd like to sleep in your own apartment," Magdalena suggested pointedly.

"Maria would never forgive me if I left you alone with a strange man."

Adam pretended he hadn't heard the old woman.

"He's not strange, he's my employer, and we'd hardly be alone with the boys in the next room."

"It wouldn't be proper. That you, a married woman, should even suggest such an idea." She eyed Adam as though he was livestock on offer. "What you do when you go off on these little 'trips' of yours..."

"We work, Mrs. Dynski," Magdalena said firmly.

"I'm sure," Mrs. Dynski pronounced skeptically. "But now that the boys are in their room I'd appreciate peace and quiet so I can watch television. Nothing but noise around here, morning, noon and night. Noise, noise, noise!" She leaned forward and switched on an LCD television that was worth more than the rest of the contents of the apartment put together. After what Magdalena had told him about her husband, Adam assumed it was one of Brunon's acquisitions.

Magdalena pushed aside a thin white curtain that looked as though it had been made from a bed sheet. She opened a glass door and beckoned Adam on to a concrete platform three feet wide and seven feet long, its wrought ironwork sides covered and roofed in by sheets of corrugated plastic.

"Interesting effect," he commented. "Bit like a cloudy fish tank."

"The cloudy is for the benefit of Maria. She doesn't like living on the twentieth floor."

Adam pulled his bag after him and laid it on top of the sheets and quilt Jan had spread on the mattress. "High enough to avoid the pollution."

"But not private. When the living room light is on, anyone looking up from below can see your shadow."

"Good. I hope that means we'll have a quiet night."

"The mattress is thin."

"After the boards we've slept on for the past couple of nights it will feel like a feather bed. And we've got Josef's luxurious accommodation to look forward to tomorrow."

"What time would you like me to call you?" She stepped back into the living room.

"What time do you normally get up?"

"Five, the boys leave for school at half past six."

"Five will do."

"You know where the bathroom is?"

"Yes."

"Adam, I do appreciate your concern for my safety..." she hesitated.

"It sounds like you're about to put a 'but' in there."

"It's what you said to the boys."

"All I suggested was they might make use of an obsolete computer that's destined for the garbage can."

"It's not just the computer, it's the offer to use the museum's facilities after school."

"What's wrong with that?"

She knew that what she was about to say was cruel, but she went ahead and said it anyway. "There are ways for rich Americans to get kicks in Poland that don't involve dispensing charity to poor disadvantaged natives."

He crossed his arms and met her steady gaze. "Is that what you think of me?"

"Can you blame me for not wanting the boys to grow up thinking the only way to get ahead in the world is by acting as a doormat to the rich?"

"Who's rich? I live off my salary."

"And you can spend every last grosz, secure in the knowledge that if you need more all you have to do is fax your family."

"So this is about resentment?"

"It's about the boys. I'm all they have, and I want them to receive the right kind of education. One that will equip them for this rotten, corrupt world."

"I was trying to help."

"You were setting them on the same road Brunon is traveling down. It's easy to be honest when you have no reason to steal, but I'd like to see how you'd behave if you'd been born into this cesspit."

"You've survived."

"Because I've worked hard. Twenty hours a day and more. I want the boys to learn the same lessons I have. That privileges have to be earned, not stolen or begged from wealthy benefactors."

"That puts me in my place." He folded back the quilt. When he looked up she'd shut the door and closed the curtain. Pulling the gun from his holster, he checked the chamber before stowing it beneath the mattress. Leaning against the rails he lit a cigar. When his eyes became accustomed to the distortions of the plastic sheeting and the gloom, he gazed down the dizzying heights to the grid of street lights twenty floors below. They illuminated a miniaturized world of diminutive, matchstick figures and toy-like cars.

The accusations Magdalena had made simmered in his mind. Did she really see him as some kind of corrupting god-father-like figure? Was he using his position as director of the Salen Institute to massage his ego? Was he self-indulgent, patronizing, looking to boost his "feel good" factor by dispensing largesse to the poor? Was it a subconscious ploy to restore his self-esteem after Courtney's betrayal?

The seeds Magdalena had planted germinated into poisonous thoughts that tainted the pleasure he'd taken in everything he'd thought he'd achieved in Poland.

He finished his cigar, stripped off his shirt and shoes, made a pillow of his bag and lay on the mattress. He was tired, but not tired enough. Magdalena's face, contorted by bitterness and anger, persisted in intruding into his mind and, all the while, he was conscious of the light burning in the room behind him and the incessant drone of not only Magdalena's television, but what sounded like a chorus of every other television in the block.

After four hours he felt suffocated by the plastic sheeting and yearned for fresh, cold, clear air. He sat up and examined the roof. It had been bolted into an aluminum frame, but by dint of careful maneuvering he managed to slide one of the top panels open. Above him a pale gold sliver of new moon shone down surrounded by a fine powdering of stardust. He felt in his shirt pocket for another cigar. A shout echoed from somewhere below. He waited but there was no answering cry. He had thought the old quarter of Gdansk noisy but compared to this concrete wasteland and rabbit hutch of a building it was a mortuary.

An alarm rang somewhere in the building. He pressed the button on his watch. Three thirty. The televisions were still buzzing and, tiny, shadowy figures moved beneath the street lights far below. There were so many noises in the building it was difficult to determine whether any were sinister or not.

"Coffee?" Magdalena opened the door and handed him a mug.

"You can't sleep either?"

"The change of guards outside the door woke me, and I heard you moving around in here."

He slipped his shirt on. She was wearing a thin cotton nightgown. The intimacy embarrassed him after the formality she insisted on in the office. Even during their incarceration they had never been alone, or seen one another without the all-enveloping boiler suits.

"Is the building always this noisy?"

"Always. The walls are paper thin. That's why most people keep their televisions on all night. They'd rather hear what's on the box than the neighbors fighting."

"Is Mrs. Dynski asleep?"

"She's been snoring for hours."

He sipped the coffee. It was freshly ground and tasted superb. "There doesn't seem much point in trying to get back to sleep."

"I doubt that I could. I think I did all my sleeping in advance in that cell."

"In spite of Elizbieta's griping?"

"She's not that bad."

"I thought you two didn't get along."

"What I said to you earlier about rich benefactors. I'm sorry. I'm just angry about what's happened to Poland. Westerners coming in and buying up all the best houses next to the sea and lakes. Our works of art, everything that we as a country should value, being shipped out. And Poles who should know better lining up to sell our heritage to any for-eigner with cash in their pocket. At least you are trying to help us to hang on to our history."

"I thought I was, but after what you said I'm not too sure."

"I was angry."

"You were also right. One of the reasons I live here is that it does make me feel good. It came as a shock to realize the natives had found me out."

"Without the Salen Institute..."

"I'm not the Institute, just one of the workers. I've been kidding myself that I was the one doing the giving. After you closed the door on me I did some thinking. Poland's given me far more than I can ever give back to the country through my work. The truth is I'm here because I've fallen in love with the place."

"Poland or Gdansk?"

"Both. I like living in an old city. Every time I walk through the streets I see something that reminds me of the great tides of humanity who've lived, worked and died here throughout long centuries we Americans can only dream of."

"I never had you down as a romantic."

"Hasn't it occurred to you that westerners flock to Poland because they envy what you have here? You've managed to hold on to something we lost a long time ago."

"Poverty?" she mocked.

"A sense of family, of tradition, of belonging not only to a people but a place. I'm happier here than I ever was in the States. Here, I have time to think, to live life instead of talk about it."

"That's down to lifestyle, not the country you're living in."

"One day you'll visit America and meet a breed of people who are too busy looking for the meaning of life to enjoy it while they have it. They're all terrified of missing out on something, just like the down-and-out who won't eat what's on the plate in front of him in case there's something better stuck to the tablemat beneath it."

"You're painting a harsh view of your fellow countrymen."

"You met Courtney and Georgiana."

"Met—I don't know them."

He held up his hand to silence her. Twitching aside the curtain he was just in time to see the living room door burst inwards. A man stood framed in the doorway. Dressed in a police officer's uniform, he pointed a gun at gibbering, terrified Mrs. Dynski.

Adam shoved Magdalena behind him and yanked the Glock out from beneath the mattress. The intruder walked to Magdalena's rumpled bed and pushed aside the bedclothes. Adam brushed aside the curtain at the same instant Wiktor opened the boys' bedroom door.

The officer swung round and cocked his gun in Wiktor's direction. Wiktor threw himself to the floor. Adam didn't wait for a second opportunity. Setting his sights in the center of the intruder's back, he fired.

The room was suddenly filled with noise and flame. Flashes of light and bullets pierced the balcony walls, thudding into the plastic and shattering the glass door. Grabbing Magdalena, Adam pulled her into the living room and lay over her, protecting her body with his own. Slivers of lead and shards of glass hailed down all around, drowning out Mrs. Dynski's screams and Wiktor's sobs, yet all he was conscious of was Magdalena trembling beneath him, and a fear born of absolute terror.

CHAPTER THIRTEEN

"THE SURGEON SAID you recognized him?"
"His name is Casimir Zamosc. He's an artist." Adam
closed the boys' bedroom door behind him and sank
down on one of the chairs.

Josef was standing in the middle of the room, barefoot
and bare-chested. He'd taken charge as soon as he'd appeared,
disheveled and panting, minutes after the first shots had been
fired; if the police surgeon or the officers who'd crowded into
the apartment saw anything humorous in their overweight
captain directing a murder enquiry dressed in nothing but a
pair of trousers with an unzipped fly, they were either too
polite, or too wary of their superior, to show it.

"My sister introduced us," Adam explained. "He's one of
her protégés."

"Was one of her protégés." The police surgeon rose to his
feet. "Bullet in the back of the skull. Body temperature and
angle of entry endorses Mr. Salen's statement.
Straightforward shooting of intruder. You couldn't have done
it better, Mr. Salen. Death was instantaneous." A blood-
chilling scream echoed from the boys' bedroom followed by
high-pitched hysterical laughter.

"Are Magda and the boys all right?" Josef asked.

"As all right as you'd expect them to be after something like this. That's Mrs. Dynski," Adam explained.

"You said you'd surprise me, and you did. I'll need your gun so we can cross-match the bullet."

Adam handed Josef the Glock.

"Very nice. You have a permit for it?"

"The papers are in my apartment."

"I'll look them over later," Josef said, ensuring he was in the surgeon's earshot. "I wonder who this guy was working for."

"And I wonder where your guards were?" Adam said dryly.

"The two in the car downstairs noticed nothing out of the ordinary."

"And the three outside the door?"

"I cut them down to two for the graveyard shift. They're in the stairwell."

Something in the tone of Josef's voice checked Adam's anger. "Dead?"

Josef nodded grimly. Murdered villains were an everyday fact of life, murdered police officers, especially men he worked with, were not.

"You can move this one out, Josef." The surgeon tossed his instruments back into his bag. "I'll take a look at the others."

"Bag that carefully, don't remove the silencer," Josef ordered a sergeant who'd snapped on rubber gloves and opened a plastic bag in readiness to remove the gun from Zamosc's hand. "I want a comparison match between the bullets that killed the guards with ammunition fired from that weapon."

"Anything on the hail that came through the balcony?" Adam asked.

"Nothing in the block across the street except empty casings. The fingerprint boys are working there now. Not that they'll find anything. This is the work of professionals." Josef stepped aside to allow two men to lift the body onto the stretcher. After the surgeon and officers left, the apartment fell suddenly and eerily silent.

"Was Zamosc a professional?" Adam asked.

"If he was, he wasn't known to us. But we'll run his prints through the records in the station. Does Magda keep brandy? You look like shit."

"I've never killed a man before."

"Next time shoot to maim, we might have wormed something out of him."

"I tried, I'm a lousy shot. And I'm not waiting around for a next time. After seeing Polish police protection in action, I'm shipping Magdalena and her brothers out on the first available plane."

"She's prepared to go?"

"I haven't told her yet."

"We'll never resolve this bloody case without her."

"Find someone else to play decoy."

"You two making my decisions for me again?" Magdalena emerged from the bedroom.

"Adam's sending you out of the country."

"Is he?" Avoiding the chalked body outline on the floor Magdalena went to the sink and filled the kettle.

"You can't stay here."

"I have a job to do."

"You're on leave as of two hours ago. Take your brothers,

pick up Brunon's grandmother, and take them anywhere you like. The States…"

"The boys have school examinations."

"We'll find them another school."

"I can't just up and change my life at a moment's notice."

"You're damned lucky to have a life left!" Adam exclaimed.

"Shouting isn't going to help," Josef said quietly.

"And don't you dare say another word." Adam turned on Josef. "Not while we're standing in a room littered with the results of your protection."

"I agree with Josef, shouting isn't helping." Magdalena poured a pot of tea and carried it to the table.

"Packing your bags will," Adam declared.

"Do you really think I'll be safe anywhere after this?" Magdalena's face was grave.

"Yes, on my grandfather's ranch. He's installed more security measures than Fort Knox. In fact, they have the same advisor."

"He has a nervous disposition?" Josef reached for the sugar and heaped three spoonfuls into an empty cup.

"A daughter snatched and murdered by kidnappers."

"I'm sorry," Josef murmured sincerely.

"It happened twenty years before I was born." Adam didn't want to talk about the tragedy that had cast a long shadow from his grandfather's and father's generations into his own. "Be sensible, Magdalena, the boys will have a great time there. If you're worried about their school work I'll get them a tutor. You could take a holiday, enjoy the pool, exercise the horses, or just sit in the sun and read."

"All right. You can send the boys and Brunon's grandmother there," she conceded. "But not me."

"What's the point when it's you they're after?" Adam asked.

"We don't know that for sure," she insisted.

"First the car ambush, now this. What will it take to convince you?" He took the tea she offered him without thinking. He loathed tea, never drank it, something he forgot until he took the first sip.

"You were with me on both occasions," she reminded him.

"No one knew I intended to sleep here tonight."

"Only half the police department and anyone who cared to follow us and look up at the balcony," she contradicted.

"I'd know if anyone had been checking on Adam's movements." Tired of waiting for Magdalena to offer, Josef poured tea into a cup and took it.

"You can't possibly know what every man who works in Piwna Street gets up to." She picked up her cup and walked to the window.

"Don't!" Josef and Adam shouted simultaneously.

Deliberately standing in front of the bullet-shattered balcony door, she turned to face them, her gray eyes glittering, frosted steel in her pale face. "I have no intention of changing my lifestyle because of the antics of a few thugs." She pushed her dark hair away from her face. "If the boys want to go to America, that's up to them. I'm packing for an overnight stay at the Wolfschanze."

"The trip's off," Adam growled.

"If you won't take me, I'll go alone. The Amber Knight is part of Poland's heritage. If I can restore it to Gdansk, I will."

"Tell her she can't go?" Adam pleaded with Josef.

"Poland became a free country after the Revolution. Everyone can do what they want. Even women."

* * *

Jan and Wiktor heard the magic word "America" and started emptying their slim wardrobes into sports bags, but Magdalena sat on Wiktor's bed, watched the bustle around her, and calmly announced that no one, and nothing, was going to drive her out of her home. After half an hour of futile argument Josef motioned his head to the door and Adam followed him into the corridor.

"We can send the old lady on when she turns up," Josef said.

"You still haven't tracked her down?" Adam asked in surprise.

"Oltzyn as an address is a bit vague even for us. But she must be safe. If she'd been killed or kidnapped we would have heard by now."

"And Magdalena?"

"I can't force her to go anywhere she doesn't want to. Just occasionally, I regret the passing of the old ways. Life might have been tough under the Communists, but it was a bloody sight easier when people did what uniformed officials told them to."

"So, you'll put a round-the-clock guard on Magdalena again?" Adam mocked him.

Josef didn't even hear him. "Why would anyone, especially the Mafia, go to such public lengths to kill a museum director?"

"To get at her thieving husband?"

"Brunon's small fry in the grand Mafia scheme of things."

"Small fry who's stolen a big chunk of their loose change and amber."

"Which will eventually cost him his head. Word is out. No one in Poland who values their life will lift a finger to help or hide him."

"But he hasn't surfaced, so someone must be covering up for him," Adam said.

"Until we find him I can't do a damned thing."

"You could try looking for him."

"You think we haven't?" Josef's temper surfaced. "There isn't a stone in this city that hasn't been lifted."

"It takes a great deal of confidence, or police protection, for a man in his position to walk around openly."

"Edmund must have been mistaken."

"And I still say that's unlikely. I think it's time to set up another meeting with Radek and Melerski."

"And your sister," Josef mused. "If she knew Casimir Zamosc, it's possible she knows more than she realizes."

Adam arranged the flight to America, Josef an escort for the boys. In a last-ditch attempt to persuade Magdalena to leave with her brothers, Josef announced that he needed to close off her apartment for at least a week for forensic tests. Her reaction was to pack everything she wouldn't need in the Wolfschanze and move it across the hall into Mrs. Dynski's apartment. Once the initial excitement at the thought of visiting America wore off, the boys began to sense Adam and Josef's concern for their sister's safety. Much to Magdalena's consternation Wiktor and Jan decided not to leave her, and it took a stern reminder from Adam that it was easier to mount a guard on one, than three, to get them into the car.

Adam had booked an internal flight for the boys and their escort from Gdansk to Warsaw, and a transatlantic flight from there. Five minutes' conversation with Adam's grandfather's housekeeper, Betsy, on Josef's mobile phone did more to reassure Magdalena of the reception the boys would receive in

California than all Adam's protestations that they would have the time of their lives there.

Less than two hours after leaving Magdalena's apartment they waved goodbye to Wiktor, Jan and their police body-guard as they walked through the boarding gate at Gdansk airport.

"And now the Wolfschanze." Magdalena turned to the main doors.

"The Grand Hotel first," Josef said. "It might help if you were there when I talked to your sister, Adam."

"In that case I'll go to the office for an hour," Magdalena declared casually.

Adam gripped her elbow as he led her out into the car park. "Until Brunon's found, we're an item."

"You can't go everywhere with me," she smiled.

"I'll give you an armed female officer to go to the places he can't," Josef said grimly, "as well as a driver and two guards. But I'd be happier still if you postponed the trip to the Wolf's Lair."

"We're running out of time to make a bid for the knight," Magdalena reminded him.

"See if you can set up a meeting with Radek and Melerski in the Grand Hotel." Adam helped Magdalena into Josef's car. "As the lady's set on leaving Gdansk, I've a feeling the sooner we go, the better, for the sake of all our nerves."

Adam opened the mini-bar and removed a miniature of brandy. Unscrewing the top he poured it into a glass and handed it to a sobbing Georgiana. "Goddamn it, Georgie, you only knew the guy for twenty-four hours."

"He was the one." She gulped the brandy. "I knew it the

first time I heard his voice on the telephone. He was the one. There'll never be anyone else..."

"You said that when you married your first, your second and your..."

"Casimir was different." She glared at him through tear-stained eyes.

"The one good thing that can be said in his favor is that he's no position to claim palimony."

"You're a callous bastard, Adam. I don't know how you live with yourself." Georgiana abandoned the empty brandy glass on the coffee table that lay between her chair and the sofa Josef and Magdalena were sitting on. "You said he was shot, captain," she moved closer to Josef. "Was it an accident? I can't believe anyone would want to kill such a talented artist."

Josef cleared his throat awkwardly. "It's possible he was mixed up in something."

"Like the Mafia, you mean? My God, do you think I could be in danger?"

"It's possible, Georgiana," Adam picked up her glass.

"The children? I had no idea Poland was this dangerous..."

"It isn't," Josef interrupted.

"Oh, but it is for foreigners. You should return to the States immediately, Georgie. Who knows what Casimir was mixed up in," Adam broke in smoothly, trying to strike a balance between Josef's fear that the Salen family were about to wreck the Polish tourist industry with unnecessary scaremongering and his own desire to be rid of his wife and sister. "Until the captain finds out exactly why Casimir was killed, it might be as well if you leave."

"I suppose we could go back to Paris...or on to Prague or Rome..."

"Brilliant idea," Adam enthused.

"But Courtney came all this way to see you, and all you've done is ignore her."

"We're here to talk about Casimir, not Courtney."

"Where did you meet him?" Josef removed a notebook and pencil from the inside pocket of his jacket.

"Here."

"In the hotel?"

"In Gdansk." Georgiana glanced at Josef, decided a man with his looks was worth flirting with, crossed her legs, hitched her skirt higher and smiled coyly beneath her tears. Adam only just managed to stop himself from groaning. "I saw these darling little paintings and I knew right then and there I simply had to have them."

"Saw them where?" Josef asked patiently.

"In a gallery. That's why I'm in Europe. To tour galleries. I'm the buyer for the European section of the Salen Academy of Modern Art in Texas."

"So you met Casimir in a gallery?"

"Not in the gallery I saw his paintings in. I had to ask the gallery owner..."

"In Paris," Adam supplied, reading confusion on Josef's face.

"Of course in Paris," Georgiana chipped in testily. "I asked her who the artist was and she told me Casimir, and then we telephoned him..."

"In Gdansk?" Josef checked.

"Naturally in Gdansk, that's where he lives—lived." She took the tissue Adam handed her. "I reached him right away.

He said... he had the most gorgeous voice..." her voice quivered as she dabbed her eyes. "He was so pleased that someone had finally recognized his talent. We spoke for hours and I arranged to meet him in the gallery at Mariacka Street."

"Waleria Gabska's gallery?" Josef looked up at Adam.

"Nothing to do with me," Adam said. "I only met Casimir Zamosc when my sister brought him to my apartment."

"Casimir was waiting in the gallery for us when we arrived from the airport." Georgiana discarded the tissue Adam had given her and he handed her the box.

"When was that?" Josef asked.

"Yesterday morning," Adam answered.

"And Casimir took us out to dinner last night, which was more than my brother did." Georgiana glared at Adam again.

"Us?" Josef probed.

"Me and my sister-in-law, who's desolate because her husband won't even talk to her." She gave Adam another hard look. "Casimir wanted to make up for the horrid reception Adam had given us. My brother was rude, but if you know him you don't need me to tell you that. Casimir took us to this enchanting restaurant in the old town. We were so happy," she blotted her eyes again, "and had such a heavenly time..."

"From the way he died I think he's in the warmer place, Georgie."

"Casimir brought you back here?" Josef prompted, annoyed by Adam's interruption.

"Of course. He was such a gentleman."

"What time did he leave?"

"It would have been about midnight. I was absolutely bushed, all this traveling makes for the most horrendous jet lag."

"Did you meet any of his friends?"

"Waleria in the gallery. Although he seemed to know everyone. The barman here, the manager in the restaurant, the croupier at the Casino..."

"You don't happen to know where he lived." Josef pressed.

"Gdansk."

"Gdansk is a city, Georgie," Adam pointed out wryly.

"I have his telephone number somewhere." She patted the sofa in search of her handbag. "I think Niklas put it in this little electronic thing. Now let's see—Niklas," she called out. "My son," she explained to Josef. "He's the only one who can understand how this thing works. He puts in all the names and addresses for me."

"Give it here." Adam held out his hand.

"You know how to work it?" She looked at Adam in surprise. "But then of course you would." She dropped it into Adam's hand.

"I'm into the address section, but there's nothing under Z," Adam said after a few seconds of searching.

"Niklas may have put him under Casimir."

"No."

"Gdansk?"

"No."

"Perhaps Niklas forgot..."

"There's a section marked 'toy boys'," Adam interrupted.

"Niklas's attempt at humor. He's a little devil." Ignoring Magdalena, Georgiana tried to catch Josef's eye.

"Here it is." Adam handed Josef the electronic notebook.

"Number's in the town center," Josef said.

"It should be, it's the Jantar Hotel," Adam informed him.

"You sure?"

"Take my word for it."

"He must have been fairly well off to live there."

"Or he booked in just to wait for the call," Adam suggested.

"I'll have it checked out. Mrs...." Josef looked enquiringly at Georgiana.

"It's Ms. Salen. I reverted to my maiden name after my last divorce." Georgiana moved her knees closer to Josef's.

"Think hard, is there anything else you can tell me about Casimir Zamosc?"

"Only that he was an immensely talented artist."

"He didn't mention what he did for a living?"

"Painted, of course."

"I doubt he'd have made a living from that," Adam said dryly.

"Really?" Georgiana was genuinely surprised. "But he was so good."

"Did he ever talk about a wife, or a family?" Josef pressed.

"No, but he hinted at some sort of tragedy." Georgiana sniffed back a tear. "When I suggested he return to the States with me, he didn't mention any encumbrances that would prevent him."

"I bet he didn't," Adam said.

"Adam, the poor man is dead, why do you have to be so horrid?"

"Because the poor man was mixed up with some very nasty people."

"Nasty people" reminded Georgiana that she could be in danger. "I must have Nanny paged so she can organize the packing."

A door that led to one of the bedrooms in the suite opened.

"Packing? You're not going to let Adam drive you out of Gdansk, are you, Georgiana? We haven't seen a single sight you marked in the guide book yet." Courtney beamed at the assembled company, while reserving one very special, significant, smile for her husband.

CHAPTER FOURTEEN

DAM WALKED TO the window and stared out at the deserted beach. Any view was preferable to looking at his wife. As silence fell, and embarrassment mounted, he was conscious of Josef's and Magdalena's eyes boring into his back.

"This is a policeman. Captain..." Georgiana had forgotten Josef's name.

"Josef Dalecka." He rose to his feet and kissed Courtney's hand. "You must be Adam's wife?"

"Soon to be ex-wife," Adam said quickly. Too quickly he realized, when he saw everyone staring at him.

"Magdalena, how nice to meet you again," Courtney gushed insincerely.

"Captain Dalecka came to tell us that Casimir is dead. Shot," Georgiana added dramatically.

"Dead! We were with him until after midnight..."

"He left us before midnight." Georgiana corrected.

"You were tired. We went to the Casino again after you went to bed, Georgiana. Only for half an hour. I wanted to play blackjack." She looked fondly at Adam. "It used to be Adam's favorite game. I asked Casimir to take me. All he did was talk about you, Georgiana. He was so looking forward to exhibiting in the States."

"So he left you at twelve-thirty?" Josef asked.

"About then."

"And you didn't see him again?"

"Not after I said goodbye to him in the lobby. How dreadful. What happened? Was it an accident?"

"He was trying to kill someone. They stopped him with a bullet." Josef put away his notebook.

"Casimir a murderer!" Georgiana's eyes widened in horror. "I simply refuse to believe it."

"Try," Adam interposed dryly.

"Did he say where he was going after he left you?" Josef looked at Courtney.

"No." She shook her head sending her blonde curls tumbling around her shoulders. "All he said was he'd call us in the morning. He'd promised to show Georgiana the medieval town."

"Did he tell you anything about his personal or private life?" Josef questioned.

"Only that he was an artist."

"Did he mention where he lived?"

"Just Gdansk. We spent most of the time talking about art." Courtney looked to Georgiana who tearfully nodded agreement.

"And in the Casino?"

"We played blackjack."

"Did you stake him?"

"I bought a hundred dollars worth of chips and gave him half," Courtney walked into the room and stood close to Adam.

"Either of you win?"

"Does anyone ever win at blackjack except Adam?" She gazed at her husband again.

Adam moved to the door. "Time we were going, Josef, they'll be waiting for us downstairs."

Courtney laid a hand on his arm. "Could you possibly spare me a moment?"

"It's a bad time."

"Just a moment," she pleaded, looking around the room for support.

"We're not in that much of a hurry, Adam." Josef left the sofa. "Don't worry about Magda, I'll look after her. We'll wait for you in the restaurant."

"I must look for Nanny." Georgiana tactfully followed them out of the room.

Adam returned to the window, folded his arms across his chest and glanced at his watch. "You wanted to talk. I can give you five minutes."

"That's very generous of you."

"I think so," he replied, refusing to allow her sarcasm to rile him.

"You seem inordinately concerned about Magdalena, considering she's only an employee."

"A valuable employee," he emphasized, "and Josef and I have every reason to be worried about her. Casimir was shot last night trying to kill her."

"Kill Magdalena?" Courtney's light silvery laugh reverberated around the room. "Why on earth would anyone want to kill that blue-stocking? Aren't you being just a little melodramatic, Adam?"

"No," he said flatly.

"How intriguing." She sat on the sofa and the slit in her skirt fell open. She saw him eyeing her thighs and crossed her legs to give him a better view. "I had no idea Gdansk would prove so exciting."

"It isn't usually." He turned his back on her, furious with himself for giving her reason to think he still enjoyed looking at her.

"Do you really think Georgiana and I are in danger?" she asked seriously.

"You could be."

"So you want us to leave?"

"It would be a prudent move," he said.

"Are you worried about Georgiana and the children, or me?" she questioned archly.

"All of you."

"Then you still consider me family?"

"Ex-family."

"Casimir was Georgiana's acquaintance, not mine, so I fail to see how I could possibly be implicated in anything that's happened. But if you really are worried, I could move out of here and into your apartment until we thrash out a settlement. That's if I can't persuade you to change your mind about divorcing me."

"After the meeting downstairs, I have to go away for a few days."

"Running away from me again?" she pouted.

"Long-standing business trip."

"With your lady friend? I could be wrong about her. Perhaps you do find that particular kind of blue-stocking attractive."

"It's strictly business, Courtney." He opened the door.

"And there's no settlement to thrash out. I've made my offer. Take it or leave it." He stepped outside and almost fell over Georgiana, who was crouched at the keyhole.

"Eavesdropping?"

"I didn't want to walk in on a reconciliation, or something even more private," she explained.

"There's no danger of you stumbling into either scenario, Georgie."

"Adam, you're a fool." She reverted to the hectoring, older-sister, school-marm voice that never failed to irritate him. "Be sensible and make up with Courtney. You'll never find anyone who loves you more."

"That's why I'm considering taking Holy Orders."

"For once in your life, be serious. At least give her a chance," she said earnestly.

"Like you did with numbers one to seven?"

"My husbands never looked as gorgeous as Courtney."

"I'd be worried if they had. In case I don't see you for another year or two, bye, Georgie." He kissed her on the cheek. "Take care of yourself and the brats."

"You aren't angry with me for springing Courtney on you?" she asked, suddenly solicitous.

"You did us both a favor by bringing our ugly abscess of a marriage to a head."

"Where are you going—just in case we need you?"

"Warsaw," he lied.

"Perhaps..."

"Don't even think about it, Georgiana. Remedy your own love life before mine."

"Then Courtney's right, there is someone else?"

"No one. I'm serious about taking orders. Between the

two of you, you've succeeded in putting me off women for life. I have to go, there are people waiting."

A sacrosanct tradition of the Grand Hotel is a buffet breakfast which is served until two in the afternoon to accommodate casino patrons who make a late start to the day. Adam found Josef and Magdalena sitting with Radek and Melerski at a window table in the deserted side restaurant.

"Coffee?" Josef purloined a clean cup from the table behind him. "I recommend the frankfurters if you're hungry. Magda and I were starving."

"So I see." Adam helped himself to a roll from the basket and a slice of ham from Josef's plate.

"Get your own," Josef growled.

"I'd be in danger of missing more than I already have." Taking a spare chair, Adam set it at the head of the table. The view from the window opposite him was breathtaking. Miles of silvery gold sands, sparkling sea and cloudless, deep blue sky.

"We had nothing to do with last night."

"Give me time to ask the question before answering it, Melerski." Adam bit into his roll.

"We're as interested as you are in finding out who's peeing on our patch," Radek asserted crudely.

"Casimir Zamosc for one." Adam opened the mustard pot on the table.

"He wasn't an artist." Josef picked up a brown, government-issue file that lay next to his plate.

"That come from the station?" Adam asked.

"It does," Josef confirmed. "Preliminary inquiries suggest Zamosc never painted a picture in his life, much less the ones in Waleria's gallery."

"So who did?" Adam took another bite of his roll.

"Some poor devil desperate enough to sell his name as well as his work. The only artistry Zamosc could lay claim to was in the con department. He had a string of convictions for petty theft, pimping around tourist hotels, living off girls and defrauding rich, old women."

"Georgiana always did know how to pick them," Adam said.

"The only surprise was last night. If anyone had asked, I wouldn't have said that murder was in his repertoire." Josef finished the ham on his plate lest Adam take more.

"Someone must have put him up to it," Adam commented.

"I wish we knew who," Radek murmured.

"You don't?" Adam raised his eyebrows skeptically.

"Not us. We lost a good man last night."

"Who was wearing a police uniform," Josef divulged grimly.

"He was a good policeman," Radek asserted defensively.

"Who worked both sides of the law?" Adam finished his roll and helped himself to coffee from the pot on the table.

"Last night wasn't down to any of the locals." Melerski succeeded in diverting Adam's attention away from Radek. "Some people have good reason to slit Kaszuba's throat. Sorry," he apologized to Magdalena, who'd paled. "But even they would prefer to settle for their money rather than his blood. Besides, we passed on the message that Brunon doesn't live with his family. Anyone who knows him would realize the futility of trying to put the squeeze on him through you or his grandmother."

"Then last night had to be organized by someone who doesn't know him. Perhaps someone who already tried to get

Magdalena and failed. Someone who drives a black Mercedes with Russian plates." Adam looked Radek in the eye.

"Do you think we'd kill one of our own men just to throw you off the scent?" Radek said testily.

"Since you're asking..."

"All our investigations point to an independent organization." Josef handed Adam the file.

"Kaszuba's shat on someone besides us." Melerski picked up the coffee pot Adam had emptied and waved it at the waitress.

"And the car in the forest?"

"None of ours have been near the border for weeks." Radek kept his cold, dead eyes focused on Adam.

"Someone knows something," Adam insisted. "No one sneezes in Gdansk unless one of you gives them the go-ahead."

"There's no word out on the street about last night," Radek said in a tone Adam wasn't tempted to argue with.

"So where does that leave us?" Adam asked.

"Treading carefully," Josef cautioned. "With everything that's going on, I advise you to postpone your trip."

"You've told these two where we're going?" Adam looked at Josef in surprise.

"Not yet. I hoped you would."

"Like hell I will!" Adam exclaimed.

"One of our men died trying to protect your ass last night," Melerski reminded him.

"I saw the expendable label."

Radek reached across the table and gripped Adam's throat.

"Put him down, there's a good fellow. Adam didn't know he was your brother." Josef shoveled the cheese on his plate onto a piece of bread, feigning nonchalance while counting off an interminable sixty seconds before Radek relaxed his grip.

"We'll be able to protect you if we know your itinerary," Melerski said.

"I'd sooner spit in my coffee." Adam rubbed his neck.

"I advise you to take them up on their offer."

"You might enjoy going to bed with the Mafia, Josef, I don't. I've put myself in your hands because I had no choice, but I'm telephoning America before we leave. If anything happens to me, or her," he pointed at Magdalena, "in the next couple of days, there'll be embarrassing headlines in the press. And all three of your names will be up in block capitals alongside mine."

"The American lady and her companion did play blackjack last night, sir. Miss Leman's table." The waiter slipped Josef a piece of paper. In return Josef pushed a bundle of bank notes into the top pocket of his tuxedo.

"I can trust your usual discretion?"

"You can rely on me." The waiter washed his hands and left the men's room.

"You have spies everywhere," Adam observed sourly.

"You have any objection to stopping off to talk to Helga Leman?"

"What do you expect to get out of her?"

"Me, nothing. You, on the other hand, might do better."

"I'm the man before yesterday. Besides, I don't know her address."

"So you always stayed at your place. I did wonder. Never mind, I have it." Josef took the paper the waiter had handed him from his pocket.

"We're on our way to the Wolfschanze." Adam went to the door.

"You can go after seeing Helga. It won't take long."

"I can't leave Magdalena."

"She'll be safe in Piwna Street."

"Like Kaszuba."

"You'll never let me forget that, will you," Josef snapped. "I'll order six men to sit with her."

"Radek's employees or yours?"

Josef lost control. "I'm the one who's busting my ass trying to keep her alive. I've already lost three men..."

"Seems to me you could have done with losing one of them."

"To hell with you and your bloody wisecracks. Zamosc wanted to kill Magda badly enough to risk breaking into her apartment when she had police protection and before then he took your wife to the casino. The obvious next step is to interview the croupier, unless you want to forget the whole thing, in which case I suggest you put a bullet in Magda's brain now. With a little care you should make a painless job of it, which is something the opposition might not do the next time they try."

"Have it your way, but do me a favor first." Adam reined in his temper. "Check out the six policemen before you entrust them with Magdalena to make sure none of them are on Radek's payroll. Then I'll give you an hour, not a second more, before we head for the Wolfschanze."

"You and Magda can go on ahead to Hitler's lair. I need to interview Waleria and examine the ballistic reports. And you'd better have this back, just in case." He handed Adam his Glock pistol. "We've kept one bullet."

"Looks like poor Mariana's going to miss her mini-break."

"Can't be helped. But don't worry, I'll send plenty of muscle with you."

Adam thrust the Glock back into his shoulder holster. "If last night was anything to go by, it's more guns and bullet proof vests we need, not muscle."

Helga lived in an art deco villa in a narrow street that ran from the main Sopot thoroughfare to the beach. The location would have been desirable in Sopot's heyday, now it was merely quiet. The building sported the usual signs of neglect and decay; peeling paint, decomposing wood, broken and boarded windows and walls green with mold and damp.

Adam left the car and scanned the column of doorbells next to the front door. Most looked as though they'd been installed when the house was built, but there was nothing to indicate which ones were still working, or any names to help a caller. Josef, who knew the area better than he wanted to, pushed the door and it opened.

"Trusting residents," Adam commented.

"Ladies out to make as many male friends as they can," Josef amended. Like most of Adam's acquaintances he disapproved of Helga.

Very little light shone through the few panes of glass that hadn't been boarded up. The hallway was dark, gloomy and stank of urine. The floor was tiled with the original 1920s mosaic tiles, which had lifted and crumbled in more places than they had clung to. The stairs were painted. Some of the flakes that clung to Adam's shoes were green, some brown. Peering into the darkness he tried to decipher the name plates on the doors.

As Josef had prophesied, they were all female. Helga's room was on the top floor. There was no bell. Josef had to knock three times before a sleepy voice cried, "Get lost."

Josef signaled to Adam. Adam had never felt so reluctant to approach a woman in his life. "It's Adam. I've brought your earrings."

"Why didn't you telephone? I would have met you somewhere." There was a flurry of movement before the door creaked open a scant two inches. The window in the room couldn't have been boarded, because light flooded around Helga, spilling out into the hall. She looked exactly as she'd done when Adam had last seen her; naked, mascara smudged in large dark circles beneath her eyes, lipstick smeared over her cheeks, her hair wild, tousled. She saw Josef standing behind him and moved back behind the door.

"I'd ask you in, but it's not convenient."

"We have to talk to you, it's official business," Josef insisted.

She pointed to a door opposite. "Go in there. I'll be with you after I've put some clothes on."

Josef opened the door on a small, obviously communal sitting room. Coffee mugs half-filled with cold, congealing liquid lay dotted around on scarred, Formica-topped tables. An upholstered sofa and chairs sagged on a heavily stained carpet. He walked to the window and looked down.

"My mother told me that this was an exclusive suburb in its day." He gazed over the tops of a scattering of pine trees to the sea.

Helga appeared in the doorway. Her face was still streaked with yesterday's make-up, but she had thrown on a robe. A shiny blue nylon affair held together by a belt that slipped every time she moved. She opened a pack of cigarettes and tapped one out. Josef lit it for her. She raised her eyes to Adam. "You brought my earrings?"

He handed her the box Feliks had given him. "They're not the ones you wanted. I couldn't run that high."

She flipped the lid open, and gave them a cursory glance. "Pity, these aren't a patch on the ones I wanted."

"I won't bother next time," Adam leaned against the door post.

"There was an American woman and a Polish man at your blackjack table last night? They played for half an hour some time around midnight." Josef launched into his questioning without any further preliminaries.

"A lot of Americans come to the casino."

"You should remember this woman. Tall, blonde, blue-eyed, with the looks of a movie star."

"She wasn't that pretty." Helga inhaled her cigarette. Her robe fell open revealing more flesh than either Josef or Adam could cope with at that time in the morning.

"Mr. Salen here thought so. He married her."

Helga lifted her head and stared at Adam. "You never told me that you were married."

"You never told me that you lived here."

"I'm not a whore, if that's what you're thinking."

"You know who I am?" Josef asked.

"Everyone knows who you are, policeman." Helga managed to make "policeman" sound worse than any of the insulting nicknames bestowed on the force.

"I'm interested in the man who was with the lady."

"Casimir Zamosc, why, what's he done?" she asked coolly.

"Got himself killed. You know him?"

"Seen him around the last couple of weeks. Lousy tipper."

"Seen him with anyone?"

"Adam's wife."

"Very funny," Josef snapped. "Anyone else?"

"Guys," she flicked the ash from her cigarette on to the floor.

"Guys?"

"Men."

"Any of them have names?" Josef persisted.

"You any idea how many people I meet in a night? Now if that's all, I have to go and change into my uniform. I'm on duty at two."

"If you think of anything..."

"I know, call Piwna Street."

Josef pushed past Helga, stepped across the hall and burst open the door to her room. A double bed dominated the limited floor space. A man sat up, a furious expression darkening his face.

"What the hell..."

"Sorry, wrong room." Josef closed the door.

"You bastard!" Helga spat sourly.

"Just checking." Josef glanced at Adam.

"I'll get you for that," Helga threatened.

"Your security clearance for the casino in order?" Josef threatened.

Using a word no Polish lady should know, she flounced off. Josef waited at the top of the stairs.

"What's the matter?" he asked Adam, who was still standing outside Helga's door.

"That man in Helga's room."

"Tall, slim, with dark eyes, Slavic features, black hair,

straight cut, combed back. I can't blame Helga, he's prettier than you. I'll check the description against the wanted files when I get back, but I don't expect to find anything. Don't tell me he came as a shock to you."

"No."

"Believe me—you're better off without her."

"It's not that. I've seen him somewhere before."

CHAPTER FIFTEEN

THE ASSERTION THAT Adam had seen the man before was enough to halt Josef in his tracks, it made no difference that Adam couldn't remember where. To Adam's dismay Josef insisted on turning back and hammering on Helga's door. This time there was no answering sound from inside.

"You have ten seconds to open up before I smash my way in." Josef pulled out his gun, "six—seven—eight—nine—ten—"

The door caved in as Josef's shoulder hit it. Standing, gun in hand, his back to the corridor wall, surrounded by girls in various stages of undress who'd left their rooms to see what all the commotion was about, Adam felt as though he'd strayed into a melodrama.

Cautiously holding his gun at arm's length, Josef moved in front of the open doorway. The bed was empty. Tattered lace curtains fluttered limply in the light breeze that wafted through the window.

"Adam, shut the door. Check the closet and the bed."

Adam did as Josef asked. There was nothing under or on the bed. The wardrobe held Helga's clothes and shoes. He was surprised how few there were. As he closed the door on the stale, musky scent of her favorite American perfume, Josef moved to the window.

"Damn the bastards."

Adam stood alongside him. A sliver of window box held a few shriveled, trampled geraniums. It was an easy step away from the fire escape. "They can't have gone far."

"I'll put out a general alert, but there's a black hole in this town that swallows people I want to question." Josef holstered his gun. "You sure you can't remember where you saw him?"

"You know how many places I go to. It could have been an auction, a museum sale, the casino. In fact that's probably it. I have a vague recollection of him wearing a tuxedo. But you can't go around harassing people just because I've seen them, and can't remember where."

"Can't I?" Josef moved away from the window. "If he's so bloody innocent, why has he run away?"

"How long did you work here?" Adam asked Magdalena as they drove along a narrow road towards the car park of the Wolfschanze.

"Three summers when I was a student. I even lived here in the old SS barracks, above the cafeteria."

"Peculiar to think of anyone living in SS accommodation."

"You think the country was fumigated after the Second World War? Germany doesn't have a monopoly on Third Reich monuments. When a country is in ruins, the last thing people can afford to do is pull down serviceable buildings."

The driver slowed at the barrier and Adam opened the back window, first checking that the car with the guards Josef had assigned to them was close behind them. A man approached with the car park attendant. Adam slid his hand under his coat and loosened the holster on the Glock.

The attendant elbowed the man aside, but he proved persistent.

"For only twenty euros I'll show you over the site."

"Staff." Magdalena flashed a card at the attendant and both men retreated. "While you were talking to your wife, I arranged for us to have access to the site," she explained to Adam. "I'll tell them we've arrived."

The driver parked opposite a row of tourist buses. A party of children ran towards them, heading for the ice cream and snack shop at the side of the old barracks. Adam left the car. It was a clear, warm day, more like mid-summer than spring. A party of Germans were crowding around a souvenir booth that sold DVDs of the ruins, cheap amber jewelry, and a selection of books on Hitler. Birds were singing in the trees, a Vivaldi concerto played softly on a car radio.

"It's not easy to imagine this place as it must have been fifty years ago," he said, when Magdalena emerged from the office with her police guard in tow.

"It will be once we get further into the complex." She crouched down and tucked the bottoms of her jeans into her socks.

"Local custom?" he asked.

"Mosquitoes." She rummaged in the bulging knapsack she'd brought and handed him a spray. "When the local breed attack, it feels as though they've come armed with knives and forks."

"They don't like me."

"Then you don't have sweet blood."

"Sour, like the rest of me." He looked back at their two guards and resigned himself to being dogged by them for the rest of the day.

"I told the warden we'll contact him if we need help. Here." She handed him an official-looking badge. "Pin that to your jacket and no one will stop you going into dangerous or restricted areas."

"What dangerous areas? I thought this place was a bona fide tourist attraction?"

"It's safe if you stick to the paths but some of the parts we'll be crawling into are unstable." She soaked her scarf with the spray and tied it around her neck. He looked ahead and saw the beginning of a woodland walk. "You'll need a map to get your bearings." She pushed the spray back into her bag and handed him a plan of the complex. "We'll walk around so you can get the feel of the place and also look for signs of recent disturbance. Fresh scratches or marks in the concrete, churned up ground or tire marks, anything that looks suspicious."

"What's that on our left?" He unfolded the plan which had been written in German, a language he was barely acquainted with.

"The SS escort detachment barracks. Ahead is the site of the old inner gates."

"Hitler knew what he was doing when he built his HQ here. It would have taken a brave spotter plane to have ventured this far over enemy territory."

"They wouldn't have seen much, even if they had. Camouflage nets were slung above all the main areas and changed with the seasons."

As they walked forward he caught glimpses of towering blocks of gray concrete shimmering through the trees. He blinked and they were still there. "I can't make up my mind whether those are real, or shadows."

"It gets even more confusing at twilight."

"How convenient, they numbered the buildings for us."

"Number two is the Security Service and SS barracks."

"More barracks?"

"It took fifty thousand people to build this place, and several thousand lived here when Hitler was in residence, including a large contingent of civilians. You need a lot of space to accommodate that many staff."

"But surely the whole complex has been thoroughly explored?"

"Depends what you mean by thoroughly," she qualified. "When the Red Army came into East Prussia they found the surrounding areas heavily mined. It took ten years to clear them."

"You really have studied this place."

"My father's brother worked with the bomb disposal squads after the war. The officer in command of his unit believed that the charges had been laid by the SS to deliberately block a lot of the tunnels and bunkers."

"There's no number on that bunker." Adam pointed to a structure opposite the second barracks.

"Unnamed bunker, there are a lot of them, and you'll find more marked as general purpose bunkers."

"You must have some idea what they were used for," he said.

"Can you imagine this place during the war? It was a self-contained city. Thousands of troops, typists, telephonists, secretaries, barbers, valets and personal servants lived here who all needed food and accommodation. Just think of the storage space that was needed for supplies alone."

"Were the bunkers connected underground?"

"We believe some of them were, but I told you, the German commander who blew this place up knew his business. More than half the underground tunnels we know about caved in when the SS engineers blasted the place and most of the ones that remain are in danger of collapse."

He paused before a low mound of lichen and weed-encrusted stones. In front of it lay a modest memorial slab carved in the shape of an open book.

"The Claus Schenk Graf von Stauffenberg memorial. This is all that's left of the wooden conference room where he tried to kill Hitler," she explained.

"Poor guy, shot by firing squad in 1944, lauded as a hero now."

"The way of the world, just like my father. Now he is a hero of the revolution, but, when he died, all my mother received was clandestine sympathy." Realizing she had allowed the conversation to become personal, she reverted to her tour guide persona. "To the left are the offices of the security detective detail. The building behind it housed Hitler's personal servants and SS guard detachment, to the right is a guest bunker. Mussolini visited here five times."

"With big noises like that arriving, the locals must have known about this place."

"There was an inner, middle and outer ring of defenses. What you've seen is only the inner ring. No one without security clearance was allowed through the outer ring which was over 1200 meters from here. None of the low-ranking staff who worked here were given leave lest they talk, and the locals were turned back as soon as they reached the guard placements in the outer ring. They may have suspected that something was here, but they didn't know what."

Adam stopped walking and absorbed the atmosphere. The trees grew closer and taller here than on the perimeter of the complex, almost blocking out the sunlight. It was cool in the shade and there was a dank, musty smell of rotting vegetation. Magdalena had been right. It was easier to picture what the complex had been like during Hitler's reign here, where the forest cloaked the ghostly ruins.

"If we walk past the old typists' offices and post office, we'll come to the bunkers constructed for individual members of the High Command."

"I'm beginning to understand why you think the knight could have been hidden here. It would take a flame thrower to shift some of this undergrowth."

"An entrance to a tunnel could easily be missed."

"Even if it does exist, what makes you think we stand a chance of finding it in three days, when it's lain undiscovered for fifty years?"

"Because whoever took those photographs of the knight must have left evidence of recent entry."

"And if they removed the knight?"

"Why would they risk doing that before they have to? Where are they going to find a more secure hiding place than this?"

"I hope you're right. So, where do we start looking?"

"The bunkers. If a passage has been opened up from any of them, there'll be marks."

"We've just passed –" he checked the plan, "ten bunkers and buildings."

"All near the main gate. Not a good place to hide the entrance to a secret tunnel. If there is one, it's my guess it will be further in. Close to the Führer bunker and the railway line."

As they penetrated deeper into the complex, Magdalena's trained eye missed nothing. She drew his attention to the remnants of barbed wire nailed high on the trees, wires that had originally been fastened a meter above the ground. Enormous slabs of concrete, four and a half meters thick and six meters high, lay at alarming angles on the site of the former Führer bunker, strands of steel reinforcing splaying out from the great masses, like the spindly legs of upturned beetles.

They crawled over concrete surfaces patterned to resemble grass and peered into moss and lichen encrusted cracks. Adam ran his flashlight over stalactites that grew down from the damp, moldering ceilings of blacked-out narrow tunnels, and delved into underground passages that traversed remarkably intact buildings. He followed Magdalena past signs warning people to stay out of the bunkers as she climbed steel rungs sunk into the concrete sides of the buildings and onto rooftops that had served as placements for anti-aircraft gun batteries or, more bizarrely, cultivated gardens.

They stepped over odd remnants of domesticity; bulky heating radiators, all but the top few inches embedded in the earth, and smashed concrete tubes that had once held the wires for the internal and external telephone systems. As they walked through the forest littered with one vast concrete ruin after another, Magdalena told him all she could remember of the internal layout of the bunkers. When her memory failed, she referred to the notebooks in her bag. And, all the while they explored, they examined the area around every step they took for signs of recent disturbance of earth, undergrowth or concrete.

"Present for you." Adam presented her with a small posy of delicate purple flowers.

"Vandal."

"They'd be dead tomorrow," he assured her.

"How do you know? They might have continued to bloom and give pleasure to other visitors."

"I'm starving."

"You should have eaten more at breakfast."

"I didn't like the company. This looks like a good place to take a break." He sat down and leaned against a tree. "Is this the boundary of the inner fence ring?" He pointed to a clearing in front of them that was bisected by railway tracks.

"It is." She sat alongside him and pulled the insect spray out of her bag.

"Is the railway still in use?"

"I doubt it."

"It's occurred to me that if the Amber Knight is here, there's no way anyone could come in and fish it out without the staff noticing. All we have to do is ask."

"No excavations, investigations, or research has been carried out here for the last four years."

"So no one can come in without the authorities knowing?"

"If you have a four-wheel-drive vehicle you can leave the road and drive across country. Hitler's fences weren't replaced."

"No security?"

"None worth speaking of. Come on, rest over."

"Slave driver." He followed her across the railway track. She led him into a building on the other side that was little more than a shell, its doors and windows blown out by Hitler's engineers.

"Air Force High Command Office. Behind is the cemetery."

He walked across the concrete floor to the holes where the

windows had been. "No headstones?" he commented as he looked out over the expanse of uneven ground.

"There were wooden markers but they were removed years ago."

"How many people are buried here?"

"Your guess is as good as mine. Even archaeologists balk at digging up sixty- to seventy-year-old bodies."

"Although, if you think about it, there's not much difference between sixty- and six-thousand-year-old corpses."

"Depends on the soil they've been buried in."

"What's that building across there?"

"The Naval High Command Office."

"Not behind, to the right." He pointed to another smaller shell, with the metal window frames intact.

She shrugged her shoulders.

"Don't tell me, it's another general purpose bunker." He returned to the entrance, kicking aside last year's leaves and debris. "There's some peculiar smells in here."

"And none pleasant."

Avoiding the rough ground of the cemetery, he led the way out of the building, across the path to the building opposite. "A fire's been lit here recently. I can smell wood smoke. Look, here's charred sticks."

"Probably kids. I told you, this place isn't secure."

He kicked through the litter on the floor. "Rich kids who can afford imported canned beer and –" he picked up a butt end of a hand-rolled cigarette and sniffed it. "– joints."

"Must have been quite a party."

"And it ended over here." He reeled from the stench of urine in the corner.

"See anything?" she asked.

"Dirt, leaves, wood, this is damned impossible. An army could have slept here last night, dirtied the place up and left nothing for us to find." Stepping outside, he walked around the building and looked down to the right. Two huge bunkers loomed through the trees.

"There were anti-aircraft guns mounted on the tops of those, presumably to safeguard the railway track." Magdalena stood beside him.

"I'm not sure what I was expecting Hitler's Wolfschanze to look like, but it wasn't this. It's so damned big."

"Over eighty buildings and it goes on for miles. There are bunkers scattered in fields all around here. Outposts, lookout vantage points, hideouts for troops, but if I'm right and the knight was hidden in a tunnel here, there has to be an access and it would have made sense for the builders to hide that access in a bunker." She opened her rucksack and pulled out two heavier duty flashlights than the ones they'd been using. Handing him one, she looked down at his plan. "I suggest we start there."

"The fire water reservoir?"

"We'll go over every inch before working our way backwards through every building until we reach the main gate again."

He glanced at his watch. "We only have a few more hours of daylight."

"You don't need daylight to search a bunker. Hurry up. We don't want to waste any time."

The warning bells that heralded the closing of the Wolf's Lair had rung hours ago. The tourists had long since been herded along the paths and out through the main gate. Shadows had fallen, shrouding the trees and bunkers in a dense, compassionate darkness that softened and blurred the edges of the buildings.

Their police escort had given up dropping gentle hints in favor of outright demands that Magdalena continue her search in the morning, but it took a threat from Adam to down tools before she capitulated. As Adam followed the path back to the main entrance, he found himself aching in places he hadn't been aware he had muscles. His hands, knees and elbows were rubbed raw, his nails were torn and broken to the quick, and he had a foul headache from scrabbling in airless spaces and peering into holes as black as the grave. But what hurt most was the knowledge that their effort had been in vain. They had come up with precisely nothing.

"I wish I'd been soaking in a hot bath for the last hour," he grumbled, stumbling in the uncertain light.

"You must have been brought up soft," Magdalena countered.

"Is this is your idea of a fun day out?"

"It would have been if we'd found the knight. There's nothing like the excitement of an archaeological dig. Never knowing what or when you're going to turn up something momentous." She stopped to speak to the warden who'd been watching for them from his living quarters. He handed her a package.

"DVDs of all the excavations that have taken place here in the last fifty years," he explained to Adam.

"I can't wait," Adam enthused insincerely.

Magdalena glared at Adam before thanking the warden. "It will be all right for us to come back in at six tomorrow?"

"No hotel serves breakfast at that time in the morning," Adam protested.

"We'll eat here."

"The restaurant doesn't open until ten," the warden warned.

"We'll have a chance to put in a few hours work in first. Thank you for your help, and goodnight."

Adam nodded to the warden before following Magdalena across the floodlit car park. "Hasn't it occurred to you that we might be too late for dinner as it is?"

"All you ever think about is food."

"All I've had today is two cups of coffee and a roll I stole from Josef's plate."

"Knowing Josef, he will have booked us into an expensive hotel that caters for German and American tourists. They'll have room service." She stopped next to the police car. "We can eat while we watch these." She climbed in and laid the package of DVDs on the seat between them.

"My mother warned me never to watch television while I eat. It interferes with the digestion."

"Then we'll watch them afterwards."

"How long are they?"

"Tired?" she mocked.

"First you deprive me of food, now you want to deprive me of sleep. Well, there's one thing I'm not going to do without, and that's my bath."

"I'll give you half an hour." They sped from the darkness of the forest road towards the brightly lit facade of a modern hotel.

"That long?"

"I need half an hour to shower and telephone the boys."

"Not everyone moves at your speed. I doubt they'll be in America yet."

She glanced at her watch. "They should have landed two hours ago. Your housekeeper gave me the number of your grandfather's security guards."

"Why do you always have to be so efficient?" he griped as they drew up outside the main entrance. He waited for their police escort to make a move before prying himself painfully out of the back seat.

"If we're going to find this knight, one of us has to be," she snapped as she left the car. "I'll order dinner to be served in your room as soon as I go in. I suggest you do the same. That way we may get around to seeing all the films before we go to bed."

CHAPTER SIXTEEN

DAM WAS SOAKING in the bath when the telephone rang, but Josef never spared any expense when the Institute was picking up the bill. The suite was equipped with a cordless telephone in the bathroom.

"As you've gathered I'm not with you."

"I haven't had time to miss you, Josef." Adam settled back into foamy water that smelled more like creosote than pine.

"Find anything?"

"Muscles I didn't know I had. What about you?" he questioned guardedly, conscious of the switchboards the call was being routed through.

"No sign of our mutual friend, but the two parcels arrived safely in the States. You remembered where you saw your girlfriend's boyfriend yet?"

"I'm trying to work out who you're talking about."

"Cut the crap. Do you remember?"

"Unfortunately not." Adam turned the hot tap on with his toe and picked up an iced vodka tonic he had set within easy reach.

"I bet you haven't given him a thought."

"I've been too busy trying to stay in one piece. I spent the afternoon crawling into holes even rats would run from."

"I paid your colleague a visit. The description of the man he saw with our target fits the stud in your girlfriend's bed."

"So you finally admit my colleague wasn't mistaken?" Adam knew how meticulous Edmund Dunst was and couldn't resist crowing.

"You went on about it so much I thought it was worth checking out. What are your plans for the evening?"

"Dinner."

"In the suite?"

"I'm too exhausted to walk to the restaurant."

"And your companion?" Josef asked.

"The same."

"How romantic."

"We have films to watch."

"All the better."

"Work films."

"I'll expect a full report tomorrow."

"Go to hell."

"You'd halve my baby-sitter problems by bunking in one room," Josef teased.

"Forget it. How's your wife?" Adam enquired maliciously.

Josef dropped his bantering tone. "The ballistic reports are in. The item you disposed of, was not, I repeat not, working alone and I'm not talking about what came in through the balcony. I'll be with you as soon as I can. In the meantime be careful."

"As a virgin in a police station." Adam replaced the telephone and slid back into the scalding water. It was useless. The more he tried to concentrate on the identity of the man he had seen in Helga's bed, the more elusive his features became. He tried closing his eyes and relaxing, but the only image that floated into his mind was one of Magdalena as she'd been that afternoon; disheveled, grubby and angry, as she'd flung insults at him in response to his complaints about rough concrete, hunger and discomfort. For Magdalena, the search for the knight had taken precedence over her own safety.

He couldn't understand the intensity of her obsession. He wanted the Amber Knight, but not in the same way that she and Edmund Dunst did. For him, the Amber Knight would add to the prestige of the Museum collection and the name of the Salen Institute; for them it was a crusade akin to the search for the Holy Grail.

Opening his eyes he reached for the soap. The more time he spent with Magdalena, the less he knew her. A psychologist would probably attribute her overdeveloped work ethic to the breakdown of her marriage, but he didn't think it was that simple. There was something else, something deeper. The result of growing up in a country in turmoil as it shook off the Communist yoke? Or having to cope with the side effects of her husband's criminal career?

He tried to imagine the young girl she'd been, the one who'd rushed into an early marriage to escape a dismal home life. So much of Magdalena was a mystery. Her reluctance to enjoy the good things in life. The principles that wouldn't allow her to break the vows of a marriage that had died almost before it had begun. The need to be faithful to a husband who was anything but.

Pulling the plug on the bath, he wrapped himself in towels and padded into the bedroom. He and Magdalena had adjoining, interconnecting, en suite bedrooms on the second floor of a wing of a hotel that overlooked a lake. Their guards had laid claim to the sitting room that separated the bedrooms from the corridor, transforming its baroque-style elegance into a masculine, cigarette smoke-filled atmosphere more suited to a barracks.

He opened his bag and rummaged through his clothes, before settling on a well-worn pair of jeans. Tucking the Glock into the waistband, he pulled on an old sweatshirt and picked up the wine list. He was ordering a bottle of German white when Magdalena knocked on the communicating door. She hadn't been happy with the idea of sharing a suite with him, but after his conversation with Josef he was glad of the arrangement. Even the raucous conversation in the sitting room sounded more reassuring than irritating.

He replaced the receiver, walked over to the window and closed the blinds, shutting out two of the guards who were sitting on the balcony. "I feel like an exhibit in a zoo," he complained to her.

"I can't wait to get back to normal."

"I can't remember normal."

"For me it's the museum and the boys."

"You spend a lot of time with them?" he asked.

"Not as much as I'd like to. You know how it is with boys their age. They're always off with friends. But I check their homework every night."

"Big sister, as opposed to big brother."

"It's easy to mock when you've never had to struggle for an education or a job," she rebuked him.

"I think everyone should work at their own pace," Adam said shortly, weariness making him oversensitive.

"In an ideal world where everyone was given the same opportunities at birth, I'd agree with you."

A knock at the door that led into the sitting room interrupted their brewing argument. One hand on the Glock, Adam asked who it was before opening the door. An armed police officer escorted in two waiters and a trolley.

"We watched over the chef while he prepared your food, Mr. Salen."

"Did you sample it, too?" Adam asked.

"Sir?" The policeman gazed at him blankly.

"Shall we lay the table, sir?" the waiter asked.

"Just leave the trolley, please. Once you've opened the wine you can go, we'll help ourselves."

"As you wish, sir."

"We'll be outside all night should you need us, Mr. Salen."

"Two of you?"

"Changeover at midnight. There are two on the balcony as well."

"I saw, thank you."

Adam checked the DVD player and television while Magdalena laid the table.

"Can't we even eat in peace?" he asked, as she picked up the parcel of films.

She glanced at her watch.

"Just half an hour without work. Is that really too much to ask?" he persisted.

"As long as it is only half an hour."

Adam turned the key in the outside door and slid the bolt across the connecting door to Magdalena's room. "A precautionary measure," he answered, in reply to her quizzical look.

"Neither of those locks will stand up to a battering," she warned.

"Any intruder will have to disable the guards before they get to us. Even if they're well armed and determined, they'd make some noise. Enough time for me to reach for my gun and hide you under the bed." He tried to sound flippant, but after the trauma of the previous night Magdalena wasn't fooled by his nonchalance.

"I haven't thanked you for saving my life."

"You have nothing to thank me for." His hand went to the Glock. He eased it into a comfortable position as he sat on one of the chairs the waiter had pulled to the table.

"We would have all been killed if it hadn't been for you."

"I doubt it. Josef would have got there."

"But not in time." She sat beside him. He noticed her hand trembling as she reached for the wine glass he had filled.

"The boys are safe. Betsy will make sure they enjoy their summer, and there are four police officers outside the door, and me inside."

"Damn Brunon!"

"You angry with him, or worried about him?" He piled rounds of puff pastry stuffed with caviar and smoked venison pate on to his plate.

"Both."

"You obviously still care for him?"

"Concerned would be a better word. Brunon's stupid, thoughtless and he can be cruel, but he's still my husband. I can't get the sight of that man last night out of my mind. The blood, the hole in his head. One minute he was alive, the next dead..."

"You'd rather it had been us?" he questioned.

"No. Of course not..."

"Do we have to discuss this over dinner? After all that fresh air and exercise in the woods you should be ravenous."

"Sorry." She took a pastry. "There are six films..."

"I don't want to talk about the Wolfschanze either." He lifted a red rose from a vase on the trolley and handed it to her. "We might not be lovers but we are two intelligent beings. There has to be something other than work and murder that we can talk about. My brain is suffering from overload. I look down at the pastries and all I see is gray concrete. I look at the salad and see pine forests..."

"Have you compiled a list of suitable subjects?" she interrupted.

"If we were in England we could talk about the weather."

"The weather is uncertain in Poland too. We never know if our springs are going to be hot or cold, they vary enormously. In 1945 –" her voice trailed as she realized he was staring at her. "Sorry, I can't seem to get away from the Amber Knight. How about you choose the topic? I'm happy to talk about anything as long as it doesn't involve politics, religion or sex."

"You've just excluded conversation."

"Nonsense, there's art, literature, music, sport..."

"They all hinge on one of your forbidden themes. Why don't you tell me about Helmut von Mau?"

"Now who's bringing up work?"

"As you can't stop thinking about him, I thought I'd steer the conversation on to something I know nothing about, medieval Baltic States."

"You didn't study them in school?"

"My parents never agreed about anything, including my education. My schooldays were split between an English public school and an American military academy. The former gave me a deeper and more thorough understanding of the Industrial Revolution in England than I appreciated then, or now. The second forced me to follow an exhaustive course of Roman and Napoleonic military theory, most of which I've mercifully forgotten." He pushed his hors d'oeuvres plate aside and lifted the cover on the main dish. By coincidence they'd ordered the same, duck stuffed with apples, potato dumplings and a mix of vegetables. "I've heard the legend of the Amber Knight from you and Edmund, and researched it in my Child's Guide to Polish History."

She smiled. "You read children's history books?"

"Always. My attention span is short and my intellect lacking. Where else could I find simple unvarnished facts?" He began to recite, 'When Hermann von Balk embarked on the Teutonic Christian Crusade to convert the Pagan Prussians in 1231, his lieutenant, Helmut von Mau, won the love of the pagan Princess Woburg, who converted to Christianity and changed her name to Maria. It was a great, platonic love as Helmut, a warrior monk, had taken a vow of chastity. Maria became his faithful camp follower. Helmut was mortally wounded during a battle with Pagan Prussians at Elblag. Before he died, Helmut made his fellow knights swear that they would strap his body to his horse and send it into the pagan stronghold. They did as he asked and every pagan who looked upon Helmut's face was struck dead. When Hermann took possession of the fort, he burned it, the amber in the burning treasury melted and Hermann ordered his knights to pour it into Helmut's stone coffin, embalming his lieutenant's body and turning him into the Amber Knight."

"Well done." She picked up her knife and fork and cut into her duck.

"There's more. Maria founded a convent and chapel on the site of the battle and devoted the remainder of her life to God and Helmut's relics. The chapel became a place of pilgrimage until the last Grand Master of the Teutonic Knights adopted the Protestant Faith in 1525. Dissolving the order, he pulled down the chapel, dispersed the nuns, and moved the Amber Knight to Konigsberg Castle where it remained on display until 1944. The Nazis admired Helmut von Mau and the chivalry and heroism he represented, which was why Hitler ordered the removal of the Knight to safety during the last months of the war. End of story, but it still doesn't explain the fanaticism I see in every Polish eye as soon as the name von Mau is mentioned."

She sprinkled salt on her dumplings. "You know the legend. Do you want to hear the real story?"

"There's a truth as well as a legend?"

"A documented truth. Helmut's brother Konrad wrote a biography of the Amber Knight. It was kept in the library at Berg Grun, the von Maus' family castle, until the end of the war when it was moved to the Berlin Document Center. I've read it."

"You're about to shatter my illusions by telling me that the Amber Knight wasn't brave or chivalrous?" Adam guessed.

"Brave maybe, foolhardy more like. At sixteen Helmut von Mau could out-drink and out-fight any knight in Germany and no woman was safe from him. When Konrad, who was two years older than Helmut, discovered that his wife was carrying Helmut's child, he went to his father who gave Helmut a choice—join the Teutonic Knights or be disinherited. Helmut joined the Knights. He took the vows of Obedience, Poverty and Chastity but avoided the customary castration by bribing the Grand Hospitaler. Throwing himself wholeheartedly into pillaging and fighting in Prussia he was soon promoted. Women came easily to him, except for Woburg. After Helmut killed her bridegroom she fought like a fury. He raped her and afterwards she tried to smother him. But she must have succumbed to his charms eventually, because she did change her name to Maria and she did, as your children's book so quaintly put it, become his 'camp follower'. Despite Konrad's desire to discredit his brother for seducing his wife, Konrad was forced to accept the Teutonic Knights' version of Helmut's death and their assertion that all the pagans who looked at his face died. But his claim that Helmut had not been castrated was borne out by a 1930s X-ray and documented evidence that Konrad's wife bore Helmut twin sons and Maria bore him twin daughters. The family of von Mau in Germany today are direct descendants of the Amber Knight."

"So much for chastity," Adam commented. "But I'm still no nearer to understanding why the recovery of his body is more important than say, the Amber Room, or any one of half a dozen other missing artifacts."

"Your mother is English, you've lived in England?"

"Two to three months a year at most. My father didn't want me hanging around him, but he was bloody-minded enough to want to keep me from my mother."

"Can you imagine the excitement in England if the perfectly preserved body of King Arthur was found? That's what von Mau is to us. There are many similarities between the Arthurian and von Mau legends. One story has it is that our von Mau, like your Arthur, is not dead, merely sleeping, and when Poland is in peril he will break free from his amber shroud, wake and rally his knights and ride out to vanquish our enemies."

"A pretty myth and totally at odds with the unprincipled seducer Konrad painted."

"People prefer myths to reality and the myth of the Amber Knight gives the Polish people something to hold on to at times of national crisis. God only knows Poland has had more than its share of those."

"I suppose I can see more likelihood of von Mau breaking free from his amber shroud than Arthur emerging from some unknown grave," Adam conceded.

"Some say that when Helmut von Mau wakes he'll take the reins of government and restore Poland to prosperity."

"You've never needed him more."

"We are a nation of dreamers who had nothing to dream about for fifty years in the last century. I can't honestly say that the Communist regime was entirely bad. Some people suffered more than others, particularly the intellectuals who valued free speech, and yes, there were chronic food shortages, but outside of the prisons no one lacked an education or a roof to sleep under during those years. Not even me and my mother after my father was arrested during the Solidarity protests. But as a people we were crushed in spirit, so crushed we lost our dreams and with them our hope for the future. Freedom has to mean more than just the liberty to shout what you like about politicians in the street. It has to mean freedom to dream, too."

"And you think the Amber Knight will give Poland that?"

"People don't want to know the story of Helmut von Mau, seducer, murderer and lecher. But they do want to know about the brave, courageous, Amber Knight. He symbolizes a nationalism every Pole can identify with. Pensioners with worthless pensions, workers without work, students who can't afford to study, even the Mafia..."

As Adam listened, he realized that beneath the austere image lurked the soul of a romantic. A woman who desperately wanted to believe that good can, and does, always ultimately triumph over evil.

It was a comforting delusion. One he'd been forced to relinquish when he had seen his father fall prey to an avaricious gold digger who'd done everything in her power to hurt and humiliate his mother and make his father disinherit him and his brother. Before his fifth birthday he had learned that money could buy anything, including principles and integrity. And he'd seen nothing since to make him change his mind.

"I find Helmut von Mau's relationship with the Prussian Princess Woberg somewhat odd, given that he raped her," he said thoughtfully.

"As she took the veil on his death she must have forgiven him."

"She must have done more than that. I can't believe that any young girl, let alone a princess, would willingly take the veil and devote the rest of her life to guarding the corpse of a man, unless that man had shown her a good time first."

"And what's your idea of a medieval good time?" she smiled.

"A convivial house-party of like-minded people, including musicians and poets, in a relatively small, easy to heat and clean castle with a view of the sea. It would have to be built off the beaten track to keep plagues, pestilences and war at bay. But it would also have to be surrounded by productive fields full of plump well-fed animals, vines and happy, smiling serfs to ensure a plentiful supply of food and drink."

Her smile broadened. "It never happened. Hermann von Balk killed Woberg's father and brothers, Helmut von Mau cut the head off her bridegroom and she, like many other pagan Prussian noblewomen, was held hostage to ensure the good behavior of her tribe."

"So, she was put in the dungeons and von Mau met her down there one evening when he was filling in the tedious hours between dinner and bedtime by torturing a few heathen captives."

"What dungeons? He was an officer in an invading army. They didn't carry castles with them."

"The prison tent?" he suggested.

"More likely she was kept in the kitchen tent and made to scrub pots and bake bread."

"A princess?"

"It takes a lot of work to keep an army on the move fed."

"We'll go for a compromise, von Mau went to the kitchen tent one night for an extra helping of swan stew after a hard day spent cracking enemy heads with one of those ball and chain things monk soldiers used. He saw her scouring a cauldron with sand and lent her the wire wool he used to burnish his armor. One thing led to another and they fell in love during a mutual metal polishing session." He picked up the wine bottle and emptied it into their glasses. "Then he took her out of the kitchen tent..."

"Into the barrack tent with all his men?"

"The lieutenant of Hermann von Balk would have had his own quarters."

"I doubt it."

"So, he found a cave, and they set up house there. If she was happy with Helmut, you'd think she would have gone off with one of his fellow knights after he died. Particularly if she was left with twin daughters to support. There was Hermann..."

"Who unlike Helmut von Mau took his vows seriously and, to avoid lapses, castrated himself and offered his offending organs to God." She picked up his empty plate and stacked it on top of hers. "Coffee and cheese?"

"You've just killed my appetite."

"You must have known that some medieval monks castrated themselves?"

"I try not to remember it. Anyway what was the point, when they took a solemn vow of chastity?"

"No one trusted vows, even in those days. The medieval church was an institution much patronized by noblemen with large families. For half the cost of a modest dowry, younger sons could be cloistered and educated away from the insecure, inheriting eldest, and castration ensured they didn't stray or pass on their intelligent genes via any troublesome young peasant wenches who might be tempted to bring up their illegitimate offspring as revolutionaries."

"And how old were these poor bastards when they were gelded?"

"The younger the better. The death rate from the operation soared among novices who'd reached puberty." She poured herself a coffee. "For someone who doesn't believe in marriage you seem to enjoy weaving 'happily ever after' stories."

"Who says I don't believe in marriage?" he asked.

"You want to divorce your wife."

"All that signifies is that I don't believe in marriage to Courtney."

"So you'd marry again?"

"If a sweet, loving, subservient, selfless and attractive woman exists and I found her, most certainly. And you?"

"I have a husband."

"Do you?" He reached across and took her hand in his. When she didn't pull it away, he lifted it to his lips.

"The films..."

"What films?" he whispered as he bent his head and kissed her. To his utter astonishment she kissed him back.

CHAPTER SEVENTEEN

SEDUCTION HAD BEEN the last thing on Adam's mind when Magdalena had entered the room, but as soon as she was in his arms it felt so right he was disinclined to stop. He couldn't have explained why he was so suddenly attracted to her after a year of working alongside her. There was none of the ruthless intensity of Helga's embraces in the kiss they shared, or even the soothing, if rather perfunctory, perfumed allure that characterized his infrequent bouts of lovemaking with Waleria. There was passion but, unlike his relationship with Courtney, there was also peace. A profound, sensual peace that permeated every aspect of his being, relaxing his battered muscles and tranquilizing his fraught mind. As he held her close, not even the imminent threat of death, Brunon or the Amber Knight seemed to matter.

Magdalena destroyed the mood and his illusion. Breaking free, she pushed him away. The telephone rang. Mentally cursing whoever was at the other end he watched Magdalena disappear into the bathroom before picking up the receiver.

"Adam Salen," he barked.

"Hold for Captain Dalecka."

Adam's temper heightened as precious seconds ticked

past. "You know how to pick your bloody time," he complained, as Josef came on the line.

"Don't tell me you were bedding the ice-queen?"

"Early night," Adam lied.

"With company?"

"Don't be ridiculous."

"Remind me to check the guards' notebooks in the morning."

"Next time you're looking for salacious gossip ring the guards direct."

"They've found Krefta's body."

"Where?" His irritation melted at the news.

"Not far from your hotel as it happens. He was lying in the woods three miles outside Gierloz. They've taken him to the mortuary in Ketrzyn."

"What did he die of?"

"All I could get out of the locals is what I've just told you. The only reason they notified us, was the 'wanted' bulletin we'd circulated on Krefta in relation to a possible art fraud. Police surgeon's doing an autopsy in the morning. Want to sit in?"

"That's not the best invitation I've ever had, but yes."

"Pick you up at eight." The line went dead. Adam turned to see Magdalena gathering up the DVDs. "You're leaving?"

"We're both tired. I thought I'd carry on with this in my own room."

"And I thought we were working on this together?" He stepped towards her as she went to the connecting door and pulled back the bolts.

"I don't see how we can after what just happened."

"Unfortunately, nothing happened."

"You call that nothing? I'm married and I've just kissed a man who isn't my husband."

"Unless I'm mistaken, it was something we both wanted." He reached out and touched her shoulder, "Magda..."

She whirled around. "Don't call me that. Don't ever call me that. You're not family, or even a friend."

"Where are you coming from, Ms. Janca?" He deliberately emphasized the Ms. "I know you've studied medievalism, but I didn't realize you had adopted its morality. Wake up. This is the twenty-first century."

"A sin is still a sin in the eyes of the church."

"And what is a husband who abandons his wife, takes up thieving and worse, and refuses to support his family?"

"Brunon's failings are no reason for me to stoop to his or your level."

"Who are we hurting, Magdalena? Brunon? He couldn't give a shipyard worker's fart for you. And my wife doesn't know the meaning of the word faithful. I kissed you, you kissed me back, I enjoyed it as far as it went and frankly I wouldn't mind more."

"More? That word characterizes your life. It covers wine, food, luxury and women. All I am to you is an experience. Another female to scratch yourself against. Duller and dowdier than the others, but what I lack in looks I make up for in intelligence. Just one more notch in the Adam Salen crotch."

"Sounds painful."

"Damn you and your jokes!"

"Magdalena, please." He put the full weight of his arm against the door to prevent her opening it. "Don't ask me to say I'm sorry I kissed you, because I'm not. If the thought of making love to me repulses you, I apologize. But none of it alters the fact that if we're going to find the knight, we have to work together, and that means watching these films. If it will help, I'll promise not to go near you again. If that isn't enough, you could try tying my hands."

The eyes that gazed back into his were dark, serious.

"What else can I say?" he pleaded. "I didn't mean to offend you. The only excuse I can offer for kissing you is—" he almost said "the softness of your skin, the loneliness in your eyes that I thought mirrored something of my own feelings" but he recalled her loathing of personal conversation and said, "—sheer bloody weariness and an excess of wine on an empty stomach."

"And the lack of a more willing woman in the vicinity?"

"It won't happen again."

"You have quite a reputation."

"That was Josef on the phone." He changed the subject. "They've found Krefta's body in the woods outside Gierloz."

"That's only a few kilometers from the Wolfschanze." She sat on the arm of the sofa as she thought through the implications of the news. He watched the expression on her face change, and wondered if she cared—really cared—for anything outside her work, her brothers and the search for the knight.

"They're holding an autopsy in Ketrzyn tomorrow. I told Josef I'd go with him. This could be the break we've been looking for. There might be something on Krefta's body that will lead us to the knight."

"What did he die of?"

"Josef didn't know, but Krefta must have been carrying something to enable the police to make a positive ID."

"His passport and identity card weren't in his apartment."

"It's pointless talking about it. We'll find out more tomorrow." Crouching on the floor, he pushed a DVD into the machine, then sat on the opposite end of the sofa to the one she was perched on. It was a very long sofa. Three people, even Germans of Herr Dobrow's ilk, could have sat comfortably between them.

The film opened with a shot of a man standing in the parking lot of the Wolf's Lair as they had seen it earlier that day. The stream of statistics that poured from his mouth was in Polish, but Adam was conscious only of Magdalena, sitting, poised and strained a few feet away from him, and the kiss they'd shared that might have led to so much more, if she hadn't pushed him away from her and Josef hadn't chosen that moment to telephone.

"The Wolfschanze covers 250 hectares—Organization Todt was given the responsibility of construction and building began in the autumn of 1940—"

The voice droned on, covering ground they had already picked clean a dozen times and more, as the man paraded in front of bunker after bunker. The tedium of the shots was relieved by occasional inserts of black and white stills taken sixty years ago at the same locations—Hitler greeting Mussolini—Hitler greeting his generals—Hitler greeting von Stauffenberg.

"I was hoping we'd see more of this," Adam commented as the camera followed the guide into an underground tunnel.

"Preferably the one that will lead us to a previously undiscovered treasure chamber," she agreed.

"Failing that, a map of the complex with a spot marked X will do." The film ended. Rising to his feet he went to the mini-bar, opened the fridge and took out a miniature of bourbon. "Drink?"

"After all that wine at dinner?"

"I need something to loosen my muscles. I'm sure yours are in the same state, for all your puritanical ideals."

"Perhaps I'm fitter than you."

"I don't doubt it." Returning with his whiskey he removed the DVD from the machine and inserted another.

"Can I see those photographs of the knight again?"

He handed them to her as an amateur film filled the screen. This time there was nothing but tunnels, and wobbly ones at that. "They must have picked a cameraman with the jitters. If you're trying to match the color of the concrete, you'll find that concrete is concrete."

"I'm beginning to see that," she agreed.

"And that swastika behind the coffin is no different from the neo-Nazi..."

"Let's not go over that again."

He leaned back and emptied the bottle into a glass. "The autopsy tomorrow shouldn't take long. We could go on to the Wolfschanze afterwards."

"You sound as though you've already given up on finding the knight there."

"Serious treasure hunters have been searching for the Konigsberg Castle loot for sixty years. What chance do we have of finding them in a few days without a tip-off from someone in the know?"

"None if we have to rely on this." She nodded at the screen. "They haven't even told us which bunker they were filming in."

"Let's see what tomorrow brings." He finished his drink and returned to the mini-bar.

"You're probably right." She glanced at her watch.

"You're exhausted. Why don't you go to bed?"

"Because I know I won't be able to sleep. We're so close, and yet..."

"Sleep on it," he said. "If the Amber Knight's anywhere for the finding, I promise I'll do my damnedest to locate it."

"Adam, about earlier—" the intensity of her look was more than he could bear.

"Sleep on it," he reiterated dully.

"I'm a senior police officer. You are obstructing my investigation." Josef eyed the raw recruit from the toes of his polished boots to the shorn hair beneath his brushed cap. "Do you know what that means, son?" he confided in a conspiratorial whisper. "It means I can have your ass kicked from here to Warsaw. You'll be lucky to get traffic duty outside a badger's set after this."

"Very sorry, sir. Just following orders, sir."

"It's not 'sir', it's Captain Dalecka of the Gdansk squad. I suggest you make a note of the name. You're going to be hearing it a lot."

"It wouldn't make any difference if you were the President, sir," the absurdly young man replied in a faltering voice. "I've had orders to keep everyone out of this area."

"But we're here for the autopsy. Surely someone told you that an autopsy is scheduled to be carried out here this morning."

"The only timetabled autopsy has been postponed, sir."

"I demand to see your senior officer..."

"I've never seen Josef like this before." Magdalena edged closer to Adam as the captain's face darkened in rage.

"Looks like he's been taking tips from Mariana." Adam stepped aside to make way for a man wearing more brass on his uniform than an English shire-horse rigged for a county fair.

"Josef," the officer interrupted. "I thought I heard your croaking."

"Bronski, old friend." Josef clamped his hand on the officer's shoulder. "Will you tell this young idiot I'm here for the autopsy?"

"Come into my office."

"I don't want to go into your office. I want to attend the autopsy and we're already late."

"The body never reached here."

"You idiots lost it..."

"Change of plans." Bronski walked down the corridor and opened a door. "Coffee for four," he shouted back to the rookie. "Please, come in, sit down. The lady should have the most comfortable chair," he suggested, as Josef was lowering his bulk into it.

"Magdalena Janca and Adam Salen of the Salen Institute, this is Stephan Bronski, the most inept recruit the Polish Police force has ever had to cope with."

Unabashed by Josef's introduction, Stephan flashed a smile at Magdalena and took his seat behind his desk. "You been transferred to the stolen antiquities squad, Josef?"

"Homicide, same as always." Josef sat on a hard chair.

"If the autopsy on Krefta isn't being held here, where is it being held?" Adam asked.

"The area institute for contagious diseases. We're not certain yet, but it's possible your Mr. Krefta died of plague."

"Plague, as in foot and mouth?" Adam looked inquiringly at Josef.

"How do you know about the outbreak of foot and mouth?" Stephan asked sharply.

"This is the idiot who drove straight into it," Josef divulged.

"Across country?" Stephan looked at Adam with renewed interest.

"You have heard of him?" Josef asked.

"Of his exploits, yes, but all I can tell you about Krefta is what the institute told me this morning. The forester who found Krefta's body is in isolation, as are the police who handled it and the staff of the mortuary they stored the corpse in overnight."

"Come on, this is me you're talking to." Josef left his chair to answer a timid tapping on the door. "Coffee? Good." He took the tray and shut the door in the rookie's face.

"Official..."

"Official quack," Josef interrupted. "I know you, Stephan. Tell us more?"

"You didn't hear this from me, but rumor has it the corpse bears all the hallmarks of plague. Black malignant pustules, swellings in the groin and armpit, darkening of the skin..."

"We get the picture." Josef dumped the tray on top of the files that littered the desk. "I don't suppose you know if he was carrying anything interesting on him, like documents, or maps?"

Stephan pulled a fax from his in-tray. "They sent us a list of items found on the body. There's nothing unusual. The passport and identity card are top of the list, which is why I contacted you. Unlike some people I could mention, I read the reports that land on my desk. You wanted to question him in connection with an art fraud?"

"So you've proved you've got a good memory. Can I see?"

"Be my guest." Stephan handed him the list.

"ID card—passport—name—address—occupation, amber-smith—brown trousers, green jacket, gray pullover, shirt, socks—" Josef ran his finger down the list until he came to the end of the clothes. "One key, no ring, that's it. You can't give us more?"

"They said on the telephone this morning it looked as though he'd died where he was found. There were brambles and dirt in his shoes and grass wound around his fingers as though he'd been trying to claw his way to the road. It could be connected to the other cases." Stephan handed around the coffee cups.

"What cases?" Josef asked.

"The foot and mouth you talked about earlier."

"The animal bodies? Were they deer or cattle?"

"Animals, so that's what they told you." Stephan shook his head. "They were human. Found in a wooden hut. The remains bore the same marks, black malignant pustules. That's why the area was cordoned off. The Institute of Contagious Diseases said it was plague."

"And was it?" Josef pressed.

"You know the authorities, particularly in a tourist area. As far as I know they're still doing tests."

"You misled us," Adam reproached Josef.

"I only repeated what I was told. How many were found in that hut?" Josef asked Stephan.

"Two, both men. There were no ID cards, and we found nothing to indicate who they were, or why they were in the hut. But we have descriptions." He rummaged through the papers in his tray. "Here we are, both heavy build, middle-aged, brown haired and eyed. Fingerprints are being checked, but as there was no indication of foul play we saw no reason to mount a full scale investigation. The contagious diseases boys took over. Cordoned off the area..."

"And kept it quiet," Adam murmured.

"At the beginning of the tourist season, you bet your sausage we kept it quiet. There was no risk to anyone outside the area, and everyone inside the area was quarantined."

"We have firsthand experience of that." Adam looked at Magdalena.

"How can you say there was no risk when you could be talking about plague?" Josef demanded.

"If it is plague, the contagious diseases boys have it under control. What I've just told you is supposition, and confidential. Sorry, Josef, can't do more, you know how it is."

"I need to speak to the people in the isolation unit," Magdalena insisted.

"They don't talk to anyone," Stephan protested. "Besides, what would you tell them? The rumors I told you? All you'd succeed in doing is making trouble for yourself and, incidentally, me, for telling you as much as I have."

"We know Krefta identified the Amber Knight. We have photographs of him with the coffin," Magdalena reminded him.

"I've seen the photographs," Josef agreed.

"And the legend says that everyone who looked on the corpse of Helmut von Mau was struck dead. Don't you see?" Magdalena looked at the police officers. "Supposing he died of..."

"Plague!" Adam exclaimed.

"No one's going to buy medieval fairy stories," Josef

snapped. "And even if they did, I've never heard of a plague that can survive seven and half centuries."

"Some medieval scholars believe that at least one of the plague outbreaks that swept across Europe in the thirteenth century wasn't plague at all, but anthrax."

"And anthrax spores can survive for centuries." Adam followed Magdalena's train of thought. "There's an island off the coast of Britain that was used as a testing ground for World War II experiments in biological warfare. It's still sealed off, contaminated by anthrax spores, and likely to remain so for centuries." He pulled the photographs of the knight from his briefcase. "Feliks said something about fissures in the surface of the amber. He thought they might have been caused by frost or damage when they moved the knight out of the castle because amber can become brittle once it's been polished and exposed to the air for any length of time."

"If those fissures run as deep as the body it's feasible that spores could have risen to the surface," Magdalena said authoritatively.

"Anthrax is airborne?" Josef ran a finger round the inside of his collar.

"At least one type is airborne," Magdalena confirmed. "That's why some medievalists believe in the anthrax over plague theory. Bubonic plague is passed on by rats and physical contact between victims. Even rats didn't travel far in those days. Give them an environment with enough food and they stay put."

"Like the surfeit of corpses you get in a plague outbreak," Josef observed gloomily.

"Quite."

"And few people traveled further than a day's journey from their village..."

"Apart from soldiers like Helmut von Mau," Adam broke in.

"The anthrax theory makes sense, doesn't it?" Magdalena looked to the men for confirmation.

Stephan sat back in his chair for a moment, then picked up the telephone.

CHAPTER EIGHTEEN

IME CRAWLED AT a Trans-Siberian train's pace while Stephan's calls were shunted from one extension of the Institute of Contagious Diseases to another. All Josef, Magdalena and Adam could do was fidget, listen, and stare out of the window at the uninspiring view of the car park. After twenty frustrating minutes, during which Bronski got precisely nowhere, Josef pulled out his cigarettes and Adam his cigars.

"No smoking in this building and especially my office," Stephan warned.

"Then we'll go outside." Josef moved to the door. "Call us if anything happens?"

"Don't hold your breath." Stephan settled back in his chair as Adam and Magdalena followed Josef out of the room. The rookie, who'd been joined by Magdalena's police escort, was still standing guard over the empty corridor, but the foyer was crowded with people reporting petty crimes and property thefts.

"Democratic Poland," Josef observed, as he fought his way past the line into the comparative peace of the parking lot.

"You wanted to join the EEC." Adam leaned next to

Josef against a low wall that marked the boundary between the station and a small, unkempt park.

"I can't understand why it's taking your friend so long to get through to whoever's in charge," Magdalena complained, standing next to Josef rather than Adam. "If I'm right and Krefta and the other two victims did die of anthrax, then anyone who goes near the Amber Knight is in danger of catching and spreading the disease. The sooner the whole area where Krefta and those other bodies were found is quarantined, the sooner that risk can be contained."

"Seems to me they're doing a pretty good job of containing it already." Josef lit a fresh cigarette on the stub of his old one. "They looked after you, Elizbieta and Adam all right, didn't they?"

"I suppose so," she allowed grudgingly.

"Just out of interest, how are they going to get those anthrax spores out of the amber if the knight is contaminated?" Josef asked.

"I don't know much about anthrax but I'd say it would be madness to even try." Adam looked to Magdalena for confirmation.

"If the spores have been released because the amber is decaying, Adam's right. The knight will have to be destroyed."

"You couldn't skim the top with amber to reseal it?" Josef asked.

"You'd have to check that out with Feliks but I doubt it will be tried, because no museum would be prepared to take the risk of causing an outbreak of anthrax. And there'd be no point in skimming it if the knight will never be put on public display." Magdalena paced restlessly alongside the wall. Two of their police escort, who'd remained in the second car while they'd been in Stephan Bronski's office, opened the car windows and scanned the surrounding area.

"So all those telephone calls I made…"

"Who made?" Adam interrupted.

"The department made," Josef amended irritably. "Not to mention all the man hours your escort spent chasing around the Wolfschanze yesterday, could all be for nothing?"

"Could be," Adam agreed.

"If Magda is right, this is it. The end of the road. Even if the Amber Knight was wheeled in here right now on a cart pulled by two gift horses, you wouldn't be able to exhibit it?"

"Not if it's contaminated," Magdalena agreed tersely.

"The exercise hasn't been entirely wasted," Adam commented. "As a serving police officer you have to do something to earn your pay."

"I like tidy jobs with no loose ends. And there's been nothing but frayed edges for the last week. Rat's murder, the three unidentified men who were shot on the boat when the amber shipment and Mafia money was hijacked, two officers killed outside Magda's apartment, and now you tell me that even if by some miracle we should find the Amber Knight, it's likely to be worthless."

"You could always donate a corpse so Feliks could make a copy."

"You wouldn't be a party to fraud?" Magdalena reproached him.

"Why not, if it will pull the crowds into the museum?" Adam teased. "I doubt that one in a thousand would be able to tell the difference between a copy and the real thing."

"I'd know," she said seriously.

"You're a purist."

"Josef?" Stephan called from his office window. "Gdansk on the telephone. The Historical Museum for a Ms. Janca."

"I told them I'd be here." Magdalena set off across the parking lot. One of their police escort left the car and followed her.

"Wait!" Adam cupped his half-smoked cigar in his hand.

"For God's sake," she snapped. "No one's going to try anything in the parking lot of a police station."

"You thought the same about a crowded apartment block, remember," Adam called back.

Josef ground the remains of his cigarette to dust beneath his shoe and went after Magdalena and Adam, catching up with them in the foyer. "I'll go in with Magdalena, if you want to finish your cigar."

Happy to postpone entering the claustrophobic, disinfectant-ridden atmosphere of the police station, Adam stepped out of the noisy mass of humanity. He stood on the topmost step and looked around. Like yesterday, it was a perfect spring day. Warm sun, cloudless, pale blue, sun-washed sky, and all the sense of inadequacy and futility of a search turned sour. Josef was right. They would end up with nothing to show for their efforts. The Amber Knight would never be exhibited in either of the Gdansk city museums if it was contaminated, because, despite his teasing, he'd never dare commission a copy. Any institution claiming ownership of the knight after an absence of sixty years would be inundated with requests from experts to examine it. And, even if they succeeded in fooling the general public, they'd never succeed in deceiving medieval specialists.

But it wasn't only the knight. There were so many other precious and priceless artifacts on the list of the missing

Konigsberg treasures; perhaps not as deeply rooted in legend and national identity, but of almost equal artistic and archaeological merit. The Amber Room that had been looted by the Nazis from the Imperial Russian palace at Tsarskoe Seloe. The missing thirteen crystal cut amber beads from Princess Dorothea's early seventeenth-century necklace, along with her other jewelry. Schrieber's seventeenth-century amber and ivory altar and crucifix. The paintings—sculptures—the ornaments of kings and princes, the tangible historical and artistic wealth of three nations, all lost forever in an anthrax-contaminated vault. It didn't bear thinking about.

Crushing his cigar against a metal bin fixed to the side of the steps, he turned his back to the parking lot. A policeman who was comforting two weeping, elderly women blocked the entrance to the building. Adam lingered awkwardly on the top step, while the uniformed officer tried to lead them inside. Both women were dressed in widows' weeds that belonged to the Europe of the 1930s, not the early twenty-first century. He didn't want to think about the crime they had fallen victim to, or the criminal who had sunk low enough to take advantage of them.

The police officer saw him and gently drew the women aside, making room for him to pass. Adam stepped forward and bumped into a man who'd been lurking behind the door. A tall, well-dressed dark figure with slanting, Slavic eyes. Adam recognized him at once. He stepped forward, fists clenched in case the man moved in on him. The man smiled, and Adam hesitated warily when he realized that the recognition was mutual. Then something exploded in his chest.

He fell back, fighting for breath as air hissed from his lungs. He looked down. A ruby stain was spreading over the left side of his linen jacket. The foyer darkened as though the lights had been dimmed, although it was still bright, sunlit morning. He looked from stranger's face to stranger's face, registering the horror mirrored in their eyes, as each set of features receded into a thick gray mist. His knees buckled and he sank downwards.

Everything around him was moving so slowly he felt as though the entire station had been submerged in water. The last thing he saw was the police officer who had been talking to the women bending over him. He tried to smile, to say that he was all right, but his mouth refused to open and the words remained locked in his throat. Then a crimson tide of pain blotted out everything, even the gray mist.

"You're one lucky son of a bitch."

It was Josef's voice, but there was another close by he didn't recognize. A high pitched, sing-song voice distorted by a strong country accent. Adam opened his eyes and blinked. His surroundings swam into focus. He was in a spartanly furnished cell, lying on a back-breakingly hard surface. His ribcage felt as though it had been steamrollered with burning flat irons, something bound his chest so tightly he could hardly draw breath, and he had a pounding headache.

Josef's face hovered above his own. "It's all right, you can talk, you're still in the land of the living."

A small, gnome-like man wielding a syringe bobbed in front of Josef.

"No injections," Adam croaked.

"You've hit your head, Mr. Salen, and your rib cage has

taken a pounding. I've strapped you up, but you'll need painkillers to help you withstand the stress of the journey to the hospital."

"No painkillers," Adam mumbled thickly. "Magdalena?"

"Is fine." Josef looked at the surgeon. "We need to speak to him, alone."

"I really wouldn't advise it. He needs to be hospitalized."

"We'll see to it, doctor. You can go."

For the first time Adam noticed Stephan Bronski standing behind Josef.

"But..."

"You can go, doctor," Stephan dismissed the man. "Remember, not a word to anyone about this."

The doctor packed his instruments and left the cell.

"Where is Magdalena?" Adam demanded weakly, as soon as he was alone with the two officers.

"Safe in Stephan's office with the rookie and the escort, but it's not Magdalena I'm worried about, Adam, it's you." Josef sat on the edge of the bunk. "Looks like it was you they were after all along. Did you see the man?"

"You didn't get him?" Adam struggled to sit up. Lying down was agony, movement pure torment. "For Christ's sake, he was in the foyer."

"Stay still. The bandages aren't rigid enough to contain the damage."

"A member of a police force as inept and inefficient as yours has no right to tell me what to do."

"What did he look like?" Bronski cut in.

Adam closed his eyes against the rampaging pain in his chest. "Tall, six-three – six-four, black hair, long nose, thin lips, slanting, Slavic eyes..."

"The stud in Helga's bed?" Josef asked urgently.

"And I still can't remember where I saw him before."

"May the Holy Madonna preserve me from idiots!"

"I'm trying!"

"Not hard enough!" Josef reprimanded.

"What do you remember?" Stephan asked.

"I was walking into the foyer. My path was blocked by an officer and two elderly women who were crying…"

"They're hysterical now," Josef informed him.

"The officer drew them aside. I stepped into the building and brushed against this man. I recognized him and I'm sure he recognized me. Then something hit my chest. I must have passed out."

"You were shot at close range." Josef held up the Glock pistol Adam had worn in the shoulder holster. The chamber had been shattered by a bullet. "Powerful construction, but not robust enough to withstand ammunition designed to explode and fragment on impact. The Glock absorbed most of the force of the bullet, but not all. You have a couple of splinters in your chest. The doctor removed the ones he could see, but there's a small piece embedded in one of your ribs. You need an X-ray before it can be removed. You've got a couple of painful hours ahead of you, but look on the bright side. If you hadn't been carrying a gun, you would be dead."

Adam took the shattered Glock from Josef and turned it over in his hand. He saw his bloodstained jacket draped over a steel table next to the bed. "The photographs of the knight. I pushed them into my jacket pocket."

"There are a few pieces left." Josef consoled him. "We gave them to Magda to play jigsaws with."

"Damn. They were the best clue we had."

"Better the Glock and them than you. Underneath those bandages you're a mess. As I said, you're one lucky son of a bitch."

"Do me a favor, Josef. Keep Magdalena..."

"Away from you?" Josef interrupted. "Why do you think she's sitting with the rookie in the other room? If these monkeys can get to you in the foyer of a crowded police station, they can get to you anywhere. I'll switch the guards from her to you."

"No." Adam heaved for breath as though he'd run a marathon.

"Every attempt that we assumed was being made on her was obviously aimed at you. The apartment, the forest..."

"We could be dealing with two factions."

"One after Magda and one after you, at the same time? That's crazy. Do you know what the odds are against that happening?" Josef said scornfully.

"Pretty small, given who she's married to. We know there's a price on Brunon's head."

"Brunon's, not hers," Josef reminded him.

"She'd only been out on the balcony a short while when the hail of bullets hit us. That could mean someone was keeping her under surveillance."

"Or they were after you and not too bothered about your company."

"You said on the telephone yesterday that Casimir Zamosc wasn't working alone."

"Because it wasn't his gun that killed the officers we found in the stairwell."

"And the bullets that came in through the balcony door?" Adam asked.

"I've got people working on them."

"You think Radek and Melerski tell you everything?"

"What I'd like to know is why anyone would be desperate enough to attempt a murder in the foyer of a police station." Stephan was lost in the intricacies of a situation Josef hadn't briefed him about.

"Think, Adam? You must have crossed someone?" Josef urged.

"As I keep telling you, no one I know anything about."

"Then you must be involved in something."

"Only the bidding for the Amber Knight."

"That can't be it. Whoever's got the knight would want to keep you in good health until you've handed over the cash."

"Unless they know I'm an awkward devil who wants guarantees before he hands over millions of dollars." Wincing, Adam leaned forward and tried to draw breath. His chest felt as though he was being stabbed by several red hot knives with serrated blades. "Get me home, I need to make some calls."

"Hospital," Josef said authoritatively.

"The ambulance has arrived." Magdalena appeared in the doorway. Her eyes darkened when she saw the pain registering in Adam's face.

"Time to get the invalid into it." Josef patted Adam's hand.

"I'm coming with you." Magdalena moved to the other side of Adam.

"Oh no you're not," Adam asserted forcefully.

"You promised to stay with me."

"That was before I found out that I was the target."

"Suppose we both are?"

"It was what you suggested yourself." Josef shrugged on his jacket and loosened the gun in his shoulder holster.

"I don't think it's wise for us to travel together."

"There's something we haven't told you." Josef eased Adam gently back on the narrow bunk. "Officially you're dead. You weren't breathing when you were carried in here, and it seemed appropriate to announce that you'd been killed. It wasn't difficult to fool the witnesses. The doctor's sworn to secrecy and, knowing what Stephan does about the doctor's grubby private life, not a word will escape his lips."

"You've issued a press release?"

"Of course."

"You idiot. My grandfather has a weak heart. There's no telling what news like this will do to him."

"We didn't identify you," Stephan reassured him. "The statement was the standard, "a foreigner was shot dead in a police station. His name is being withheld until his family have been informed"."

"We figured that if whoever 'killed' you thought they'd succeeded, you'd have a breathing space until we've thought this thing through," Josef said.

"The last thing it feels like I have at the moment is breathing space."

"We've alerted the local hospital that you're coming in. You're booked under my brother's name," Stephan added, "just keep your mouth shut so no one hears that American accent of yours."

"Someone is bound to see me leaving here."

"That's the general idea." Josef produced a body bag. "Don't worry, Stephan and I will wheel you out as quickly as we can. These things aren't airtight. Provided Helga's lover boy isn't lurking around anywhere, you'll survive."

CHAPTER NINETEEN

IGHT FELL BEFORE they left the hospital. Josef drove Stephan's squad car around to the back of the building while Stephan wheeled Adam out through the deserted mortuary entrance, Magdalena, carrying the bags that held the shattered Glock and Adam's ruined jacket and shirt, trailing in their wake. It had taken six torturous hours to X-ray Adam's chest and extract the last bullet and pistol fragments from below the skin, before the doctor could begin to check that his cracked ribs weren't splintered. And, by the time the last bandage had been wound into place, Adam was convinced he'd never be able to breathe in deeply again.

Josef and Stephan helped Adam into the front passenger seat of the police car which had conveniently blackened and, so Stephan assured him, bullet-proof windows. Josef had ordered their police escort back to Gdansk after the shooting and Stephan saw no reason to accompany them, so for the first time since the attack on Magdalena's apartment, Adam and Magdalena found themselves alone with Josef as he drove them west, to Gdansk.

"Our clothes are still at the hotel," Magdalena reminded Josef from the back seat.

"No, they're not, they're in the trunk. Stephan had you both checked out. And you'll be pleased to hear that the Institute of Contagious Diseases has taken your theory seriously, Magda. Mind you, it might have had more to do with the shooting than your professional status. Witnesses who've been used for target practice while in police protection have more clout than those who wander in off the street. The Wolfschanze together with a ten-kilometer area around the stretch of woodland where Krefta was found was sealed off this afternoon, and that's in addition to the zone around the hut where the other two bodies were found. The official story is that a cache of leaking, World War II gas tanks have been found. Twenty people have been taken to the Institute for tests and health monitoring."

"I suppose it's better than nothing," Adam said cynically.

"I agree with the Institute. Why start a panic? Also, all doctors in Poland have been alerted and told to look out for symptoms of plague."

"Has a systematic search of the Wolfschanze been instigated?" Magdalena demanded.

"Contaminated or not, you're still convinced the knight is in Hitler's Lair, aren't you?" Adam grimaced, wishing he'd been given a stronger dose of morphine.

"I can't see where else it could have been hidden for the last sixty years," she persisted stubbornly.

"The Institute directors are advising an army search party. They went in a couple of hours ago," Josef concentrated on the road ahead. "Don't worry, all personnel will be wearing protective clothing, the directors will see to that."

"I suppose they expect me to sit around and spin sauerkraut until they come up with something," Magdalena snapped.

"I think you've done enough for the time being, don't you?" Josef said quietly.

"I've studied the Wolfschanze. I could help with the search."

"If they need you, they'll get in touch."

"I have to make some telephone calls." Adam grimaced again. Talking intensified his pain.

"You can't make anything, you're dead." Josef glanced in the rear view-mirror, as he had done every couple of minutes since they had left the hospital.

"I have to tell my grandfather I'm not dead in case someone in the press gets wind of who was shot in that police station."

"Can he be trusted?"

"That's my grandfather you're talking about. By the way, I'd almost forgotten. What did the museum telephone you about?" Adam asked Magdalena.

"To report a break-in."

"They take anything?" Aching too much to risk turning around, Adam reached out stiffly and lowered the cosmetic mirror on the passenger side so he could look at her face.

"Two suits of medieval armor and clothes."

"What!"

"The same thought has already occurred to us," Josef said briskly. "All the amber-smiths have been notified."

"And all the museums," Magdalena added. "Edmund faxed out the details this afternoon."

"Did he mention the anthrax scare?"

"No, only that suits of medieval clothes, armor and a quantity of raw amber had been stolen and an amber-smith capable of producing a forgery has been found dead. I doubt anyone will make a bid for the knight now, especially as Edmund went to the trouble of getting the notification countersigned by the officers investigating the loss of the amber shipment."

"If you want to find out if there've been any further developments, you can telephone Edmund. You have your mobile?" Josef checked.

"Yes," Magdalena confirmed.

"And you." He glanced at Adam. "Not so much as an identifiable breath or sneeze while she's speaking."

Edmund's voice crackled over a patchy line. "Most of the museums are commissioning their own experts to determine the feasibility of creating a forgery. As far as I can make out, so far they all concur with Feliks Malek."

"Any other messages?" Magdalena asked him.

"Only from Waleria. Adam's wife turned up at his apartment late last night and insisted on moving in. Waleria came around to tell me first thing this morning. I've tried to get hold of Adam and failed. Is he with you?"

"Would I be phoning you if he were?"

"Can you get a message to him? Waleria's afraid he's going to blame her when he finds out."

"I take it Adam's wife is still in his flat?" Magdalena asked in response to Adam's furious miming in the mirror.

"Waleria's tried everything short of calling the police to turf her out, but the woman refuses to go. She insists Adam asked her to move in."

"I can't see Adam doing that."

"After what little he's said to me about her, neither can I, but apart from having her physically evicted there's nothing Waleria can do. Do you think we should contact

Josef? The problem is, it could get sticky if they're still legally married. You know how the police hate to interfere in domestic disputes."

"If I were you I'd wait until Adam gets back," Magdalena advised, anxious to get off the line before Adam erupted.

"That's what I suggested to Waleria. But what do I tell Adam's wife when she comes around tomorrow to ask where he is? And she will. She's been here four times today, and Wiklaria rang to say she's been badgering the staff in the Historical Museum as well."

"Tell her the truth," she advised.

"Which is?"

"You haven't a clue where he is. Is there anything else?"

"Nothing that can't wait."

"I'll be in touch tomorrow."

"Magdalena, everything is all right, isn't it?" Edmund's voice was full of concern.

"Fine," she lied.

"The Amber Knight..."

"We're still no closer to finding it. Bye, Edmund." She switched off her phone.

"You couldn't have gone to your apartment anyway." Josef tried to calm a fuming Adam.

"Want to make a bet? It would be worth returning from the dead to strangle that bitch."

"If Helga's boyfriend has the slightest inkling that you survived that bullet, someone will be watching Mariacka Street."

"In which case I hope Courtney runs out of clothes and starts wearing mine."

"In the meantime you have to live somewhere. I can take you to a safe house," Josef offered.

"A police safe house?" Adam questioned caustically. "No thanks."

"You have to go somewhere," Josef pointed out.

"The museum apartment has a back entrance behind a high wall. You can park right next to the door. At this time of night there won't be anyone in the neighboring offices to see me sneaking in, and once I'm in the apartment I can draw the blinds, sleep and watch satellite TV all day long."

"If they're watching the museum they'll see the lights going on and off," Josef turned off the slip road into Gdansk.

"How many do you think there are of these mythical 'they'?" Adam asked. "The way you talk about them, anyone would think they're an organization of CIA or KGB proportions."

"Whoever 'they' are, they have access to police information," Magdalena commented. "First the raid on my apartment, now the shooting in the police station."

"You could have been followed both times," Josef pointed out.

"Come off it. Our escort would have apprehended anyone they'd seen following the car from the hotel this morning. I agree with Magdalena, it's more likely they knew of our movements in advance."

"I suppose it's possible." Josef looked at the clock and switched on the radio. The news item he wanted received second billing after a massacre in the Middle East.

"An American national was shot dead in Ketzryn police station this afternoon. The police are withholding his identity until relatives have been informed. The gunman has been described as tall, thin, with Slavic features, green eyes and straight black hair brushed back from the face. He is armed and dangerous and, if seen, should not be approached by a member of the public. Ketzryn police have set up an information number..."

"I'm not happy with the museum apartment." Josef switched off the radio. "I won't be able to stay with you, Adam. It wouldn't make sense, not now you're supposed to be dead, but I suppose I could assign a guard to the museum after the burglary. I'll try to find one I can trust."

"Radek has another brother?" Adam enquired.

"I'll stay with Adam," Magdalena volunteered. "You can drop me off at the front door after Adam has entered through the back. If anyone is watching the place they'll see me and assume I'm alone."

"The last thing I need right now is a woman to look after," Adam protested. "There's only one entrance to the apartment on the third floor. Give me another gun and I promise you no one will get past the front door."

"The gun is easy enough. There's a spare in the car," Josef opened the glove compartment and Adam saw a standard police issue handgun lying on a box of tissues. "But you don't leave this car until I've called the boys to search the area around the museum."

"You'll only succeed in alerting the Mafia snitches in your force," Adam warned.

"Aren't you both forgetting that there are security guards in the museum?" Magdalena reminded them.

"And where were they when it was broken into?" Adam asked.

"Probably on a different floor," she conceded.

"Quite," Josef remarked grimly. "Much as I hate to admit it, you're right about the snitches, Adam. I'll park the car around the back of the museum. You can stay inside while I go in, introduce myself to the guards and look over the building. When I'm sure it's clear I'll come back for you, then I'll take Magda..."

"On second thoughts it would be better for me to carry my bags around to the front door of the museum when you come back for Adam, Josef," she interrupted. "The guards know me and I can keep them talking at the door while you smuggle Adam up the back stairs."

"Oh no, you don't," Adam contradicted. "There's no way I'd let anyone, especially a woman, stay with me after what happened today."

"Someone has to study the plans of the Wolfschanze."

"There's an army of professionals combing the place. They don't need your help," Adam said firmly.

"But you do. Josef's right about the lights. If someone is watching the building they'll see me, and we'll make sure they think I'm alone. Besides, you're dead, so you'll need someone to answer the phone and the door."

"They won't need answering."

"Where else could I possibly go?" she pleaded. "My apartment is in police hands, that only leaves hotels. At least in the Museum I'll be close to my work."

"It would be easier to guard you both. With Brunon a Mafia target and on the loose, Magdalena still warrants police protection," Josef suggested practically.

"How many times do I have to tell you, no police guards? Nothing personal, but I'd rather look after myself than trust your colleagues, Josef."

"I can't be with you twenty-four hours a day."

"It would look strange if you were."

Josef slowed the car to negotiate the lane at the back of the Historical Museum.

"Get me to the top floor," Adam said flatly. "Give me the gun and enough ammunition, and I'll see off anyone who dares put a foot on the stairs."

Josef introduced himself to the two night watchmen in the museum and told them that he needed to make sure that the museum was safe because Ms. Janca was on her way to move into the apartment on the top floor. After they had scrutinized his ID and telephoned the police station to make sure he was who he said he was, they allowed him to examine every floor, cupboard, stairwell and basement area in the Historical Museum. They told him that the apartment on the top floor was out of bounds because there were only two key holders, Ms. Janca and Mr. Salen. While Josef pretended to examine the back staircase, Magdalena walked around to the front entrance and rang the bell. She then kept the guards talking about the robbery while Josef smuggled Adam up to the top floor apartment.

"The only door into this suite of rooms is the one we came through," Adam informed Josef, who began looking at the place with a view to defending it as soon as he had opened the door.

"Fire escape?"

"Opens out of the double bedroom window. First door on your right," Adam whispered into the darkness.

Josef walked into the room. A narrow steel platform outside the window held a collapsible metal staircase.

"We keep it folded up to minimize the risk of opportunist intruders," Adam murmured from the shadows.

"Very wise," Josef whispered back. "How many rooms are there?"

"Two bedrooms, one double, one single, two bathrooms, sitting room, conference room and small kitchen."

"Nice décor from what little of it I can see in the dark."

"Should be, I saw the bills left by my predecessor who ordered the conversion."

"He lived here?"

"Rarely. You didn't know him?"

"Met him once or twice. Unlike you he wasn't any trouble."

"Unlike me, he was hardly ever here." Adam went into the single bedroom and closed the door.

Josef stepped outside the apartment, relocked the door and waited for Magdalena. A few minutes later she walked up the stairs with one of the guards who'd insisted on carrying her bags for her.

"You've met Captain Dalecka?" Magdalena asked the security guard.

The guard nodded respectfully. "Everything in order, sir?"

"I hope it's as secure as it looks."

"Don't worry, sir, Ms. Janca will be safe with us."

"I sincerely hope so." Josef frowned at Magdalena who couldn't resist a triumphant smile at her success.

"We heard about the attack on your apartment, Ms. Janca. I'm sorry," the guard commiserated.

"This seems to be safe enough, but I'll order the regular patrols to keep an eye on the building and check with you every couple of hours." Josef said to the guard as Magdalena unlocked the door. "Allow me to check the place before you go in, Ms. Janca?"

"Of course." Magdalena waited with the guard until Josef reappeared.

"I've dropped all the blinds and pulled the curtains. Everything looks in order but I'd be happier if you allowed me to send in a female officer to sit with you."

She shook her head. "I'm exhausted. All I want is a night's sleep."

"Hit the fire alarm if anything happens, that should galvanize the emergency services." Josef checked the back of the door, registering the four deadbolts and chain. "Don't forget to lock yourself in." He ushered the guard down the stairs. "I want you to show me where the thieves broke into the building."

Magdalena went into the apartment, closed the door and fastened all the locks. She waited until the echo of footsteps on the stairs died, then whispered Adam's name. He emerged from the bedroom white-faced with pain.

"You look as though you could do with a stiff drink and a month's sleep," she dropped her handbag on to the floor.

"What do you think you're doing here?"

"Taking care of you. And before you say another word, it's too late to argue now, it's done. Is there any food?"

"I told Wiklaria to keep this place stocked with tea, coffee and a supply of frozen convenience food in case someone turns up late at night," Adam sank down on the edge of a chair.

"Could you eat something?"

"Depends on what the something is."

Magdalena went into the kitchen and examined the refrigerator. She found a couple of bottles of white wine and a half full bottle of vodka. The cupboards held two bottles of red wine, tea, coffee, sugar, cartons of long life milk, pasta, rice and a selection of canned sauces.

Adam heard the clatter of pans as he went into the hall and retrieved his briefcase from behind the door where Josef had dropped it. He turned the combination lock, opened it and pocketed the scrambler before returning to the sitting room. After fitting the device on the telephone, he slumped down on one of the sofas and dialed the international code for America. It rang just once before a voice echoed down the line.

"Who is calling?"

"Peter, it's Adam. Can I speak to my grandfather?"

"He's with his doctor. Is there a message I can give him?"

"No. Has he had another attack?"

"Nothing serious, but he's picked up a stomach bug."

"I'll hang on."

"The doctor's only just gone in. If you give me your number I'll get him to phone you back as soon as the doctor leaves."

Adam hesitated, but only for a moment. Peter had been a fixture in his grandfather's life for as long as he could remember. He gave Peter the direct line number of the apartment, remembering to prefix the international code. "Tell him to use the scrambler."

"I will, Mr. Salen. He'll ring as soon as he's free."

Magdalena walked in with a bottle of wine and a bowl of steaming pasta covered in carbonara sauce. "Did you make your call?"

"Yes and no. I didn't talk to my grandfather, but he's phoning back."

"You gave him the number here?"

"I gave his assistant the number here. Don't worry—no one can listen in, not with this gadget attached to the telephone."

"Are you going to tell him about the knight?"

"I have to, but I'm not looking forward to it. He was set on buying it for the Institute and adding it to the list of Poland's national treasures. Like you and Edmund, he's enamored with the knight's history and has been since he saw it in Konigsberg in the thirties when he toured Europe with his father."

"I've been wondering if we have been going about this whole thing the wrong way around." She sat on the sofa opposite him and piled two servings of pasta onto plates. "Instead of concentrating on Krefta, perhaps we should have been looking at the people who were in the Wolfschanze in 1945."

"You said the colonel in charge disappeared with all his men. Could he have survived?"

"If he had, he'd be in his eighties or nineties by now. But one thing is certain—someone out there knows where the knight is. If not the colonel, then someone else. It's possible he revealed the whereabouts of the knight to a captor, or perhaps he trusted another officer with the secret. If he hadn't, the knight wouldn't have resurfaced after all these years."

"You want Josef to ask every German in Gdansk if he's here to dig up the knight?"

"They may not be German. In January 1945 the forest around the Wolfschanze was teeming with Polish Partisans and Russian soldiers."

"I can hardly see a German colonel entrusting his secret to a Russian officer or Polish Partisan."

"I can, if he thought it would buy his life."

"In that case we're looking for someone who has known the whereabouts of the knight for over sixty years but hasn't been able to collect it until now." He poked at the pasta with a fork. The pasta was passable, but the sauce had a strange chemical taste and the only evidence of ham was microscopic shreds of off-putting, neon pink. "My money is still on the Germans," he pondered slowly, thinking of Herr Dobrow, and wondering at the man's age. It was difficult to tell with people as overweight as he was. Sixty–seventy?

"We know the area around the Wolfschanze was under attack in January 1945. Remember the Polish peasant who hid the altar cross in his house? Supposing a group of Partisans attacked the German convoy, found the treasure in their trucks and the surviving Germans used it and the promise of more back in the Wolfschanze, to barter for their lives? If the partisans had allowed them to live, the Germans would have hardly reported back to Berlin after losing the Konigsberg treasure."

"Poles and Germans sitting down and talking in 1945?" he queried skeptically. "Even if you're right, they in turn could have been disturbed by the advancing Russians. Let's face it, it's impossible to track down individuals after all these years."

"We have Krefta and those other two men."

"Their bodies, not them, and Josef said the men were middle-aged, which probably means they were working for someone else."

"But Krefta was old enough to have fought in the war. It might be worth looking up his military record to see if his name is linked to any others. The Germans were nothing if not methodical. First thing in the morning I'll fax Berlin for a list of the last known personnel manning the Wolfschanze."

"That's the morning." Adam winced as he leaned forward to pour out the wine.

"Let me."

"I'm not ready for the graveyard yet."

"No, but you're exhausted."

"I am. I'll move my stuff into the small bedroom."

"I'd rather you took the double."

"Frankly, after all the drugs and trauma, I'd quite happily lie on the floor and sleep right here. I have to wait for the call anyway."

Magdalena cleared and washed the dishes. When she looked into the living room, Adam was stretched out on the sofa, with his eyes closed and a pained expression on his face that suggested he wasn't asleep.

She tightened her mouth, reminding herself of his cynicism, his reputation, his womanizing and the other rumors she'd heard and rather not believe; but try as she might she couldn't forget the feel of his lips on hers.

Retreating to the conference room with her briefcase, she laid out her papers and the plans of the Wolfschanze on the table. Then she pushed one of the DVDs into the machine and began to watch.

CHAPTER TWENTY

AGDALENA WOKE WITH a start. Disoriented, she lifted her head from the conference table and knocked the pile of papers she'd fallen asleep over to the floor. The DVD player was still switched on, but the TV screen was blank.

"It's the doorbell," Adam whispered from the corridor. He'd changed his bloodstained trousers for jeans but his feet and bandaged chest were bare.

The ringing started again. A masculine voice shouted, "Police! Open the door, we have an urgent message for Ms. Janca."

Adam flicked the safety catch off the gun Josef had given him.

Magdalena went into the hall. "Josef Dalecka?" she shouted after laying her finger across her lips to remind Adam he was supposed to be dead.

"Captain Josef is not on duty."

"How did you know I was here?"

"The captain alerted the patrols to watch the building. He didn't say, but we hoped Ms. Janca would be here."

"I'm Magdalena Janca."

"It's your grandmother, Maria Kaszuba. She's very ill."

Adam pushed Magdalena into the conference room. "Tell them to get Josef," he murmured.

"But Maria..."

"The half an hour it will take to verify this with Josef can't make much difference one way or the other to Maria. But it could save your life."

The policeman knocked on the door again. "Ms. Janca?"

"I need to speak to Captain Josef."

"By the time we contact him it could be too late. Your grandmother is very ill."

"Where is she?"

"In intensive care at the Institute for Contagious Diseases."

"Wait for me downstairs," she ordered. "I need to dress."

"I'll wait for you here."

"No need, I'll be down in five minutes." When she turned around Adam had already picked up the telephone in the conference room.

"You're not setting foot outside this building until I've cleared this with Josef's office." He banged impatiently on the buttons. "Goddamn it! Bloody Polish telephone system. No wonder my grandfather didn't ring back." He looked at her through darkly suspicious eyes. "You're not going. If I have to hold you here at gunpoint, you're not leaving this apartment."

She picked up the internal telephone and buzzed the guard downstairs. "Hello, yes, I know there's a police car waiting for me, but I promised Captain Josef I wouldn't leave here without him, and I can't contact him because the main telephone line is dead. Please, go to Piwna Street and ask them if they sent—you sure his identity checks out?—How could you confirm it when the telephone is dead?—I know the lines frequently go down—all right even if the photograph on his identity card is him, go to Piwna Street—Please, just do it. I can't leave here until you do."

"I'm going with you," Adam said curtly, pulling a shirt from his bag.

"You can't go anywhere, you're dead." She picked up her suitcase from the hall.

"I can stay dead if I call down to the security guards and borrow one of their uniforms."

"All the guards are shorter and wider than you, you'd look ridiculous."

"No one gives a security guard a second look."

"They would if he was wearing a uniform that had a foot missing from the arms and legs. Aren't you forgetting you're the target, not me?" she said. "Besides, what could possibly happen to me in a police car between here and the institute?"

"The same thing that happened to me in the foyer of a police station today. Get the guard again." He held out the internal telephone.

"Adam, there's no time."

"Get him. Tell him to run around the corner to Kaletnicza Street. Number two."

"Who lives there?"

"Melerski."

"You want to bring the Mafia into this?"

"He's always struck me as an honest criminal, besides he's Josef's cousin. Go on," he pleaded, "I'd be happier if you do."

She took the telephone from his hand and dialed downstairs.

"—but my colleague's already left for Piwna Street, Ms. Janca. If I go to Kaletnicza Street the museum will be unprotected."

"I'll take full responsibility."

"But..."

"Full responsibility."

"I'm leaving now, madam."

The doorbell rang less than five minutes later.

"It's Melerski, Magda. What's the fuss about?"

Adam looked through the spy hole in the door. The guard was standing behind Melerski. "Send the guard away," he whispered to Magdalena as she emerged from the bathroom in clean clothes.

"I will, but Josef will go wild if you show yourself to Melerski."

"I'll be right behind the door." He moved back into the conference room and hesitated. "Do you want the gun?" he asked, offering it to her.

"I wouldn't know what to do with it."

"Magda? Are you there?"

"Just one moment."

She waved Adam back. He withdrew, leaving the conference room door slightly ajar after making sure there was enough room to fire through the gap if the need arose. Magdalena pulled back the bolts. Melerski stepped inside.

"I heard about Adam today. I'm sorry."

"Thank you."

"You need help?"

"A police officer called here about a quarter of an hour ago to tell me Maria's in the hospital. The telephone lines are down..."

"As usual."

"I can't contact Josef. He warned me not to leave here without him. But I have to see Maria. After what happened to Adam I'd rather not go anywhere by myself, even with a police escort."

"I can understand that, given where Adam was killed." He slipped his arm around her shoulders and gave her a brief hug. "I'm going to miss Adam, he was an awkward bastard, but I always knew where I stood with him, unlike some others I could mention."

"He used to say the same about you."

"I'm honored that you trust me enough to ask for my help."

"It does seem odd to call on the Mafia when there's a police escort outside the door."

"I'd prefer it if you thought of me as a friend."

Adam gritted his teeth as he glimpsed Melerski taking Magdalena by the arm.

"Don't worry, Magda," Melerski led her out through the door. "I'll keep you safe until Josef can take over."

"Ms. Janca." The second museum guard ran up the stairs and knocked on the open door. "Lieutenant Pajewski is waiting for you downstairs. He says he's met you. He contacted Captain Dalecka and the captain will meet you at the hospital. He's doubled the size of your police escort. They're ready to leave whenever you are."

"I'm ready." She opened the door. "This gentleman is coming with us. He's a close friend."

"Shouldn't you switch off the lights? Melerski asked as Magdalena followed him into the outside corridor.

"Of course, thank you for reminding me." She switched off the lights and closed the door.

Adam listened as the sound of footsteps died on the stairs. He went to the window of the conference room and flicked one of the blinds, watching Magdalena climb into the back of the police car with Melerski. He cursed Josef's ruse. If only he could be certain that the mysterious "they" whoever they were, had really wanted him dead, and had not merely eradicated him as an obstacle in their plan to capture Magdalena and use her as a bargaining chip in their dealings with Brunon.

The glow from the street lamps in the Royal Way filtered through the blinds, providing sufficient light for him to find the front door. He slid the bolts home, then padded uneasily from the shadows of one darkened room to another. He ended up back in the conference room. Magdalena's maps and charts of the Wolfschanze were still lying on the table, but it was too dark to study them and he dared not switch the light on now she had left the building. Trying not to think of what was happening in the police car, he turned the television away from the window. Muting the sound, he pressed play on the DVD player and watched ten minutes of a film on the Wolfschanze without registering a single frame. Switching off the television, he took a book and a flashlight from Magdalena's knapsack, and retreated into the single bedroom. He lay on the bed and tried to drum up interest in the story of the Wolfschanze's construction. After an hour he realized he hadn't absorbed a single word.

The phone rang. He sprang to his feet, only just remembering he couldn't pick it up. Josef's nasal tones droned down the answering machine.

"I had the telephone fixed. The wires were cut outside the building, at the back. It could have been vandals but I doubt it. Maria Kaszuba is dying of anthrax. The doctors are one hundred percent certain. Magdalena is as close to her as the medical advisors will allow. The end won't be long. When it's over I'll bring Magda back." The answer phone clicked off and Adam was left to stare at the wall.

With hindsight it was so damned obvious. Why hadn't he thought of it? Someone old. Someone who knew where the knight was. Someone with a grandson who had a taste for money and the experience and connections to steal a shipment of amber to make a copy or even two, so the knight could be sold three times over. Only the grandson couldn't just leave it at the amber, not when it was only part of a consignment—he had to take the Mafia's money as well.

Magdalena approached the glass wall that gave a fish-tank view of the cubicle beyond. Maria's small frail figure was lying on a narrow hospital bed covered by the transparent folds of an oxygen tent.

The doctor took Magdalena's arm. "It's a matter of minutes rather than hours. I think she would have died some time ago if you or her grandson had been here. She insisted she has to speak to one of you."

"Why didn't you send for me earlier?" Magdalena demanded.

"Because no one knew who she was until she came around just over an ago." Josef tried to blot out an image of Mariana beside herself with rage when he'd walked out on her less than twenty minutes after walking in.

Magdalena approached the glass. Maria opened her eyes and her hand moved feebly within the confines of the tent. Magdalena pressed her fingers against the glass as close to Maria's as she could get, while trying not to blanch at the dry whiteness of Maria's skin and the disfiguring, malignant pustules that covered the old woman's face and arms.

The doctor pressed a button set below the glass. "Intercom," he explained. "She can hear you."

"Magda..." Maria's voice was so faint Magdalena crashed her head against the pane in an effort to draw nearer. "...I'm sorry. I shouldn't have gone with Krefta, but I was afraid he'd keep our share. He was always greedy. My August never trusted him. With good reason..."

"August was your husband?" It was the first time Maria had mentioned her husband in all the years Magdalena had known her.

"...He called himself Jan—we were Partisans, freedom fighters for Poland..." She closed her eyes.

"What happened to him?" Magdalena questioned gently, regretting all the times she could have talked to Maria about her life, and hadn't.

"Killed—so many were killed."

"In the war?"

Maria answered without opening her eyes but she couldn't hide the pain, not even after all the intervening years. "He was shot in the street like a dog because he was a Jew. That's why I never told anyone who or what I'd been—why I could never see a rabbi—never say Kaddish for August's soul."

Magdalena sensed movement behind her and heard Josef whisper to someone to send out for a rabbi, but she wasn't optimistic enough to think one would arrive before Maria died.

"Did Krefta take you to the Amber Knight?" Josef moved close to Magdalena.

Maria opened her eyes, they were bright, feverish. "I told

Brunon all the money he could ever want was in the Wolfschanze. He didn't believe me until the Russian came."

"You knew where the knight was hidden?" Josef asked.

"I knew, but what could I, a woman alone, do? Krefta knew, but he couldn't leave the Russian territory until after the revolution. Then his wife died and he lost the will to live. But they came. They needed help from people who knew about the treasure and could speak Polish. I sent them to Brunon." Maria tried and failed to sit up in the bed. "It was for you, Magda. You—your brothers and Brunon. I wanted money for you. Living in the flat with me and your brothers, you and Brunon never had time to be alone together—" she closed her eyes again; exhausted by the effort it had taken to say so much.

"Maria." Josef moved in front of the microphone. "Who are these people who came to you?"

"Germans. I wanted to kill them, but my August allowed them to live because they told us about the treasure."

"Where did you hide the knight?" Magdalena begged. "We have to know, Maria. It's infected. It's what killed Krefta, what's killing you."

"Nine of us. Three Russians, three Germans, three Poles—August, Krefta and me. I told Brunon all the money he could spend was hidden in the Wolfschanze," she repeated dully.

"Where, Maria?" Magdalena pleaded. "Where in the Wolfschanze was it hidden?"

"I was one of the nine—the nine—"

"Was it in a bunker?" Josef urged.

"The German showed us a secret vault. He said we would go back at the end of the war and get it—but we never did. August—" her eyes clouded and lost focus. "—I wanted to die when he was killed but I was carrying his baby—Little August was like his father—always causes before family—he disappeared and I was left with Brunon. I thought about the treasure, but what could I do? One woman on her own—"

"Maria, did you go to the hidden vault?" Josef asked. "Was Brunon with you? If he was, we have to find him."

"The Russian found me. After fifty years he found me—"

"Who is this Russian? Did he go in the vault with you?" Josef demanded impatiently.

"August was too trusting. He would take anyone into his band. He used to say it didn't matter where people came from, only where they were going. But he was wrong—some carry hatred with them—hatred for Jews—"

"Maria," Josef appealed. "Who is this Russian who knew about the treasure?"

"The German sent him. The German is old—old and tired like me, he can't travel," she rambled.

"Maria, we have to seal off the vault before anyone else goes into it. Where is it?" Magdalena begged.

"Where are Brunon and the Russian? If they went into the vault with you, they need help. If they don't get it, they will die," Josef pressed. "You don't want Brunon to die do you, Maria?"

"Under the... cemetery..." the old woman shuddered. A rattling sigh escaped her lips. The doctor stepped forward and shook his head. Magdalena pressed her hands and forehead against the glass. The minutes ticked past slowly and audibly on an electric clock above the door. The quiet clicks resounded like staccato machine-gun fire in the stillness of the room.

Josef watched impotently as the last vestiges of life ebbed from the frail body. Feeling like a trespasser he retreated with the doctor.

"You know who this Russian is?" the doctor asked when they reached the corridor.

"No."

"If he and her grandson have been exposed to this disease we need to see them before they start an epidemic. I can't impress on you how serious this could be. Anthrax—"

"You don't need to impress me," Josef said wearily. "If we find Brunon and this Russian, you'll be the first to know." He looked up at Magdalena who had left the cubicle. "We'll both do all we can."

CHAPTER TWENTY-ONE

ADAM WAS SITTING in the conference room keeping pain at bay with shots of vodka that were disagreeing with the painkillers he had been given in the hospital, and watching yet another DVD about the Wolfschanze, when the telephone rang again. Expecting his grandfather's call, he waited for the answering machine to cut in. When it did, whoever was at the other end hung up.

Seconds later there was a ring at the door bell. He reached for the gun on the table. The ringing was replaced by an urgent knocking.

"Mr. Salen?"

He tensed when he heard his name. Had Josef sent one of the guards up with a message? Why would he do that when he could contact him directly through the answering machine?

As he looked into the hall to reassure himself that he had fastened all the bolts on the front door, he heard the guard protest.

"I told you no one was in there."

The bell rang again. Louder and longer this time. He held the gun out ahead of him and walked backwards into the single bedroom that overlooked the rear of the building. A crash resounded behind him. He turned as a dark mass steam-rollered through the smashed window and landed on him. He had no time to brace himself for the impact, and in his weakened state, no strength to combat it. Thrust headlong, face down on the floor, he moaned as a knee jerked into his back, compressing his broken ribs and sending razor-sharp shards of pain into his lungs. Josef's gun was wrenched from his hand and hurled across the room. He followed the sound, groaning as the weapon skidded out of reach beneath the bed.

The sound of splintering wood reverberated from the passage and he realized someone had taken a fire axe to the front door. The dead weight of his assailant's knee continued to press into the small of his back, effectively paralyzing him. A hand dug into his hair and yanked up his head. A dry, foul tasting rag was stuffed into his mouth. Ropes bit between his lips and teeth as the gag was knotted firmly into place.

The knee was lifted, but his relief was short-lived. He doubled in agony as his arms were hauled high behind his back. His teeth clenched around the suffocating gag. Whoever was working on him was fast, silent, and efficient. His ankles and legs were trussed together. He was rolled, none too gently, on to an open body bag. He recognized the smell of cheap, raw plastic from the wrapping Josef and Stephan had used to carry him into the hospital.

As if the ropes weren't enough, a black gloved hand zipped the bag up to his neck. He looked up as he was dragged, a shiny chrysalis, into the corridor. A man holding a bloodied fire axe stepped through the shattered door. Beyond its fractured remains Adam saw the decapitated torso of the guard. The head lay alongside his feet, the neck cleanly severed below the chin.

The man's Slavic features twisted into a crooked smile as he walked towards Adam and his assailant. It was the man Adam had seen in Helga's bed, the man who had tried to kill him in the police station, and in that split second Adam realized exactly where he had seen him. He cursed himself for not remembering earlier. Like Maria, it was all so bloody obvious—now.

He brought up his knees and lashed out with his bound legs in a futile gesture of defiance. All he succeeded in doing was rattling the body bag cocooned around him. He wanted to scream that they'd never get away with it—that there were police patrols outside the building, but the gag muted his cries.

The handle of the fire axe swung towards him and cracked against his left temple. Consciousness clouded, Adam was barely aware of being hauled to his feet. He lurched against the shoulder of his assailant, a hurting, helpless bag of flesh and blood. He had neither the strength nor the will to fight back as he was lifted like a sack of potatoes and pressed against the wall.

The tearing sound of a zipper closed out even the half-light. There was movement, a change in atmosphere and a sharp drop in temperature that permeated even through the plastic. The ring of footsteps on metal confirmed that he had been bundled out through the broken window and carried onto the landing of the fire escape.

There was a click of metal on metal as he was strapped into a harness that constricted his waist and shoulders, followed by a sickening, lurching sensation as he hurtled downwards.

Hands closed around him, the harness was removed and he was unceremoniously stuffed into a space too small for comfort. The stench of exhaust fumes vanquished the reek of plastic. He was in the trunk of a car. Would Josef's patrols think to stop it? If they didn't, how long before Josef returned to the apartment to find him gone? Would Josef go there after Maria died, or would he linger in the Institute talking to the doctors?

Adam's brain was too fogged by a combination of carbon monoxide, exhaustion, vodka and analgesics to think of escape. The only consoling thought was, if his assailants had wanted him dead, they would have killed him in the apartment and laid out his body alongside that of the guard. He tried to move in an effort to ease the cramps settling into his legs and arms. Whatever these people wanted of him, he had a feeling that he was going to find out—and probably sooner than he wanted to.

"Nine people knew of the Konigsberg treasure. Three Russians—"

"Maria said the Russian had been sent by a German," Magdalena reminded Joseph as they sat side by side in the back of the squad car. Consumed by guilt she murmured, "Maria might have had time to say more if I'd left for the hospital as soon as that police officer came to the apartment."

"Bloody idiot, he should never have gone to the museum in the first place. Rookies and their ideas of initiative," Josef griped, as Pajewski turned out of a side road and on to the main thoroughfare into Gdansk.

"If I'd gone with him straight away Maria might have still been lucid."

"From what the doctor told me, I doubt it. And we now know who the three Polish conspirators were."

"Were", the past tense grated. Magdalena thrust all thoughts of Maria's death aside. She would remember and mourn the woman who had been more family to her than her own, later. Now was not the time to grieve, not with Brunon and some unknown Russian at risk of dying from anthrax and, even worse, causing an epidemic.

"One in 1945, two now," Josef muttered. "It must hinge on the German who was too old to travel, but judging from what Maria said, not too old to mastermind the recovery of the Amber Knight."

"A German, who employed a Russian," Magdalena mused. "I checked on the SS colonel who commanded the Wolfschanze in January 1945. He and all his men disappeared during the Russian invasion."

"Disappeared at the end of the war didn't necessarily mean dead, as high-ranking Nazis and those who ran the concentration camps have proved time and again. Were the staff in the Wolfschanze all SS?" Josef asked.

"Contemporary documents indicate the only personnel left there in January 1945 were SS. It makes sense. The Wolfschanze was Hitler's headquarters and his bodyguard was drawn from that regiment."

"The chances are, if the colonel and his men were captured by the Russians, they were killed. No one who lived through the Nazi occupation of Poland and Russia could blame the Russians for coming down hard on all Germans in uniform, and doubly hard on the SS."

"But Maria said there was one survivor. The answer has to lie in the names in the documents I've had from Berlin. I'll go through them again as soon as we get back to the museum."

Josef looked across at her. In the half-light of the street lamps, she looked haggard, clearly emotionally and physically drained. He would have liked to have told her to forget about the Wolfschanze and rest, but with the search for the Amber Knight transformed into a race against time to contain the spread of anthrax, neither he nor Magdalena could afford the luxury of sleep. He watched as she leaned back in her seat and closed her eyes.

"I'm sorry for the way Maria died," he consoled her clumsily. "It was a rough way to go."

"What I can't bear is the thought that I never took the trouble to get to know her better. She took me and my brothers into her home, made us feel wanted and welcome even when Brunon moved out and we had no reason to stay and she had less reason to allow us to live with her. Never once in all those years did she mention her husband, or fighting with the Partisans during the war."

"I'm not surprised. Have you heard people talking about the Jews lately? Even now, when there are less than four thousand of them left in the country, they're being blamed for everything from rent rises to political unrest. God only knows why, when there are so many other, more obvious, scapegoats to choose from."

Magdalena wasn't listening to him. "Maria carried all that guilt and shame, and I had no idea."

"You can't blame yourself for that," Joseph said briskly. "Put yourself in Maria's shoes. How do you even begin to tell someone the secrets she disclosed to us tonight? She said she'd told Brunon about the Amber Knight, but I'm betting he didn't believe her until Krefta and this Russian turned up."

Pajewski slowed the car and pulled on the handbrake. Josef stared at the red traffic lights ahead. The complexities of the case were bewildering. No matter which way he turned he seemed to be spiraling in circles of confusion.

Since the fall of Communism in the Eastern Bloc, money had become the new God. He wouldn't have to look far to find men and women who would be only too delighted to terrorize, kill and commit murder and mayhem for a lot less than fifty million dollars. For that reason alone he doubted that Maria's and Krefta's deaths would signify an end to this case, especially if Brunon knew about the knight. Or was Brunon already lying dead of anthrax somewhere in the forest? He wished he'd thought to ask Maria just how many people had gone into the vault where the knight had been hidden.

So far there were four dead, but Maria had intimated there were more conspirators. There had to be, two nondescript, middle-aged men with fingerprints that indicated they had no police record worth recording, one washed-up ambersmith who had produced nothing worth exhibiting for years, and an old woman at the tail end of a tragic life, couldn't have planned and carried out the attacks on Adam and Magdalena. That's if the attacks were connected with the reappearance of the knight.

"This Russian Maria kept talking about," he said thoughtfully. "Could he be anyone Brunon knew?"

"Brunon knows Radek," Magdalena reminded him.

"It's been a long time since Brunon worked for Radek. Perhaps Maria didn't know this Russian well enough to put a name to him, and if he wasn't one of the two dead men who were found in the hut—if he was someone who had been sent by the surviving German, whoever he is. If he was the man who shot Adam—" Josef delved into his pocket for his mobile phone and pressed the button that connected him to police HQ. "Send a squad around to the museum now, at once. Warn them to expect trouble."

Magdalena looked on horrified as Josef switched on the siren and ordered Pajewski to put his foot down on the accelerator.

"Adam's a competent soul," he mumbled, in an unconvincing attempt to reassure her. "He has a gun. There are guards in the museum. Patrols in the street. He'll be fine. You'll see, he'll be fine."

The exhaust fumes that had penetrated the body bag lingered beneath the plastic, repugnant and nauseating. The car continued to lurch forward slowly, bumping over cobblestones that jarred every throbbing inch of Adam's flesh. The wheels ground to a halt after a drive that seemed short even to him. Doors opened and slammed but he remained in the trunk long enough to wonder if he'd been abandoned there. When he was finally lifted out, he feigned unconsciousness. It didn't take a great deal of effort. He was bundled head first down a flight of steep stone steps. He knew they were stone because his heels bounced against the edge of every one.

A door grated open on hinges in need of oiling. He was unzipped from the bag and propelled into pitch darkness. Hands caught at the ropes that bound him, cutting him free, before spread-eagling his body and chaining his ankles and wrists to the frame of a metal cot.

The gag around his mouth was tightened. All he could see was a faint square of gray in the darkness, and even that was blotted by shadows. The door closed and he could no longer decipher anything. Footsteps ebbed into absolute silence. He tried moving his arms and legs, but all he succeeded in doing was rattling the metal cuffs against the bed frame. He explored his body, tensing each muscle in turn. His ribcage burned with an almost unendurable pain he knew would heighten as soon as the effects of the vodka and anesthetics wore off. Cramping pins and needles shot through his limbs.

Even if he'd been able to cry out he doubted anyone would hear. The combination of steps and cool temperature told him he was in a cellar. Dressed only in jeans and band-ages, and immobilized by chains, he would soon begin to feel the cold, but there was nothing he could do to help himself except breathe slowly and deliberately, keep panic at bay and wait for something—anything—to happen. And hope that he didn't choke on the foul-tasting cloth and his own saliva.

By the time Josef and Magdalena reached the Main Town, a police forensic team was hard at work in the apartment in the Historical Museum and roadblocks had been set up on all the major and minor routes out of Gdansk. But when they drew up outside the old Town Hall, Josef knew that he had done too little, too late.

Despite the Museum's proximity to Piwna Street, the Royal Way was packed with squad cars. Josef opened his door, and the look on his colleagues' faces told him more than he wanted to know. He tried to keep Magdalena back, but she was inside the building and up the stairs before him. She reached the top landing as the police surgeon was bagging the guard's head.

Reeling back against Josef she gripped his arm so tightly

he could feel her nails digging into his flesh through the layers of shirt and jacket.

"There was no one in the apartment, sir." Pajewski walked out to meet them.

Magdalena struggled free from Josef's grasp.

"Careful," Josef warned. "You go in there and you risk destroying evidence that could lead us to Adam."

"We have to look for him," she insisted.

"Tell me where?" Josef pleaded. "We've erected road blocks. They won't be able to take him out of the main city. Believe me, I know it looks as though we're wasting time but our best chance of finding Adam is by looking for clues in the apartment." He snapped on the rubber gloves Pajewski handed him along with a pair of white paper overalls and over-shoes.

"Four sets of prints," a technician announced as he finished dusting what was left of the door.

"You have mine on record. Take Ms. Janca's and both guards for elimination purposes, and pick up a set of Adam Salen's from his office in the Archaeological Museum."

"Looks like a well-planned job, sir," Pajewski advised. "The guard downstairs said a uniformed police officer knocked on the front door and asked for Mr. Salen. They told him they were the only ones in the building. The man flashed an identity card and insisted he had an urgent message for Mr. Salen from you. He was so persistent one of the guards took him up to the apartment. They thought it was the only way to convince him there was no one there. He used the fire axe to decapitate the guard and smash his way inside. By the time the second guard arrived on the scene it was all over."

"I don't understand." Josef stepped cautiously through

the broken doorway. "Surely Adam would have heard the axe. He had a gun. Why didn't he shoot?"

"Probably because he'd already been overpowered." Pajewski led Josef into the small bedroom. "The window's broken in here. It looks as though it was kicked in, commando-style, from the outside. There's a rope tied to one of the turrets on the roof. The timing was probably coordinated between the man who posed as the officer and whoever crashed through the window. From what the second guard told us, they were all out of here seconds after the bogus policeman broke through the door."

"You have a description of this 'officer'?" Josef demanded.

"You're not going to like it, sir."

"Let me guess, tall, thin, Slavic features, slicked back dark hair..."

"Yes, sir."

Josef walked through the apartment to the double bedroom. He looked out at the narrow metal landing. "The fire escape wasn't dropped."

"There's a fixed fire escape three buildings away. They could have used the rope to get back up on the roof and climbed down to it from there."

Josef leaned forward and picked up a splinter of wood from the foot of the railings that fenced in the narrow platform. "Looks like the bastards laid planks across from next door's balcony. Send someone down to check out all the outside landings, balconies, window boxes and fire escapes to the right of this window. Wake anyone who's sleeping in any of the buildings. I don't care who they are. I want to know if they heard a car, or saw anything unusual in the last couple of hours. If they heard footsteps I want to know what direction they were moving in. If they heard a cat cry, I want to know who trod on its tail. If a dog barked I want it hauled in for questioning. Do you understand?"

"Sir!" Pajewski scuttled down the passageway.

Josef glanced into the other rooms as he walked to the door. Magdalena, dressed in a paper overall and over-shoes, was standing at the table in the conference room.

"He was watching one of the films of the Wolfschanze." Her eyes were heavy as though she was holding back tears, but Josef couldn't tell whether they were for Maria or Adam. "They'll kill him, won't they?"

"If they'd wanted to kill him they would have done it here, along with the guard."

"Who are these people?" she exclaimed bitterly.

"It looks as though one of them is the same man who tried to kill Adam in the police station earlier today. This has to be connected with the Amber Knight. First Adam wouldn't make a bid because he couldn't be certain it was genuine. Then he decided it might be worth checking out and dragged you and Elizbieta to Kaliningrad and attracted the wrong sort of attention. Now we know that it's more than likely contaminated, no one with any sense will go near it. Possibly they shanghaied him because they want him to push through the sale with the people who hold the purse strings in the Salen Institute. Would a financial decision on a purchase like the knight have to go through a board of directors?"

"I have no idea."

"Would the Institute hand over the money on Adam's authority alone?"

"I don't know." Magdalena bit her lip in annoyance. "He never discussed funding with me, he's never needed to. My job is to evaluate archaeological and educational projects and turn out reports on artifacts that come on the market. The only time he ever mentioned money was to say the Institute would have trouble raising fifty million dollars, but he did call his grandfather earlier. I don't know whether it was to tell him he'd survived the attack in Ketrzyn, or discuss the knight."

"Number?"

"Only Adam knows that."

"That sister of his, where is she?" Josef looked to Pajewski.

"She did say that she was leaving the Grand Hotel today, sir."

"She may have left a forwarding address, call the hotel."

"Sir." Pajewski reached for his mobile.

"Fuck it!" Josef exclaimed angrily. "We can't even go to the press and announce Adam's missing when we've already announced his death and leaked the identity of the 'corpse' to the Mafia." Josef turned to Pajewski who had begun to dial. "I want all leave cancelled and every available man out looking for Adam Salen, and I want them out now. Warn everyone in Piwna Street there'll be no eating, sleeping or rest until he's found."

CHAPTER TWENTY-TWO

"WE HAVE TO find somewhere safe to put you," Josef commented as he watched Magdalena pile books and tapes from the table into her bag.

"I'm not going anywhere until Adam is found."

"You can't stay here. Apart from the fact it's a crime scene, there's no door."

"My office across the hall isn't a crime scene. I'll work there."

"You could move into Piwna Street."

"Do you have a particular cell in mind?" she asked, anxiety making her even more caustic than usual.

"You could use my office," he answered, "although it's likely to be about as peaceful as Election Day until Adam's found."

Magdalena lifted her bag to the floor, then sank down on to a chair as though the effort had been too much for her. "I need to go through those Berlin documents to see if I can come up with a name that means anything. And there's still the knight. Maria said something about the cemetery..."

"You can't be sure she was talking about the Wolfschanze. It was the last thing she said..."

"It's all we have to go on, Josef," she snapped. "And I think it's worth passing on the information to the team from the contagious diseases institute. They could probe the ground..."

"I'll contact them first thing in the morning," Josef promised. He had never seen anyone so close to breaking point.

"I'll e-mail, fax and telephone them now. Someone on the team is bound to be awake. If Maria was right, it will be a difficult excavation. As the knight is almost certainly contaminated they can't risk ripping the bunker apart with a bulldozer. The only alternative is to find the entrance, and even then they'd have to move cautiously, that means slowly."

"With your knowledge of the knight, Adam and the Institute it might be a better idea to move the center of operations into this building." Josef went into the hall and looked at Adam's briefcase and bag. "You said he telephoned America after you got here?"

"Adam was waiting for him to return his call when we discovered that the telephone had been cut off."

"So he gave someone in his grandfather's house this number?"

"He used a gadget so no one could listen in on the call."

Josef stepped into the living room and picked up the phone. "A scrambler." He pulled it off the receiver and shouted for Pajewski. "Take this to the lab and find out if there's a way to put a trace on it when it's in use, then get on to the phone company. I want a list of all the incoming and outgoing calls from the telephones here tonight." Trying not to think about whether or not Adam was alive, he retrieved Adam's briefcase. "I'll be across the hall in Ms. Janca's office. Bring me the reports as they come in, and bring coffee sooner. I'm going to need something to keep me awake."

Magdalena had only just gathered up the Berlin faxes when Melerski walked into her office.

"I assumed you went back to bed hours ago." Josef acknowledged his cousin's presence without looking up from the map of the old quarter he was studying.

"I heard you cancelled all sleep."

"Only for police officers, I have no jurisdiction over the Mafia."

"You sound like Adam. I went to see Radek."

Josef lowered the map. "And?"

"I find your naivety extraordinary in a member of our family. Did you really think we wouldn't find out that Adam had survived the shooting in Ketrzyn and was hiding out here?"

"How did you know?" Josef fumbled for his cigarettes.

"Half the police force clomps round the main town in the early hours of the morning, and you ask me how I know you had Adam holed up here."

"No one knew Adam was here except Magda and me. I certainly didn't tell you."

"And neither did I," Magdalena broke in hotly.

"Come on, Melerski, who told you?"

"Does it matter? How often do Radek and I have to insist that we're on the same side as you? East against West..."

"Who told you?" Josef commanded in an icy tone.

"If I tell you, do you promise not to do anything to the man?"

"No."

"He was trying to help. He contacted me to find out if I knew anything."

"Do you and Radek have the entire bloody Gdansk police force in your pocket?"

"No, we've never had you," Melerski answered quietly.

"Where is Adam Salen?"

"Radek's men are out looking for him but there's no word on the street and that means he's in the hands of someone we've never done business with. I swear it on the Holy Virgin's nose, Josef, this whole thing with the Amber Knight isn't connected to any organization Radek or I have ever come across." He pulled a chair close to Magdalena's desk. "We all know what a pain in the ass Adam can be, but I'm quite fond of the man. He's the only westerner I've ever met who has Polish interests at heart."

"He wanted the knight for Gdansk," Magdalena asserted.

"He's also steered a lot of foreign investment into the museums which in turn has increased tourism, which has been good for the town. That's why Radek and I want to pool resources."

"You want to help the police find Adam?" Josef questioned incredulously.

"And the knight and, not to put too altruistic a point on it, our missing amber."

"And the unlaundered money Brunon stole?" Magdalena added.

"And what's left of our money after your husband's visit to the casino," Melerski agreed. "Radek and I suspect that whoever stole the amber took it to make a copy of the knight so they could sell it twice over."

"And as the amber and your money disappeared at the same time, you're supposing we're all after the same band of racketeering murderers." Josef picked up the coffee pot and replenished their cups. "All right, before I agree to pool resources, let's hear your offer."

A seductive aroma lingered in the air. The fragrant smell of pine woods basking in languid, summer heat. It was the promise of warmth that unsettled Adam. He'd tried to keep his circulation going, but it was difficult when the pain in his chest blotted every sensation other than cold from his mind, and the chains on his wrists and ankles restricted his movement to less than a skin chafing inch.

The icy chill had seeped through every pore of his being, freezing his blood and numbing his mind. It was as much as he could do to concentrate on keeping breathing and prevent himself from choking. He tried to ignore the fragrance by mulling over every incident, significant or not, since he had opened the envelope containing the demand for the knight.

Krefta, two anonymous men, and now Maria, dying because they had entered the vault where the knight had been stored. Brunon Kaszuba implicated because he had helped hijack the illegal amber shipment smuggled out of Kaliningrad and, incidentally Radek's money. Helga's Slavic bed mate to do the cold-blooded killing. And, he suspected, an avaricious woman he had taken into his bed masterminding the scheme to divert fifty million dollars of Salen Institute's money into her own pocket.

It all fitted neatly, and probably would have worked like a clockwork babushka if the Amber Knight hadn't carried death in its shroud. The knowledge that the knight was contaminated must have upset plans for early and luxurious retirements.

The smell came again, warm, resinous, redolent of woods on sunny days, and he realized what it was. Somewhere close by, the stolen amber was being heated in readiness to manufacture a replica of the knight. They had medieval clothes and armor—probably courtesy of Kaszuba. It wouldn't have been hard for a determined professional thief to break into the Historical Museum, but it would have been even easier for Kaszuba, who had access through Maria to Magdalena's keys, which might explain why the guards hadn't been alerted to the presence of an intruder. If Kaszuba had copied the keys and returned the originals before they were missed, all he would have had to do was let himself into the museum, hide between security checks and pick up the clothes and armor before slipping out the way he had entered. Not difficult, given the complex layout of the museum, and well within the capabilities of a man of even limited intellect. Adam had long since decided intelligence couldn't be one of Kaszuba's assets, not when he had abandoned a wife like Magdalena so soon after their wedding.

The smell grew in intensity, filling his nostrils and overpowering his senses. He pictured the scene that had been played out on the shores of the Baltic so many centuries before. A corpse enveloped in plague pustules—he hoped for the sake of the grief-stricken mourners it had been covered—an open stone coffin, and the melted aromatic resin running free from the treasure house of the burning medieval village. Scented smoke curling around the majestic, armor-clad figure of Hermann von Balk as he walked among his troops. And the Princess Woberg—had she been there? Or had she already donned the veil?

How did they melt amber these days? He should have asked Feliks Malek.

Footsteps, at least two sets, disturbed the icy, tomb-like silence. One tapping in the light staccato of feminine stilettos, the other a ponderous, more masculine tread. The door creaked on the rusting hinges and blinding light shone down from a single naked bulb.

He closed his eyes against the glare. When he opened them a moment later he saw artfully colored red hair, glittering green eyes and a slim, desirable body.

The woman stepped forward holding a gun to his temple as her companion unlocked the chains that bound him to the bed. Adam attempted a smile, choking on the gag for his trouble. He fought for breath.

"It's a trick."

"He's suffocating, you fool," the woman snapped. "Cut the gag. We'd be in a right mess if he died."

Brunon Kaszuba bent over Adam and sliced through the rope that held the cloth in place.

Adam spat the gag from his mouth, coughed and fought for breath before finally managing the smile that had threatened to be his last. "You're not wearing my earrings, Helga. Does that mean you've already sold them?"

"The amber never left Gdansk."

"How do you know?" Josef asked Melerski.

"Radek and I have had men checking every cargo that's moved out of the town by ship, road, rail and air since the hijack."

"Whoever took it could have had a plane waiting, a boat..."

"Take my word for it. It's still here," Melerski assured him. "We received confirmation yesterday. Friend of ours brought a parcel into the city last night. It was very heavy."

"Like a stone coffin?" Josef asked.

"Two."

"Stop spinning it out. Where were they delivered?"

"Warehouse in the Old Town."

Only a place like Gdansk could have a medieval quarter universally known as the Main Town and a newer quarter christened the Old Town, Josef reflected.

"Kaszuba picked them up before dawn this morning. He was with another man, and before you ask, the description matches the one you issued after the shooting in Ketrzyn police station."

"Transport?"

"White transit van, false plates."

Josef made a note on his pad. "I suppose it's too much to hope that your man followed them?"

"He knows Kaszuba and values his hide."

"I'll put out a description on the van. Someone may have seen it." Josef glanced up, Melerski was smiling. "As you seem to have more control over my men these days than I do, I assume you've already done so?"

"Radek wants whoever murdered his brother."

"So do I, but I want him legally, Melerski, and that doesn't mean an eye for an eye."

"Then we have to find him before anyone can exact retribution."

"If they have stone coffins, amber and medieval clothes, they are making copies," Josef guessed. "Probably right this minute. It's time we contacted the Salen Institute in America to find out if Adam has authorized payment for the knight. Will anyone be there yet?"

Magdalena shook her head. "I've tried the fax and phone. All the offices are empty. It's three in the morning in

Europe, seven p.m. in San Francisco, and ten at night in New York."

"Leave messages on all the answering machines and I'll get on to Interpol to see what they can do. Pajewski?" Josef's lieutenant came running to the door. "Have you raised Salen's sister yet?"

"She's in Prague. I've talked to the nanny. She's trying to track down Ms. Salen, but the lady is doing the night clubs with a group of artists and her mobile is switched off. It could take time."

"I hope you told the nanny that time is the one commodity we don't have."

"I stressed that it was vital we talk to Mr. Salen's sister as soon as possible."

"Call back and ask her to wake the boy," Magdalena suggested. "He can operate his mother's electronic address book. If Georgiana has Adam's grandfather's telephone number it should be in it."

"Good idea." Josef lifted Adam's briefcase on to the desk in front of him. "There may be something in this." When the combination lock proved stubborn he produced a Stanley knife.

"Salen won't thank you for ruining an expensive briefcase," Melerski admonished. "Hand it over."

"I was opening briefcases like this when you were still in kindergarten," Josef boasted.

"Not like that one you weren't."

Melerski's warning came too late. An ear piercing alarm shrieked, deafening everyone within earshot and a jet of glutinous, foul-smelling liquid shot out of the locks towards Josef, staining his face, hands and clothes a conspicuous shade of luminous green.

* * *

"We know you have the code that will release the emergency funds from the Salen Institute's Swiss bank account. All you have to do is write it down, then you can go." Helga pushed a cheap pen and pad of even cheaper paper along the table until it rested in front of Adam. Brunon had dragged him off the bed and down a passageway into a Gothic arched and vaulted cellar that looked as though it had been built to accommodate a Tsar's wine reserve. Dusty wooden racks stood at the back of some of the alcoves. An enormous electric kiln belched out heat into an atmosphere that was already stifling, prompting Adam to wonder how he could have ever considered extreme cold less bearable than a surfeit of heat.

Brunon had dumped him on a chair set skin-cracklingly close to the kiln. His ankles were still chained, and they had been securely fastened to the metal legs of the chair. His hands, cuffed together at the wrists, were resting on the surface of the table Helga had provided for him to write on.

"I'm sorry, I have an appalling memory. I can never remember names or numbers. On the other hand I always remember warnings, especially when they concern my own or other people's health. If either of you went into the vault with the Amber Knight, you're not going to last long."

"As neither of us did, that's not a problem." Helga pushed two cigarettes into her mouth, lit them and handed one to Brunon.

"What about you?" Adam asked Brunon. "Don't you care that your grandmother's dead and your wife has exposed herself to anthrax by visiting her?"

"My grandmother was old. The old die and, you're too interested in my wife."

"Someone has to be."

"I know Magda. She's so hung up on her fucking church and morality you'll never get anywhere with her." Brunon drew heavily on his cigarette and waved the glowing tip before Adam's eyes. "She won't drop her principles or her pants for anyone who hasn't put a wedding ring on her finger. In fact she's so fucking superior, she hasn't even done it for her husband in years."

"That's because her husband is an impotent bastard who can't satisfy a half-zloty whore, let alone a real woman."

The blow was powerful, swift and sudden, sending Adam and the chair he was chained to spinning on the floor. Adam held his breath and tensed his muscles against the kick Brunon aimed at his bandaged ribs, but his efforts didn't lessen the impact. An ominous cracking escalated his pain to screaming pitch.

"Kaszuba!" the Russian shouted from somewhere behind them.

"The bastard insulted me."

"We need him," Helga hissed, revealing more to Adam than she'd intended with those three words.

"Keep your fucking mouth shut," the Russian warned Helga as he hoisted the chair, and Adam, upright. "And you," he glared at Brunon, "stand on the other side of the kiln until you learn to control your temper."

Helga examined a cut that ran from the corner of Adam's left eye to his ear. She dabbed at it ineffectually with a crumpled tissue.

"If you haven't got any disinfectant I'd rather you kept your germs to yourself," Adam muttered, fighting pain.

"I'm trying to help."

"Your boyfriend to kill me?" he asked flatly.

"What makes you think Brunon is my boyfriend?" She eyed the Russian warily.

"He isn't?" Adam asked with what he hoped was just the right amount of skepticism. "You do know that if you're trying to recreate the Amber Knight, you're going the about it the wrong way?"

"Who says we're trying to recreate the knight?" the Russian asked.

"The smell of molten amber." Adam utilized his pain to stimulate his brain into recalling everything Feliks and Elizbieta had told him about the Amber Knight. "Even a qualified amber-smith would be hard pressed to recreate the knight," he lied. "The temperature of the amber has to be exactly right..."

"280 Celsius," the Russian interrupted.

"And there's the pouring. You have to be very careful not to get air between the layers or the amber will flake and crack. Look what's happened to the original. I trust you have no intention of trying without an amber-smith around." Given the expression on their faces he knew they had every intention of doing just that.

"Leave the knight to us," the Russian snapped. "I promise you'll get a very credible copy to put in your museum. All you have to do is write down the code that will release the funds to buy it." He turned Adam's chair so it faced the table and the blank sheet of coarse, grayish paper.

"You've been around Brunon Kaszuba so long you think everyone is as stupid as him. That code is the only reason you haven't put a bullet in my brain or chopped my head off," Adam said. "Once I give it to you, there'll be nothing to prevent you from contacting the holder of the Salen Institute Special Fund and collecting fifty million dollars. I hate to disappoint you but you're too late. Word is out that the knight's contaminated."

"The word isn't general knowledge—yet, and may never be, given the authorities' determination to keep the anthrax outbreak secret," the Russian contradicted. "And, in view of the extra expense we've incurred in handling the knight, the price has doubled, but the Salen Institute can stand the increase. Give us the number, Salen. In exchange you'll get your freedom and the knight."

"Don't you mean the Institute will get the knight—after a fashion?" Adam raised his eyes to the Russian. "All I'll get is an amber shroud."

The Russian laughed as he opened a case and laid the instruments it contained out on the table. "You Americans are so suspicious."

"Go back and tell the boss I won't do. Modern ultrasound and X-rays are too good. Even a cursory examination will prove you've supplied a copy."

"By then we'll be long gone."

"You'll be tracked down. The directors of the Salen Institute don't like fraud."

"In what way will it be different?" Helga earned herself a frown from the Russian.

"A probe will reveal that I have the wrong color hair. Helmut von Mau was a Teuton and every child knows they have blond hair and blue eyes." He looked at Brunon, who was lounging against a pillar.

"Fuck off, Yank," Brunon grunted, running his fingers through his blond hair.

"And for another." Adam eyed the instruments the Russian had laid out, "you believe von Mau was castrated. That's why you've brought the gelding irons. You think that the first thing an ultra-sound examination would pick up on are extra bits that shouldn't be there. But there are records that prove Helmut von Mau went to meet his maker as he'd been born, with his balls intact."

"Liar," Helga snapped.

"Legends aren't always what they seem and people dislike the truth." Light headed with pain, Adam took a deep breath despite the agony it cost him and played his last card, hoping that Feliks hadn't overestimated the amount of amber that had been stolen. Looking at Brunon he said, "who are you going to immortalize first, me, or your other sacrificial knight?"

CHAPTER TWENTY-THREE

WHILE JOSEF CLOSETED himself in the museum bathroom with a gallon of industrial solvent and a nail brush, Melerski tackled the briefcase. He had the alarm silenced in seconds, the combination lock open in less than a minute. Magdalena took the papers it contained, leaving him the electronic organizer. Beneath it was a small, narrow jeweler's box. Melerski picked it up and read the message scrawled across the lid. For Magdalena, sorry for the days you lost because of me.

"Mean anything?" He handed it to her.

"It could be an apology for landing me in quarantine."

"You'd better open it. Very nice," he complimented as she lifted out the crystal cut earrings Adam had bought from Feliks. "Your boyfriend has good taste. Nice work, expensive, but good."

"He's my boss, not my boyfriend," Magdalena retorted brusquely.

"Then he's a very generous boss."

She returned the earrings to their cotton wool bed and replaced the box in the briefcase.

"Aren't you going to keep them?"

"Magdalena's a common enough name. He probably intended them for someone else."

Melerski switched on the organizer. "You don't believe that—Damn! There's a security code on this machine."

"There would be, Adam Salen's a cautious man." Magdalena sifted through reports on the Wolfschanze and the Amber Knight that proved Adam was not as uninformed on both subjects as he had led her to believe.

"You must have some idea what he'd use?"

"I only work for him."

"Come on, Magda, keep the protests of innocence for the gossips. What password would he use?"

"I was in Adam's apartment once when the place was full of his relatives. He was furious because his nephew had cracked his PC by typing in 'Open Sesame'."

"Not the most original password I've ever heard—but no—it doesn't work."

Josef returned from the bathroom, his skin and clothes as green as when he'd left. Melerski burst out laughing.

"You look like an oversized wood sprite from a production of A Midsummer Night's Dream."

"I've set a watch on all the amber workshops," Josef countered soberly, ignoring Melerski's mirth.

"Don't you think you'd be better off setting a watch on the homes of the amber-smiths in case they're waylaid on the way to work? As Radek hasn't tracked down the Russian and Brunon Kaszuba yet, it probably means they've got a workshop somewhere in the main city. It would have to be a fair size to hold two coffins, the amber..."

"And Adam."

The note of desperation in Magdalena's voice spurred

Melerski into taking another crack at the electronic organizer. "Got it!" he announced finally.

"What was it?" Magdalena asked.

"That's between Adam and me. I'm scanning the addresses now."

"Here, let me," Josef tried to take the machine from him, but Melerski refused to relinquish his hold.

"Museums—staff—friends—America—here we are, family—"

"But nothing for his grandfather," Josef snapped impatiently, looking over Melerski's shoulder as he scrutinized the numbers. "There has to be another file."

"No doubt protected by yet another password," Melerski grumbled.

"Keep looking, I'll see to the amber-smiths." Josef left the room, rubbing at his face with a tissue that remained stubbornly white.

"What was the password?" Magdalena asked Melerski again.

Melerski grinned at her. "Magda. What else?"

"He's right," Kaszuba babbled. "You have two of everything. Two suits of medieval clothes and armor, two stone coffins and enough amber to fill both of them..."

"We planned it that way in case we mess up on our first attempt. We won't be able to sell a faulty coffin full of burnt amber. The stuff is so fucking flammable, one spark could set it off," the Russian said calmly.

"And if we mess up the body?" Brunon demanded.

"Corpses aren't a problem. We'll just go to the city mortuary and pick up a couple. I have contacts..."

While the argument tennis-balled back and fro between

the Russian and Brunon, Adam studied the cellar. There appeared to be no windows and only one door, and that was behind him. The area around the chair he'd been strapped to and the kiln was surrounded by wooden packing cases, most of which were sealed; but the one nearest to the kiln was empty and two had been ripped open, displaying piles of brown and yellowish rocks he recognized as raw amber.

Twin stone coffins lay on the floor on the other side of the kiln, their lids propped against the wall behind them. Both were decorated with the carvings Edmund had pointed out in the photograph of the Amber Knight. There was a large cardboard box on top of one of the cases, large enough to hold two sets of medieval clothes and armor. The only things missing were the bodies and, if he could keep up the pressure on Brunon Kaszuba and convince the Pole that he was here to supply one half of that need, maybe, just maybe, he could uti-lize any altercation to escape. It wasn't much of a plan, and it didn't solve the problem of the chains that fastened him to the chair, but under the circumstances it was the best he could come up with.

"Brunon, you're crazy," Helga argued. "By quarrelling with us you're playing into Adam's hands. Can't you see what he's trying to do? Once he's set us at each other's throats he's hoping we'll be angry enough to forget him and why we're here."

"None of us know Gdansk or the surrounding area the way you do, Brunon. We need you to get us out after we've sold the knights," the Russian assured him. "And we also need you to persuade Adam to give us that code, because without it there's no money, for any of us."

"Look in the mirror, Brunon," Adam taunted, "and tell me which one of us looks more like a Teutonic knight?"

"The only thing we want to hear from you, Yank, is the code." Galvanized by the Russian's mention of money, Brunon kicked Adam's chair even closer to the kiln with vicious blows that shook every damaged bone in Adam's body.

Adam bit his lip, cringing silently until the pain was just about bearable again. He tried not to anticipate what was going to come next. More pain? Torture?

The Russian picked up a cordless drill from the table and inserted a fine bit into the socket. He switched it on, set it at high speed and held it in front of Adam's eyes. "Where would you like the first hole?"

"The middle of your forehead," Adam answered.

"If that's a hint that you'd like to be put out of your misery quickly, it can work that way. All you have to do is give us the code, but make sure it's the right one. If we discover you've been wasting our time, we'll be very angry, won't we, Brunon?" the Russian said softly.

"As I've said, I have a poor memory, but then you know that. If I had remembered where I'd seen you, you would have been picked up days ago."

"By the police?" The Russian laughed derisively. "Brunon, hold Mr. Salen's hand down on the table. It's time to prospect for that code."

"Damn him for not keeping family numbers in his organizer." Josef stared at the telephone, willing it to ring. "Magda, there has to be a way of getting hold of someone from the Institute even at this hour. A procedure for emergencies..."

"In a charitable institution and museum?" Fear for Adam had made her irritable. "What emergencies? I've tried every number I can think of, and all I've reached are answering machines. Nothing's open." She glanced at her watch. "And nothing will be for at least another hour and a half, until San Francisco wakes up."

"Stupid bastard for allowing himself to be kidnapped in the middle of the night. Bloody idiot..."

"Sir?" Pajewski tapped at the door. "Krakow's on the other line. The nanny's woken the boy."

"I'm coming."

Magdalena picked up one of the faxes and began to read. Seconds later she ran to the door. "Josef!"

"Problem?" Melerski set aside the electronic organizer.

Josef appeared in the hall, Pajewski at his heels.

"I know who has the knight. Who has Adam," Magdalena blurted out urgently. "The SS officer in charge of the engineers who blew up the Wolfschanze on the night of January 25th 1945 was Erich von Bielstein."

"So?" Josef looked at her in confusion.

"Adam's wife introduced herself to me as Courtney von Bielstein Salen."

"Adam's wife?" Melerski repeated, bemused by Magdalena's train of thought.

"They're separated. Adam won't have anything to do with her. She's the reason he left America and came to Poland. He's been living off his salary here so she couldn't touch his trust fund or the family money."

"She would be in a better position than anyone to know about any extra Salen Institute funds that could be used to acquire the knight," Josef conceded.

"But only if Adam authenticates the purchase." Magdalena dropped to her knees and began searching for the shoes she'd kicked off.

"Where do you think you're going?"

"Adam's apartment. Edmund said she'd moved in there."

Melerski waited until Josef and Magdalena tore out of the room before picking up the telephone.

Everything was bathed in red. The air that wavered before Adam's eyes. The Russian's and Kaszuba's hands, the table his palm was pinned to by the screwdriver. The half dozen holes the Russian had already drilled oozed blood which mingled with his sweat, drenching both the table and his jeans.

A ringing in his ears drowned out every sound in the cellar. The Russian's, Helga's and Brunon Kaszuba's faces wafted before him. Their lips were moving but he could neither hear nor understand a word they were saying.

Brunon snapped first. He reached out and cut the bandages from Adam's chest with a butterfly knife. His fist slammed repeatedly into Adam's broken ribs until Adam slumped forward, verging on unconsciousness. Then a voice penetrated through the clanging of bells in his head.

"Stop! You'll never get him to do anything that way. He's always wanted to play the hero. You're just giving him an excuse to indulge in cheap dramatics."

Adam forced his eyes open. The ringing was still there, but fainter than it had been. His throat was parched. He croaked for water as a woman walked towards him. He'd recognize those legs anywhere, and the French silk stockings that few women could afford.

"You idiots." Courtney surveyed the bloody table.

"It's his left hand," the Russian pointed out sullenly.

"I wondered if you'd come," Adam croaked.

"You wanted to say goodbye?" She smiled the special smile

he had once been fool enough to believe she kept exclusively for him.

"I've told them I won't make a good knight."

"No, you won't, not while you've still got your balls. I've spoken to your grandfather, Adam. You failed to keep him informed of your progress in tracking down the knight."

"You're his second string." It wasn't a question.

"Who else? We both majored in medieval history and I had better grades. I'm also a member of the family."

"But a member he hasn't trusted with the release code that will free the special fund," Adam guessed.

"Yet," she stressed. "He was on the point of doing so, when you rang Switzerland—hours after he'd asked you to. I thought if you were dead he'd give it to me. But I misjudged him. He wouldn't even give it to me this afternoon when I assured him that you'd been murdered in a Polish police station. When he rang me tonight, to tell me the good news— that you were alive but he'd failed to reach you at the number you'd left, I offered to check it out for him. That's how I knew you were holed up in the museum. Given time and your disappearance I'll coax the code out of him but it would be so much easier for both of us if you save me the trouble."

"Don't underestimate him, Courtney. He's too old to be driven by his libido, like me, and this phony Russian prince."

She laughed. "You really didn't recognize Vladimir, did you? He insisted you hadn't, but I must admit I never took you to be quite that stupid."

"I told you, I didn't care who you fucked. Not even enough to take a good look at him while you were doing it."

"But you waited around to make a scene," she reminded him.

"No, only to tell you I was leaving."

She turned away from Adam and looked at Brunon. "Strip him, we've had a bid in from the Middle East, let's give them their money's worth."

Brunon went for his gun, but Vládimir got to him first, and chopped Brunon's neck with the side of his hand. Brunon fell in a crumpled heap at Helga's feet.

"Four in the vault including Maria and Krefta, Casimir Zamosc in the attack on Magdalena's apartment, and Brunon here," Adam counted off gravely, struggling to find the strength to keep talking. "Tell me, how are you planning to get rid of Helga, Courtney? A convenient bullet in the back of the skull so you and lover boy here can go off into the sunset? Or has your Russian prince insisted on Helga going along too so he can continue to indulge in his ménage à trois? You must know that he is screwing Helga as well as you?"

Courtney turned to the Russian and Adam knew he'd touched a raw nerve.

"You can't keep any man can you, Courtney? Not me, not him, not anyone. You're doomed to take second best all your life."

"Not once your family's one hundred million dollars are in my bank account, I'm not. It was good of your grandfather to tell me he'd doubled the size of the fund."

"So, you sleep with the money while he," Adam jerked his chin towards Vladimir, "sleeps in Helga's bed, which is where Josef and I last saw him."

"He's lying," Vladimir protested.

"It doesn't matter. We've more important things to do than listen to his rambling. Like get him to give us that code so we don't have to wait around for the old man to drop it in my lap."

Vladimir picked up the gelding irons.

"Start work on Brunon."

"Why?" Vladimir asked. "Salen's the one with the code."

"Let him see exactly what you have in store for him. After you've castrated Brunon dress him in the medieval clothes and armor, put him in the coffin and pour in the molten amber. Slowly." She checked the gauge on the kiln. "It will be ready in ten minutes. Brunon's screams should jog your memory and your conscience, Adam. First you fuck his wife..."

"Magdalena and I..."

"Are colleagues?" she sneered. "Whether you screwed Brunon's wife or not, if you don't give me that code, you'll be responsible for his slow—extremely slow—and very painful death. The code will buy the touch of Vladimir's hand that will put Kaszuba out of his misery. Remember that, when Brunon is staring at his own balls on the table and his flesh begins to shrivel with the heat of the amber." She nodded to the Russian. "Get on with it."

CHAPTER TWENTY-FOUR

"VALERIA, YOU MUST have some idea where Courtney went?" Josef said testily as he and Magdalena followed her up the stairs to Adam's apartment.

"She didn't see fit to inform me, and I didn't ask. I was too busy hoping she wouldn't come back. Adam's phobic about his privacy. The last thing he said to me was tell my wife I've gone, you don't know when I'll be back and I've taken my keys with me."

"Then why let her into his apartment?"

"Because she threatened to go to the police and tell them that I was keeping Adam from her. A businesswoman doesn't need gossip, even when there's no truth behind it."

"What time did she leave?"

"Late—a couple of hours ago maybe." She read the look of exasperation on Josef's face. "I was in bed," she protested defensively. "I didn't think to look at the clock."

"Did she go by car?"

"I heard her walk down the stairs and into the street. Even if she had a car it wouldn't have been parked outside. The police don't allow vehicles in Mariacka Street," she added, reminding Josef of the arguments she'd had with the traffic police when she'd tried to take deliveries for the gallery through her front door.

"But it could have been parked around the back. Please, Waleria it's more important than you can possibly know. Did you hear a car engine start up shortly after she left?"

Waleria shook her head as she opened Adam's apartment. Josef stepped inside and looked around. Courtney wasn't as fastidious as Adam. Magazines lay strewn over the tables and floor, dirty glasses and coffee cups filled the kitchen sink, clothes hung in disarray over the banisters on the mezzanine.

"I'll get Pajewski to put out Courtney's description." Disheartened by one blind alley too many, Josef headed back down the stairs.

"Adam is all right, isn't he?" Waleria asked Magdalena anxiously.

"We're not sure." Magdalena read the very real concern in Waleria's eyes and wondered if she was the only woman in Gdansk that Adam Salen hadn't slept with.

The Russian threw a bucket of water into Brunon's face, bringing him around so he could feel the steel of the gelding irons closing in on his testicles. Brunon opened his eyes, saw what Vladimir was holding and screamed hysterically.

"Give me the pen. I'll write down the code." Adam concentrated his gaze on Courtney.

"Hold off for a moment," Courtney commanded Vladimir.

Adam took the pen Helga handed him and scribbled a complex series of numbers and letters on to the paper. Courtney walked over and looked over his shoulder.

"Don't worry, it's the right one," Adam assured her.

"I don't doubt it. You might try delaying tactics if you were the one facing the irons, but you're far too noble to risk prolonging someone else's agony. Even if that someone is a worthless bag of shit like Kaszuba."

"You'll need the twenty-four hour telephone number of the bank."

"I have it. Your grandfather gave that much to me when you didn't phone Switzerland when you said you would. Pity you didn't delay longer, another couple of hours and he would have been angry enough with you to give me the code. I'm sorry, Adam."

"What for?"

"This charade. It wasn't planned this way. We intended it to be a simple, straightforward operation. Exhume the knight, sell it to the Institute and clean out the special fund, which your grandfather had so generously doubled since the early days when you used to tell me everything. I didn't envision any of this." She wrinkled her nose in distaste at the kiln, the boxes of amber, Kaszuba's naked body chained by the ankles to two Gothic stone pillars to expose his genitals, his neck roped to another pillar to immobilize his head, Vladimir tapping the gelding irons against his hand.

"Why steal the amber shipment? It was taken before you or anyone else could have possibly known the knight was contaminated. Did you intend to make a copy all along?" When Courtney didn't reply, Adam said, "Of course, you always were greedy. You wouldn't have been able to resist the chance of doubling your profit."

"Stealing the amber shipment was Brunon's idea. I didn't know he'd done it until I arrived a couple of days afterwards.

At that stage I was quite content to go for the original fifty million and leave it at that."

"I doubt you would have been content with fifty million dollars for long, Courtney. You always have had expensive tastes. How did you find out about the knight?"

"My grandfather was an officer in the SS. His last orders were to blow up the Wolfschanze."

"I thought your grandfather..."

"Was a Prussian refugee?" she laughed. "It was the story he told the US immigration board in 1946, and afterwards he saw no reason to change it. People in the States had more sympathy for refugees who'd run from the Communists and Stalin than ex-Nazis at the time." She took the paper from the table, read it and folded it into her pocket.

"You won't be long?" Vladimir called after her as she turned to the door.

"Only as long as it takes you to clean up here and me to transfer the money from the Salen holding account into the one we set up."

"I think we should go together."

"I'll take Helga with me so you can get on with what needs to be done without any distractions."

"If you wait outside until I've finished, I'll be able to go with both of you."

"What's the matter, Vladimir? Don't you trust us?" Courtney asked.

"Anyone who does is a fool," Adam said to Vladimir. "And that's coming from a man who was married to one of them for five years, and slept with the other for five weeks."

"We'll be back." Courtney walked over to the Russian and

kissed him. Adam saw Helga's eyes turn a deeper shade of green.

"You'll have to make a choice sooner or later," Adam informed Vladimir.

"I'd be happier if you'd let me go with you." Vladimir tried to pretend he hadn't heard a word Adam had said. "Anyone could be out there."

"In Gdansk at four in the morning," Helga scoffed, "you're lucky if you stumble into a cat." She opened the door.

Once the women had left Vladimir wasted no time. Throwing the bolts across the door to reinforce the lock, he returned to Brunon. Whimpering in terror, Kaszuba was thrashing around as much as his chains would allow. The Russian retrieved the irons and snapped them, testing their strength.

"I gave you the code. You promised..."

"I promised you nothing, Salen." The Russian lashed out, catching Adam on the side of the head with the irons. The chair rocked for a moment before clattering on to its side, knocking what little breath remained out of Adam's body. Too winded to cry out, he lay stunned and helpless as a loud and intensely agonizing scream tore from Kaszuba's throat.

The atmosphere darkened. There was noise and confusion. Shadows moved through a haze of reports that might have been gunshots and cries that could have been caused by pain.

Adam continued to lie on the floor curled into an all-encompassing world of torment that left no room for any other emotion. He was no longer capable of untangling reality from dream or nightmare.

Strong hands lifted him and the chair from the floor. Someone called for metal cutters. A stone passageway flowed past, dark, damp and icy after the heat of the cellar. A rug that stank of gasoline and dog hair was wrapped around him. He was stretched out on cold, hard pavement. Above him arched a vast expanse of sky, tinged with the clear, gray light of early dawn.

He could still hear screams. Frenzied and bestial like the howling of a trapped and wounded animal.

"We've sent for an ambulance. It will be here soon." Melerski bent over him and examined the damage that had been done to his chest and hand. "Don't talk. I think you have a punctured lung." He waved away a man who came towards them with a spirit flask. "I dare not risk giving you anything, you may need surgery."

Melerski's last words were drowned out by one final blood-curdling scream.

"Adam!" Courtney pushed her way towards him, dragging the man she was handcuffed to with her. "Tell your police friends I'm an American citizen. I have influence and money. And I won't keep quiet about police brutality..."

Adam smiled in spite of his pain. He pointed a finger at Melerski.

"What your husband is trying to tell you, Mrs. Salen," Melerski answered, "is that you're in the hands of an organization that's more powerful than the police. I'm Stanislaw Melerski, member of the local Mafia."

"You told Radek," Josef hissed at Melerski as they helped load Adam into the ambulance.

"I didn't have to. I warned you he had men watching the streets. Salen's wife walked into this building, his men followed."

"There's no way I can condone what went on in there."

"Why not? Salen has his Amber Knight."

"You don't think for one minute he'd use it? Magdalena, what do you think you're doing. You can't go with Adam…"

"You're always trying to keep me from where I want to be," Magdalena interrupted Josef.

"You a relative?" the paramedic asked.

"Yes," she answered defiantly.

"Then you can come with us."

A mid-morning hush had settled over the hospital. Josef's footsteps resounded like an army recruit's as he walked down the corridor to the waiting room where Magdalena sat hunched next to Melerski.

"He's still in surgery," Melerski answered Josef's inquiring look.

"Do they know any more than they did an hour ago?" Josef asked.

"A nurse came out ten minutes ago. She said it's worse than they first thought. Two ribs have pierced his right lung. And his hand is a mess."

"Do you want coffee?"

Magdalena didn't answer Josef.

"I'll come with you." Melerski followed Josef out through the door.

"You knew Radek would kill that Russian," Josef rebuked, as soon as they were out of Magdalena's earshot.

"You didn't?"

"We could have got something out of him."

"Nothing we didn't already know," Melerski said carelessly.

"Then tell me the location of the vault in the Wolfschanze where the knight's been hidden for the last fifty years?"

"Brunon Kaszuba..."

"As far as we can make out he hadn't a clue. Not that he's in a fit state to question," Josef snapped.

"Radek told me that the Russian castrated Brunon before his men broke down the door. Idiot, everyone knows the Amber Knight kept his balls."

"The Russian castrated Brunon?" Josef asked suspiciously.

"Surely you don't think Radek did it?"

"I think Radek, and you, are capable of a lot of things, when someone's helped themselves to what's yours," Josef stood in front of the coffee machine and sifted through the coins in his pocket.

"Radek was the one who staunched the bleeding and put Kaszuba into an ambulance."

"Before or after he embalmed the Russian in molten amber and turned him into an Amber Villain, as opposed to knight?" Josef demanded.

"Ask Radek. I was outside with Salen at the time. I saw nothing." Melerski shrugged his shoulders.

"Has Magda seen Brunon?"

"Briefly. He didn't want to talk to her."

"I'm not surprised. Does she know?" Josef asked.

"That he's lost his balls?" Melerski asked. "She knows, but from the impression I have of their married life, she's not going to be missing much." Tired of waiting for Josef to use the machine, Melerski pushed a couple of coins into the slot and pressed the button for coffee.

Josef took the plastic cup from his hand and waited while he repeated the procedure. They met a nurse on their way back to the waiting room, but she shook her head before they could ask any questions.

"Adam's still not out of surgery," Magdalena said when they returned.

Josef handed her one of the coffees. "Magda, I hate to press you at a time like this, but the Wolfschanze's been on to us. They've searched all morning and found no trace of the entrance to the vault in the bunkers around the cemetery. Do you have any idea where it could be?"

She shook her head. "Can't it wait until we know about Adam?"

"The director would like to speak to you now. It won't take long to drive to Piwna Street."

"Can't we phone from here?"

"There's a security blackout in case of panic. Magda, I'm sorry, but you know how important it is we track that knight down quickly."

She rose from the chair and walked towards the door.

Melerski winked at her. "Don't worry, with what he's got to live for he'll come out of this. I'll let you know the minute there's any news."

Magdalena sat in the visitor's chair in front of Josef's desk. "Courtney's grandfather must have given her a map, a plan, something that pin-pointed the Amber Knight's hiding place," Magdalena insisted. "Have you asked her about it?"

"Yes," Josef replied shortly. "It was a one way conversation."

"She must know where the vault is. Her grandfather was one of the nine who hid the knight there."

"What about the paper in the bullet Mr. Salen found in Krefta's apartment, sir?"

Josef and Magdalena looked up from the table and stared at Pajewski.

"The report came back on it?" Josef asked.

"Yesterday, sir. You were so busy I didn't disturb you. It looked like a lot of nonsense to me, but perhaps you and Ms. Janca can make something of it."

"You bloody, imbecilic..."

"Where is it?" Magdalena interrupted. Pajewski dived into the mess on Josef's desk and extricated a faded sketch on greasy fax paper. She glanced at it for a moment. "I need a map of the Wolfschanze."

"Here." Josef produced one from his drawer.

"Unnamed bunker opposite no. 25. Get me the director on the line. He has to look at the wall opposite the door. Bottom, right hand corner—there's a marking on a brick –"

The phone rang. Pajewski answered it smartly, lest Josef use tardiness as another excuse to direct his temper in his direction.

"It's Mr. Melerski, sir." Pajewski held out the receiver. "Mr. Salen has come out of surgery."

CHAPTER TWENTY-FIVE

LONG SNAKE of stationary trucks were drawn up on the forest path, they waited in almost the same spot where another convoy had lined up over sixty years before. Magdalena and Edmund passed them before entering the decontamination chamber that had been erected at the entrance to the unnamed bunker opposite the Third Reich's Naval High Command Offices. After donning the bulky protective suits they padded into the bunker. The director of the Institute for Contagious Diseases, dressed in his own distinctive suit, was waiting for them. He opened the stone trap door.

There was no need for words. Everything that needed to be said had been discussed in the warden's office. The Director lowered himself down first, Magdalena followed, leaving Edmund to bring up the rear.

Magdalena had imagined herself crouching and crawling on all fours, but there was no need. When Hitler ordered something built, it was built properly, and to last the thousand year life he had prophesied for his Reich. The subterranean staircase was as solid as the day the builders had finished their work. The passageway that flowed from the foot of the steps was intact, remarkably free from mold and damp. It terminated in a steel door. The Director opened it and stepped into a vast tomb-like vault.

A stone coffin stood against the back wall. Heart pounding, Magdalena walked slowly towards it, scarcely daring to believe that the end of a sixty-year search lay in her sights.

It really was the Amber Knight. As she shone her flash-light over its contours she recalled the warden's attempt to console her on its loss.

"It's been photographed from every angle. You have a record for the museum."

She and Edmund had tried to be grateful, but neither had fooled the other. The last thing the museums of Gdansk needed were more photographs to join the vast collection of pictorially chronicled artifacts that had been lost, stolen and looted during the war. It didn't matter which army had taken them, not now. The loss to the Polish people and their history had been, and would remain, catastrophic.

The Director laid his gloved hand on her arm and she nodded, remembering the warning he'd given her earlier.

"We've skimmed and sealed the surface with resin, a temporary measure while we shot the photographs, but don't touch the knight. Not even the coffin. I know you'll be wearing protective suits, but there's no sense taking unnecessary risks."

She tried to imagine a world without Hitler and the Second World War. A peaceful world where everyone had lived to die of natural causes, a world where the Amber Knight could have lain undisturbed—and safe—in Konigsberg castle for another five hundred years. Would its deadly secret have remained locked within the amber shroud? She glanced around the bare concrete vault and wondered where the rest of the Konigsberg treasure had gone. Both the vault and pas-sageway had been thoroughly searched. There had been no more loose bricks, no other hidden passages, no more artifacts.

But there was one now. She turned to face another coffin pushed into the furthest corner of the vault. A stone coffin identical to the first. A coffin that was rumored to have been carried out of the cellar where Adam had been tortured. When she'd asked Josef about it, all he would say was that the Russian who had tried to kill Adam and castrated Brunon was dead, and the Mafia had only retrieved half of their missing amber shipment.

The Director of the Institute motioned them to the door. She shuddered as she glanced at the knight and his com-panion for the last time. The Director wedged the steel door open and they returned to ground level.

They left the protective suits and helmets behind in the decontamination chamber, showered, dressed and walked back down the forest path. None of them wanted to wait for the trucks to move up and the pumping to begin. It was easy to imagine the ready mixed concrete oozing down the shaft and into the secret vault, filling first the tomb, then the passageway and finally the steps to the level of the trapdoor. The knight slowly drowning in the rapidly hardening concrete that would hide it from the world for a second time, only this time forever.

Magdalena heard an engine start and looked back in spite of herself. "I wish—" she began hesitantly.

"Don't we all," Edmund finished fervently.

Adam was lying on a hard, uncomfortable hospital bed in the tiny cubicle his doctor graciously referred to as a private room. Although the analgesics had softened the worst of his pain, he felt as though he'd been pounded by the hooves of a carthorse weighed down by full medieval armor.

He was also bored and angry because, after everything he'd been through, his doctor had categorically forbidden him to visit the Wolfschanze, and the authorities had refused to delay the destruction of the knight one moment longer than necessary, which meant he'd never see it, except in photographs.

He'd tried to dress that morning intending to sneak out of the hospital during breakfast, but to his shame and mortification one of the nurses had found him in a state of collapse in his bathroom. She'd returned him to his bed, clucking over him as if he were a recalcitrant child.

There was a knock at the door, and he called out, "Come in," expecting another dose of mind-numbing painkillers, or a cup of the peculiar substance the hospital called coffee. Instead Melerski and Radek strolled in.

"How's the invalid?" Melerski dropped a bottle of vodka and a bunch of half-dead roses on his bed.

"Sick of being sick, but grateful for sickness when he considers the alternative. Thank you for carrying me out of that cellar when you did."

"It was hot in there," Melerski said laconically.

"In more ways than one." Radek pulled a chair up to the bed. "I wanted to express my gratitude for leading me to the bastard who killed my brother."

"I wasn't doing anything of the kind. I was only trying to survive."

"All the same, I might not have found him without your help. And this is my thank you." He whistled, and a man built like an ox struggled in with an enormous wooden chest that could have coffined an average-sized man.

"What's in there?" Adam asked suspiciously.

Melerski opened it. On top of a glistening pile of amber, gold and ivory, were thirteen golf ball sized, crystal cut amber beads.

Adam gazed at them in disbelief. "The missing beads from Princess Dorothea's necklace..."

"And her headdress, rings, bracelets, and Schreiber's ivory and amber altar," Melerski smiled, "and..."

"Where did you get this?" Adam stared at the chest in awe.

"It was stored with our raw amber."

"In the cellar?" Adam reached down with his good hand and picked up the leather thong that had been threaded through the beads. "Did you find your money?"

"Let's say we're satisfied with the overall outcome."

"There has to be more than this one chest. Josef said, apart from the knight, the vault beneath the bunker was empty, but we know that the Konigsberg treasure was several truckloads..."

Melerski raised his hand to silence Adam. "The words you're looking for, Mr. Salen, are, 'Thank you for this chest'."

"But the rest of the treasure?"

"Do you think if we knew where it was, we'd give it to you?"

"You gave me this."

"And I'm already regretting it." Radek rose from his chair.

"Just one thing before you go. I'll accept this for the museum, but not if it's hush money."

"Hush money, Salen? As if we'd try to buy you?"

"There are still a few outstanding matters. Like the murder of Rat."

"Kaszuba and Rat annoyed many people. The Rat deserved to die."

"And Kaszuba deserved to be maimed?" Adam interrupted Radek.

"That depends on your point of view. However, I assure you I'm not responsible for the Rat or Kaszuba's misfortune," Radek smiled coldly.

"And then there's that car with Russian plates that tried to stop us on the way back from Kaliningrad," Adam continued.

"We wouldn't have hurt Magdalena."

"I only have your word for that. And Magdalena's apartment..."

"Our man was there to protect you and he was murdered for his trouble. It was Kaszuba who fired the machine gun," Melerski interrupted as Radek's eyes darkened.

"I guessed as much because none of the bullets hit a target. Kaszuba seems to have lousy luck. Nothing he touches goes right. And now..."

"Forget Kaszuba, Salen," Melerski advised. "Put Princess Dorothea's jewelry in the museum and take care of yourself and Brunon Kaszuba's wife."

"I have your blessing?"

"You know something, for an American, you're not that bad. Which is why we're allowing you to romance one of our women." Melerski led the way out of the room.

Josef came in next, looking glum and carrying a bag of grapes that he slowly munched his way through without offering any to Adam.

"Mariana thrown you out again?"

"She's working."

Adam decided not to press the point.

"Some hotshot American lawyer flew in. Your wife's going

to be transferred from our prison to a private American clinic."

"Don't think for one moment that a private American clinic is a soft option. You've never met an American shrink. They're all nuts."

"You had something to do with this?"

"She's been punished enough. She's poor and alone."

"With her looks she won't stay that way for long. And what about her grandfather?"

"He's old. Besides, contrary to what most Poles think, not all the SS worked in concentration camps."

"No, only about half of the bastards. The other half wandered around shooting civilians. I thought the United States didn't take war criminals at the end of the war?"

"Some slipped through the net," Adam acknowledged.

"Evidently," Josef concurred.

"How's Kaszuba?"

"I don't know what he's angrier at, being in jail and facing a charge sheet that grows longer every day, or losing his balls."

"And Helga?"

"She's disappeared." Josef screwed the bag that had contained the grapes into a ball and flicked it into the bin. It missed. "Rumor has it a ship sailed from the docks an hour after we raided that cellar. Apparently she was having an affair with one of the crew."

"That's our Helga."

"No one claimed the Russian's body."

"Just as well considering what Radek did to it."

"And what was that, Adam?" Josef asked.

"Just something I heard about a stone coffin and the missing half of the amber shipment."

"Slander of a well-respected businessman is a dreadful thing," Josef reprimanded.

"Particularly when it's directed at the innocent." Adam looked down at the chest.

"Your trousseau?" Josef asked.

"A few odds and ends Radek and Melerski donated to the museum. I'm planning a party to celebrate when I get out of here."

"Next month?"

"I was thinking more next week. You'll come and bring Mariana?"

"If she's talking to me." Josef rose from his chair. "Take care of yourself and do me a favor? The next time you get a demand for something that's been missing for sixty years, burn it. My marriage won't stand another strain like the last."

It was quiet after Josef left. Adam didn't have the scrambler but for the first time in days he felt he didn't need it. He picked up the bedside phone and dialed his grandfather's home, a number he stored in his memory and nowhere else.

His grandfather answered.

"No Peter today?"

"He's arranging things in the clinic for your wife."

"Ex-wife."

"I'm an old fool. I should have listened to you when you said it was over."

"The important thing is you believe me now."

"The police said you'd been hurt."

"I'll mend. I'm sorry, I didn't get the knight. It's gone, for good this time." He put aside his own disappointment and consoled his grandfather, giving him a sanitized and censored version of the events surrounding the second disappearance of the knight.

"So that's that," the old man declared philosophically.

"Not quite, the Amber Room's still missing and the Rembrandts and…"

"Someone's contacted you about them?"

"Not yet. I'm hosting a party in the museum in two weeks to launch a new exhibition of a few minor pieces that have fallen my way. Want to come?"

"You want to celebrate after losing the knight?"

"It's the Salen way. Pick yourself up, dust yourself off and get on with it, or so I was taught to believe." He looked up and saw Magdalena in the doorway. She was wearing the amber earrings he had bought for her, but had never found the courage, or the right time, to give to her. "You could bring the boys back for Magdalena Janca, now that things have settled down here."

"I wanted to talk to you about those two."

"Talk to me when you get here. I'll book you into the Grand Hotel in Sopot."

"I stayed there in the thirties."

"You can tell me how much it's changed."

"Adam, I'm sorry about Courtney."

"Don't be. It was over a long time ago. See you soon." He put down the telephone and smiled at Magdalena. "Hi."

"The knight's gone."

"But you and Edmund saw it?"

"We did."

"Magdalena…"

"That name is too long. My mother used to call me Lena. You might have to use it for quite a while when you get out of here. The doctor says you won't be able to live alone for months. Lung injuries are susceptible to relapse. You have to rest, eat properly, take care of yourself, take a little light exercise, nothing strenuous. And then there's your hand..."

"It's been remodeled as a strainer. Useful for spaghetti."

"Always jokes with you, isn't it?"

"Sorry, please go on."

"I thought perhaps you could do with live-in help. I've had the door repaired on the museum apartment."

"I prefer my own in Mariacka Street."

"It only has one bedroom."

"Sick as I am, I'm prepared to sleep on the sofa until you're ready to invite me into it." He smiled. "Go on. Live recklessly for once."

"Some would say I've lived quite recklessly enough during the past few days."

"You don't know the meaning of the word—yet." He reached out, but he couldn't have kissed her if she hadn't come to him. It was just like before. Loving, passionate yet peaceful, and he knew he had found a woman he could spend the rest of his life with. The only problem was, did she want to spend the rest of her life with him?

EPILOGUE

HE ARCHAEOLOGICAL MUSEUM was teeming with the wealthy and the powerful, which in contemporary Poland did not necessarily mean the elegant and cultured. The dry white German wine and the French red were flowing. Josef, looking distinctly ill at ease with an overdressed Mariana clinging to his arm, was eyeing all the guests as though they were potential terrorists. Pajewski, dressed in a suit far too tight for his bulging frame, never strayed far from the waiters dispensing the refreshments.

Seeing Melerski and Radek, Adam tried to sneak past Georgiana and her latest discovery, a Czech artist with a green and purple ponytail who went by the improbable name of Clovis.

"And these really are part of the lost Konigsberg hoard, Adam? You are so clever to display them this way. I must commission someone to take photographs of them for the Salen Institute of Modern Art in Texas—"

"Over my dead body, Georgie," Adam growled.

"Adam ... "

"Sorry, must dash." He gave Edmund and Helena a smile of commiseration before greeting Radek. "Come to see your donation?"

"I'm not sure I like the inscription on the door," Melerski complained. "This exhibition made possible by the generous donation of businessmen who prefer to remain anonymous."

"There is another plaque." Adam drew their attention to a large bronze plate on the central case that contained Princess Dorothea's headdress and necklace.

Melerski read, "This display is dedicated to the memory of two Gdansk police officers, Leo Radek and Jerzy Dolny, who were brutally murdered while bravely carrying out their official duties."

"I thought you'd prefer their name on it to yours," Adam said.

Radek nodded dumbly.

"Adam." Melerski stared at the case that contained the princess's rings. "There's one missing."

"It fell apart when it was being cleaned. Feliks is doing what he can with it."

"Strange, I thought they were all in pretty good condition."

Adam shrugged. "You know what a perfectionist Feliks is."

"Did I hear my name being taken in vain?"

"Feliks," Adam greeted him expansively. "Have some wine and tell these kind benefactors how you restored the pieces they so kindly donated to the museum."

"I'd rather pry Elizbieta away from that man."

Adam smiled as Elizbieta cornered a terrified Pajewski. "Don't worry, she's safe with him."

"But is he safe with her?" Feliks asked seriously.

Adam looked away from Feliks to the corner where Magdalena was talking to her brothers. "Will you excuse me?"

"You have a good man in Edmund Dunst." His grand-father waylaid him before he reached Magdalena. "We should offer him a part-time consultancy. Something he can do alongside his work here."

"I take it you intend to pay him a retainer?"

"He can't live on the pittance they pay him here."

"Most people earn pittances here."

"You don't." His grandfather frowned. "I intend to send some of our American staff over to see Edmund's work. Imaginative layout, dark blue velvet goes well with amber, and the amber studded lampshades are a superb touch."

"Perhaps you ought to consider putting Edmund's wife on the payroll as well as him. The subdued lighting was Helena's idea, perhaps she suspected that people would be better off not knowing what's in these canapés."

"Are you ever going to grow up, Adam?"

"I'm trying." He couldn't keep his eyes off Magdalena and the old man noticed.

"She reminds me of your grandmother. God, how I miss her! She was a real woman. Comparing her to some of the females you meet nowadays is like setting wholesome, plain, old-fashioned cooking that satisfies, to this fancy nouvelle cuisine that only tickles your palate."

"It's not Magdalena's cooking I'm interested in."

"But I bet she can cook?"

"She can," Adam agreed, thinking of all the meals she'd prepared and they'd allowed to get cold since she'd moved into his apartment in Mariacka Street.

"She's not the prettiest girl you've been out with, but she's good for you, Adam."

"She's married."

"I heard her husband left her."

"He'll be away a long time."

"Then there's nothing to stop you from jumping into his place."

"I've jumped."

"Glad to hear it. I called into an international school in Switzerland on the way here. Her brothers liked it. Poland needs young men of their caliber to guide it into the future. A little international education won't hurt."

"Magdalena won't allow it. She hates charity."

"What charity? The boys sat the entrance examination. They won scholarships."

"Salen Institute scholarships?" Adam guessed.

"They're the first recipients. And they both know Poland's their home if that's what you're worried about."

"That's not what I'm worried about."

"You look sick, boy, why don't you have an early night, and take her," he nodded to Magdalena, "with you. We can manage perfectly well without you here."

"I'll take you up on that. Lunch tomorrow?"

"Maybe, if I don't get lucky with one of the croupiers in the casino tonight."

"Believe me. You'll be a lot luckier if they leave you alone."

"Your grandfather's great, Adam," Jan said.

"Mr. Salen," Magdalena interrupted.

"He's promised to take us to the casino tonight."

"Neither of you are old enough," Magdalena objected.

"That won't stop my grandfather," Adam smiled. "He took me to a Texas whorehouse for my twelfth birthday treat."

"Adam!" Magdalena exclaimed, shocked.

"You two told your sister your news?"

"Yes, but she won't let us go." Jan's mouth set into a thin line of disappointment.

"Really?" Adam leaned against the wall because he was tired of trying to support himself and his aches and pains.

"I told you we don't accept charity," Magdalena lectured Jan.

"Didn't they tell you they won scholarships?"

"Yes, but ... "

"Be a shame to let all that money go to waste."

"I don't know ... "

"If my grandfather picked it out, it's a good school. Georgiana and I turned out the way we did because he wasn't allowed to have a say in our education."

"Please, Magda," Wiktor pleaded.

"Now is not the time to discuss it."

Adam winked at the boys. "Help yourself to wine and whatever food's going, we'll see you tomorrow."

"You and your grandfather are undermining my authority with them," Magdalena complained.

"A little spoiling and grandfatherly corruption never did anyone any harm."

"It's an expensive school."

"They're always the most brutal." He steered Magdalena towards the stairs.

"Where are we going?"

"My office."

"You should be back in bed, not climbing stairs," she scolded as he winced.

"I'll not argue with that, provided you join me." He stepped inside, closed the door and drew the blinds before opening the cupboard that concealed the safe. He removed a small box. "Something to go with the earrings."

"I can't possibly accept any more presents from you."

"It didn't cost me a penny. It's a gift from grateful citizens who know that you single-handedly and courageously averted an anthrax outbreak that could have decimated the population of Poland."

She opened the box and stared down at the contents.

"Princess Dorothea had a lot of jewelry. No one is going to miss one small ring."

"It's not small—it's—"

"The shank had to be replaced. It wouldn't have been authentic. Feliks renovated it for me. I thought it could be our unwedding ring."

"What's an unwedding? Some strange American custom?"

"You're married, I'm married, it's messy, but it doesn't have to be. It could be gloriously simple. I've become accustomed to having a nanny looking after me again. I'm asking you to stay with me, Lena. Forever," he added, so there'd be no mistake.

"I'll have to think about it."

"Take all the time you want." He bent his head to hers. "Preferably the rest of your life."

Áccent Extras

Conversation with the author
Get to know Katherine John

Setting the Scene
Historical background

Reading Group Guide
Get more out of your reading experience

Read On
An excerpt from Katherine's next book

www.accentextras.com
sign up for our newsletter
learn about upcoming events
keep up with your favorite Accent authors

Katherine John is the daughter of a Welsh guardsman
and a Prussian refugee mother who met at the end of the
Second World War. Although she grew up and was
educated in her native Wales, she spent long vacations
in Germany with her Prussian born grandmother, and
was always conscious of her dual heritage. Her
favourite hobby is traveling to her mother's birthplace
in Eastern Europe to research her novels.
Katherine lives with her family in Wales on the Gower
Peninsula near Swansea.

Talk to the Author!
If you have any questions for Katherine John or
would like to invite her to speak to your reading group or
participate in an online chat session, please feel free to
contact her at her website where you can also check out
the latest news!
www.katherinejohn.com

CONVERSATION WITH THE AUTHOR

How did you get the idea to write Amber Knight?

Katherine - The inspiration for the Amber Knight came in 1995 when I accompanied my mother back to her East Prussian homeland which she fled in 1945 when the Russian army invaded. We stayed in towns and villages where she knew every street, every house, and could remember every person who had lived there during the war. Yet, every name on the map had been changed. And, as a result of the ethnic cleaning carried on during the final months of the war, not a soul she knew remained. After walking the streets, visiting the museums, and talking to the locals about the enormous impact wartime events still had on contemporary Polish life, I began to weave a story that blended fact with fiction in an attempt to capture the mood of modern Poland.

Modern-day Poland now covers much of Prussia, where exactly did you visit and what did you see?

Katherine - I hired a car and in three weeks we drove EVERYWHERE. From the German border in the west to the Russian Border in the East, and the Baltic coat in the North to the border with the Czech Republic in the South. Our first stop was my mother's home town of Allenstein (now Olsztyn) and also Rastenburg where my uncle lived, (now Ketrzyn). A short drive away is Hitler's ruined Bunker's city where he spent most of the war. I wasn't prepared for the size, it had its own railway station, airfield, cemetery, casinos, brothels, etc. and everyone in High Command

Get
to
know
Katherine
John

had their own detached bunker. We spent a day exploring the site, an experience I used when writing the Amber Knight. We stayed in Malbork and visited the largest red brick castle in Europe, which the Teutonic Knights began to build in 1380. Part of the castle now houses one of the world's finest amber museums. I could have spent a week there.

We toured the Mazurian lakes, drove to Sopot and Gdansk, where my mother had enjoyed many summer holidays as a child and I fell in love with the medieval quarter of Gdansk. At the Dluga Street gate to Gdansk is a Medieval Torture house (now an amber museum). In the sixteenth century criminals were brought from all over Poland to be tortured and /or executed in the circular courtyard, for the amusement of the local populace who could watch from an encircling platform. (There are even channels for blood in the cobblestones).

As an author, the entire time we were in Poland I fervently wished stones could talk.

The legend of the Amber Knight is so compelling, where did you track it down?

Katherine - One of the most beautiful streets in Gdansk is Mariacka Street, where every house resembles a poem in stone. There, highly skilled Ambersmiths work in studios behind their shops. One of them told me that when the Teutonic Knights sacked the Prussian stronghold of Elbag during the Teutonic crusade (which began in 1231 with the aim of bringing Christianity to the Pagan Prussians), they fired the town. The amber in the treasury melted, ran out in a golden stream and was used to preserve the head of a brave and saintly knight.

I failed to track the legend to recorded fact, but.my imagination went one step further and I used the legend and the Nazi obsession with the Teutonic Knights to create the Amber Knight by encasing an entire Teutonic Knight's body in amber in a stone coffin.

Where did the inspiration for your American hero, Adam Salen, come from?

Katherine - Even now, more than half a century after the war the Gdansk museums are pitifully bare. Many have posters and photographs of artefacts, with

HAVE YOU SEEN THIS, IT DISAPPEARED IN 1945 AND WAS STOLEN EITHER BY THE NAZI OR RUSSIAN ARMIES.

I thought it would be wonderful if there was an organisation dedicated to tracking down Poland's missing treasures and restoring them to the nation. That thought led me to create my American hero, Adam Salen, who works for the fictional Salen Trust. A charity set up by his wealthy Polish born grandfather with the aim of preserving Polish heritage and culture.

Amber plays an important part in the story, how did you learn about this highly unique material and art form?

Katherine - When my grandmother was forced to leave the family home in the face of the advancing Russian army, she had ten minutes notice. Ten minutes to decide what to pack. She left her valuable jewellery behind and packed my grandfather's briefcase (he had been killed by Hitler in 1940) with family photographs, the plans and keys of the house she would never see again, and some of the amber my grandfather had given her when they first met. He had picked up the pieces of fossilized resin on the coast of the Baltic (You can still find it now). As a child I was allowed to play with the amber and fascinated by the glimpse of prehistoric worlds I spent hours gazing into pieces that held tiny insects and fauna.

Unfortunately since then and thanks to Jurassic Park the price of amber has rocketed. But it hasn't stopped me from collecting amber jewellery. Last month I visited Gdansk again to research the next Adam Salen novel, The Amber Pawn and also The Prodigal Knight a medieval mystery featuring the Amber Knight, Helmut von Mau. As it was my birthday my husband insisted I add to my collection. I didn't protest too much although I noticed he blanched when the ambersmith told him the price of the earrings I had chosen.

The Russian and Polish Mafia appears in the story. How did you research those characters in order to portray them as realistically as you have?

Katherine - when we visited the dream house my architect and master builder grandfather built for our family in 1936 we found it standing as though it had been frozen in time. It had been turned into apartments. Three had been created in my grandmother's old wash-room and preserving cellar. The apartment on the third floor had been bought—you could buy apartments even in the communist era—by a civilian worker for the Polish police. Mr. Rodzina and his wife Helena were most welcoming and fascinated by the keys and house plans my mother showed them of their home. (The keyholes remained and new locks had been drilled above the old). When we discovered that they accommodated tourists to supplement their income we not only stayed in the house but also slept in my mother's old bedroom.

I talked to Mr. Rodzina at length about his work with the Polish police and he introduced me to Polish "businessmen" who had thrived during the Communist era and continued to thrive after the fall of the Communist party. Entrepreneurs survive in every society.

When I returned to Poland a year after the trip with my mother to do further research for the Amber Knight, I stayed in the Grand Hotel in Sopot, a magnificent hotel that had been built to cater to Polish pre-war high society. It has a Casino and I visited it with my husband (we didn't play after they confiscated our passports). There I saw two Polish gypsies lose ten thousand dollars in less than five minutes by blanket bombing the roulette table. It was an incident I used in the Amber Knight.

Later I sat in the bar and talked to the patrons. Just after the fall of Communism the only people who could afford to stay in the hotel were—I'll use the same term to describe them as Dalecka, the police officer in the Amber Knight—Polish "businessmen".

Get to know Katherine John

Setting the Scene

Hermann von Balk is an actual historical figure. His thir-teenth-century Teutonic Crusade, which began in 1231, led to the formation of the Prussian State.

Helmut von Mau and the Princess Woberg/Maria are creations of my imagination. The legend of a canonized Teutonic Knight's head encased in amber is widespread in the Baltic States; unfortunately, I failed to track it down to any recorded historical fact.

Several prominent medieval historians believe that at least one of the plagues that swept across Europe between the twelfth and fourteenth centuries was anthrax.

The contemporary amber workers, Krefta and Malek, are fictional. The artifacts produced by George Schrieber's seventeenth century Konigsberg workshop can be seen in the world's finest museums. Princess Dorothea existed in the sixteenth century and ten of her crystal cut amber beads are on display in the Amber Museum in Malbork Castle.

Very little of the treasure the Nazis looted from Russia and Poland during the war and stored in Konigsberg castle until the Russian invasion in January 1945, when it disappeared, has been seen since. It included the leg-endary Amber Room (which has since been recreated and completed in Tsarkoe Selo in St. Petersburg), but my theory that the treasure was taken to the bunker city

Hitler built at Rastenburg and named the Wolfschanze, or Wolf's Lair, prior to the invasion of East Prussia, is pure speculation.

On the ground floor of 52 Mariacka Street is a well-stocked modern art gallery. Adam Salen's apartment on the top floor is the office of the Gdansk Branch of the Union of Polish Writers.

All the museums in Gdansk are characterized by their lack of exhibits. The Salen Foundation and its funding are, unfortunately for Gdansk and Poland, figments of my imagination. The Historical Museum in the main town in Gdansk has an entire floor devoted to photographs of exhibits which disappeared during the Second World War and appeals along the line of "If you see this, please contact..."

The Wolfschanze is only fenced off along the main road out of Gierloz. If you drive down a side road you can enter the bunker area, and it would be possible to drive a truck there at night.

Katherine John
September 2006

Historical
Setting

READING GROUP GUIDE

1. Do you think that Katherine John was successful in her intertwining of medieval, wartime and present day Poland?

2. What was your opinion of the Legend of the Amber Knight? A believable medieval romance, or not?

3. Hitler and the Nazis had a particular fascination with Teutonic Knights, their history and their legends. Why do you think they were so obsessed?

4. The people of Poland, both Jewish and non-Jewish Poles alike, suffered terribly during World War II. The suffering and persecution continued after the war's end under the Russian occupation and Communist regime yet this is not given much attention in history books. Why do you think that is?

5. Did you guess the identity of the person behind the sale of the Amber Knight? If so what clues in the book led you to finger the culprit? Did you suspect anyone else? If so, why?

6. Adam Salen gives up a comfortable life with a beautiful wife in America to stay in his ancestral homeland of Poland. What do you think draws him to the people and the country his grandfather had left behind? Can you relate to his choices?

7. The novel is set in modern day Gdansk. Did Katherine John succeed in capturing the atmosphere of the town? If so, how do you think she did it? Is it a

place that you think you would like to visit after reading the novel?

8. How would you describe Katherine John's writing style? To what extent do you feel that the novel's structure is successful?

9. Did you find any humor in the Amber Knight? Were there particular passages that you found amusing, if so which ones?

10. The Mafia is pretty violent in some scenes, but in the end they help Adam. Does this fit with your image of the Mafia? Do you think they are capable of doing good in real life?

11. One reviewer has described Adam Salen as "being attractive, and aspirational from a male point of view, and being rather weak and vain at times - which Magda's reactions to him holds in relief" Do you agree with that statement?

12. Magda is a very proud and independent woman who holds tightly to traditional values. What do you think draws her to Adam Salen? Do you think their romance will last?

13. Would you like to read more about Adam Salen's life as an American exile in Poland, or Helmut von Mau's life as a Teutonic crusader? If so which aspects interest you most?

14. What did you think of the novel's dénouement? How satisfying did you find it?

Get
more
out of
your
reading
experience

COMING SOON FROM KATHERINE JOHN

AMBER PAWN

The second in a series of contemporary thrillers featuring
Adam Salen the Director of the Salen Institute, a charitable
organisation funded by the wealthy American Salen family
with the aim of conserving the cultural and historical heritage
of Poland.

Separated from his wife, Adam lives in a tiny apartment in
Mariacka Street in the medieval quarter of Gdansk with the
love of his life, museum curator Magdalena Janek. He receives
an anonymous letter and maritime map pinpointing the position of ancient artefacts unearthed by the Teutonic Knights in
twelfth-century Jerusalem. Enclosed with the letter are pawns
from a thirteenth-century chess set.

But when Adam sends down a diving team to investigate,
instead of artefacts, they discover a container containing the
corpses of 200 illegal immigrants. Forensic tests indicate the
immigrants died days before of asphyxiation and drowning.

After Adam is introduced to a girl who was trafficked by the
gang that murdered the immigrants he embarks on a quest.
Not only to track down the Teutonic Knights' treasure, but
also the traffickers. A quest in which he finds himself not
only risking his own life, but those of his friends, and even his
beloved Magda.

CHAPTER ONE

VEN IN SUMMER, Gdansk nights are cold when the wind blows in from the sea. They are colder still for those who come from sunnier climes. There was no moon and there were no tugs to guide the freighter that edged out of the open sea into the sheltered bay that housed the shipyards.

Capitalism had brought dereliction to the once thriving center of industry. The seventeen thousand strong workforce that had laboured under Communist rule had dwindled to less than three thousand. The result could be seen in the abandoned docks, warehouses, and rusting cranes that reared, silhouetted against the blue black of the starlit night sky like giant locusts.

The crew that remained on deck of the freighter ranged themselves against the ship's rails. Some stared blindly into the cold swirling depths of the sea below. Others strained to make out figures on the approaching bank. None spoke.

One, who might, or might not have been Russian—it wasn't the sort of ship where the crew socialized—stood apart from the others; just as he had done throughout the voyage. His features were dark, possibly Arab; possibly Spanish. Someone had suggested he was Russian because he understood the language. But, as the rest of the crew had discovered during the course of the short voyage out of an Eastern Baltic port, he also understood Turkish, English, Greek, Spanish and various Baltic dialects. Understood but rarely used.

Because they had to call him something, the cook had christened him, Krak—after the Slavic Dragonslayer of mythology. The nickname had stuck because Krak had knocked the first mate out cold when the man had tried to rob him on their first night at sea.

Krak's reticence wasn't unusual. Even those men on board who liked to hear the sound of their own voices didn't talk about themselves. No one signed on to crew a ship like this if they could find another that paid as well. Some took the job for the money. The pay was four times the going rate. Most were

Áccent Extras

From Katherine's next book Amber Pawn

running from something or someone. Perhaps the law, perhaps one of the many mafias that operated globally, one or two romantics were trying to escape bitter memories of a woman.

The Captain didn't ask questions when he hired and none volunteered information. Only Krak knew that he was different from the others. He wasn't running or escaping from anyone. He was searching for someone.

The freighter drew alongside a dock and juddered to a halt. A command was passed down softly from the captain in the wheelhouse. So softly it didn't disturb the sleeping gulls; white dots in a shadowed landscape. Anchor was dropped. The engines died.

Ahead, in the distance the sailors on deck could make out the twinkling lights that marked the way to the main medieval town of Gdansk. Behind them lay the vastness of the Baltic.

The Captain stepped out and spotted movement on the quayside to their right. He waved. An answering light flashed on shore. The gangplank was dropped and the Captain was the first to walk down on to dry land.

The men on deck heard snatches of whispered conversation too faint and indistinct to make out the language.

One of half a dozen transporters parked in front of a warehouse roared into life. It moved sluggishly up to the gangplank and parked. The doors to a container it was hauling were opened. It was a signal to the first mate waiting at the stern of the freighter. He passed down an order to seamen who opened the doors to the hold.

Whispers in several languages buzzed.

"Damen . . . Filles . . . Señoritas . . . women . . ."

"Women . . . women only . . . women first."

Figures emerged on deck. They walked as they'd been ordered to, in silence, head down in single file. The men on deck moved in either side of the column. They ushered the women to the container, watched those fit enough climb inside and helped those who needed assistance.

Krak and one other man continued to lean on the rails. Their duty would come later and they were grateful for jobs that kept them away from contact with the cargo. Their conscience pained them enough as it was. They smoked and turned their heads to look out to sea while they waited. The sea at least was clean—cleaner than the land.

The stream of humanity leaving the hold dwindled to a trickle. When the last woman had been lifted into the container, the doors were slammed, sealed, locked, and bolted. The driver leaned out of the window. On receiving a signal from a man at the back, he turned the ignition and drove the transporter back towards the warehouse. Passing it, he entered the maze of tracks that criss-crossed the shipyards which separated the town from the sea. Soon the vehicle was lost to sight.

Another transporter drove in and parked, taking the space that had been occupied by the first.

The captain flashed his light a second time. A few minutes later a second stream of humanity left the hold and climbed up on deck. Like the women the men walked quickly, silently, head down, looking neither left nor right.

It took less than ten minutes to fill the container. The doors were closed and sealed. When the driver received the signal, he gunned the engine and drove the few yards to the end of the dock. He pulled on the brakes, shut the engine, climbed out of his cab, and walked away. He knew what was about to happen and like the seamen was reluctant to witness it.

Krak and his companion continued to look doggedly out to sea and the horizon. They were waiting for the first cold grey rays of the false dawn that precedes the real one.

Behind them, out of their line of vision, men moved, swarming over the container unbuckling, unlocking and freeing the fastenings that married it to the transporter. When their work was done, they retreated. A crane poised above the container whirred into life. It swooped down like a giant heron homing in on a fish. Its hydraulic grabs seized the container and lifted it from its bed on the vehicle.

The sound of the crane was accompanied by a welter of muffled screams, shouts and bangs that echoed from the outsize box. The crane swung round until the container hung over a deep-water channel that cut between the yard and its neighbour. The Captain and the mate waved to the crane operator and spoke to him on mobile phones. After ten minutes of shifting and lining

Accent Extras

From Katherine's next book Amber Pawn

up the container in response to the Captain's orders, the operator lowered the burden until it dipped into the water. Then, in response to a final sharp command from the Captain, he released the hydraulic grabs.

Although the base of the container was a few inches below the surface, there was a loud slap of displaced water when the weight was dropped. The noise startled the men on deck and the shore, although they had been expecting it. The container remained static, poised on the water for a minute or two, moving with the waves. Then slowly, inexorably it began to sink. The banging and cries grew gradually fainter as the container dipped lower—and lower—only ending when the roof finally disappeared in a froth of flotsam and air bubbles.

Krak and his companion turned to watch the last moments of the container's journey. They knew the bay and the currents. They also knew about the deep channels between the yards; channels that had been cut decades ago to accommodate the draft of ocean-going vessels. The channels were now obsolete. They wouldn't be needed for years—if ever again—since the post communist government had discovered just how uneconomic the shipyards were.

Krak tossed his cigarette end overboard and lit another. He wondered if it was his imagination or if he could still hear shouts and bangs.

The transporter, minus its container drove off. He watched it go. The men on the dockside dispersed. The Captain and the crew returned to the ship. Krak went to his bunk.

His fellow sailors dressed for shore leave, stashing the bundles of cash they had been paid, in the inside zip-up pockets of their leather coats. But he did not join them. He pulled a blanket to his chin and continued to wait for dawn. When someone spoke to him he closed his eyes but he did not sleep.

Half an hour after dawn broke, Krak was in his wet suit and goggles. He checked his air tanks and went over the side with his companion—the other diver employed by the Captain. The water in the channel was murky, visibility poor, but they had both seen the container enter the water and knew where to look.

They hit the top five meters down. The Captain had briefed the crane driver well. The container was neatly parked on the sea bed, beside another, which in turn was sandwiched next to a third. In all five containers lay side by side. There was room for another two, possibly three if the Captain and crane operator were careful in their positioning. A fourth would project perilously near the quayside and might impede the flow of traffic to the dock.

Krak's companion made a "thumbs up" and headed for the surface. But Krak lingered. He had noticed something floating beside the container. Something that gleamed in the darkness. He swam towards it. The container had scraped the mud from the bank on its way down to the seabed, exposing the rusting outline of a ship—no not a ship.

He swam closer and ran his hands over the remains of a submarine turret. Most of it was still embedded in the mud. Whatever he had seen danced and glittered a foot before his mask. He reached out and his hands closed over a net. A net caught on a rusting spear of metal. The contents floated in the water, moving and bobbing with the currents. He stuffed the net into his belt and surfaced.

Alone in the head he washed the contents of the net while he showered away the filth of the dock water. Lumps of mud and algae dissolved to reveal exquisitely carved amber chess pieces. A queen, a knight, a bishop, and two pawns in pale gold amber. A king, a castle, a knight and three pawns in dark brown amber.

Like most East Europeans, he knew about chess, amber and carving. And a little about history. Were they medieval? Or facsimiles? If they were copies they were good ones. But the decay around the edge of the carvings suggested original.

They were sailing east at nightfall. He had a few hours to go on shore. He was close to breaking point. He knew he wouldn't be able to stand back and watch another container crammed with living human beings dropped into a watery grave. But neither could he go to the authorities without risking everything he had spent the last year working towards.

He didn't care about his own life . . . but Krista . . .

Somehow he had to alert the authorities to the existence of

Accent Extras

From Katherine's next book Amber Pawn

the tomb beneath the waves without compromising his own position. When they reached the next port he'd sign off and look for another ship—another gang—and hopefully the police would investigate and close in on this one. Arrest the Captain and his contact in the shipyard.

He was too astute to think that his actions would do more than make a slight dent in the trade. There were too many gangs involved in human trafficking and too many ports in Europe and along the Baltic for the coastguards and police to monitor. But he had to do something before another container would be dumped in the channel on the next moonless night.

He tried not to think about the women. He knew what had happened to them because he'd made it his business to witness one of the "auctions" that periodically took place in one of the deserted warehouses. Women fetched a high price, young girls even more. They were needed to fill brothels. The women too old or ugly for the sex trade were sold as domestic servants.

The profit for the gang masters was high. The prices they charged their human cargo for passage to a Western EU country, ensured that the women would labour for decades without earning a penny more than the interest on the loan they had taken out to buy their "ticket" to a better life.

Slavery was more lucrative and less risk than drugs these days.

It was a short walk from the shipyards to the medieval town of Gdansk. Krak bought an apple from a fruit seller who had set up a stall on the banks of the Mottlau canal. He skirted the dense groups of tourists who marched resolutely behind guides bearing flags, banners and in one case a teddy bear on a stick. Sidestepped past crowds of Russians who were examining the "Made in China" souvenirs in the tourist shops and Japanese, who stood in droves around everything that looked remotely old, photographing it from every angle. And he bypassed Germans who gazed, fixated, at the glittering displays of gold and amber jewellery and artefacts in the overpriced jewellery shops.

He stopped at a cafe on the Royal Way, sat at an outdoor table in a corner away from the crowds and ordered kielbasa, cabbage and fried potatoes. While he waited for his meal, he took a newspaper from the rack provided for patrons. He hadn't read a paper in nearly a month but the international headlines were just as he remembered. Bombings and murder in the Middle East—drunken celebrity antics in London—deaths of NATO soldiers in Afghanistan—the Aids epidemic in Africa—the Russian bear growling at NATO.

Bored, he exchanged the national newspaper for a Gdansk local. On the front page was a photograph of a good-looking man in his early thirties. But it wasn't the man that interested him. It was the background of cranes and warehouses and the banner over an enormous set of gates. SALEN INSTITUTE SHIP-BUILDERS INC.

He read the article below it slowly and carefully, making sure he didn't mistranslate a single word.

SALEN INSTITUTE SHIPBUILDERS BRINGS JOBS AND MILLIONS OF DOLLARS INVESTMENT TO GDANSK

A year ago, Adam Salen, managing director of the Polish branch of the archaeological and educational Salen Institute ignored all cautionary advice and invested twenty million dollars in the old Plock shipbuilding yard. That investment is now paying off, and handsomely. The yard has received firm orders from European and American universities to build six, five-million-dollar archaeological marine vessels. Each will be equipped with the latest radar technology and attendant mini submarines.

Mr. Salen said, "These are purpose-built vessels designed by marine experts to explore the tens of thousands of ancient and medieval shipwrecks that litter the sea and ocean beds of the world. Our own Salen Institute prototype vessel, The Magda, is already in operation along the Baltic coast between Gdansk and Kaliningrad searching for thirteenth-century wrecks that could yield more information about the maritime activity of the Teutonic Knights."

When questioned by our reporter, Mr. Salen admitted that he was aware of the legend that credits the Teutonic Knights with discovering the gold altar of Solomon's temple. It is generally accepted that the land the Teutonic Knights built their castle on in Jerusalem was formerly the site of the temple. It has even been

From
Katherine's
next
book
Amber
Pawn

suggested that King Simon of Jerusalem ordered the knights to use the pretext of building their castle to fully excavate the site.

Mr. Salen added that although it is rumored that 270 tons of gold were used in the construction of King Solomon's temple, much of it to decorate the altar, the value of any antiquities found would lie solely with their artistic and religious merit.

Looking around to make sure that no one was watching him, Krak tore out the page, folded it and pushed it into his pocket. He ate his kielbasa, potatoes and cabbage and washed it down with a half liter of beer, paid his bill and left the waitress a modest tip.

He then went in search of a stationers. He felt for the pieces of amber. He had pushed them into his rucksack with the intention of having them valued. They were there in the bottom still wrapped in toilet tissue.

He needed to buy notepaper and a large envelope. He checked the pieces again, a very large envelope, and he needed to find somewhere quiet where he could write a letter and draw a map.

A guide in the Gdansk town museum in Mariacka Street showed Krak the back staircase that led to the offices of the Salen Institute. Halfway up Krak heard a voice raised in anger.

"Teutonic shipwrecks my arse, Adam. You built that boat so you could go nosing around World War Two wrecks to look for looted Nazi treasure. They are designated war graves . . . "

"Dalecka, Dalecka," a smooth American-accented voice interrupted in Polish. "Haven't you read the interview I gave the local paper? I built the Magda for two reasons only, as a prototype I could show other museums and institutes to gather orders, and to search the Baltic look for medieval shipwrecks."

"My arse!" his companion repeated. "The paper printed what you told them to print, Adam."

"That would be a first," the American-accented Polish drawled.

"You're a lying, junk food eating Yankee . . . "

"There are worse things to be." The American clearly wasn't in a mood to be angered.

"You're a foreigner, here on sufferance. I don't like your attitude, and I don't like what you're doing."

"What you mean is Melerski and Radek don't like it," the softer voice drawled. "Sometimes I wonder if you and your police force spend more time working for the mafia than you do the honest citizens of Gdansk, Josef."

"Radek and Melerski are businessmen."

"And I'm Mickey Mouse."

"A Mickey Mouse who's playing stupid games . . ."

Krak didn't wait to hear any more. The newspaper article had set him on the right track. He wouldn't find a better fish than Adam Salen. All he hoped was the man would take the bait he'd placed on his hook.

The door to the outer office was open. A pretty young blonde was sitting working behind a desk, apparently impervious to the argument raging inside the inner office, although the connecting door was open.

Krak turned up his collar, pulled down his sailor's cap and walked in. He dropped the package he had made on to the secretary's desk.

"Urgent delivery for Mr. Salen."

The blonde glanced up and smiled. "Thank you, Mr. . . ."

"I'm just the errand boy."

He turned and ran down the stairs. Seconds later he was in the thick of the crowd heading out of Mariacka Street for Warzywnicza street that bordered the canal.

The blonde knocked on the door between the outer and inner office.

"Package just arrived for you, Adam."

"Thank you, Wiklaria." Adam took it from her, slit the envelope open and upended it. The medieval chess pieces landed on his desk. But he was too busy reading the map and note that had been packaged with them to examine them.

"Nice." Josef Dalecka picked up one of the pieces. What's in the letter?"

"Nosy aren't you?"

"It's my business to be nosy," Josef growled.

Adam smiled. "Someone's kindly me drawn me a maritime

Áccent Extras

From
Katherine's
next
book
Amber
Pawn

map of the dock area around the shipyard. And, if they are to be believed they have pinpointed the exact spot where I can find the altar from Solomon's temple."

"And you believe it?"

Adam picked up the pale gold "white" queen. It glittered in the sunlight that streamed through his window as he held it up to Josef.

"Unlike you, Josef, I pride myself on keeping an open mind."

Krak set aside his doubts when he stepped back on board the freighter. A fool could find the container from the map he'd drawn. And, from what little he'd heard Adam Salen say, Adam Salen was no fool.

Some victims of the traffickers at least would receive a Catholic burial.